EIGHT KINKY NIGHTS

XAN WEST

CONTENTS

About This Book
Content Notes
A Brief Note About Trans and Non-Binary Terms

1. Friday evening, December 13
2. Friday evening, December 13
3. Friday evening, December 13
4. Saturday night, December 14
5. Saturday night, December 14
6. Saturday night, December 14
7. Saturday night, December 14
8. Sunday morning, December 15
9. Sunday afternoon, December 15
10. Sunday afternoon, December 15
11. Monday afternoon, December 16
12. Monday afternoon, December 16
13. Monday afternoon, December 16
14. Monday evening, December 16
15. Tuesday evening, December 17
16. Wednesday evening, December 18
17. Thursday afternoon, December 19
18. Friday afternoon, December 20
19. Saturday morning, December 21
20. Saturday afternoon, December 21
21. Sunday morning, December 22
22. Sunday evening, December 22
23. Sunday evening, December 22
24. Sunday evening, December 22
25. Monday afternoon, December 23
26. Monday evening, December 23
27. Monday evening, December 23
28. Monday evening, December 23
29. Tuesday morning, December 24
30. Tuesday morning, December 24
31. Tuesday afternoon, December 24
32. Tuesday afternoon, December 24
33. Wednesday morning, December 25
34. Thursday morning, December 26
35. Thursday afternoon, December 26
36. Thursday evening, December 26
37. Thursday evening, December 26
38. Friday morning, December 27
39. Friday morning, December 27
40. Friday afternoon, December 27
41. Friday afternoon, December 27
42. Friday evening, December 27
43. Friday evening, December 27
44. Friday evening, December 27
45. Friday evening, December 27
46. Saturday morning, December 28
47. Saturday morning, December 28

48. Saturday afternoon, December 28
49. Saturday evening, December 28
50. Saturday evening, December 28
51. Saturday evening, December 28
52. Saturday evening, December 28
53. Sunday morning, December 29
54. Sunday afternoon, December 29
55. Sunday late afternoon, December 29
56. Monday afternoon, December 30
57. Tuesday late morning, December 31
58. Tuesday evening, December 31

A Note for Readers
Cast of Characters
Drink Recipes from Eight Kinky Nights
Ginger Lime Fizzy Drink Recipe
Cherry Lemonade Recipe
Grapefruit Ginger Drink Recipe
Ginger Lime Drink Recipe
Songs Referenced in Eight Kinky Nights
Books and Movies/TV Referenced in Eight Kinky Nights
Acknowledgments
I want to extend particular thanks...
Also by Xan West
Praise for Xan's Work
About the Author
About Their Troublesome Crush
Their Troublesome Crush Excerpt

Copyright © 2019 by Xan West

All rights reserved. No part of this publication may be reproduced, distributed, or transmitted in any form or by any means, including photocopying, recording, or other electronic or mechanical methods, without the prior written permission of the publisher, except in the case of brief quotations embodied in critical reviews and certain other noncommercial uses permitted by copyright law.

For permission requests, write to the publisher, addressed "Attention: Permissions Coordinator," at the address below.

XanWest@Gmail.com

This is a work of fiction. Names, characters, businesses, places, events, locales, and incidents are either the products of the author's imagination or used in a fictitious manner. Locales and public names are sometimes used for atmospheric purposes. Any resemblance to actual persons, living or dead, business establishments, locales or actual events is purely coincidental.

The author acknowledges the copyrighted or trademarked status and trademark owners of the following wordmarks mentioned in this work of fiction:

"Perhaps, Perhaps, Perhaps," Doris Day, Fetlife, Coyote Grace, "Glory Be," "Ghost Boy," Doc Martens, Joe Stevens, Queen, "Killer Queen," "Fat Bottomed Girls," "Leavin on a Jet Plane," James Bond, 007, The Goo Goo Dolls, "Iris," Labyrinth (1986), David Bowie, "As the World Falls Down," Lena Hall, Becks (2017), Sting, Alicia Keys, "If I Ain't Got You," Goldfinger (1964), "Goldfinger," Shirley Bassey, Sade, "By Your Side," Regina Spektor, Sara Bareilles, "She Used to Be Mine," Sarah MacLachlan, Rihanna, Adele, Skyfall (2012), "Skyfall," Bond girl, Earl Grey tea, "Misty Mountains Cold," Stim Ray, The Princess Bride (1987), Count Rugen, Buttercup, Prince Humperdink, Merry, Pippin, Lord of the Rings: The Fellowship of the Ring (2001), Play It Again by Aidan Wayne, That Kind of Guy by Talia Hibbert, The Indigo Girls, "Closer to Fine," Hercules (1997), Twitter, Return of the King (1980), Rankin Bass, Gandalf, "Less Can Be More," The Hobbit by J.R.R. Tolkien, Bag End, Bilbo, The Shire, Janet Jackson, "Miss You Much," "You," "Birdhouse in Your Soul," They Might Be Giants, Into the Woods (2014), Tangled (2010), "Clever Girl," The Doubleclicks, The Muppet Show (1976-1981), Beaker, "Clifford is Not Too Big," Clifford the Big Red Dog, Fame (1980), "Red Light," Zabar's, Prince, "If I Was Your Girlfriend," "I Am A Rock," "Perfect Day," Lou Reed, Nick and Nora, The Thin Man (1934), Myrna Loy, "The Kiss Waltz," Ruth Etting, "Maoz Tsur/Rock of Ages," "Chanukah Oh Chanukah," Mollena Williams-Haas, Chub Rub Club, Beauty and the Beast (1991), Macbeth, Doughnut Plant, "Haneiros Hallalu," Lesley Gore, "My Secret Love," "Bridge Over Troubled Water," Avant Pride collection, Fatties Against Fascism, Two Fat Ladies (19960-1999), Jean-Luc Picard, "Ner Li," "Ocho Candelikas," "Sevivon, Sov, Sov, Sov," Fiddler on the Roof (1964 stage musical), "Miracle of Miracles," "Latke Recipe," The Maccabeats, High School Musical (2006), YouTube, Fluevog, Brave (2012), "Touch the Sky," Bullet Journal, Big Gay Ice Cream Shop, Mermaid Sundae, Society Dame, Guys and Dolls (1950 stage musical), Marie's Crisis, Disney, Mia Mingus, There's No Wrong Way to Have a Body, Disneynature, "Black Velvet," Alannah Myles, Kushiel's Dart, Jacqueline Carey, "A Dream is a Wish Your Heart Makes," Gollum, "Everything Stays," Victoria sandwich, Anne Hathaway, The Devil Wears Prada (2006), Settle In Babies, Great British Bake Off (GBBO) (2010-present), Mary Berry, Pam Tillis, "Blue Rose Is," Gay Straight Alliance, "When Will My Life Begin," Fat Bitch, Merida, Rapunzel, Tracy Chapman, "At This Point in My Life," "Yours," KD Lang, "At Last," Nina Simone, "Here Comes the Sun."

Digital version 1.0

Cover design and illustration by Hannah Zayit

All rights reserved.

Image Description of the cover:

Illustrated cover with a lavender background shows two figures illuminated by the light from a menorah. Leah is kneeling on a pillow in chaps, jeans and a tank top, wearing cuffs and a collar Jordan is sitting in a chair in a vest & dress shirt, holding a leash attached to the collar. Title at the top reads: EIGHT KINKY NIGHTS: An f/f Chanukah romance. Author name Xan West in tan letters at the bottom of the image.

Created with Vellum

ABOUT THIS BOOK

Sometimes the perfect Chanukah gift can change everything.

Newly divorced stone butch Jordan moves into her friend Leah's spare room, ready, at 49, to take on a new job and finally explore kink and polyamory. But moving to NYC during the holidays sends grief crashing through her, and Jordan realizes that when she isn't solely focused on caring for others, her own feelings are unavoidable. Including her feelings for Leah.

51 year old queer femme Leah, an experienced submissive kink educator who owns a sex shop, has recently come to terms with being gray ace and is trying to rework her life and relationships to honor that.

Leah has a brainstorm to help them both: she offers Jordan eight kink lessons, one for each night of Chanukah, to help Jordan find her feet as a novice dominant, and to create a structured space where Leah can work on more deeply honoring her own consent, now that she knows she's gray ace.

She'd planned to keep it casual, but instead the experience opens cracks in the armor Leah's been using to keep people at a distance and keep herself safe. Now she needs to grapple with the trauma that's been impacting her life for years.

Can these two autistic queers find ways to cope with the changes they are making in their lives and support each other, as they build something new they hadn't thought was possible?

CONTENT NOTES

- Autistic characters getting overwhelmed, going non-verbal, experiencing meltdowns and shutdowns. Includes references to memory difficulties related to meltdowns.
- References to and descriptions of chronic pain.
- Both MCs have PTSD and experience nightmares, flashbacks, panic attacks, intrusive thoughts.
- MC with depression. References to depression flares in the past.
- References to MC with depression experiencing suicidality in the past in the following chapters: 5, 55
- References to parental depression and child neglect stemming from that depression.
- References to parental death in the past. Death was from suicide. Suicide is directly discussed in the following chapters: 19, 21
- Grief from loss of parent in the past is a significant part of the story; death anniversary occurs and is honored during the course of the story.
- References to parental emotional abuse and norming around autism. References to familial fat hatred and fat hating abuse from family. References to family being controlling.
- Alcohol use. References to being drunk, and fuzzy memory due to alcohol.
- Use of the term "queer" as a reclaimed slur.
- References to an ex being anti-kink.
- References to sexual partners in the past that pressured the stone MC to be sexually receptive and touch receptive.
- References to an ex being a TERF, a public confrontation around her TERFiness, and discussion of transmisogyny in queer kink community, and activist efforts to change it.
- References to ableism and norming from allistic partners, including setting expectations of masking in the context of kink.
- References to D/s relationship in the past that included elements of dubious consent, sexual pressure and emotional abuse, and trauma from that relationship. Details recounted in the following

chapters: 42, 45, 55, 56.
- Moment in the story where the MC is in the same space as her abusive ex and scared what she might do.
- References to having sex that was technically consented to but not wanted, and that causing trauma.
- Moment of accidental non-consensual service, challenged on the page.
- Sex on the page, including fisting, group sex, strap-on sex, masturbation, mutual masturbation. All of the sex in this book involves some element of pain play or power exchange. Sex occurs on the page in the following chapters: 3, 6, 7, 27, 28, 30, 59
- Consensual kink is central to the story, is discussed and depicted throughout the story. Kink depicted includes D/s, pain play, sensation play, orgasm control, genital torture, bondage, collaring and using a leash, play with sharps (scissors). Kink includes solo play, pair play and one group scene. Some of the kink takes place at a play party.
- Some of the kink is sexualized and involves sexual activity. Chapter references for sex are above. Sexualized kink (but not sex) occurs in the following chapters: 27
- Much of the kink is non-sexual. Non-sexual kink occurs in the following chapters: 12, 23, 24, 33, 46, 47

A BRIEF NOTE ABOUT TRANS AND NON-BINARY TERMS

This book has three trans women characters: Erica, Ellie, and Rebecca. This book has five trans men characters: Marcos, Tyler, Xavier, Ernest and Gideon. This book has two non-binary characters: Shiloh and Tal, and a genderqueer butch character, RJ. (There are a few other minor trans and non-binary characters, but they don't get significant page time in this book.) These characters use different terms to refer to themselves and each other, so I thought I would include a brief note about each, including a pronunciation guide (in italics) for potentially unfamiliar terms. While some non-binary and trans folks shift between pronouns, all of the trans and non-binary characters in this story use one set of pronouns.

I'm including a full set of pronoun examples (nominative, objective, possessive adjective, possessive pronoun and reflective) here, so you can see how they are used.

So, for a character like Leah, Jordan or Erica, who uses she/her pronouns, you would use them thus: She knows. I ask her. Her friends are great. That is hers. She likes herself.

Similarly, for a character who uses he/him pronouns, like Ernest or Gideon, you would use them this way: He knows. I ask him. His friends are great. That is his. He likes himself.

Shiloh uses ze/zir pronouns, which are used this way: Ze (zee) knows. I ask zir (zhere). Zir (zhere) friends are great. That is zirs (zheres). Ze likes zirself (zhereself).

Tal and RJ use ze/hir pronouns, which are used this way: Ze (zee) knows. I ask hir (here). Hir (here) friends are great. That is hirs (heres). Ze likes hirself (hereself).

1

FRIDAY EVENING, DECEMBER 13

JORDAN

"You don't have to go," Leah said. "Your flight just got in this morning. I know you must be fucking splatted."

"I want to go," Jordan insisted. "I've never gotten to see you do your thing before. I've been dying to, for years."

Leah curled into a new position on the couch and pushed her long black curls out of her face. It drew Jordan's attention to the color Leah had dyed her grey streaks this month, and she almost got lost in the bright blue and the way it echoed the tattoo of blue roses that twined from one arm to the other across Leah's chest. Were the blue streaks perhaps in honor of Chanukah? Perhaps, perhaps, perhaps. The old Doris Day song began to run through her head. Perhaps Leah was right and she was splatted. Whatever, she still wanted to go to the class.

"Are you sure? It might make you uncomfortable."

Wait, perhaps Leah didn't want Jordan to go. Perhaps, perhaps, perhaps. "Is it me you're worried about, or are you thinking it might make you uncomfortable?"

"Oh! No, I've taught this so many times, I honestly think even if my first girlfriend showed up I wouldn't blink."

"Kyra Rabinowitz? Wasn't she the rabbi's daughter?"

"Yep."

"And you wouldn't blink if she came to your fisting class?"

"Well, probably not," Leah shrugged. "Maybe she could use a little fisting in her life. Many of us could, don't you think?"

Jordan did. Very much so. Which is why she really wanted to go to the damn class. Because fisting hadn't been part of her life, but she was going to change that as soon as she could.

"So, if Kyra Rabinowitz can go to your class, why don't you want your best friend to be there?"

Leah was tapping her fingers against her thigh, and Jordan tried not to pay attention to how very form fitting those yoga pants were on her. Damn, she loved queer femme style, in pretty much all its iterations, including these yoga pants, which covered the curves of Leah's fat thighs in the softest cotton and made them even more distracting. But wait, why was she tapping? Leah usually rocked to stim.

"Look, I know you aren't into this kind of thing, and I just…I'm so damn glad to see you, so excited you're moving here. I don't want to make things weird because now suddenly you have memories of seeing my hand inside someone, okay?"

Aren't into this kind of thing. Of course Leah would think that. Because Jordan had never told her otherwise. Had never talked about it, with anyone, since that awful conversation with her ex-wife 12 years ago. It was past time to tell her then, wasn't it?

"So. Okay. That thing you just said…it's not exactly accurate."

"Which thing?"

"You said I'm not into this kind of thing," Jordan muttered.

"Yes, I have been under that impression," Leah said slowly, carefully. "That's not exactly accurate?"

"No." Jordan said. She could feel her chin sticking out, knew she was wearing her most stubborn stoic stone butch face.

"Can you tell me more about that, Jordan?"

"It would be more accurate to say that Dani wasn't into that kind of thing. So I tried to stop thinking about it."

"Ah. And now that you're divorced?"

"Well, let's just say that I no longer have to stop thinking about it. Or any of the other things that Dani wasn't interested in."

Leah nodded. "So it sounds like I shouldn't assume I know what kinds of things you are into, then."

Jordan laughed. "I honestly think I shouldn't assume that I know, even. Just because you've been fantasizing about a thing forever doesn't mean you'd actually like doing it, right?"

"Well, I'd say that depends on the person, and on the thing."

Jordan nodded.

"Look, I'm trying not to pry or say anything too blatant here, but…in most of my life, I speak pretty openly about this kind of stuff. Not just because it's my job as a sex and kink educator who runs a sex shop, but because that's part of kink culture. We talk about what we like with each other, fairly bluntly."

Jordan nodded, trying to imagine what that might be like. Bluntness sounded really good. "I don't mind blunt," she ventured. "I prefer blunt, really. You know that."

Leah nodded, smiling. "Yeah, I do. So do I."

They chorused together, "It's an autistic thing." And grinned at each other. "And really, an Ashkie Jewish culture thing, too," Jordan pointed out.

"Yeah, true," Leah said with a grin. "Especially us New York Jews, we're really fucking blunt."

"And foul-mouthed."

"You love me for it," Leah said. Then she shifted back to the subject at hand. "So it sounds like you had a sex life with Dani that didn't include some things you think you may be into, and might want to try now. And some of them are things you have been fantasizing about forever."

Jordan nodded. "But it's not like I can just go on Fetlife and say I'm a dominant and make a date with someone. I don't know what the hell I'm doing! I'm not even sure if I actually am a dominant. Or into fisting. Or any of the other stuff I've been wanting to try. And who would want a divorced 49 year old pansexual stone butch dom that's new to kink?"

Leah raised her eyebrows. "So I see you found Fetlife, and have words to describe some of what you want."

"It was part of my job at Terry's Place to train staff to know the differences between kink and abuse and to help them serve survivors of violence who were queer, trans, kinky and polyamorous. I had to know a lot, in order to do those trainings. And I did a lot of research about kink, once I said goodbye to my marriage. I know things. It's just all theory, right now, and stuff I know from other people, not for myself."

"Okay, okay. I knew that, about your job, I just hadn't really thought about what it meant in terms of this."

"I know you don't like me to talk about my job much. That it upsets you to hear about it. It makes sense that it wouldn't occur to you. And it's not like most agencies that serve survivors are really working to serve kink communities."

"Yeah, folks here are pretty wary of trying to go to get help from agencies that serve survivors; it would be cool if your work here changed that some."

"I'm excited about this job at Safe Haven, because it will have a wider impact, and hopefully will lead to that kind of change."

"I'm glad you're here, Jordan, and I'm glad you get to find out what you're into now. I just am a bit caught off guard here with the kinky stuff. I'd put you in the no kink box in my brain, and my brain is stubborn with shit like that. So bear with me as I adjust, okay?" Leah looked sad. Why did she look so sad?

"Did I say something that hurt your feelings, Leah?"

"Oh, Jordan. I just. I've been so fucking worried that our friendship might not survive you moving here, because it would become clear how central kink is in my life."

"Oh. I. Wow, Leah." Jordan noticed she didn't say that her feelings weren't hurt, she just talked about something else. They could get back to that.

"Yeah. You know, when you would visit each year I'd make my apartment Jordan-safe?"

"What?"

"I'd put away the shit I thought might make you uncomfortable. I did that yesterday, too."

"Okay, so basically, despite DMing pretty much every day, regular visits, and sending letters through snail mail every week for close to thirty years…we've been hiding important things about our lives from each other?"

"It does sound like it."

"But Leah, you offered to let me stay in your spare room for the next six months until I was ready to look for my own place. I was going to find out."

"Yeah, that's why I was worried!"

Jordan laughed, it just struck her as the most hilarious thing. Leah joined in not long after, her slightly nasal giggle filling Jordan with memories of being college housemates and all the times they'd pulled all-nighters trying to finish a paper and gotten laugh drunk together from sleeplessness. How the fuck had they ended up like this?

She knew how, could see the fault line clear as day, could mark it to the exact minute, that phone call that had yanked her back home, that had led to all these years in different cities, living such different lives, keeping all this from each other.

She'd be thinking about it all week, as she did every year, leading up to her dad's yartzeit next Friday. So, while Leah started getting ready, Jordan pulled out her phone and texted her sister.

Jordan: I got to NYC ok, will call tomorrow to check in.

Erica: Oh good! <3<3<3

Erica: Give my love to Leah. No need to call tomorrow if you've got stuff.

Jordan: I just want to check in. It's our first time not being together for dad's yartzeit.

Erica: I'm ok, really. You made the right decision, moving now.

Jordan: But we're missing Chanukah too.

Erica: I'm 35 years old. I'll be just fine. And you need time to settle in. Change is hard, you don't want to be moving and starting a new job all at once.

Jordan: Change *is* hard. I feel weird not being there with you for this.

Erica: We're gonna be okay. You'll be much less likely to have a meltdown if you don't do all this change at once. Plus you have that party your boss wanted you to go to. I helped you pick out a suit and three different ties. AND we packed your tux, so you have options.

Jordan: True. Your fashion expertise is much appreciated, sis.

Erica: You just remember our motto: pics or it didn't happen.

Jordan: I won't forget.

2

FRIDAY EVENING, DECEMBER 13

LEAH

Leah tried to focus on making sure she had all her supplies. Thanks, past me, she thought as she checked things off on the list she'd made for the class. She was certain she'd have forgotten something essential like gloves as she was obsessing over the conversation with Jordan, turning it around and around in her head. In fact...she double-checked that gloves and lube were in the bag, just in case. Whew. They were there. Now she could go back to the obsessing.

It was one thing to be aware that she was toning down parts of who she was around Jordan. It was a completely other thing to learn that Jordan had been keeping things from her too. Leah wasn't even sure why that hurt, but now wasn't the time to try to figure that out. She had to suck it up, get herself ready to teach. A fisting class. With Jordan in the audience.

You can do this, she repeated to herself as she got in the shower, putting on Coyote Grace's "Glory Be" because it always helped her breathe through the sensation of the water. The water and the music drove everything else out, the kind of stim that overwhelmed her sometimes but was a welcome relief right then. By the time her shower was done her skin felt alive and tingly and she could feel it soaking up the lotion like it was parched for it. Which it honestly probably was, her skin got so damn dry in the winter.

The music shifted to "Ghost Boy," and Leah made her way to the closet. She chose her favorite purple dress that accentuated her ass, because when a fat femme like her carried her weight in her ass and thighs she wanted clothes that showed them off, damnit. She decided on her rainbow glitter Docs, grey ribbed tights, and of course she'd wear her signature burgundy lipstick that perfectly matched her cat-eye glasses and leather gloves. She didn't need much else; she'd let her hair be the main event tonight. Just a pendant. Garnet or sodalite?

Leah had a habit of wearing the garnet when she was doing a fisting demo. Sometimes she was scheduled to teach about sex when she was leaning sex-neutral, and upping her connection with the sensual helped get her through. Sometimes she wasn't up for the demo and she asked friends to do it. On sex-repulsed days, she had to change her plans; she either cancelled, or taught something non-sexual. Leah used to push herself and do them anyway, but she was working on breaking that habit since she'd accepted that she was gray ace. It was an ongoing thing she was still figuring out, how to adjust her life to be true to that part of herself.

Today she was feeling energized and connected to her body sensually. The way the dress slid all soft and cool against her skin made her feel very aware, and her hair brushing against her shoulders was delicious. Joe Stevens' voice slid all sultry into her like hands gripping her firm, and moving her exactly where they wanted her to be. She didn't think she needed the garnet, but she tucked it into her bag just in case that changed. Instead, she held the sodalite, letting it warm in her palm as she sunk into the blue of it, and felt like it was the right choice. She wasn't sure why she needed a grounding bolster to her self-esteem, but it surely would only make her a better teacher. When it came to rest in the center of her chest, she felt her shoulders relax. Alright, then.

She stood in front of the mirror, doing one last check, and traced the vine of blue roses tattooed across her chest, renewing her vow to herself like she did every time she got dressed. "My body is mine, my heart is mine, my submission is mine to keep," she murmured to herself, the words familiar in her mouth. "No looking for the moon in someone's eyes."

When Leah emerged from her room, she saw that Jordan was ready, and sitting on the couch playing with one of Leah's fidgets from the bowl on the table, eyes closed. Leah just stood at the edge of the living room, taking her in. Black jeans, motorcycle boots, a magnificent blue button down with a black pinstriped suit vest, her fatness taking up all the room she needed, no attempt to make herself smaller. Jordan's curly hair had fallen over her eyes like always, and Leah was struck by a memory of Jordan's much younger face of 30 years ago, when they'd first become friends. Her hair was pretty much the same, except it was salt and pepper now. Her large nose was still the focal point of her face unless she was smiling. She hadn't smiled since she'd arrived. If anything, Jordan was more handsome now than she'd been at 19, but then Leah had always been partial to salt and pepper hair on butches. Her face just had more lines: on her forehead, on the sides of her mouth, crinkling at the edges of her eyes. It was truly unfair of her to look this good, Leah decided.

"That's my favorite kind of fidget," she said quietly. Jordan startled a bit, then responded, her eyes still closed. "It's great, and my favorite colors. Can I bring it to the class?"

"You always did like jewel tones. Of course you can bring it. I've got a bunch of them in different colors. You can keep that one."

"Jewel tones are the best. They make my brain happy. Thanks, Leah."

"I like jewel tones myself, as is evidenced by this room." Leah said, gesturing.

"Yeah that painting, I could look at it forever. The way the colors swirl together like that..."

"Rebecca made that for me, for my birthday."

"Is she going to be there tonight?"

"Nope, she has a thing to go to. But if you go to shul tomorrow, she'll be there."

"I was hoping to go to shul; come with me?"

"I'll see how I feel after tonight. These classes can eat all my social spoons sometimes. And there's a party Saturday night I'd like to go to."

"Oh really?" Jordan finally opened her eyes and looked at her. She actually bit her lip, like she was staring at something she wanted to devour, and said. "Damn. Talk about jewel tones."

"You like?" Leah asked, smoothing down the skirt a bit.

"Fuck yes. You look gorgeous, darlin'."

Whoa. Jordan hadn't called her darlin' since she'd gotten married. Leah had always figured Dani didn't like it, or the way their friendship held flirtation in it, because both had stopped after the wedding. But now darlin' was back, and perhaps the flirtation with it?

"Thank you. Folks expect the teacher to shine. It's part of the deal."

"You definitely shine, no question about it."

"You are looking damn good yourself."

"I am? I wasn't sure what to wear, honestly. It's my first time going to a leather group." Right. She was a novice, and that's the way Leah would try to treat her. Like a friend who was a novice, and needed support and a safe way to enter kink community. Leah knew how to do that; she'd done it many times before. She would just ignore the fact that it was Jordan. No big deal.

"I wouldn't say so if it wasn't true. I don't do false compliments, you know that."

"True." She looked so nervous. Leah wanted to hug her. If they touched like that. Which they never had. So, yeah. No hugging.

"Don't worry. There's no dress code; you can wear whatever to this. The party on Saturday has an unspoken dress code, but this isn't like that."

"I can go to the party?" Jordan sounded so unsure.

"If you want to."

"I just...you never took me to a party before." All this time, Leah thought she was respecting Jordan's vanilla-ness, but it was clear that Jordan had felt rejected.

"Well, you never told me you were kinky before. New rules now."

3

FRIDAY EVENING, DECEMBER 13

JORDAN

It was like getting to know Leah all over again. Jordan soaked up all the details, from the way she greeted people—gloved hand out for a clasp or a kiss, redirecting them from the hugs that everyone else seemed to be exchanging like they were nothing—to the way she put on Queen during set up. Killer Queen kicked off the mix, and it felt a bit like a magic spell, transforming Leah from her best friend to this spectacle of a performer who shone so bright everyone else faded into the background. When Fat Bottomed Girls came on, it seemed like it must have been written about her, and she knew it.

Jordan had already laid out the supplies per Leah's instructions. She had checked out the sling; it was her first time seeing one in person instead of just pictures on the internet. She was resting in the chair Leah had put in the front corner of the room for her, where she'd get to have her back against the wall but also be able to help out. The walk from the train had been a bit much after the steps. Her knee was hurting, probably from the cold, so she rubbed it, and watched Leah dance her way across the room, talking to the woman who was hosting this, shaking her ass in time to the music as she did. She truly was a fat bottomed girl, in the most spectacular way, and Jordan couldn't keep her eyes away from that deliciousness.

It had been Leah's ass all those years ago that had Jordan fantasizing about using her belt, leaving her marks, claiming Leah as hers. It had scared the shit out of her at 19, and she'd never pursued anything with her because of it, had let the school year end and just done nothing. When she'd returned to school that fall, Leah had been in her first D/s relationship, with an older butch named Bev, a serious monogamous relationship that had lasted for five long years. By the time she was single again, Jordan had been deep into her monogamous vanilla marriage.

She was done with monogamy now, probably for good. She was definitely done with pretending vanilla did it for her. The divorce may have shattered her life, but it had also freed her to go for what she wanted. She was feeling just reckless enough to admit—at least to herself—that she wanted Leah, and she wasn't scared of wanting her like she'd been at 19. She just wasn't sure if it was real, if it was about who Leah was now. Especially since she was fairly certain she didn't know this Leah. So she'd get to know her, and figure it out.

When the class began, Jordan tried to focus on what Leah was saying, but kept getting distracted by the movements of Leah's hands, the way her mouth pursed over certain words, how her large nose felt like it made her wide mouth, big hair, dark eyebrows and pointed chin all come into perfect balance. It was like Queen had kept playing and filled Jordan's head, and all she could do was look at Leah. There were all these guitar crescendos and soulful melodic voices harmonizing and the piano just kept building on itself as she honed in on the way Leah's hair moved when she laughed, how her dress slid along her thick thighs, the electric nature of her smile.

An Asian man dressed all in leather broke into her line of sight. She realized that it was Tyler, and he had a huge grin on his face. She and Leah had eaten dinner with him and his partner Marcos the last time she'd visited, from Marcos' favorite Brazilian restaurant; he'd said they made coxinhas that rivaled his mom's. She'd really liked both of them, and it was a relief to see people she knew.

Marcos was right behind Tyler, and gave her a little wave. When Leah had told her he'd be there, Jordan had been a bit surprised, figuring an aroace person wouldn't really want to be at a fisting class, or be there when his partner got fisted. But when she'd asked about it, Leah had said that Marcos generally preferred to be there when Tyler was acting as a demo bottom, to support him and do aftercare, and wasn't sex repulsed, just wasn't interested in sex.

It was time for the demo. Leah asked for water, so she handed it to her, and then took a slow breath. She really wanted to pay attention, not get distracted by this new Leah in front of her. And to learn at least the basics of fisting.

Leah was asking everyone to make a shape with their hands and hold it up, and she went around correcting how people held their hands, making jokes about ducks. When she circled back to Jordan, who'd been struggling to get it, Leah gently adjusted her forefinger, the leather of her burgundy glove smooth and cool on Jordan's skin. The position wasn't very comfortable at all, and she wondered if that was her arthritis or if it was something she just had to get used to. She murmured something to Leah about that, and Leah smiled at her like she'd said something smart, and straightened, repeating her question to the whole class. She took a few minutes to talk about ways to adjust play to go easy on hands, ways to work on increasing grip strength, and the fact that this was definitely going to feel weird for folks who don't do fine motor skills with their hands much.

Jordan was glad she'd mentioned it. From what Leah said, it sounded like fisting was a thing that wouldn't be easy for her, especially when it was cold, and especially if she wanted to do other things with her hands beforehand. That was kind of disappointing. In her head, it had seemed like the next thing to try. After all, she'd been fucking with her hands for her entire adult life. Fisting at least meant she didn't have to go buy a bunch of new supplies. Well, even if it was going to be a special occasion activity, she still wanted to learn how to do it.

Tyler had settled himself in the sling. He'd kept his boots, leather vest and red t shirt on, but had stripped down to his red and black striped boxer briefs, and was clearly packing hard. His legs were splayed open. It takes guts to just lay there like that, Jordan thought. Especially as a trans guy in a group of cis, trans, and non-binary strangers, she figured.

At least Tyler wasn't alone. His dominant and queerplatonic partner Marcos was right next to him, hand stroking Tyler's shoulder. Marcos whispered in Ty's ear, and he smiled up at his dom, saying something that made Marcos's low chuckle swirl into the room. There was this lovely warmth between them, the same one she'd witnessed at dinner on her last visit; it felt like they carried home together.

Jordan knew that Ty and Leah had been playing for years, and they had a sexual and kink relationship where Ty was dominant. She wasn't sure what being dominant while getting fisted would look like, and it definitely wasn't something she was interested in doing herself. As a stone butch, she was never sexually receptive. If she could step into anyone's boots in this scenario, it would be Marcos's.

Leah and Marcos were negotiating, and she paused at several moments to draw attention to how they were doing that, and the ways she was also checking in with Ty, as it was his body, even though his dominant was calling the shots in this scenario. She and Marcos seemed super comfortable together, made several jokes Jordan didn't quite get, one of which seemed to be about zucchini? There weren't any zucchini around, so this wasn't a food sex thing. Jordan would ask about it later.

Then the leather gloves came off and the nitrile ones went on. Leah was cheerfully talking about the importance of lube when fisting the front holes of folks on T, and Marcos was brandishing a shiny pair of large sharp sewing scissors, which he used to cut Tyler's boxer briefs off, and to tease his throat, coax him to ask permission to get fisted. Oh my. Yes, she wanted to be Marcos in this scenario. Wanted to hear that throaty Sir from her submissive's lips, wanted to tease and threaten like he was doing with those scissors, wanted to be the one who was in charge of everything that was happening, wanted to claim someone so deeply that they needed to ask permission to get fucked.

She wasn't going to be able to focus on technique at all.

4

SATURDAY NIGHT, DECEMBER 14

LEAH

Her bags were packed and she was ready to go, she was standing there outside her door, and Jordan was going to have to meet her at the party if she didn't get her fucking boots on and get out the door in the next thirty seconds. They had a subway to catch. And damned if she wasn't going to make Jordan sing "Leavin on a Jet Plane" with her as they walked to the station because now it was in her fucking head.

She hummed the song as she waited, remembering how she'd been obsessed with it in 1991, and had sung it to Jordan incessantly the last two weeks before Jordan had gone home that summer. Changing the lyrics of course, because Jordan was the one leaving, not her. It had been her last ditch effort to goad Jordan into admitting that she was into her, and it hadn't worked, of course. Oy, she'd been terrible at communication. It had felt like everything was changing, and it was her last chance with Jordan.

Leah had just graduated and had all summer to do what she wanted, before she had to go to B school, like her parents wanted. It had felt like her last moment of freedom, and she'd immersed herself in the queer leather scene in NYC, wanting to soak up every experience she possibly could. Which truly had changed everything for her, and had led her to her first dominant, Bev, who she still had such complicated feelings about.

Leah could still remember being in that room at Leather And Power (LAP) eleven years ago, how she'd taken such a clear stand against Bev in public, how much it had hurt because it felt like something dear to her had shattered on the floor of that room. It was hard when someone who you had ingrained respect for, and had been in service to for years...when she turned out to have fucked up politics. It had shifted things, at the core, to learn that about her former dominant, made her question if she'd known her at all.

Bev had looked at her with such helpless rage and shock, like she couldn't believe Leah had betrayed her like that. She'd do it again, in a heartbeat. That awful transmisogynist rule had needed to go, and Bev (and all the rest of them) had needed to be called on their TERF bullshit. (They hadn't used the word TERF back then, but that's definitely what Bev had been.) Hadn't she tried a private approach first, drawn on that old connection to try to change her thinking, and been dismissed? Had Bev really thought that Leah would be quiet simply because she'd told her to?

After eleven years, and a supposed change of heart from Bev, it still ached. There was a loss there. Of respect…of adoration, really. She had thought of Bev as someone honorable, admirable, back then, even if she'd been shattered by the way their relationship had ended, and the things that Bev had said to her on that last night. And while they had eventually found their way back to tolerating being in the same space, there was a finality to the way Leah felt now. And yet, they still were in the same community.

Eleven years after that awful LAP meeting, she was taking her oldest and best friend to a LAP play party, and would likely run into Bev there. Jordan had always disliked Bev, so she should give her a heads up about that.

Was she thinking about Bev because they might see her, or was something about this situation with Jordan pinging her in a similar way? Was that why she'd felt hurt and vulnerable yesterday? Because it was difficult to reconcile the Jordan she'd thought she'd known with a Jordan who was kinky, and had just not been acting on it for years?

It was a familiar thing, this dramatic shift in understanding about someone. She'd been experiencing it since she was a kid, realizing that people who acted like they were your friend were not actually your friend. It was shattering, to recognize that you'd gotten it wrong for all that time. That you'd misunderstood a relationship that much, or a person. She'd come to dread it, had even bonded with Jordan over that kind of realization, years ago. Nobody got how destabilizing it was like another autistic person. Jordan had really gotten it, maybe especially because she'd been making sense of these experiences with her new autism self-dx. It had never occurred to Leah that Jordan would someday be one of those people she'd realize she had misunderstood.

But had she? She'd stepped away from showing Jordan much of her kink life because talking about it would create this spark in Jordan's eyes, a spark that would quickly get shut down. She'd begun telling herself a story of discomfort. Had decided to respect Jordan by not being in her face about kink. But it wasn't like she hadn't seen that spark.

She hadn't been wrong about the discomfort, about what was going on with Jordan. Her friend hadn't been ready to accept it in herself, and Leah was nothing if not willing to be where someone was at, regardless of information that might be poking out to say perhaps there's something else going on underneath.

So if it wasn't the same, wasn't actually shattering her sense of knowing Jordan, where did the hurt live? Mostly it was the feeling that she and Jordan had lost out on something, on a connection that they could have had. Leah decided to try to let that go. There was a doom and gloom aspect to it that was likely framed by her depression, and she thought her therapist would be damn proud of her for recognizing that. He'd say she knew how to handle it then, didn't she? Reframe. So she gave that a try.

Wasn't Jordan trusting her now, with her vulnerability, with being a novice? Giving her the gift of letting Leah show her the kink scene? Couldn't they have that connection she'd been mourning now, only deeper because of the foundation of years they brought to it? Those felt like good questions, so she typed them into her phone, to remember them.

She was just tucking it into her coat pocket when Jordan finally emerged, face flushed, an apology on her lips for making Leah wait. Leah just grinned at her and told her that she was now obliged to sing along all the way to the subway. Jordan offered her arm, which itself was a surprise, a gesture of chivalry she hadn't offered in a very long time. So Leah linked her arm with Jordan's, a bit breathless, and led the way, beginning the song.

5

SATURDAY NIGHT, DECEMBER 14

JORDAN

The dungeon wasn't as dark as she'd expected; it was actually really well lit. It wasn't all black, either. Each smaller room had a theme, so one might be opulent and French while another looked medieval, and yet another was filled with children's things except in adult sizes. There was even a room with a communal shower, and one with a cage big enough for at least three fat people. Each had different music playing, and when Jordan asked, Leah told her that folks could select from different themed playlists.

They settled in a larger room that was kind of like a cafe, with a dance space that had hardwood floors, cozy looking chairs and sofas all along the edges, a few fourtop tables, and food spread on one end.

"This is a room set aside for socializing, dancing, negotiation, and aftercare," Leah said. "Though some aftercare happens in the individual rooms too."

"This isn't what I'd pictured a play party space would look like."

"Ah, well, it's actually two different spaces, except when they rent it out for parties. This large room and the other two larger ones with mirrors belong to a dance studio and rehearsal space, and the small rooms are used by pro dommes."

Bev walked past them and paused to say, "Leah, Jordan. I can't stop, I have a date with this one here," she gestured to the woman crawling behind her, with her boot. The woman kept her eyes on the floor and her head bowed as they left. Bev always rubbed Jordan the wrong way, and today was no exception. She was glad to see her go.

"Anyway," Leah said, shaking her head. "I have a date with Iris, for clips and fisting."

"Fisting?"

"Yeah, I often want to bottom to it after I teach it, and it's one of Iris' favorite things. It's like teaching it puts it in my head or something. There's something about the intensity and catharsis that can be part of a fisting scene that makes more sense to me than other kinds of sex. In some ways the demo could be misleading, because it's all about technique and when I do it in play it looks really different."

"Oh. That's useful to know. I might want to watch, then. If that's really okay."

"Oh, yeah, you're totally welcome to watch us. You can also hang out here, watch any other scenes as long as you don't interfere or disrupt, or play yourself if you feel comfortable. Whatever you want."

"I doubt I'll play, not without a guide. Maybe if the bottom was experienced and willing to teach me, or if there was another top who could guide me."

"Good for you, being clear on what you want, and careful with yourself and others," Leah said, which made Jordan blush.

On the train going there she'd explained the rules of the space, going over the ones listed on the website for the party, and a few of the social norms nobody would write down but just assume that people knew. Leah was really good at making sure Jordan had the info she needed to navigate new social spaces as an autistic person. It was one of the reasons she'd decided to go to the party, even though Leah had a play date. Well, that and it was a chance to wear her tuxedo, as it had a 007 theme. She always felt especially handsome and dominant in her tux.

Leah was wearing a two piece gold dress with a long full skirt, a plunging neckline, and long sleeves. It draped beautifully, bared just a hint of her midriff, and flowed in gorgeous lines when she moved. She looked every inch the Bond girl in it, especially with her dark burgundy lips and dramatic eye makeup, and her curls in an elaborate twist.

She was just working up the courage ask Leah more about her play date, when a fat desi butch wearing a gorgeous tux stopped in front of Leah.

"Iris," Leah murmured, "you remember my best friend, Jordan."

"Oh yes. Very good to see you again," Iris said, giving Jordan a friendly smile, and winked at her, before offering her hand to Leah.

Leah said, "Well, they are playing your song," and took her hand, rising.

That's when Jordan realized that the Goo Goo Dolls had come on. Iris led Leah over to a table on the café side, and they began to chat, deeply focused on each other. They were probably confirming the details of the scene. Jordan wondered what they were planning, and if it was something she would want to watch. She'd never gotten to see Leah play, though she had seen her with Bev, years ago, and had watched her dance with Iris before, at a party, years ago.

Iris was Leah's main dance partner, and Jordan hoped she would get to see them dance tonight. They spoke all throughout the song, and transitioned easily to the next one, which was from Labyrinth, she thought. Except it wasn't David Bowie singing this time, and she thought she might even like this pared down version better than the original. She turned to someone sitting nearby, a superfat genderiffic white person wearing a swirling rainbow of colors. "Do you know who's singing? I don't think that's Bowie."

She was rewarded with a tremendous grin. "No, that's definitely not Bowie. It's Lena Hall, she's been doing pared down tributes, usually in amazing outfits." They pulled out their phone, like they were looking something up.

"That name sounds familiar."

"She was in a queer indie film that was in all the festivals a couple years ago, Becks. Maybe that's how you know her name."

"Ah, yes, I saw it. She was brilliant."

"I absolutely agree." They seemed to have found what they were looking for on their phone. "Here, see? She has a channel. I can send you the link if you want?"

Jordan rattled off her email address. Her phone pinged, and there was a new email from someone named Shiloh, who had ze/zir pronouns in zir signature, and a website under it that looked like a blog of some sort. "Shiloh, I presume?"

"Yep that's me. I use ze/zir pronouns," Shiloh said with a grin that showed zir dimples.

"I'm Jordan. I use she/her pronouns."

"Very nice to meet you, Jordan," Shiloh purred. "Very nice, indeed. And are you here with someone or someones tonight?"

"My best friend. She's..." Jordan looked over at the table, but Leah wasn't there anymore. She scanned, and found her on the dance floor, with Iris. "She's on the dance floor. In the gold dress." Jordan gestured, and then got distracted by the way Leah's neck looked in the light as she moved. She and Iris had this gorgeous chemistry as they danced, and Leah was luminous, gathering light with every movement. Then Leah threw back her head and laughed, joyous and sultry, as the music shifted to a Sting song she didn't recognize. Jordan couldn't take her eyes off of her.

They were doing a tango, and it was riveting, the fluidity of their movements, the way she saw the D/s dynamic build between them as they moved along the floor. They seemed to barely be touching the floor, and the way their bodies intertwined as they tangoed was one of the hottest things she'd ever seen in her life. Wow, she could watch them dance for hours. She definitely wanted to watch them play; to see how this dance dynamic translated into kink.

Then the song shifted and Alicia Keys came on, and they shifted into a waltz, though Leah wasn't laughing anymore.

Jordan remembered taking a bus to NYC to be with Leah after she'd broken up with Bev, the way Leah had played this song incessantly all weekend, until Jordan heard it whether it was actually playing or not. "If I Ain't Got You" would always be Jordan holding Leah in her arms as she sobbed, devastated by the end of her first D/s relationship, feeling completely unmoored. She had melted down at least five times that weekend, and barely ate.

It was the first huge depression flare Jordan had witnessed in Leah, and it had scared the shit out of her, the lyrics of the song evoking a world without Leah in it, which Jordan refused with all her being. She'd had to force herself to get back on the bus and go home. Leah had been okay, she had other supports, local ones, and had started therapy again within a few weeks. She'd been okay.

And she was still dancing, clearly taking comfort from the close hold, from attending to the ways Iris invited her to move. She looked certain she was safe and cared for. It was good Leah had that, she wanted that for her.

"Oh, I know Leah. She's your best friend?" Shiloh said softly.

"Yes, for almost thirty years," Jordan said absently, focused on watching the way Leah's dress shimmered as they stopped dancing and Leah moved towards her, Iris going in another direction.

"And are you going to play tonight?"

"I might watch. I'm not sure."

"Alright. If you want company, for play or just someone to hang out with, feel free to seek me out."

Jordan turned to Shiloh. "Thank you. It's my first play party. It's a bit... daunting. I might come find you later."

Shiloh grinned. "I'd like that."

Leah sat next to Jordan, a bit breathless. Jordan handed her a bottle of water.

"Thanks," Leah murmured. "Hi Shiloh," she said, shooting zir a smile.

"Well, hello there, Leah. Nice to see you. I've got some serious spy business to attend to in the other room. But I'll be around." Ze almost seemed to float away in waves of color, dress flowing.

"I see you met Shiloh," Leah said. "Ze is lovely. One of my favorite people at Femme Brunch, and a great asset to the store, especially where education is concerned."

"Yes, ze seems great. Mentioned play, too. But I'm not sure about playing tonight. It's like I told you."

"It's up to you. I was thinking about what you had said about wanting to be guided by an experienced person. I had an idea about that."

"Well, I definitely want to hear it."

6

SATURDAY NIGHT, DECEMBER 14

LEAH

She just had to say it. Why did it seem so hard? When she'd been discussing it with Iris it had felt like the right thing. Because she did want to support Jordan to learn, and Iris was a great person to learn from, and this was a way to support Jordan that had boundaries around it. One scene, two elements, them co-topping her, Jordan getting to learn, her getting to support that without it getting complicated, Iris getting to co-top with another butch that she thought was hot and getting to mentor, which she loved doing. Win-win-win.

But now it felt hard to say. She tried closing her eyes, not trying to read or anticipate Jordan's expression, just to get out the words. That helped.

"Well, Iris and I were thinking perhaps you could join us tonight. She could show you some things about clips, help guide as you try fisting for the first time. And you could trust that I know your experience level and will support you through the scene. I thought it might be a good way to get a bit of experience in a safer context, with less pressure on you."

"Oh. Wow. I wasn't expecting you to say that."

"I don't want to make you uncomfortable, so if it feels weird or wrong that it would be with me, just say so. I promise it's okay to say yes, no, whatever."

"No...it doesn't feel weird or wrong. It feels...safe. Though having people watch, I'm not sure about that."

"Oh, there are rooms where if you close the door, you get privacy. Iris is securing one of those already, because I prefer privacy when I get fisted."

"Oh, that's good to know. I really wouldn't be intruding? You two seem so in sync. I figured she was your dominant, and maybe your primary romantic partner."

Leah chuckled. "Oh no, she's married, actually. We aren't in a romantic relationship at all. Mostly, we are dance partners, and we play every few months or so. We've been doing it that way for years."

"And her wife—"

"Husband, actually."

"Silly of me to assume. Her husband would be okay with me joining in?"

"Definitely. She and David have an open marriage, and casual play is a regular part of her life. She also mentors other dominants fairly frequently, so if you wanted that, it might be an option. Not something to decide now, of course."

"Mentor...okay, I will ask more about that later. This is a lot of new for me at once."

"I know. Go at your own pace. I know it's a lot just even being at a public play party."

Jordan seemed to relax a bit when she said that. Her shoulders had been slowly rising to meet her ears, but now they were coming back down. Leah just let her sit with it for a bit, holding space as Jordan thought it through. That's how it always had been; Jordan needed to go through her own process before she decided things. If you rushed her, she'd be much more likely to melt down or go non-verbal. You just needed to give her space, and wait.

The Goldfinger theme song came on, and Leah got lost imagining that she and Iris were dancing to it. The horns were great, and Shirley Bassey's singing was so dramatic. Perfect for a tango.

She shook herself out of hyperfocus when Jordan cleared her throat, turning to look at her. Her heart was racing. Why was her heart racing?

"I would like to try it," Jordan said shyly. "With the option to stop if I need to."

"Of course. For something like this I'd be in favor of direct communication, but I'd like to have a safe signal, in case talking is hard. I usually do a double tap, for that."

"A double tap?"

"May I demonstrate on your thigh?"

Jordan swallowed, and nodded. Leah kept herself focused on the task, showing her the double tap, then inviting her to practice on Leah's thigh. They touched each other so rarely that even this practical touch carried something in it, some kind of electricity. Well, there was definitely going to be more touching tonight. Leah took a long slow shuddering breath, and stood, grabbing her bag. "Shall we?"

Jordan stood, and offered her arm, and Leah got to do that trick of traveling through a space on a butch's arm where she was the one who was subtly leading the way. She loved getting to use that trick, and as long as she kept pace with Jordan, it worked wonderfully. When Iris opened the door at her knock, she had a big grin on her face. She'd slung her tux jacket over the arm of the sofa in the room, removed her tie, and had rolled up her shirt sleeves. She often waited to do those things until Leah was there, because she knew that Leah thought it was sexy to watch. She had also laid out a bunch of clips on a table by the sling. They must have taken longer than Leah had even noticed, but she didn't seem impatient or annoyed, just focused.

Iris had set up a banquet chair by the sofa, and she asked Jordan to try it out, see if it was comfortable. Jordan wouldn't be able to stand for the whole scene, so having a chair that was accessible and could be pulled close was important. The banquet chair was okay, so they settled in on the couch. She lifted her skirt when she sat down, and Jordan's gaze slid to her metallic peep-toe heels. And lingered there. Well, well. Perhaps she would keep them on then. They talked over what they were going to do, and then Iris gave a 5 minute tutorial on clip safety, using the low neckline of Leah's dress to bare enough skin to demonstrate different ways to take off clips, and how to put them on, asking Leah to describe what each felt like.

Then Leah took a few moments to go to the restroom, and check in with herself, to make sure she was still up for fisting. Ever since she'd come to terms with being gray ace, she'd been trying to do that before any kind of sex, to really give herself room to change her mind, or say no in the middle. She did a bit of mental rehearsal, forming the words in her lips, to see how they felt, to make it easier to say them, reminding herself that nobody wanted her to be having sex she didn't want to have. Especially her.

Then it was time, and Iris used the remote to put on the song they always started with. Sade's voice grabbed ahold of her, and Leah approached Iris who was still seated on the coach, handing Iris her glasses. She kneeled, like usual, sinking into headspace. Iris cupped her face, her calloused thumb stroking Leah's cheek, and the world receded to the two of them.

Iris gathered her close, and Leah wrapped her arms around her, face buried in her chest, and just breathed as "By Your Side" wrapped around her. One of the things she loved the most about playing with Iris was the way she made the scene flow through music. From the very beginning, where they started out dancing, through this ritual that began every scene, every step of their play moved with the music, including the aftercare. There was definitely something to be said for playing with your dancing partner, even if you only did it four times a year.

Iris tugged her head so that she looked up and to the side, and there was Jordan, looking particularly tall and fairly blurry as she stood over her. Jordan put a finger under her chin to lift her face a bit more and Leah's bones went a bit more languid. Just that small movement, that assertion of control, and something had shifted between them. This was a different Jordan, one she had never met before. What would she do? Damn if she didn't make her wait on her knees in front of her as she took off her jacket, undid her bowtie and the top couple buttons of her shirt, and then slowly removed each of her cufflinks. They were lapis lazuli, and picked up the blue notes in her tie and vest. Jordan reached down to cup Leah's chin in her hand and run her thumb along Leah's lower lip.

"Open," she said, in a growly voice Leah had never heard before. When Leah parted her lips, the cufflinks were placed between them, cool stone against her tongue and metal gripped in her lips, and she was told to hold them between her lips, not let them fall. Oh my. What the fuck did Iris say to Jordan while she'd been in the bathroom? She had never played with a novice dominant who actually got that it wasn't about what you did but about the control, taking it and giving it, and that creative ideas were not just fine but actually wonderful because they provided opportunities to give over control in ways that felt fresh and new. Jordan was fucking brilliant and maybe it was that, but Leah was pretty sure that Iris had given her a few nudges in the right direction. Damn. Putting the two of them together was dangerous, in the best way.

Jordan was rolling up her sleeves, very slowly, and just as slowly was describing how good Leah looked with her cufflinks between her lips, that it felt like marking her, that she hoped to leave another kind of mark on her soon. That she couldn't wait to see what the clips would do to her skin, to know that she had been the one to put marks there. The stones were warming as she held them, smooth against her tongue, and holding the cufflinks built a pool of liquid in her mouth. By the time her sleeves were rolled up to just below her elbow, Jordan had Leah all gooey, and drooling just a bit. Jordan slowly removed one cufflink, then the other, took her pocket square and gathered the drool carefully. Her lips felt tender, wanting, her mouth empty and aching to be filled. She couldn't stop thinking about the fact that the next time Jordan put on those cufflinks, she would think about how Leah's lips had pursed around them. Jordan wrapped the cufflinks in her pocket square and put them in her pocket, as Iris told Leah to remove all her clothes. She started taking them off automatically, then stopped, and said, "Sir, may I please keep my shoes on?"

"If you tell me why, I will consider it," Iris said.

"I think Jordan likes them," Leah whispered.

Iris chuckled, then turned to Jordan. "Would you like our girl to leave her shoes on, Jordan?"

"Yes," Jordan said, simply. Not playful like Iris, but also not hiding exactly what she wanted. Jordan didn't use extra words, unless she was talking about stones or Disney, so it wasn't a surprise, but again...not usual for a novice dominant. Leah was going to need to stop expecting her to act like the other novices she'd played with.

They helped her into the sling, and she sighed. There was such comfort in equipment that you knew you could trust would hold you, especially as a fat person. Iris put her glasses on the side table, and let her know they were there. Then Iris got Jordan set up on the side of the sling, waiting for the music to shift to the next song. When the piano started, and Regina Spektor's ethereal voice slid into the room, Leah sighed. There were two mixes Iris favored for play, one that played more with rhythm that she used for impact play, and this one, which leaned on melody and emotion, and was about a different kind of scene. A scene oriented towards peeling emotional layers back, slowing things down and creating room for her to feel splayed open and rubbed raw, to have that kind of helplessness wash through her. Damn, she needed this, and somehow it was the music that made it feel real and touchable and as inevitable as a freight train coming her way.

Clothespins were like nothing else, a sharp electric almost grating pain that stole her breath and made her feel angry and helpless all at once, with a scraping sadness that followed in waves. They were an irregular dance, one fading as the new one came in, hitting her nerves differently in different parts of her body, and sharpening as she began to anticipate them. The sling cradled her body so she was most comfortable looking at the ceiling. There was plenty to look at; one of her friend Blaze's gorgeous rope bondage mobiles lazily swung and spun with the music. It was the perfect visual stim to focus on as the pain moved through her.

Between the music, the two tops dancing pain along her skin, and the mobile, there was no room for anything else. All she could do was feel, and the sensation built in this odd architecture that didn't really make sense but gave her just enough structure to hang these devastating feelings on, drew them out of her like poison. Jordan smiled down at her, murmuring that she looked so beautiful this way, that Leah took her breath away. The music shifted to a low lilting voice and quieter piano, and it took until the chorus for her to recognize it. The lyrics reached into her and pierced her heart, which the pain from the clips only intensified, as Sara Bereilles sang about how Leah was imperfect but she tries, and is hard on herself and won't ask for help, and is messy and lonely most of the time and it was so much she wasn't sure she could take it.

Then she heard Iris say the word zipper, and reached for Jordan's hand, gripping it tight, because she knew what was coming. Waves of fire bit into her skin, and she held on tight, and screamed, tears finally flowing, and the chorus came back to punctuate it and wring her dry. Then the music shifted and it was that song she'd fallen for the year she'd come out as queer, Sarah MacLachlan's voice crooning and soothing, and the tears just flowed as Jordan lifted the hand she was still holding to stroke it along her own cheek, almost like a cat scent marking, and Leah started giggling because really Jordan was so catlike in so many ways and now she couldn't unsee it.

She could tell Jordan was exchanging looks with Iris, trying to understand this latest reaction, having no clue that after a while this kind of pain pretty much always made her laugh. Iris gestured to the clips covering Leah's chest and suggested that Jordan play with them a bit, wake them up.

If it'd been Iris, she would've done it to the beat, but Jordan worked her own rhythm in counterpoint, so the pain built in swirls and built her giggles into open laughter. Which only made her whole body vibrate, and all the clips move, which made the tears flow faster and her breathing get ragged. When the music shifted to Rihanna, Iris began to twist the clips off, driving sharp bursts of electricity into her and making her beg for more. This was the best part and she wanted it to drive her into her first orgasm, if they would let that happen.

Iris had slicked up a glove, telling her she was doing it, making her wait, aching, as she begged, and cursed and called her a handsome sadist and began begging again, and was that Jordan who was laughing delightedly? Then Iris was inside her, sliding three fingers in like it was nothing, and she was sure she could come if she could just have more of that pain, now that she had something to thrust towards, to clench around, so she started to beg for the pain to make her come, not just to beg Iris but both of them, calling them both Sir and telling them she'd make it good for them if they would just give her the pain she ached for.

Jordan looked at Iris, and they seemed to come to an agreement because Iris began working four fingers into her, which was almost too much until Jordan took off two clips at once, and then it was perfect, exactly right, the pain glorious and the fullness exactly what she needed. She was saying thank you, Sir over and over, with each thrust of Iris' fingers, each clothespin that Jordan took off, and she felt herself getting louder. Iris put a small plastic clip on her clit, and she came, unable to be still, screaming at the top of her lungs, and then whispering a litany of thanks as Iris tapped the clip on her clit in tune to the music. This delicious pain seared through her in big bursts, and she felt herself open, and then Iris' hand was inside her where it belonged. She lifted her head, and smiled, and Iris gave her the best damn grin in the world and told her she was beautiful and deserved to be treasured.

She was full, and content, and surrounded by people who cared about her, and getting exactly what she needed, and the raw scraping sadness that had found her at the beginning of the scene was drifting away. The music shifted to something dreamy with Adele's voice caressing her skin as Jordan traced the marks on her chest with her fingers and Iris shifted her hand in minute movements that felt amazing. It wasn't until the first chorus that she even realized what the song was: the title theme for the film Skyfall. She started laughing, couldn't believe there was actual 007 music playing, when it had never been on this mix before.

"Now I really am a Bond girl!" she exclaimed, and they started laughing with her.

"Now would a Bond girl get fisted like this?" Iris asked.

"She would if she had any fucking sense because that feels incredible, Sir."

7

SATURDAY NIGHT, DECEMBER 14

JORDAN

Jordan's knees were not doing so well, but she didn't want to disrupt the scene. She felt a bit stuck, but she knew Leah would be pissed off if Jordan didn't do something about it, so she said she'd be right back, and brought the chair over, so she was sitting next to Leah, and could still touch her. Iris smiled at her, and started talking about what it felt like to have her fist inside Leah, how she was moving, and in a teasing tone, told Leah to describe what it felt like.

Leah was trying, but it was clearly hard for her to make words, though she did manage to say things like full, and pulsing, and glorious, and Iris began playing with the clip on her clit again, which led to some fervent begging to take it off so she could come. Iris suggested that Jordan take over playing with the clip, and it was amazing how just the tiniest of movements created really intense reactions. She was a bit shocked at how much she liked hurting Leah, and making her beg, forcing her to wait until she was sobbing.

The tears reached into Jordan's gut, and made her throb, and she was growling at Leah that she had to wait, that Jordan was in charge and would be deciding when she could come. She felt herself shudder after she said that, like she couldn't even fathom that she actually had said it. It had felt amazing to tell Leah some of the things she'd muttered to her submissive in her fantasies, and to hear Leah say "your decision, Sir," and know that she'd given over that control. Iris grinned at her, nodding that she was ready whenever Jordan wanted to do it, and Jordan just savored that for a moment, that the power rested in her hands. She breathed that in, then removed the clip, and Leah screamed, her body shuddering. Iris was using the moment to slide out of her, strip off the glove, and slick Jordan's hand up, forming her fingers into the elusive shape she'd struggled with in the class. Jordan scooted her chair into position, and began to thrust her three fingers into Leah, awed by the pulsing heat around her hand, and the electric feeling of intensifying her connection with Leah, actually being inside her for the first time. Jordan had barely touched her for thirty years, and now her hand was actually inside Leah. It was so intense and amazing to feel her cunt pulsing, to hear her moaning as Jordan fucked her, while Iris whispered in her ear that it was a process, not a goal, and all she had to do was enjoy the ride.

What a fucking ride, it was completely different from what she'd thought it would be, which was at least partly because Leah had already been fisted tonight, but still. She had thought of it mostly as being about control and surrender and this felt ferocious and claiming, like she wanted to snarl and bite and scratch and…claim. It kept coming back to that word, claim, resounding in her head. It had felt like that earlier, when she had been looking down at Leah kneeling before her with Jordan's cufflinks in her mouth. And again, when she'd been touching the marks she'd made on Leah's glorious breasts. But this was even more intense than either of those experiences, like a maelstrom was building inside her, and she dug her boots into the ground trying to keep it contained.

It was like Iris could tell what was happening, because she came to stand behind Jordan and rested her hands on Jordan's shoulders, pressing down, helping her ground. It felt good to have Iris at her back, watching over them both. She didn't just feel connected to Leah, all three of them were connected, and Jordan leaned her head back to rest it against Iris' belly, soaking up that feeling coursing through her.

The urgency faded, and everything got all slow and languid, like time had melted and there was no rush at all. Iris coaxed her through the next stages calmly, and it turned out that her fingers could make the right shape, they just needed this context, needed it not to be abstract. So she was able to get four fingers in, no worries, and had tucked in her thumb, was just at the point where the largest part of her hand was almost there. Then Iris produced a clip, and offered to help her put it on Leah's clit. They managed it, and Leah made the most gorgeous sound, and then…Jordan's entire hand was inside, this intense pressure at the wrist, a gloriously silky slide in, this amazing sense that they were doing something miraculous.

She kept very still, and felt Leah clench around her. Whoa. She was actually doing it. She had her entire hand inside Leah, and Iris was describing the different ways she could move, emphasizing the need for tiny movements, encouraging her to focus on the reactions each one brought. It was like learning sex all over again from scratch, the how of it, the person she was fucking, the way it reverberated through her, the tremendous high of the power that was part of it this time. She was in charge of leading this dance, she was experiencing this immense trust. It was like her hand was moving inside her own chest, as it moved in Leah. Leah would react, and it would move through her, and then Jordan would react, and she could almost feel it wrap Iris in, too. Like one huge feedback loop.

Iris was encouraging her to try a pulsing movement, and that got a huge reaction, a wave of moaning sobs that awed Jordan, and this sense that big feelings were building, that she was holding Leah's heart in her palm. She definitely felt something huge building in herself, so big it scared her, and she leaned into Iris, looking up into her face, asking for help.

"You've got this. I'm right here. The only thing to do is ride it out, and make sure your feet are on the ground. Press your boots into the floor, okay?" Iris said softly.

Jordan nodded; she could do that. Then Iris began tapping against the clip on Leah's clit, drawing out a staccato of moans from her that got louder as she went on, and Jordan pulsed her hand in counterpoint, just trying to breathe as she kept doing exactly what she had been doing, and Leah began to beg again, her voice hoarse and thick.

"Not until Jordan says it's time," Iris told Leah, and Jordan felt this rush of power that drove through her, making her moan. Because damn it, she did want to be in control of this, she did want to hold the leash of it in one hand while the other wrapped around Leah's heart. She had this image in her head of driving a chariot across the sky, like a goddess, holding reins in each of her hands, taking them all over the sun. The sense of power built right alongside the emotions as she drove that chariot, growling the word now when it felt like they were reaching the sun, and using the burst of pain to take them all over it. Iris was shuddering behind her, and Leah was a pulsing flame around her and she could feel tears streaming down her own cheeks as an orgasm sliced through her.

Then Iris had her hand on Leah's thigh and was coaching Jordan through withdrawing before the orgasm stopped, helping her discard the glove and clean her arm. They each took one of Leah's hands, as she moved through the last waves. Iris was petting Leah's hair and praising her, and Jordan followed that lead, stroking her cheek and telling her how amazing she was. Once Leah could walk, they gathered her up and brought her over to the sofa, seating her between them. They stayed like that for a good long time, just holding her, telling her how good she was, before Iris turned to Jordan and said,

"You are such a good dominant already. So attentive, creative, and connected. It was a joy to co-top with you. Thank you for trusting me to guide you through it."

Her words landed somewhere in Jordan that felt tender and unsure, and she felt her eyes fill. She knew she was supposed to make words but she couldn't, so she just reached for Iris and buried her face in Iris' arm, holding on tight.

"It's okay, you don't need words right now," Iris said. "Just listen to mine, okay?"

Jordan nodded against her arm.

"This was such a pleasure. You are already such a good dominant, and you are just getting started. I would be glad to co-top with you again, and also just to help you become the dominant you want to be. You can think about that, and decide later. I feel so honored by everything you brought to us tonight. I bet Leah does, too."

Then Leah spoke for the first time since the scene had ended. "Seriously, Jordan, you are so damn good already. That thing with the cufflinks...fuck that was perfect. Thank you for trusting me, for letting me be the first person you dominated. It was a wonderful scene, and you were wonderful in it."

Leah wrapped her arms around Jordan's waist, and just held on, as Jordan slowly made her way back towards earth, her face buried in Iris' arm, with Iris' hand stroking her hair. She was never going to forget this. Now if only there were a way to teleport herself into bed, because she felt completely spoonless.

8

SUNDAY MORNING, DECEMBER 15

LEAH

Leah wished that she didn't have to be out in the world all day today. But she couldn't miss Femme Brunch and afterwards she had to cover for one of her managers, who had the flu. Unless Amaya was miraculously free and checked her texts before noon. What Leah really wanted to do was to sleep in and stay home all day eating her favorite post-scene foods and let herself just be with Jordan, settle in to being roommates and best friends, maybe do a movie marathon or something. Something that didn't require being on and looking good and being out in the fucking world.

She was going to get onion rings and a rare burger, and a chocolate shake, damnit. If she had to drag herself into Manhattan for brunch, she was going to have her favorite diner stuff. At least the train to the shop was right by the diner, so she wouldn't be rushing from brunch. She just needed to pick out what to wear. Something that wasn't too much for the shop.

After much consideration, she decided on her favorite patterned skirt and a black top that had a high neck and shoulder cut-outs, because she always tried to keep her tits under wraps a bit at work. The skirt reminded her of one of her grandma's gorgeous Russian scarves, red and grey on black, and stopped at the knee, so she decided just to wear her knee length grey boots with it, with one of her favorite silly socks underneath for a touch of whimsy only she knew about; today's had red pandas on them. The key was makeup; she took her time with her eyes and her contouring, putting her hair up so her eyes would really pop.

She saw no sign of Jordan, so Leah left her a note detailing her schedule today and when she likely would be back, and included her handout on scene drop, with a sticky note saying that she should text Leah or Iris if she was dropping, plus Iris' number, in case she'd lost the card Iris had given her. Jordan was probably still sleeping, and rest would be the best thing for her. Jordan would be fine, Leah told herself.

She was twenty minutes late even though she'd left extra time, because she'd missed her damned stop on the subway, thinking about last night's scene. So she'd decided to stop thinking about it. Right now she needed to soak up all the femme community she could get.

She slid in between Shiloh and Ruth, and after ordering she closed her eyes, just let herself settle. She focused on drinking the water in front of her; it was cold and grounding and helped her manage the noises swirling around her. Damnit, she felt fragile, which meant scene drop. It always seemed to hit especially hard after sexual play. She needed to plan better so she wasn't dealing with drop out in the world.

Something was just different, lately. Since she'd admitted to herself that she was gray ace, she felt more thin-skinned about sex, more aware of how intense and risky it felt, and she dropped harder afterwards. She wasn't sure she liked this new normal. Feeling needier after play, and for longer, wasn't something she'd built her life to accommodate. Damnit, she needed someone to hold her right now. She looked to the left; Ruth was deep in conversation with Liliana and would likely be awhile. So Leah looked to the right, and saw that Shiloh was smiling at her.

"Hey there, you," ze said.

"Hi," Leah said, unable to smile back, knowing her voice sounded small.

"Seems like all is not good in the Leah-verse. What's going on?"

"Drop," she said miserably.

"What can I do?" ze asked, zir voice gentle and easy like it was no big deal if she needed something from zir.

"Can you hold me and maybe rub my back?"

Ze turned zir chair toward her and opened zir arms, and Leah sunk into them, resting her head on Shiloh's large belly. Zir arm was a comforting weight on zir back, and it felt so good to be protected by zir body. There was something about being a fat person and cuddling with a much larger fat person that helped her relax. It felt like Shiloh's supersize body could envelop her, and keep her safe. Right now, that was exactly what she needed.

By the time the food arrived, she felt more solid, a bit thicker-skinned. Her phone signaled a text just as the burger was placed in front of her, and she almost didn't look. She was glad she did, though, as it was Amaya, asking if she still wanted her to cover this afternoon. Once that was arranged, it felt like a weight had been lifted. After this she could go home. She texted Jordan to let her know, trying not to worry that she hadn't heard from her, and concentrated on her food.

Ruth asked after Jordan, and Shiloh chimed in that ze had met the very handsome Jordan last night at the 007 party. That had Ruth raising her brows and wanting the news, so Leah blurted out that it seemed Jordan had been a dominant all along, but her vanilla marriage prevented her from doing anything about it, and now she wanted to learn everything she could.

"Well, she couldn't have a better teacher than you," Ruth said. "You taught me so much."

"Yes, your D/s workshop series helped me and Liliana figure important things out," Violet chimed in.

Leah blinked. "What do I know from novice dom problems? She's better off learning from another dominant. I hooked her up with Iris."

"Leah, aren't you the one who gets all indignant when people assume all kink educators should be tops?" Liliana said.

"Why is it either/or?" Shiloh asked. "Why can't Jordan learn from a bunch of sources? Isn't that one of your core principles?"

Ruth nudged her and said, "I think you might be getting in your own way here, darlin. Or…perhaps there's something we should know about your relationship with Jordan that you haven't told us?"

Leah blinked a few times, trying to clear her head. They were all being logical. She didn't know why she'd been focused on other folks teaching Jordan. "I don't know why I hadn't thought of it. Maybe I'm still trying to make sense of not knowing this about her for all these years. But all of you are right, it might be exactly the kind of thing she needs."

After brunch, Leah went on one of her favorite walks through Chelsea. Her sense of direction was mostly terrible, but she loved to walk through the city with her ear plugs in, as long as she stuck to routes she knew. If she didn't stray off course, she wouldn't get lost. Walking helped with drop. Plus, she could pick up food to share with Jordan, and not have to worry about cooking. She called in an order to one of her favorite Chinese restaurants, and began walking, gloriously alone in the city that she loved.

The cold air felt good to breathe, and as she passed the gift shop she'd gotten Jordan's last birthday present, she realized that she hadn't made her final decision about what to get her best friend for Chanukah. She'd found a couple gifts that might be funny, but this was a big Chanukah, the first they were spending together in a long time, and Jordan had all this change going on. She wanted to get her something that showed she got it, and was supportive, not just something she could have gotten her any other year.

After picking up the Chinese food, Leah stopped at one of her favorite bakeries for treats. Just being in the bakery and breathing in the scents, looking at the deliciousness in the case, made her feel less frazzled. She was surrounded by comfort, would be taking some home. She'd make a pot of Earl Grey, curl up on the couch, hopefully with Jordan, and watch something long and cozy with hobbits in it.

9

SUNDAY AFTERNOON, DECEMBER 15

JORDAN

Jordan knew it was going to be a bad pain day right from the start. She'd pushed it too hard last night, plus it was winter. The sense of being made of lead and having skin like paper, that wasn't expected. It felt a bit like the aftermath of a meltdown/panic attack combo, but she hadn't had either. She'd gone to bed feeling wrung out and pleased with herself, and had slept hard. So why did she feel this way? Was all the change catching up to her? Getting up felt impossible, but she managed to grope for her phone, only to realize that she hadn't plugged it in last night and it was completely dead. She fumbled with the cord, yanking it out of the outlet by mistake before getting the phone plugged in. In the process, she realized that she hadn't even taken off her clothes, had just gone to sleep in her tux, sans tie and cufflinks.

Cufflinks! Jordan reached into her pocket and took them out, their coolness soothing something that was flickering in her chest like panic. She stroked them against her cheek, remembering the feeling of power surging into her, intense and beautiful, and the shining awe in Leah's eyes. She fell back asleep with them cradled in her hand.

When she woke again, her head was pounding. It felt like she had been sucked dry of all moisture and she had passed right through hunger into nausea and trembles. Fuck. What time was it? She fumbled with her phone and groaned, because it was almost two. She'd slept 11 hours, and before she tried to get to the kitchen, she really needed to eat something that would make her less trembly. Her backpack was on the desk chair nearby, so she maneuvered into a sitting position, grabbed her cane, and used the handle to slowly bring the chair to her. With any luck, she had a juice box and a few snacks in there, stashed for when she was in too much pain to get proper food.

Score! She had a box of apple juice and pretzels filled with peanut butter. That would get her to a place where she could walk to the kitchen. Though in a pinch...Jordan eyed the desk chair speculatively. Hard wood floors, no carpet, wide hallways and doorway, no clutter. Huh. That could be a makeshift wheelchair if she really needed one. It was a relief to know she could deal with that on her own if she needed to. That settled in her mind, she drank half the juice before starting on the pretzels. She was just finishing them when she heard someone come in, and Leah calling her name.

"In my room," she said loudly, hoping Leah could hear. A couple minutes passed, and then there was a soft knock on her door. "Come in," she said, smiling when Leah's face appeared in the doorway.

"Hey there, if you're hungry, I brought food."

"Well, aren't you good to me?" she said with a grin.

"I figured it might be just the thing. I got someone to cover at the store so I took a walk on Eighth Avenue…"

"What did you get me?"

"Oh just the pea shoots you love, and scallion pancakes, cold noodles, that braised beef you like, and…"

"And? Oh wow, did you go to…"

"Yup. A chocolate snowball and a lemon snack cake just for you."

"You are the best friend a ravenous butch could ever have."

"I do my best. Are you just getting up?"

"Yeah, basically. Why?"

"Oh, I left you a note, but it didn't look like it had been touched."

"Do I still get it?"

"I mean, if you want it, it's yours. I left it in the kitchen."

"Ok, it's going to take me a few to get there. Moving slow, and I want to get out of this tux."

"You do look a bit like a debauched groomsman who doesn't remember which bridesmaid she slept with last night."

Jordan chuckled. "Oh I remember, don't you worry," slipped out before she thought it through. Had she just made it awkward?

"I remember, too," Leah murmured. "So…how about I fix you a plate and you can eat in comfort on the couch. Maybe we could watch a movie?"

"Yeah, that sounds perfect. You pick the movie."

Leah nodded, and closed the door behind her. Jordan could hear her singing "The Misty Mountains Cold" as she made her way to the kitchen.

Guess she was in a hobbit mood. Which meant the comfort food was for her as well as Jordan. She always wanted hobbits when she was feeling fragile or sad. Did she wake up feeling thin-skinned too? And then went out and was social for a couple hours. Yikes. Well, whatever processing they might need to do about last night could wait until they both were a bit more solid.

When Jordan was in her favorite sweat pants that were worn and soft, her Stim Ray t-shirt and cozy socks, she walked creakily toward the living room. She might be turning 50 this year, but her walk today was more like her grandma's had been when she was in her 70s. Well, arthritis did run in the family, so that made sense. When she was settled on the couch, Leah brought her the note, which seemed kind of thick, and held up two bottles, one coconut water and the other a very green athletic drink.

"Pick your poison," Leah said brightly.

"Um. Neither?"

"No, really, you're probably dehydrated after last night. It will help."

Huh. Well, that would explain some things. No way could she do coconut water, the texture was...ugh. But she could maybe do the athletic drink.

"Hey could you put the green stuff in one of those opaque glasses you have with the straws, and a bunch of ice? I can probably get it down that way."

"Absolutely. I'll bring you some water, too. And I'm brewing Earl Grey if you want?"

Caffeine would be good. "Yes, you know how I like it."

"As if I'd forget."

"Thanks, Leah. Just...thanks."

"I'm glad to do it, J. Truly."

She did genuinely seem to be happy to do it, too. There was a bounce in her step that hadn't been there before. Like doing this for Jordan made her feel good. A marked contrast to the way Dani used to seem so aggrieved when Jordan asked her for help on bad pain days. She wasn't going to think about that right now. Or about the way that she now had to rebuild systems for getting things done. At least here she had a job that was easier on her physically, and a place to stay that was more accessible, with a friend who wanted to support her. She could ease into things, here, had a soft place to land.

Jordan focused on the note, which was actually pretty brief. The long part seemed to be a handout about scene drop, which hadn't shown up much in the books she'd read but had been on a couple of websites. She tried to concentrate on reading the handout, but couldn't get her brain to do that right now. So she sat, and drifted, running her fingers over the cufflinks, until Leah asked if she needed anything else. She opened her eyes to find a tray table in front of her with food, three beverages, and a napkin that had been folded into a bowtie.

"Wow," she said softly. "I'm so lucky." Then she turned to Leah and smiled. "No, this is perfect. Thank you."

10

52

SUNDAY AFTERNOON, DECEMBER 15

LEAH

Leah decided to say something about drop, especially since she was still feeling it herself, and was hoping Jordan might be up for cuddling.

"So. Um. I don't know if you read the note, but I wanted to mention scene drop, in case you didn't know about it."

"I have a vague sense, and I see you left me a handout, but my brain is all fuzzy and made of lead right now, plus I'm hungry, so it's not a good time to read."

"Let me explain. No, there is too much. Let me sum up."

"Buttercup is marrying Humperdink in a little less than half an hour?"

Leah grinned. They had watched The Princess Bride about forty times throughout the course of their friendship, and often recited whole chunks of it to each other. "So all we have to do is get in, break up the wedding, steal the Princess, and make our escape..."

"After you kill Count Rugen."

"Well, yes, that tiny detail. I do have a wheelbarrow, though, so that should help."

"It should indeed."

"So basically, kink has a big impact on your biochemistry and emotions and it's common to experience a thing we call drop, which feels a bit like having the flu and recovering from a meltdown."

"So what you're saying is, the fact that I feel like I'm made of lead and like I'm on the edge of tears is normal?"

"Well...kinda, yeah. There are things that help lessen the drop & help you when you feel the drop. But those are kind of individual so you need to experiment for a while until you figure out what works for you."

"Is this like a physics thing? What goes up must come down?"

"Didn't you feel a bit like you were flying?"

"Yeah. I really did."

"You gotta come back down to earth. For me what helps is hydration, touch, praise, red meat, veggies, & comfort rewatching my favorite movies."

"We have hydration, veggies, and beef, and we're going to watch hobbits. What are we missing? I'm partly responsible for you feeling this way, I want to help you get what you need."

"Maybe after we eat, we could cuddle as we watch the hobbits?"

"Actually, that sounds really good," Jordan said, her voice holding a note of surprise.

"We'll experiment to see what might help your drop too. Perhaps this'll be like a romance novel where we are perfectly suited and what I need is exactly what you need."

Jordan snorted. "Um, when you are reading that in the story do you actually buy into it? I'm not sure I could."

"No, of course not. But it's not about that being real. It's more...a symbol of a good fit, but they often force it into a monogamous context where you have one perfect partner who meets all your needs and you meet all of theirs."

Jordan sighed. "Maybe the divorce has made me cynical, but I'd rather build a family of folks where we can all lean on each other and no one person is solely responsible for another person's happiness or needs. And, y'know, build a society where everyone has access to free health insurance that covers mental health options and gender transition options and reproductive health care options, and everyone has access to housing and basic income and can access disability care services independently if they need to."

"Preaching to the choir, my friend," Leah said, and tucked the idea that Jordan might be polyamorous into her pocket to think about later. "Now it's hobbit time. I decided I wanted Merry and Pippin in my life today so we are going for Fellowship first, and see where we end up."

After Fellowship, Leah needed a nap, so she headed to her room. She thought about asking Jordan to spoon her while she slept, but that felt a bit too openly needy, so she squashed the idea unspoken. Besides, she'd rather spoon when she was going to be awake.

She put on the audio of one of her new favorite comfort read romance novels, a romance by Aidan Wayne with an ace protagonist who was adorable. She remembered to set both the sleep timer and her alarm so that she wouldn't nap too long. As she gathered the covers around her exactly the way she liked, so they felt like a solid, heavy barrier, she thought about the fact she'd instinctively reached for an ace spectrum romance that had no sex in it, instead of finishing the Talia Hibbert romance she was in the middle of rereading on audio, which had a demisexual MC and did have sex. She was too sleepy to figure out what that meant right now. She'd put it in a box to think about later.

Her subconscious clearly wasn't buying that, because of course she had... well, it wasn't exactly her usual kind of nightmare, but it still left her all jangly and feeling unmoored. She'd been in some room she didn't recognize, half naked, with some woman she didn't recognize, who'd been expecting her to have sex, and her heart had been racing and her head pounding and she couldn't make words to try to explain that she didn't want to, and was contemplating whether it might be easier to just do it. When she woke up, her hands were fluttering a mile a minute and she was full of self-loathing and despair and felt like she had no skin at all and was barely attached to the ground. Like she wasn't solid enough to have gravity. Her eyes flung themselves around the room so fast that they didn't really see anything, but couldn't stop watching. Finally, they landed on her purple and blue weighted blanket, a bright spot at the edge of the bed, and she tugged it over herself, put on the audio book to give her brain something to sink into, and started to rock. Her hands were still fluttering, and that was okay. The blanket had gravity and would keep her tethered to earth.

Oy, what a day, she thought, when she'd found her way to more solidity. Drop, and brunch, and meltdown, oh my. At least there were cuddles and milkshakes and hobbits, too. And audiobooks. She loved this one, the performer's voice was so soothing, and there were all these bad jokes and sweet moments, and a guy figuring out his aceness in a context of no sexual pressure and lots of support. She might be a bit jealous that he got to have that. Maybe it was a good time to listen to music instead. So Leah put on her oldest most reliable self-soothing music, an Indigo Girls mix she'd made 25 years ago. As the beginning notes of "Closer to Fine" began, she grabbed her lotion, putting it on methodically, using the task to give her skin the kind of pressure that would ground her. She tried to put on lotion at least once a day in the winter, anyway.

By the time she was done with the lotion, she was in her body enough to realize she was hungry. Food would be good. Perhaps there could be food and treats and another movie. She'd gotten her hobbit fix; maybe Jordan wanted to watch one of her own comfort movies.

"I heard the Indigo Girls...seems like you're having a hard day," Jordan said, when she made her way into the living room.

"Yeah, I don't think it's just drop. There's more, but I don't have words."

"That's okay. You don't need to make words. Want to do something quiet over dinner, together? Like, maybe another movie or reading, or listen to a podcast or book?"

Leah nodded, her eyes filling. Jordan made it so easy for her to just be. She'd missed this, so much.

"Maybe we could watch one of your movies this time," she whispered.

"Okay, I will pick one out, if you can get the food?"

Leah nodded. She knew how to get the food, there were no decisions to make, and getting it together would feel good. When they were all settled and ready to start watching Hercules, she remembered something.

"Oh! One more thing can help with drop."

Leah grabbed her play bag, rooted around in it for a moment, and then brandished the chocolate at Jordan.

"Try some dark chocolate. It really helps," she said, breaking off a piece for herself before passing it to Jordan.

"Like we've seen a dementor?"

"It kinda does feel like magic, to me anyway. Like it's giving my body something it needed and was missing and now I'm a bit more solid." She let it melt slowly on her tongue, smiling to herself.

"Ok!" Jordan said, sounding flustered. "Let's get this show on the road."

Leah let her eyes close as the movie started, letting the opening music of Hercules wash over her as she focused on the way the chocolate felt like it was seeping into her, warming her up from the inside.

11

MONDAY AFTERNOON, DECEMBER 16

JORDAN

When Iris had texted, offering to take Jordan to a late lunch and to pick out some things for her toy bag, Jordan hadn't really known what to expect. She'd been sitting on Leah's couch, feeling adrift and alone, and wishing she'd asked to do some more cuddling before Leah took her nap. She hadn't been aware of how intense her skin hunger was until they had stopped cuddling, and she wasn't used to feeling like this.

Jordan had never felt like she needed to touch Dani to feel solid. She had felt like hugging her baby sister Erica was reassuring, met a need that couldn't be met other ways, and she'd liked it when Erica had made it clear that she wanted to grow her hair out, because then she could offer to brush it, and braid it. But that was different; hugging Erica was Jordan reassuring herself that Erica was okay. And with the hair, it was not just saying, but showing that she supported Erica in her decision to transition in high school. Showing was an act of love, and she loved her sister ferociously.

But this...this felt selfish and needy and desperate, wrapped into this sense of intense loneliness, and she didn't usually need touch that way. It was still a very stone experience of needing touch, because what she wanted was to touch Leah, not be touched by her. But usually she was touch averse enough that cuddling was more of a challenge than a need. Not right now, though. Jordan grabbed one of the throw pillows on the couch, an emerald green velvet one, and hugged it to herself, stroking her cheek against the velvet. That helped a bit. Maybe she needed to invest in a velvet body pillow or large velvet stuffie. Did they make weighted stuffies covered in velvet?

She had begun a search on her phone when the call came through from Iris, who was checking in on her after the scene. After they talked for a bit about Jordan's drop and the things she'd tried to do to help with it, Iris had asked if she liked playing with clips. When she'd responded enthusiastically, Iris had suggested that perhaps she might like to grab a meal with her and go shopping for her own clips. Jordan had the immediate urge to say yes, and so she had, without thinking it through much. After they had made a plan to meet up in Chelsea near Iris' office, she realized that would make the day rather packed with being social, as Leah had already arranged for them both to go to R&R's place for dinner that night.

Iris was at the restaurant when she arrived, and after asking permission, gave her a rather long hug in greeting. It felt good, more necessary than she wanted it to. They had a corner table, so Jordan could just slide in, not worrying about whether there was room.

"I know folks usually don't go to NYC for the chain restaurants, but I really wanted a steak, and this place is pretty quiet at this time."

"No, no, it's fine. This was one of Erica's favorite places to go for special occasions when she was a tween, so I have fond memories."

"Is Erica your kid?"

"Well, not precisely. She's my younger sister. But I stepped in to be her parent when I was 21. So kinda?"

"How old is she now?"

"Oh, she's 35. She lives in the Boston area with her two spouses and their two kids."

"She's polyamorous?"

"Yup. She figured it out before I did, about myself. The younger generations, I think they see the options more clearly, yknow? I didn't know I was queer until I went to college, and wasn't sure I was kinky until I was deep in a vanilla marriage. But Erica, she knew she was bi and trans as a tween, and she told me she was polyamorous when she was 21, but she may have known even before that."

"Yeah, I think it depends on a bunch of factors, how early folks figure stuff out. It's not as simple as being about age, but that's definitely a factor," Iris said.

"True. Anyway, I'm going to get what I always used to order when I went here with Erica, which is a sirloin, medium rare. Leah said red meat was a good idea."

"Yeah, that's why I wanted steak, it helps me to have red meat after I play."

Jordan nodded. "She gave me a whole handout on drop yesterday."

"She's definitely got great handouts. I'm glad she talked to you about drop. So...you still feeling it?"

"Yesterday was worse, but yeah. I am. Got any tips?"

"Sure. My biggest one is don't just suck it up and hope it will go away."

"Damnit, that's my best life strategy!"

Iris laughed. "I'm not surprised. It's a thing butch dominants often do. But it's important that you treat your own needs as important. Otherwise you're letting down your play partners."

Jordan blinked. "If I don't treat my own needs as important, I'm letting down my partners? I'm going to need you to explain that one to me."

"Ok, let's order first, though."

After they had ordered, and were devouring the bread in front of them, Iris continued. "I'm going to talk about scenes with two people first, because that's easier. Your submissive play partner is counting on you to be attending to them, of course, and making sure that you are being careful with their safety. That's basic. But with D/s, they want to give themself over to your control. They are trusting you to see to your needs within that framework, because they aren't driving the play."

Jordan sat with that for a minute. "So, because I'm in control, I'm expected to watch out for my own needs alongside theirs."

"Yes. I mean, I'm simplifying. But, yes, that's part of your job as the dominant. Most submissives would be upset to learn that the dominant they were playing with was orchestrating the scene purely for the submissive, and wasn't treating their own needs as important."

"They would?"

"I mean, there are always jerks who don't actually care about the people they play with, of course. But most submissives would value your needs very highly. Especially where service was involved."

Jordan contemplated her salad as she tried to take this in. Well, she had wanted to actually focus on her own needs, for once, go after the things she wanted. That was the driver behind all of her choices in the last six months. She just hadn't bargained for this when she had thought about finally doing kink.

"So that's during the scene, right?"

"It's throughout the process connected to each scene: the negotiation, the scene itself, the aftercare, and checking in the next day or so to see if there's drop or unresolved issues. A scene isn't just the part where you are playing."

"I bet Leah has a handout about that, too."

"Probably."

"Okay, I will ask her for it so I don't start taking notes while I'm eating this awesome salad. So when you asked me to lunch, was that the check in part?"

"Well, yes. And, also…we don't know each other that well, but I wanted to see if you might be interested in some informal mentoring. I could be a dominant you could talk to, could get questions answered, or ask for advice. I could help you find your feet, as a new dominant. Help you build up your skills."

"Did Leah put you up to this?"

"She suggested it as a possibility. She knows it's something I enjoy doing, with other butch doms."

"What do you enjoy about it?"

"Hm. I like teaching, and it's a way to do that, without the kind of formal stuff Leah does. It's fun." Iris grinned, and continued. "I like supporting other butches, and building connections with other butches. That's important to me. I promised the butch who mentored me that I would pass on what she taught me, so it's a way to honor her memory. She died a few years ago." Iris inclined her head, perhaps in prayer, definitely in memory.

"I get that, about legacies."

"I thought you would, given what you told me about your family."

"It's my dad's death anniversary this week," Jordan offered.

"Ah, Leslie's was last month. I discussed my promise with Leah around then. I think that's why she mentioned this as an idea."

Jordan nodded. She didn't know why it felt so raw and snarly that Leah had talked to Iris about this, had pushed them together. I do need more friends here, she thought. More of a support system. And it's good to learn this from someone trusted. It just feels…so intimate to learn from someone who is almost a stranger.

"I want to think about it, if that's okay?"

"Of course. We can leave it at lunch, or if you want, I had the thought of helping you to begin to build up your toy bag today, starting with the clips we discussed on the phone."

Oh wow. Her own toy bag.

12

63

MONDAY AFTERNOON, DECEMBER 16

LEAH

Leah had been feeling weird all day, ever since she'd started scrolling through Twitter that morning on the train into work. Thin-skinned and grumpy and like every noise was too fucking loud, and each tweet she scrolled past with the latest news had made her flinch. But you couldn't hide your head in the sand completely, could you?

Now she finally had a moment to breathe and eat some of the ropa vieja her lovely employee Lisette had brought in for everyone. It was cozy and warm and delicious and made her decide she really needed to have brisket soon. She needed more food in her life that made her feel like a warm hug.

The collar of her sweater felt too tight, and she tugged at it, wishing she'd been up for doing laundry this weekend. She hadn't had much time to herself since Jordan arrived and definitely hadn't been able to do chores. It was important to remember that Jordan lived here now, it wasn't a short visit separate from regular life, but it was hard to break the habit of soaking up all the Jordan she could.

Overscheduling leads to meltdowns, she recited to herself in her old therapist's voice. It was one of those things she knew sometimes, but forgot a lot of the time. Especially when there were changes going on.

She pulled out her phone to check her calendar: dinner tonight, concert tomorrow, Jordan's work thing Wednesday, date with Ellie Thursday, shul with Jordan Friday, dreaded dinner party Saturday, and then Chanukah began. Oy. She was definitely setting herself up for a meltdown. Time to clear things out. What could be cancelled? She was already closing the store from December 22-January 2. She could actually only come in on the 30th to do her clean and inventory day. Or maybe even put that off until the new year. She could give Octavia the extra hours she'd been asking for and take more time off this week.

She was just about to text Octavia when she saw a text from Iris, asking her to share her anatomy of a scene handout with Jordan. With a follow up text explaining that Iris was having a late lunch with Jordan and was going to take her to buy some things for her toybag. Somehow that made Leah want to cry, that they were together without her, that Iris was mentoring Jordan just like she'd asked her to, that neither of them had even thought to let her know they were getting together. She tossed her phone onto her desk, yanked her office door closed, and buried her head in her arms, letting the tears fall.

She hated feeling this way, all droppy and needy and churned up and just...raw. She wasn't going to make it through this workday, much less dinner at Ruth and Rebecca's. So she gave herself permission to leave work, to cancel on dinner, to take the night for herself. Something more was going on than just the scene drop, and it was time to tend to it. She pulled out an index card and made a list: 1. Text O about taking shifts. 2. Text R about dinner. 3. Text J and suggest she go to dinner without me. 4. Go home, pick up pizza on the way. 5. Eat. 6. Figure out what to do next.

Leah took care of 1-3, then let the staff know she was feeling sick and heading home. She put on her noise cancelling headphones once she was on the train, and just counted the stops until she got to hers. Her neighborhood pizza joint smelled incredibly good, and she got herself enough for leftovers for the next couple days. There was nothing like pizza when she felt sorry for herself, it had been her go-to since she started sneaking slices after school at age 11, when her mom started being especially awful about her fatness. She wasn't going to think about her mom, though. Tonight was about her, and what she needed, and right now she needed to watch hobbits and have some garlic knots while they were still hot.

Leah put on the animated Rankin Bass Return of the King because it was the coziest. She'd had the vinyl read along album as a kid, and listened to it over and over, so she pretty much had it memorized. She wrapped herself in a velvety blanket and savored the garlic in her mouth as Gandalf began to set up the story.

Octavia was taking all her shifts this week, she had a stretch of days with maybe only one thing to do, and she might even cancel some of those things. The tightness in her chest had eased at the thought. She was glad to have realized she needed to clear things off her schedule. After food, she'd see what else she could clear. But first, it was time for her beef patty. Between this and the garlic, her mouth felt so alive. Taste stims were the best, they really cleared things out. Like certain kinds of pain did.

In fact, maybe what she needed was some pain to clear things out, and help her find clarity. Nothing like clips, those did something else entirely, and were mostly for the dominant she was playing with. What she needed right now was the pain that was for her, not for anyone else. The pain that brought her calm and clarity. Yes, this was a good idea. After the hobbits.

She made a list when the movie was done: 1. Pain. 2. Velvet blanket. 3. Weighted blanket and audio book. 4. Journal. 5. Plan next steps. Leah was glad that Jordan wasn't going to be home for a while, but she locked her bedroom door just in case. Then she got her blankets ready, and her audiobook—she didn't mess around there, went right for the Tolkien—and laid her quirts out on the bed. She moved her cushy bench far enough from the bed that she could sit on it comfortably, and decided against music. She wanted to hear the strikes.

Leah sat and braided her hair so it would be out of the way, singing the song from the hobbit movie about how less can be more as she concentrated on the feel of her curls between her fingers. When she was done, she took a slow breath, shedding all of her clothes, and sat, picking up the lightest quirt. She struck her pillow a couple times, making sure she had the fine motor control she needed to use the toy, and then began, savoring the whistling sound it made as it ripped through the air, and the light slap of it on her back. It didn't hurt at all, just felt good and right, except maybe not sharp enough. But she made herself be patient as she warmed up her skin before increasing the intensity of the strikes. Yes, that was lovely, covering her with this layer of calm, driving everything away.

Soon the light quirt was more frustrating than satisfying, so she picked up the purple one with more sting. Oof it was perfect, this wonderful biting pressure that was exactly what she needed. And she could have as much as she wanted, for as long as her arm was able to strike. Just that thought made her giggle, and grin, and she paused just letting herself laugh, wrapping her arms around herself, filled with joy. Quirts were the best stim ever.

She switched arms to give herself a rest, and just savored the lovely feeling of giving herself exactly what she wanted, exactly what her body needed, with no obligation or expectation or pressure, just the joy of sensation that hit just the right spot. Yes, she thought to herself. You deserve this. You deserve to get what you need, what you want. And answered any doubts that rose up by giving herself just that, until the purple quirt wasn't enough, and it was time for her favorite quirt, the one Rebecca had handmade and given her for her birthday. It was black, with a woven leather handle in white, and thick supple strips of leather that were heavy and did more than bite, they drove into her skin in this superb slice of intensity, thud and sting beautifully intertwined.

She grunted with each blow, letting the full wave of it wash through her before she gave herself the next, building so the waves overlapped and spiraled, a cyclone of hard slapping water driving into her and through her in this tremendous swirl of sensation that brought the most luxurious calm in its wake. Leah crawled onto the bed and slid under the velvet blanket, savoring the sensation of it along her skin, not too light anymore, but exactly right, like a gigantic cat was scent marking ever bit of her and she got to cuddle with it for as long as she wanted.

When she had floated on sensation long enough, she pulled the weighted blanket over herself and started the audiobook, letting the beginning of The Hobbit wind around her, and hold her close, her mouth saying the words right along with the narrator. Just the description of Bag End made her feel cozy and comforted and peaceful, and she soaked it in, the weight of the blanket bringing solidity.

13

68

MONDAY AFTERNOON, DECEMBER 16

JORDAN

They were finishing lunch when Jordan got a text from Leah telling her to go to dinner without her, she needed alone time. Jordan stared at the text for a moment, feeling bereft and worried, wondering if Leah was okay, nervous about going to dinner on her own. She did want to give Leah space, though, and thought about taking herself to the movies instead of dinner, having some alone time out in the city in a neighborhood she knew. But, she was already in Manhattan, and she'd been looking forward to seeing Rebecca and Ruth, maybe asking some questions. She got a text from Rebecca urging her to please still come over for dinner, so she let her know she'd be there.

"I brought you a present," Iris said. That was a bit surprising, but Jordan went with it.

"You did?"

"Yeah, in case you wanted to start building your toy bag today. This was my first toy bag." She handed Jordan a brown leather bag that was shaped like a teardrop, with a thick shoulder strap. "It's got some great pockets, and it's supposed to be good for your back. I thought it might feel nice to have a smallish bag to start out, especially one you could wear on your back so your hands were free." Jordan looked through the bag, slowly. The leather was soft, and worn in a few places, and it felt good to hold. There was something comforting about knowing the bag had been places, wasn't as brand spanking new as she was.

"Thank you," she said, and her voice cracked a bit.

"I'm glad to pass things down. That's a big part of leather tradition, for me."

Jordan nodded, at a loss for words. Her hands found something hard, a small box, in the next pocket.

"I put a small first aid kit in there, for you. Plus one more thing." Iris produced a red handkerchief, one that was clearly well loved.

"This is the hanky for fisting; if you're a top you wear it on the left. I figure you earned it."

Jordan nodded.

"This was the hanky I was wearing on Saturday. I had it washed and ironed, for you. It's good to have a hanky on hand, even if you don't flag with it. They're pretty good makeshift blindfolds, for one thing." She smiled at Jordan.

"Thank you. Just...thanks." Jordan couldn't make more words come out. There was something so intense about being honored as a dom by another butch dom. It made her breathless and stole her words. Jordan folded the hanky carefully and put it in her new toybag, which luckily fit right inside in her backpack. Then she retreated to the bathroom to compose herself before they headed out.

At Jordan's request, Iris took her to the dollar store. As they walked through the aisles, Iris talked about the different kinds of pervertables you could get in a store like this, pointing out a range of things including candles, spatulas, dog toys, cutting boards, and a star shaped plastic magic wand in the children's toy section. She stopped when they got to the section that had clothespins, and talked Jordan through how to test them, helping her pick out a few different kinds.

She emerged from the store with her mind spinning possibilities, like the world had tilted. Pretty much anything could be used for kink, and she had clothespins, a hairbrush, a wooden spoon, and a ruler to go in her toybag. They stopped to rest and have some tea, and Jordan was glad for the quiet corner and the time to regroup after the visual loudness and overwhelming scentedness of the dollar store.

Iris asked if she wanted to see a kink shop, not necessarily to buy, just to get a feel, and she couldn't resist that. Jordan was led into a store full of corsets, latex, and leather, that had scary looking things in a glass case, and a great set of books, and was way more brightly lit than she expected a kink store to be. She guessed she shouldn't be surprised by this, after the play party, but she still was.

Iris explained that it was good to wait to invest in higher cost items, that if she wanted to buy something, it might be good to consider a lower cost item like a paddle, crop, quirt, or cane, depending on what appealed to her. She pulled out a selection of each and brought Jordan over to a bench to sit, so she wouldn't feel rushed, saying she'd be glad to answer questions, but it was also okay if Jordan just wanted to take some time to hold things and see how they felt to her, first. That sounded perfect. She was glad Iris seemed to get that how things felt was an important thing for her.

Jordan started by rejecting things based on sensory experience, because she knew if a toy felt wrongbad to the touch, she'd never use it. That got it narrowed down to four items: a heavy rubber paddle, a leather crop with a teardrop shaped end, an item that was crimson and black braided leather that ended in two leather strips—she didn't know the name for that one, and a supple smooth stick she thought was probably a cane. She wondered what they felt like, and asked Iris.

"I can show you how to test them on yourself, if you want."

Jordan nodded, and Iris walked her through it, asking if she felt comfortable before retreating and giving her space to try them out. The paddle felt wrong when she tried using it, too heavy, and it felt completely different on her thigh than she had predicted. Nope, not that one. The crop felt comfortable, and made a nice sound. It was closer to what she was after, the sharpness of it. That was a maybe. The cane was hard to use, she felt clumsy and like she would need to practice a lot. But the sound of it was awesome. It had this glorious slicing sensation that she liked. That was a maybe. She wasn't sure she wanted to start out with something that made her feel clumsy. The quirt—that was what Iris called the braided leather thing—felt really good in her hand, zingy. It made a beautiful sound. The sensation on her back was bitingly sharp, in this really satisfying way. Yes, this was probably the winner.

She asked Iris for her opinion, between the crop and the quirt, and listened carefully, weighing the information about quality, and was the pricing fair, and which toy was easier to use, which needed more practice. Amidst all of this, one piece of information stood out: Leah loved quirts. That felt like it settled the question. She was definitely getting the quirt. It would be her Chanukah present for herself. Because damnit, she was starting a tradition of that. Every Chanukah, she would get—or make—herself a gift. Not just any gift, either. One that honored who she was and what she wanted.

It wasn't until she was on the train to R&R's for dinner that the reality of what she had done really hit her: she had bought the quirt with Leah in mind, because she wanted to use it with her. She had bought her first real toy—not a pervertable but something created specifically to do kink— driven at least partly by her desire to dominate Leah again. Whatever happened between them, Jordan knew that her early memories of kink would be connected to Leah. Which was already true, actually. Had been true since she first started fantasizing about her all those years ago. But this made it more tangible, somehow. The question was...did Leah even want to play with her again? Or help her learn how to be a dom?

14

MONDAY EVENING, DECEMBER 16

LEAH

Leah must have dozed off, because Bilbo was caught by the trolls and she didn't even remember them leaving the Shire. She sang "Misty Mountains Cold" to herself softly, just savoring the feel of the welts on her back against her soft flannel sheets. When the song was over, she sat up, and reached for her water bottle, making herself take slow languid sips. Time for tea, coconut water, and toast, she thought, so she pulled on her softest pajamas and padded barefoot into the kitchen, deciding to melt cheese on the top of her challah toast.

It smelled amazing, just like the cheese toast she used to love as a kid before they wouldn't let her have it anymore. Such a complicated sensory memory, as it was intertwined with her mother's fat hatred. I get to have as much cheese toast as I want now, she reminded herself. This is my house, and my life, and I decide what I eat. Leah sighed, knowing that she'd be dealing with memories like this all damn week because she was going to the dreaded dinner party on Saturday, where she'd have to deal with her mother's shit in person. Three times a year she'd been showing up for this shit, for way too fucking long.

Now her stomach was roiling and her throat was all closed up. She wasn't going to be able to eat the damned toast. So she would focus on the next things: 1. Clear her schedule. 2. Figure out what to do about Jordan. She set out her supplies on the kitchen table, deciding to stay in there where the light was best, and busied herself making a calendar of the rest of December in her bullet journal. Then she took out her smallest sticky notes and made a key for herself: blue was low stress, green was medium stress, orange was fun plus spoon suck, and red was highly stressful. Leah pulled out her phone and began labeling the sticky notes with her current plans. When she looked at the rest of this week, her heart started racing. Orange, green, orange, green, red. Not a blip of blue. Even with no work on those days, she was courting a meltdown bigtime. She was going to be ruthless and cut 2 things, maybe even three.

Leah stared at the post its, watching the slow build of them to that awful blaring red on Saturday, and thought, what if I just didn't go? It was this incredibly radical thought that felt almost ridiculous in its simplicity. What if I told my mother I couldn't make it? Or just...didn't let her know in advance at all, dropped the news at the very last minute?

"What if I just...didn't...go?" she murmured to herself, and began to giggle, because even the thought was freeing. Why had this never occurred to her before? So she took her purple marker, and put a big X over the words "dreaded dinner party," grinning to herself, and deciding that it was time for a dance break.

Leah decided to put on an old favorite, one of the first songs she ever danced to in public. She hadn't ever gone anywhere where she might be expected to dance until she turned 21, and her fat activist friends dragged her to a queer club and cajoled her out onto the dance floor. She'd had enough to drink and was in a big enough group of fat queers that she could shout down her mother's scorn in her head and just close her eyes and let her body move to the music. Which is exactly what she did now, in the center of her living room, as Janet's voice wound around the beat and pushed her into the familiar steps. After that night, she had watched the video for "Miss You Much" over and over, studying the moves, and teaching herself how to do them, until they were perfect. Now they were in her muscle memory, and she could just enjoy doing them, as she had for so many years. Old school dance breaks were the best, so full of joy.

When the music shifted to "You," she stopped dancing, turned off the music, and went into the kitchen for some ice water. The song kept playing in her head, because let's face it she knew all of Janet's music by heart. When she sat down at the table to write in her journal, it was still going, so she wrote out the lyrics, because that usually made a song stop doing that. Then she turned the page, and started fresh, letting whatever had been building pour onto the page, barely aware of what her hand was writing until it had been written down. When she stopped, her breath was ragged, and her hands were trembling, and she needed to rock. So she let herself rock, and sang her favorite rocking song, "Birdhouse in Your Soul," which had the perfect rhythm for the kind of rocking she did when she was upset.

By the time the song was over, she had found her calm again, and sending a silent thanks to They Might Be Giants, she switched back to practical mode, and put an X through the show she'd planned to take Jordan to the next day. She was in no shape for a punk-klezmer band right now, too loud, crowded and overwhelming. They had plenty of time to catch the band in the new year. Which meant there was only one more question to settle: her date with Ellie on Thursday. She had meant to schedule a pre-date conversation with Ellie, but had forgotten. Or blocked it out. It was honestly hard to tell how much was unconscious self-protection and how much was executive dysfunction. But anyway, she hadn't made sure there was time to talk.

Going forward with a date without talking was not a good idea, as she hadn't told Ellie about realizing that she was gray ace, or attempted to navigate a conversation with her about what that meant in terms of her needs around their play. Leah had spent time in therapy working out where to start with these conversations, developing a script, choosing which of her regular partners to tell first. Ellie was supposed to be the first person she told, she'd planned it that way, because Ellie was a good listener, and had ace and aro spec folks in her life, so at least had a handle on what gray ace was. But then she hadn't set up the conversation. Now their date was a few days away, and her play with Ellie often leaned sexual, so it was really not a good idea to just go forward with the date without the conversation.

She thought about cancelling the date, and her whole body relaxed. Well, that made it clear, didn't it? There was something about the weight of expectations that was especially hard to navigate. It felt like there was no room for her to be unsure or need to figure it out as they went, because there were layers of previous scenes shaping their play. It would be easier with a new play partner, Leah thought. Wouldn't come with that kind of weight.

Which brought her to the question of Jordan, and helping her learn to be a good dom. If she were in teacher mode, she could set things up the way she needed them to be, and already be in a position to give feedback around meeting those needs. She could see what play was like in that kind of structured context, decide lesson to lesson whether sex was on the table or not, or set things up so that there was plenty of room for her not to know and for them to see how it goes, change their minds about the sex part at any given point. And it wouldn't risk their friendship, or be anything but casual, because the structure of lessons would keep it in the pedagogical zone.

Jordan had so much potential as a dominant, she'd experienced it firsthand, had even been surprised by how much she'd wanted to submit to her, how wonderful it was to hand her the control. Sure, Iris could mentor Jordan, and there were workshops she could go to, other people Leah could connect her with. But it felt like she'd be missing out on something. She'd been so upset thinking about Iris and Jordan getting together without her. Sad, and jealous that she'd been left out of the picture. She didn't get jealous often, so it was notable. It meant some important need or want was going unmet. She was pretty sure she knew what it was. Underneath it all, she wanted to be one of the people helping Jordan learn to be a dom. Which meant she had some planning to do.

15

78

TUESDAY EVENING, DECEMBER 17

JORDAN

Jordan was relieved that Leah wasn't up for the show tonight. She couldn't do the crowds or the noise herself, not with so much social this week, and this way she hadn't needed to save her spoons for it. She'd made them both cottage cheese pancakes that morning, and then spent most of the day in her room, unpacking, because the bulk of her stuff had arrived this morning. She wouldn't feel right until everything had a place, but she was trying to be methodical about it so she didn't get overwhelmed. Checklists helped, and so did the Into the Woods soundtrack playing as she worked. She set alarms to remind herself to rest, stretch and hydrate, and eat, but even with them she forgot several times, and hit the end of act one (the third time) feeling tense and suddenly ravenous, noting that the sun had gone down as she'd worked.

When she stretched, Jordan realized that her knee was unhappy, and it was going to scream at her all the way to the kitchen. Leah noticed immediately that she was in pain, and offered to make dinner, so she could rest and put her leg up on the couch. Jordan agreed to the plan, relieved to be able to rest and still have dinner soon. She didn't have to worry about Leah making her something she couldn't eat, either.

"I thought I'd do breakfast for dinner, if that sounds good?" Leah bustled in with a heating pad for her knee, a cup of apple juice, and a bag of garlic bagel chips that made Jordan grin when she saw them. Bagel chips were the best, and exactly right in combination with breakfast for dinner.

"That sounds amazing. Thanks, darlin'. You are very good to me."

"I try. Sweet or savory toast?"

"Maybe just with butter. I want sweet afterwards, and I have these for savory." Jordan shook the bag of bagel chips.

"Bet you want cream cheese for those."

"Well, I sure wouldn't object."

Leah brought the cream cheese, along with a knife and a plate, and smiled at Jordan. "It's your job to pick a movie to watch with dinner."

That was easy. It had to be Tangled, after listening to that soundtrack all day. But it might be triggering for Leah. Well, she'd ask, and if needed, they'd pick something else. The heat felt achy, but in a good way, and she knew it would help, if she could tolerate it. The bagel chips were really wonderful with the cream cheese, made her mouth so happy and had this gorgeous crunch.

Leah had made scrambled eggs with cheddar cheese, and the texture of the eggs was perfect. Jordan couldn't ever get it this perfect when she made them herself, so she usually just fried the eggs. They watched Tangled in companionable silence, focused on eating. The challah was toasted exactly how Jordan liked it, it all felt cozy and like she was being cared for. It was so good, after a day of trying to settle in here and feeling frustrated by how long it was taking, to sit next to her best friend, watch a Disney movie, and eat something that made her feel like this was home.

"You mentioned wanting something sweet. Maybe we can pause here and see about that," Leah murmured.

Jordan paused and looked at Leah, who rarely asked to pause movies.

"It's upsetting you, isn't it?" she asked.

"Yeah, it kind of is. I mean, I know she gets free in the end but wow terrible abusive mom is a LOT."

"This scene is really heartbreaking, too. It feels like it really makes room for the trauma."

"Yeahhh."

"Ok, I'm turning this off, then. Maybe it's time to stim, before we have cookies?"

"Wait, there are cookies?"

"Yup! Ruth sent some home with me last night. They are chewy and gingery and awesome, with that granulated sugar stuff on top."

"Oh she makes amazing ginger cookies. Okay, yes to cookies but yeah, stimming is a good suggestion."

"What kind?"

"There's one that really worked yesterday. An old standard."

"Birdhouse?"

"Yup. Wanna stim with me?"

"Sure." Jordan smiled at Leah. She pulled the song up on her phone so they could just sing along, and more easily stay in sync with each other. It had been a while since they had done this, and she'd missed it. There was something really intimate about stimming together. It felt tender, and connected, and joyous. When the song ended she was grinning, and felt all sparky. Time for cookies!

Leah made licorice spice tea, and suggested they eat the cookies in the kitchen, so Jordan slowly made her way to the table, elevating her leg on a nearby chair. The tea was wonderful, the spices woke up her mouth in a delightful way, and the cookies were actually better tonight than they were yesterday. They were super zingy and exactly the right kind of chewy, and she loved the sugar crystals on top.

"So I had this idea and I wanted to see what you thought about it," Leah said.

"Okay, I'm listening."

"I was thinking about Chanukah, and had this idea for a present for you. You said you wanted to learn how to be a good dominant. I thought I could give you lessons, as your present. One lesson per night of Chanukah."

Jordan felt her eyes go wide. She really had not been expecting that. "But, I thought you didn't want to, so you told Iris to do it." She hadn't even decided to say that, had just blurted it out. It probably came out wrong. "I'm sorry. I don't mean to sound ungrateful."

"No, no it's fine. I just want to make sure I understand what you meant. You thought I was rejecting you?"

"Well. Yeah. I mean, I'm used to it. You never took me to kink things. You didn't really want me to go to your class. You seemed all weird after the party."

"Oh, fuck. I've made a mess of this. I'm sorry. I didn't take you to kink things because I was trying to be respectful of your vanilla-ness. Now that I know you're kinky…I think I've been playing catch-up. I don't change how I think of things very fast, you know that about me. So…I've acted all weird, not because I'm rejecting you, but because I'm awkward with change."

"That's the only thing that's going on? Nothing else is making this weird?" Jordan wanted to be sure.

"Well, I think that's the main thing that's going on."

"Uh huh." Jordan knew there was something else.

"There's this other thing I've been dealing with, and I'm still figuring out how to handle it. It might've had some splash over."

"Okay. Do you want to tell me about it?"

"I'm not sure I have the words. But yeah I would, maybe. Though not right this minute."

"Okay. So you really want to give me kink lessons? I don't want you to feel obligated."

"Yes, I really want to."

"That would actually be great. It was okay getting stuff for my toybag with Iris, and I like her and everything, but if you were up for teaching me, I think that would feel...safer, if that makes sense?"

"Yeah, I get that. We have such a deep friendship, it could make a safer place to learn."

Jordan nodded. "I trust you, and it feels better learning from another autistic person, honestly. You won't expect me to learn in an allistic way."

Leah grinned at her. "I definitely will not expect that. I didn't even consider that aspect of this."

"It feels like a big deal, for me anyway. I haven't had the best learning experiences. You know that, you saw how hard college was for me."

"Yep, I remember. So I was thinking about eight lessons, one per night, though eight nights in a row might be too much, so they can always be postponed."

"Sounds good."

"How would you feel about a structure where I do some teaching, then we do a short scene where you get to practice what we covered? And then we could do follow-up, if you have questions or want feedback."

"So a bit like where Iris taught me some safety stuff about clips, and then I got to try it out?"

"Yeah, but a bit more formal than that. I might even make a handout for the lesson, and it would be a bit longer, probably. Not quite so quick and dirty."

"I do better if I get to practice, and a handout would help me, actually. I also get things better if you can lead me to realizing them myself, and help me connect to other things I know."

"Okay, I can work with that. So it sounds like this is something you want to do, then?"

Jordan took several slow breaths and held the idea for a few moments, just to be sure. "Yes. This is a really wonderful present, Leah."

"I want to be sure it doesn't fuck things up with our friendship. You mean so much to me, Jordan. I don't want this to ruin what we have. So we need to keep it strictly about learning, okay?" Leah's voice was raw.

"I don't want us to ruin what we have, either. It's been thirty years, darlin'. We made it this far; I really think we'll be okay. Our friendship might change, might have new layers to it, move slightly differently. But then, that's already started, and it seems okay so far, yes?"

Leah nodded. "I might need you to reassure me about this," she whispered, closing her eyes.

"I can do that. We have a solid foundation. I truly believe that. We're just adding new aspects to what we already have. Sex, kink, romance…none of that is more important than friendship." Jordan watched Leah's face carefully to see how she reacted to the fact that she'd snuck the word romance in there. A small tentative smile grew on Leah's face, like she was rolling the words around in her head, wanting to believe in them. She definitely didn't seem to object to the word. Jordan would just leave it there, for now.

16

WEDNESDAY EVENING, DECEMBER 18

LEAH

"You're sure it's okay my ink is showing?" Leah asked, smoothing her dress.

"Yes, I'm sure," Jordan said, smiling at her. "You look beautiful, darlin'. I'm proud to have you on my arm."

"I can change into one of my mother-approved dresses, it would only take me about fifteen minutes to change," Leah said quickly.

"Leah, I don't want you to change. Especially not into one of those dresses you hate that make you feel shitty about yourself."

"But this is a fancy party, with the people from your new job."

"Yes, and I want them to be clear about who I am. Hence my favorite suit, & a date I love dearly who I will always be proud to be seen with."

"But are you sure?"

"Yes. I'm a stone butch, and I don't want to hide that, or the fact that I date queer femmes. I could care less about respectability politics and the folks at my new job should know that upfront."

"So what you're saying is that I don't need to come up with a palatable lie about what I do for a living?"

"Nope. Tell the truth to your comfort level. Be exactly who you are. You are my best friend. If you are not welcome as yourself, then neither am I."

Leah took a slow breath. "I just…I really don't want to disappoint you."

"My only wishes for you this evening are for you to be yourself, and to support me as you are able in this social situation. You have a lot of practice at both, and will do just fine. We are autistic Jewish queers who don't fit most social norms and are very butch and very femme…perfect compliance with social norms isn't doable here; we aren't even shooting for it."

That got through somehow. This was fucking with her head in a way that reminded her of both Bev and her mother, which was a terrible combination.

"I'm sorry. I think this is bringing up old shit for me."

"Yeah, I can tell. It's really okay if you aren't up for going, you know."

Leah took a long slow breath. Thought about it. "No, I want to go, and support you. I also want to see who these folks are that you'll be working with. I'd be surprised if I didn't know anyone."

"Yup, it's a tiny queer world in NYC. I'm sure you'll run into a few people you know. Leah, how can I support you, given that this is bringing up old shit?"

"Hmm. I guess, maybe you could say the velociraptor thing to me?" They had a bunch of things they often said to each other, and had happened upon this one from a Doubleclicks song after her mother had been particularly awful a few years ago. Jordan really got how helpful this kind of repetition could be, and that made it easier to ask for it.

Jordan sang softly, "Don't judge yourself too hard, velociraptor. You are good the way you are, velociraptor."

They roared together like velociraptors, and Leah broke into giggles. "Yeah. That will help. Though maybe we don't need to roar at your work party."

"We can use our discretion about the roaring. You know it's true, right? You are good the way you are."

"I do, most of the time. My trauma brain doesn't, though."

"That's okay. I'll just keep reminding your trauma brain."

"Thanks. Okay, I'm going to do one last makeup check and then I'll be ready."

The cold air on her face helped. When they arrived, she immediately realized that the biggest problem was the space itself. Standing tables were the norm, and it was mostly set up for dancing which meant loud pounding beats and yup...a strobe light.

Well, at least the access issues gave Leah something else to focus on right after they checked their coats, so she wasn't even thinking about the impression she was making. She spotted a rectangular elevated space that wasn't very close to the speakers and had bench seating all around the edge, with tables that had chairs she wouldn't want to try sitting on. There were a few steps, but given the other options, this was the best bet. She did the I'm on your arm but I'm leading thing, and maneuvered them over to comfortable seating at a corner by a table, pulling two pairs of ear plugs out of her purse, and handing one to Jordan, who smiled at her gratefully.

"I can get us drinks, what would you like?"

"Something I can sip for a long time, no alcohol. Surprise me."

That certainly gave Leah something to contemplate as she made her way to the bar. Something light, and tart, she thought. Citrus, not too sweet. Well, the best plan was to get two different ones and let Jordan choose. So she looked at the menu, picked two out that she'd be glad to drink herself, and then requested a little tray from the bartender, who was surprised, but went with it. She filled up the tray, stopped by the food table and made a plate for them to share, and after carefully balancing it on the tray with the drinks, headed back.

"You got them to give you a tray?" Jordan chuckled in disbelief.

"Of course. Never doubt a service submissive in action," Leah murmured.

"I see. I was not aware of this superpower. I need to learn more about it,"

"I'll add that to my lesson planning then," Leah said, grinning.

"Yes, see that you do. Now tell me about these drinks."

"That's a grapefruit ginger spritzer; it's one of their specialties here, and is sparkling and not very sweet. This is a frozen cherry lemonade, on the sweeter end of things, but still pretty tart, I've been told. Whichever you want is yours."

"Tart, eh?"

"Well, I figured tart was a good plan."

"Tart is always a good plan in a crowded place like this. I think I will go for the ginger, but let me taste both before I decide."

Leah found herself a bit too damn focused on Jordan's reactions, so she forced her gaze away, to see who else was around. They were bantering like this was a date. How did that happen? She hadn't been on a date in more years than she could even count. She didn't do dates. She did play dates. And service weekends. She did things where it was clear kink was the main agenda, with buddies. So how had she ended up being Jordan's date for this work event, where they were flirting like a couple? And why did she like it so damn much?

Right, people, she was looking at the people. They weren't the only fat queers sitting here. In fact, she was pretty sure she knew that butch/butch couple across the way, but she couldn't place from where. Wait a minute, was that Jax and Zak? She tilted her head, squinting.

"Spotted someone you know?"

"I think so. Did you decide on your drink?"

"This ginger one has my name all over it. So stimmy. Here, give it a try."

So she did. Jordan was right, it had this lovely heat and sourness to it that completely woke up her mouth. "Oh wow," she murmured.

"Yeah, it's really great. I love taste stims."

"Me too. Okay, looks like I was right. It is Jax and Zak." And they were approaching.

"You know them?" Jordan asked. "Jax is one of the people I'm supposed to work closely with on this big project they hired me for, but I haven't met Zak yet."

"Yup, I met Jax when I was dealing with that situation with Bev about ten years ago. He was part of the group that was trying to change that TERFy rule. He's great."

Jax gave her a big hug, and smiled at Jordan. "Welcome aboard. It seems we already have someone in common. It's a tiny queer world, isn't it?"

Jordan replied, "It really is. Please, sit with us. It will make me look like I'm being social."

"Well, it would mean actually being social, at least a little bit," Jax said, pulling up a couple chairs so they formed a closed group of four around the table.

"Sure," Jordan said. "A little bit social is about right for me, especially with my back to the strobe."

"You have a point there," Jax said, angling his chair a bit more so his back was to it as well. "Ugh, I'm going to have a migraine if I don't leave soon. Though honestly the bass is just as bad."

Leah chimed in, "Between them both, I'm not going to be able to stay long, either. Autistic life. You get all dolled up, you plan your route perfectly, and still when you get there, you often can't stay long because there's something in the space itself that makes that impossible."

"You said it," Jax and Jordan chimed in unison.

"What is this, the neuroatypical corner?" Zak joked. "Can I join? I'm allistic but I've got ADHD, PTSD and depression."

"Of course, of course," Leah said.

"Wait so this means I lucked out and the colleague I'm working with the most closely is also autistic and queer?" Jordan asked.

"Yup. We can actually pick venues for working lunches based on how quiet they are."

"I am looking forward to those."

Leah grinned. Jordan was smiling, and relaxed, and had already almost finished her drink. This was going very well, indeed.

17

THURSDAY AFTERNOON, DECEMBER 19

JORDAN

Jordan was pulling the tater tots out of the oven when Leah emerged. She's so predictable, Jordan thought. The scent of tater tots makes her appear.

"Is that tater tots?" Leah said sleepily, like she always did.

"Of course it is."

"Does that mean you made…"

"Why yes, I did make kosher hot dog puffs."

"My mom always called them pigs in the blanket."

"Yes, I know she did. I don't eat pig, so I call them kosher hot dog puffs."

"Yeah, I know. You also don't make jokes about wrapping me in blankets."

"No, I don't. Once again we establish that I am not your fat-hating mother. I love your fatness. And my own fatness. Fat people are awesome. Yay for being fat! We will eat delicious things to celebrate!"

"They sure smell delicious."

Jordan put together a plate for Leah and placed it in front of her on the table with a flourish. Then she pulled out sour cream and ketchup and spoons, and put those in the center of the table.

"Yknow, tater tots are so good with sour cream. I wonder if they're like latkes and are equally good with apple sauce," Leah said.

"I will not hear this blasphemy. Apple sauce is not worthy of tater tots or latkes!"

"Hmm. You're prejudiced against applesauce."

"Yes I am, the texture is wrongbad. But I tolerate you eating it, so why do you care?"

"You're so benevolent."

Jordan bowed deeply, and fixed herself a plate. She'd tried to make a ginger lime fizzy thing akin to the grapefruit one they'd had last night, and wanted to see what Leah thought, so she got both their glasses ready.

"I have been experimenting," she said solemnly.

"I'm Beaker in this situation, aren't I?"

"Well, of course. My head is rounder. And your nose is more Beaker-like than mine."

"Hmm. I wear glasses, and I'd argue that your nose is as much like Beaker's, actually. Beaker had a classic Ashkie Jewish nose, like both of us. But I'll be Beaker. For you. So are you going to tell me what this is, or do you just want me to try it?"

Jordan grinned at her, not answering. After a minute, Leah tried it. "Lime... and ginger, and fizz, and is that honey?"

"Yup!"

"It's like the one yesterday, only better! Also it would be great if I was sick."

"Are you sick?"

"Nope, but I probably will get sick this winter."

"And I will make this for you!"

"Yay! Because you live here now!"

Jordan sipped at hers contentedly, and began to eat. She wasn't sure why she felt so damn happy this morning, but she was going with it.

"So listen..." Leah began, and Jordan focused on her. "I've gotta have this difficult conversation today, with Ellie. I was wondering if maybe I could try it out on you first?"

"Do you have a script?"

"Yeah I wrote it in therapy."

"Sure, I'd be glad to help. Is this the thing you've been struggling with that you mentioned a couple days ago?"

"Yeah."

"Okay. So, since it relates to me in some ways, maybe you could try out your script on me, as me, instead of me pretending to be Ellie."

"Oh." This clearly hadn't occurred to her. "Yeah, I could do that. Okay."

They sat in silence for a few minutes. Then Jordan asked, "So, not during brunch then?"

"Oh. No, I want to just eat first, if that's okay."

"Of course," Jordan said, and pulled out her book, trying to focus on the advice it was giving about negotiating kink scenes. Nope, she wasn't nervous at all about what Leah was going to say.

When she'd finished eating, Leah had a bit more, so she decided to play her the song she'd found. "So you know yesterday we were singing that Doubleclicks velociraptor song?"

Leah nodded.

"Well, I couldn't get it out of my head so I went to listen to it, and I somehow missed the album they put out recently. Have you heard the song about Clifford?"

"Nope, I missed it too."

"Lemme play it for you."

She pulled it up on her phone, and moved her chair so they both could watch the video as they listened. She put her head on Leah's shoulder, and Leah leaned into her, resting her cheek against Jordan's. Jordan felt Leah's breath catch as she listened, and wrapped her arm around Leah. The song got to her, too, just as much this time as when she'd first heard it last night. There was something about it that just got inside. She wasn't surprised when Leah's tear touched her cheek; Jordan's eyes were full too.

"Wow, okay," Leah said, pulling away to wipe her eyes. "You've been cutting onions."

"You can't have latkes without onions."

"You're getting ahead of yourself with the latkes buddy, Chanukah isn't for a few days."

"Latkes are a year round food and you know it."

"Can't dispute that, it's just fact," Leah smiled, and took another sip of her fizzy drink before continuing. "So, thanks. I actually needed that. My mom shit is all activated, and I decided not to go to the dreadful dinner party. I'm sure it would be worse if I actually went, but damnit, I'd hoped not going would be less stressful."

"Are you sure you are up for the hard conversation, then?"

Leah sat with that for a moment, wheels turning. "No, I'm not, really. I thought about cancelling my plans with Ellie, then I was like, well at least have the conversation even if you cancel the date."

Oh, she'd had a date? Jordan thought about it for a moment, and realized that it didn't bother her at all that Leah had a date. Which was surprising. She'd never been the jealous type, but she'd also never dated anyone polyamorous before. Was dating the right word? They sure were doing something new, even if she didn't know what to call it. She figured it was good this didn't bug her, though. "What made you think about cancelling?" Jordan asked.

"Well, partly because I need to have the conversation before the date, but partly I was clearing out some stressful things on my schedule."

"Sounds like both the date and the conversation are stressful."

"Yeah, that's really true. I just subbed in one stressful thing for another."

"I'm assuming you were clearing off stressful things for a reason..."

"Meltdown prevention. I've been struggling." Ah, that explained some things.

"Hmm. That's a good reason. And the dinner party is still stirring up your mom shit, even though you aren't going."

"Yeah, that was supposed to help with stress but it hasn't."

"What would?"

"Cancelling my date and going to dance class instead. I usually go on Thursdays but was going to skip it."

"Keeping your routine is good. What else would help?"

"Hyperfocus."

"Can you do some of that?"

"Yeah, I was going to work on lesson planning Saturday but if I can sort out a few things with you today, I can do some planning tomorrow."

"Is that the conversation we were going to have?"

"Um, no. That's a different conversation. We should have both, but can the other one wait?"

"Of course."

"I have a questionnaire, and we can talk about it, or you can fill it out. Which do you prefer?"

"Filling it out, electronically if possible."

"Okay, I'll email it. It will help me figure out what lessons to plan."

"I'll work on it today."

18

FRIDAY AFTERNOON, DECEMBER 20

LEAH

After she got off the phone with her therapist, Leah needed a dance break. She put on one of the albums she'd danced to in her room as a kid. She'd only had to get caught dancing by her mom once to make Leah realize she never wanted to go through that again, so she'd always waited until her mom was gone before putting on the Fame soundtrack. Red Light had been her favorite, because it was so long, and when she needed to move to get things out there was nothing better. It still held up as a great dance release song even after all these years, and after talking about her mom in therapy it felt especially defiant to dance to it, like she was reclaiming her fat body and her right to dance for herself. By the time she was done, she was pleasantly sore, instead of tense the way she'd been during her phone session with her therapist.

That was mostly from dance class the night before, but it was also because being tense wore her muscles out. She liked feeling sore, it was one of the pleasures of dancing, that it brought her into her body and left her aching, like a good scene left her with aches and bruises.

Jordan had sent the questionnaire back in the middle of the night, and she'd been thinking about it all morning, as she focused on planning out the first lesson, an adaptation of her class on scene structure and planning. But now she really needed to figure out the rest of the lessons, and the ways they would interlock and build on each other. She pulled out her sticky notes and began writing things Jordan had expressed particular interest in. The key was to have the different lessons build on each other, but also to give Jordan a range of experiences and skills, so that she'd know more about herself and what she was into, and have a foundation to build on, one that would hopefully have her feeling confident.

Leah put all the sticky notes on the board she used for planning, and immediately removed the ones that were things she couldn't teach, wouldn't do, or thought were too advanced. She looked at the ones that were left, and added some of her own, the soft skills and theory that a novice wouldn't know were part of the kinds of kink Jordan was into. Some of those would be part of the first lesson, but some she thought might be better later on. She played around with the sticky notes until she had a sense of which things might go together, and then she brought over a chair and sat.

This next part wasn't about Jordan, but about her. She wanted to dovetail both of their needs, and that meant thinking about which things felt sexual, which felt like they could go either way, and which ones she was into non-sexual aspects of. She wanted a mix of each thing, so she would get to try out setting different kinds of boundaries and taking risks. This part was hard. It made her heart race, thinking about deliberately planning to do kink in a way that was flexible based on her own sense of whether she was up for it to be sexual or not. It felt both scary and...selfish. Her therapist was going to have a field day with that one, but it was true. Somewhere in there she didn't really believe that it was okay for her to honor whether she was up for something sexual or not, or to ask a dominant to wait and see, and go with where she was at in the moment.

She knew it was bullshit, that of course her consent mattered, and it was just one of many things that people doing kink need to be flexible and responsive about. Like her sensory needs, or Jordan's spoon levels, or the way sometimes trauma was too close to the surface to do something edgy but she was into doing things in her comfort zone. This was just another thing like that. But somehow, it didn't feel like it. Maybe this was a thing where she needed to act as if until she believed it. It had worked before.

She'd plan two lessons that felt sexual, three that could go either way, and three that were not sexual for her. Leah labeled each of the sticky notes and began to weed things out, group others together, and build her loose plan for the eight lessons. The more concrete it felt, the less her heart raced, and by the time she had typed it up, she felt pretty grounded. Now she got to grab pieces from the classes she taught, and put together handouts for each lesson, which was going to be fun and hyperfocusy, so she should probably grab a snack, drink some water, and stretch first.

When she emerged, she saw that Jordan had left her a note: Going to a Judaica store in Manhattan because I still can't find the yarmulke my mom crocheted for me and I don't want to wear a generic one at shul tonight. I'm getting a yartzeit candle too, and stopping for bagels and lox at Zabar's on the way home. If you want me to get anything else, text. Leaving for shul at 5:30 (services at 6:30), will be back by 4pm. -J

Right. She was going to shul with Jordan tonight because it was her dad's yartzeit. She had been so into the zone with her lesson planning that she'd forgotten. She set an alarm for 4:30, laid out her clothes for that evening, and grabbed a quick snack. She put on her favorite planning music—

Prince, of course—and sank into the fun of working on handouts as he crooned "If I Was Your Girlfriend". She was just printing out the handouts for the third lesson when Jordan called that she was home. It was a good place to stop for now, so she called back a welcome and went to give Jordan a hand with whatever delicious things she'd not been able to resist at Zabar's.

She ended up leaving out half of what she found because she was suddenly ravenous. Soon she was sitting at the table across from Jordan, listening to her recount her adventure, and eating bites of fresh raisin bagel with cream cheese, full sour pickles, grape tomatoes, and this amazing smoked gouda that made her mouth very happy. Leah loved eating a bunch of small things, especially if they were a range of textures and flavors, and she could rotate among them and make them come out even. It was grounding and helped her mind quiet down. Just arranging them on the plate in their little areas helped. Especially because she had these cool plates with sections.

As she ate, she checked in with herself about whether she was up for going to shul. She really wanted to try if she could, because it was Jordan's dad's yartzeit, but going to shul was hard for her, loaded with triggers and not something she was always up for. She had usually tried when Jordan was visiting, and it mostly had been okay, but recently, she had felt less able to go. Figuring out she was gray ace had stirred up a bunch of stuff around boundaries and pushing herself beyond what she was up for and old trauma, making it feel even more risky to go. She really didn't want to have flashbacks tonight, or a meltdown at shul when Jordan was there to mourn. She didn't want to draw her friend's attention towards taking care of her instead of focusing on her own grief.

Leah was pretty sure that was one of the reasons why she kept forgetting they had planned to do this. She wasn't actually up for it. Once she thought that, she knew it was true. Just thinking about not going had her muscles relaxing. Now she just needed to find the words to say that, and hope Jordan would understand.

"So, I was really hoping I'd be up for going to shul tonight with you, but unfortunately, I'm not," she said softly. Jordan had been staring into her mug of tea, and didn't seem to react at all. Had she even heard? Leah continued, "I still would like to light a candle with you tonight, if you want?"

Jordan nodded. "I got a yartzeit candle at the store." Her voice sounded wooden.

"I'm pretty sure Ruth and Rebecca are going tonight. If you want, I can text them to save you a seat?"

"Yeah, they said they would be there. A seat would be good."

"Okay, I'll do that now. No subways tonight, okay? I'm going to call the car service I like, and have them take you there and wait, and then take you home."

"Okay." Jordan rarely let her pay for that kind of stuff, it mostly felt too fancy for her. She must really be in bad shape. Maybe she overexerted when she went shopping? Or maybe she was always like that on her dad's death anniversary, and Leah hadn't witnessed it before because she hadn't been in the same place.

"You know, if you aren't up for it, it's okay to say kaddish here, or go to shul tomorrow instead."

"I want to go today. Erica and I always went today."

"I know. You must miss her very much. Have you talked to her today?"

"This morning. We talked before I went out." Jordan's voice was so dulled, it felt almost like she was talking to a different person.

"Oh good. I know it has to be weird to not be with her today."

"This whole day hasn't made any sense. It never does. I'm going to get ready."

"Okay. I'll make those arrangements."

Was she really not up for going? Leah checked in with herself again, just to be sure. Just thinking about it made her breathing get all wonky, and she felt dizzy. Okay then. She would support Jordan in other ways. She arranged for R&R to save her a seat, and for one of them to be waiting outside to meet her. She called the car service and set things up. Then she stared at her phone for a full minute, trying to decide if she was going to take this next step, listening to the sound of the shower.

It took only one ring before Erica answered. Leah expressed her condolences, asked how she was doing. Erica thanked her, rushing her through that to ask if Leah knew where Jordan was going to shul tonight.

"Yes, of course," Leah said, and gave her the information.

"Good. I thought so, but I wanted to be sure. Services are at 6?"

"No, 6:30."

"Oh, perfect. I can just show up, right? I don't have to be a member?"

"You're in town?" They always left out the important details when they were in a hurry, the both of them.

"Yep. I knew Jordan wasn't okay when I talked to her this morning. I'm just here for tonight and Saturday night, then I'm off Sunday morning. I can stay with you, right?"

"Of course you can. You're family, you know that. I'm so glad you came. Are Avery and Caro with you?"

"Nope, just me. They're on their own with the kids. They told me I had to go, when I got off the phone this morning. She sounded terrible."

"Yeah, she still sounds terrible. I was worried, because I'm not up for going to shul tonight. She's meeting a couple friends of mine there--I'll let them know you're coming too. Text me a selfie so they know to look for you?"

"Yup, will do. I am barely going to make it to the shul--was planning to surprise Jordan. I know she doesn't usually like surprises, but I really wanted to come and didn't want her to tell me not to."

"She doesn't like surprises, it's true. I'll think on it, and if I think it's better to tell her, I will, if that's okay?"

"Yeah, sure, that's fine. I gotta go, otherwise I'll be late."

Well, then. Leah was glad she'd called. She didn't need to worry as much about Jordan and she could get the place ready for Erica's visit.

19

102

SATURDAY MORNING, DECEMBER 21

JORDAN

When Jordan went into the kitchen to make coffee, her head was pounding and her throat was dry. The flickering light of the candle had the kaddish rolling through her head, and she sat at the table waiting for it to pass through. Then she did what she always did; she started singing "I Am A Rock," the song her dad had always sung to her ever since she was a baby. By the time she had gotten to line about poetry protecting her, Erica had come to stand behind her, and joined her in singing it.

"Again, from the beginning?" Erica asked, so of course they sang it again, Jordan's hand reaching up to clasp her sister's, both of them staring at the candle as it flickered. They rolled right into the song that had been Erica and their dad's ever since he took her to the zoo when she was five: Lou Reed's "Perfect Day." Tears were rolling down both their cheeks by the end, and Jordan stood to pull Erica into a hug.

"And people were surprised he killed himself?" Erica said softly. "Those songs scream depression."

Jordan nodded against her cheek, still holding on. "They really fucking do."

"Okay, I need coffee."

"I was going to make some."

"No, let me. I will make coffee, and waffles—if you can locate a waffle iron—to thank you both for letting me crash here this weekend so I could spend it with you."

"I'm really glad you did, sis. I was in bad shape yesterday."

"Yeah," Erica said. "You looked it. You look a bit more human now. Still fucked up, but not quite as, if that makes sense."

"I agree with that assessment," Leah said from the doorway.

They both turned to smile at her. "My wonderful sister is making coffee, and waffles," Jordan informed her, and then went to go digging through boxes to find her waffle iron. She didn't even bother looking, because she knew Leah wouldn't have one.

"Well, then. Erica, you're welcome any time," Leah quipped. But they all knew she meant it.

The waffles were delicious, though Erica complained about the lack of mimosas, and said she was definitely going to need a drink later. Then she was scheming a theme and spinning an event from that, and before they knew it, the plan for the evening was set. Jordan was glad to have her here; she filled up space and made this day seem less interminably bleak. Plus, it would be good to have a plan for tonight as Leah was sure to be freaking out over not going to her mother's dinner party. Structure would help.

Erica took inventory and made a list of supplies, and then like a whirlwind she was off running errands, ordering Leah to keep Jordan company.

"And then there were two," Leah murmured.

"Well, not really, not til Sunday morning when she leaves. But yes, for now."

"I'm sorry I wasn't up when you got home last night. I tried to stay awake, but you went out for such a late dinner, I just conked out."

"Oh I didn't expect you to be up; we got home at 1."

"I meant what I said, you look better than yesterday. How do you feel, though?"

Jordan took a few moments to take inventory. "Not like an empty wasteland anymore, I'm more...here. That has its good sides, and its not so good. More here is more feelings."

"Yeah, I get that. Numb comes with less pain."

"And a rock feels no pain. And an island never cries." Jordan sang softly.

"Yeah. It's alright to cry, though. Even stone butches cry sometimes."

"That's a rumor that's never been proven."

"Uh huh. We'll just pretend I've never seen it happen, then."

"That would be best. Have I taught you nothing?"

She was saying the right words, the same ones they always said, but they felt like dead leaves in her mouth. She could barely get them out. She was supposed to be strong for Erica, but instead her baby sister had come all this way to rescue her, because she couldn't get through this fucking day. Being here on her dad's yartzeit had fucked her up bad, and she hadn't even seen that coming until it was a train flattening her. She'd been so out of it yesterday with all the flashbacks that she'd thought Erica wasn't real when she'd first seen her. And now instead of the flashbacks, the mourner's kaddish was messing with her.

The kaddish spiraled in her head, twisting around itself and not letting go. The songs hadn't helped. They usually helped. But they hadn't helped today. Nothing was helping. She was a failure of a parent and a person and she couldn't handle this. She couldn't get through this fucking day. She wasn't going to make it. Jordan screwed her eyes shut and hid in the circle of her arms on the table. Her heart pounded in her ears, and her lungs felt stuck. She didn't even decide to do it really but her feet were crossed and they were going fast under her chair.

When the time she emerged from the meltdown, the room seemed different. Oh. The lights were off, the room was lit by the light coming through the window; it wasn't an outside window but one that looked out onto an air shaft, so it was pleasantly dim. And the place was silent, no music or TV, just Leah sitting nearby, reading silently, her energy calm, grounded. Not asking for Jordan to do anything, just present in case Jordan wanted her. Leah did that incredibly well. Most people didn't.

Was that a submissive thing? She'd never let herself think about Leah's submission, and how it fit into the friend she'd known for so many years. But now, she felt free to wonder. Maybe even to ask. Asking would at least give her something else to think about, give her brain something else to do.

"I have a question." Jordan's voice was hoarse. Had she been making noises and not even been aware of it?

"Alright. Ask."

"You do this thing, where you're here, and it seems like you're really present, available if I should need something. But not...asking anything of me, not pushing into my space, letting me be."

Leah smiled. "That's a lovely compliment, as it's exactly what I was aiming for just now. But it's not a question..."

"I was getting there."

"Okay."

"Is that a submissive thing?"

"Hmmm. It's a skill I use as a submissive, but I also use it outside of a power dynamic. A lot of D/s is like that. If you're asking if I was doing it out of submission just now, I'd say no. That was friendship. In particular, that was about being an autistic person who has a sense of what another autistic person might need during a meltdown."

"I wasn't thinking you were submissive just now. I was more thinking...it's a rare skill, and wondering if it was something you're good at because you're a submissive."

"Ah. I know some doms that are very good at it, actually. I'm going to guess that you've been reading about 'true submissives' and 'true dominants'."

"I've been trying to do research."

"Some sources are more reliable than others. I generally recommend folks access a bunch of sources, learn from a range of teachers. You should decide for yourself, of course, but I find the concept of 'true sub' and 'true dom' a terrible lie, as well as a red flag. People aren't born to be submissive or dominant, and the idea that they are reminds me too much of eugenics not to turn my stomach."

"Oh. I hadn't thought of it that way. Thanks. I will think that over."

"Sure. We can talk about it more if you want."

"Maybe later. Can I ask one more thing?"

"Sure."

"When you do that thing as part of submission...what does that look like? What does it feel like?"

"That's two things."

"Yes, I guess it is."

"I use it most often when I'm doing personal service of the sort that's more about waiting in attendance and being...well essentially arm candy, in public. Unobtrusive, but present if needed. Not drawing attention or needing it, there to serve when it's desired."

Oh. That idea was utterly delicious. Jordan's tongue traced along her teeth slowly, contemplating this, as Leah continued.

"It feels like...being in hyperfocus, but instead of on a task, it's on a person. Giving them every bit of my attention, but in a calm grounded way, not one where they feel my gaze. It's not sexual, but it is sensual. My skin feels...alive. But more, it's like the rest of the world disappears except for where it's relevant to serving them, like all I am is theirs, and I'm so glad to be."

Jordan bit her lip. Well, she'd wanted distraction. This would most definitely do.

20

SATURDAY AFTERNOON, DECEMBER 21

LEAH

Leah spent the morning so focused on Jordan that she didn't think about her mother until after lunch. She'd decided to wait to let her mother know she wasn't coming until late afternoon, had gotten her therapist's help drafting the text. It was sitting in her notes app, waiting for her to cut and paste, and she couldn't stop staring at it.

She didn't say no to her mother. She never had said no to her mother, not outright, not like this, not so very deliberately. She avoided, she maneuvered, she made choices that her mother disapproved of so intensely that the family barely demanded her presence anymore. But refuse a command performance? She hadn't tried to get out of one since she was thirteen and had stomach flu on Pesach. But she was going to say no today, damnit. She was going to put her own well-being first. And she didn't even have the fucking flu.

But wow was she nauseous. Plus her head was pounding. It was a mother-induced flu. Erica plopped down on the couch and nudged her. "You have your phone in a death grip and have been staring at it, frozen, for like twenty minutes. What's up?"

Leah blinked and tried to make words. "I have to send this to my mom." She handed her phone over to Erica so she could read the text.

"You don't actually have the flu," Erica said.

"No. That part is for thirteen year old me."

"Okay. Wanna tell me about that?"

Maybe she did. "So when I was thirteen, I had the stomach flu on Pesach, but my mom made me go to the seder anyway, even though I was as green as my olive dress."

"That color green is all wrong for you."

"Tell me about it. It was the 80s, there were slim pickings for fat girls. That dress was horrifying."

"The pickings were slim for me too, at thirteen."

"Yeah. I know. I remember taking you shopping for your bat mitzvah dress." Leah put her arm around Erica's shoulders, smiling at the memory of her at thirteen, and her obsession with ruffles.

"You were so good to baby trans me that day. Let me go on and on about exactly what I wanted, and took me to places that didn't even blink."

"We found something great, didn't we?"

"Yeah, we did. Though I wouldn't be caught dead in it now. And I bragged for days about buying my dress in New York City."

Leah smiled, squeezing her. "So yeah. Olive green. With this bodice that was all ruffles. It was way too tight, too, because my mom always stuffed me into the smallest sizes she could, even if they were too tight. I had this terrible flu. Just sitting at the table smelling the charoset made me rush to the bathroom to puke."

"Uh oh."

"You guessed it. Some of it got on my dress. On the ruffles of course. And I didn't notice, just went back to the table. I was so out of it, dizzy, felt terrible. And then my mother pointed it out, and this whole table of adults was laughing at me."

"Fuck. That's awful. I'm so sorry."

"I never wore ruffles again."

"Well, I'd regret the ruffles too, after something like that! And you were so sweet, helping me find this ridiculously ruffle-filled dress, not even mentioning this."

Leah shrugged. "I knew your family would never do anything like that to you."

Erica turned, and hugged her. "You're my family, too, you know. I always thought of you that way."

"Aw, thanks hon. I love you to pieces, you know."

"I love you, too. Okay, I feel like I'm missing a bit of the picture, beyond your family being awful."

"My mom never let me miss any occasions, all throughout my childhood, and I never tried to convince her otherwise after the ruffle incident, because I knew she got them to laugh to punish me for trying to skip dinner."

"Okay, I hate her."

"Join the club. So anyway. I have been commanded to be there tonight for a dinner party and I decided that I wasn't going to go, this time."

"Ohhh. And you're letting her know last minute so she has less time to do anything about it."

"You got it."

"This is a big deal. I get why you were frozen like that. I'm glad you're staying home with us instead. This feels right."

Leah nodded. It did feel right. And somehow...she had always thought of herself as Erica's family, but it hadn't occurred to her that Erica was her family, too, until just now. That she was now an adult that Leah might lean on a bit. If that was a new thing for her, how was Jordan was dealing with leaning on her sister?

"So how can I help?"

"Actually, I think telling you about it already helped."

"You know..." Erica said softly. "You deserve a family that wouldn't do that to you, either."

Leah gave in and just let herself cry. Fuck it. Erica patted her back and let her cry for as long as she needed to. Just like a sister would.

"Thanks. I'm really glad you're my family, Erica. We should visit more, okay?"

"Yes. We should. Now, do you need me to hit send? I can even hold your phone so you don't see what she says, if you want."

Leah took a slow breath. "I will hit send, but yeah, if you could hold my phone for me, that would be good."

"Okay. Ready when you are."

Leah stared at the message one last time, and then sent it. She handed over her phone, and Erica shoved it in her pocket.

"Alright, we're basically set for our evening of Nick and Nora. The only thing left is to get dressed. Do you have something I can borrow? I hadn't planned on this when I was coming out here."

"I have just the thing," Leah said, grinning.

"Remember what dad used to say about Myrna Loy?" Erica asked.

"As if I could forget," Jordan replied. "She was a good friend to the Jews!" she trumpeted.

"Well, he wasn't wrong."

"No, he wasn't. I remember you did a paper about her for some class, didn't you?"

Erica smiled. "Well, I basically wanted to be her, so any excuse to watch the movies and learn about her life."

"You do make a great Nora," Leah said. She had found a steel gray dress that worked really well, even though Erica was a size smaller and shaped a bit differently. Erica's hair was always rather thirties, so it fit the theme perfectly. Leah had put hers up, and found a black satin gown that had a thirties flair to it at the back of her closet. The key was the makeup. It was all smoky eyes, mascara and a rosebud mouth. Her mother would hate this ensemble, right down to the peeptoe heels. Nope, she wasn't going to think about her mother. A martini would help. Except Erica insisted that they wait until Nick has a martini in the film, then pause and put on a waltz so she could shake them to the proper time.

Leah put on one of her favorite thirties waltzes, The Kiss Waltz, and danced to it, as Erica made their martinis. Jordan just sat and watched her dance, and as Leah listened to Ruth Etting sing she couldn't help but think about kissing Jordan. They had played, and were going to play again, and Jordan knew her better than practically anyone, except for her kinks, which she was getting to know…but they hadn't ever kissed. Leah rarely kissed her play partners, and didn't often kiss her friends, but still. She had been thinking about Jordan kissing her since she was 20. What harm could it do, to put kissing on the table as a possibility?

The song ended, she had a perfect martini in her hands, and was about to watch some of the best banter in the world. She'd think about that later. But first, before they started the movie, she had something to deal with.

"Hey Erica? Can you look at my phone for me?"

"You got it," Erica said, giving her fingerguns, which made her giggle. Okay maybe the giggle was partly nerves.

Erica stared at the phone, doing her best to have blank face, but the corners of her mouth turned down, and her jaw got really tight. So it was probably bad. Erica raised her head, and her face softened as she looked at Leah, her eyes going sad.

"So I read it. She sent one text acting like you must be joking, and a couple texts about twenty minutes apart demanding that you call her. Then several missed calls. Then she moved on to insults, manipulation and guilt, from her and it looks like several messages from your dad echoing her, and one from your brother that says basically the same thing. She's a fucking piece of work, your mom. I mean, I'd gathered that, but this..." Erica shook her head.

"Yeah, Leah's mom is awful," Jordan said quietly. "And the rest of them all back her up."

Leah sighed. Well, she'd known she would get a response like this. But damn, it was like an anvil on her chest. Erica took her hand and counted breaths with her until she was breathing steadily, then pulled out a gold box, and opened it, offering it to Leah.

"My secret weapon. Dark chocolate truffles."

Chocolate would help. Her mother was basically a dementor, after all.

21

SUNDAY MORNING, DECEMBER 22

JORDAN

Jordan asked Erica to go get breakfast sandwiches from the bodega nearby and eat with her in her room before heading back to Boston. She wanted to check in, see how Erica was doing, without Leah around, and she just wasn't up to going out, not with how fuzzy and worn down she felt. Yesterday had kicked her ass.

They'd always done movie nights on her dad's yartzeit, it was a way of honoring a family tradition that he had started, and Erica had been especially into the idea of dressing up like a character in the movie and serving some kind of snack or beverage that was appropriately movie themed. Dani hadn't participated, she left this to Jordan and Erica to do alone, but once Erica moved in with Avery and Caro, they'd gotten into it. They were all cosplaying geeks, so it was right up their alley. It had been nice to have Leah there this time. It felt like bridging. Even if she'd had too many martinis, and was paying for that this morning. And had been a complete wreck in other ways.

"So..." Erica drawled.

"So?" Jordan responded wearily.

"So the stuff you said last night...is that how you really feel?"

Oh no. Jordan tried to clear her head and remember what she'd said, but it was fuzzy. She'd lost her shit again, had another fucking meltdown. But damned if she remembered what she said during it.

"I have a hard time remembering what I say during meltdowns, even when I'm sober."

"So you don't remember."

"No, I'm sorry. I really don't. I had two meltdowns yesterday. I barely remember the spaces in between them, honestly. It's like the whole day is fuzzy. What did I say?"

"You apologized to me for needing me and being a complete wreck, said that you felt like a failure because it was your job to take care of me but

I'd been taking care of you."

"Oh. Well, actually, I do feel like that."

"You know that's fucking bullshit, right?"

Jordan blinked and tried to follow along. "It is?"

"Yes. Look, I know you were my parent when I was a kid. And I'm glad. You made a safe family for me, when I really needed it, after dad fucked off and left us alone. You did a much better job than he ever could, definitely a better job than mom ever did."

"I-"

"I'm not finished."

Jordan put her hands up, and waited, listening.

"But. I'm an adult now, have been one for a long time. I'm 35 years old. And yeah, we're never going to be regular siblings because of our history, but damnit, Jordan. I have the right to take care of my sister when she needs me. She has the right to need me."

"I do?"

"Yes," Erica said crisply. "You do. I'm good at taking care of people, you know. I'm a fucking awesome parent, and partner, and friend. Let me really be your sister."

"I...taking care of me is part of being my sister?"

"Older sisters aren't the only ones who need to take care of their siblings, you know. You should see how Caro is with her older sister. It goes both ways. Let it go both ways, Jordan. Just because we had fucked up parents doesn't mean we can't find a way to be sisters."

"This is complicated for me, okay? I'll try, but I'm probably going to fuck it up."

"Yeah, I get that. It's okay to fuck it up. Just...don't apologize to me again for needing me."

"Okay."

"And just to be extra clear, I was glad to be able to support you. Dad's suicide, it fucked us both up, and for years you focused on supporting me around it. You get to need support too. And who knows the specific ways it fucked us up better than me?"

"You have a point. Thank you for dropping everything and coming out for this."

"You're welcome. Now get some rest today, okay? You must be wiped out from those meltdowns." Erica leaned in and kissed Jordan on the cheek. "I'll text when I get home, and we'll take pics of the kids lighting the candles, and send them your way."

"I want pics, and reports back about my presents."

"Of course, of course. Need your weighted blanket?"

"I...haven't unpacked it yet."

"Well, then, I'll do that before I go. I know exactly what box it's in."

"Thanks, sis."

"Not a problem at all."

After Erica left, Leah appeared in her doorway.

"So, she's off," Leah said.

"Yup. She had words for me this morning."

"Yeah, she was upset about what you said yesterday."

"Until she told me, I didn't even remember saying it."

"I remember," Leah said sharply.

"Sounds like you have words for me too."

"Are you up for that?"

Jordan nodded, and reached for her water. Water would help.

"Jordan, I just. It sounds like you have some stuff around meltdowns. Like you think it's not okay to have them."

"But-"

"I'm not finished."

Jordan nodded. "You apologized for having meltdowns, for being in such bad shape, emotionally. Like you thought it was bad. That hurt. I have meltdowns. I'm sometimes in bad shape. You've seen it. You've supported me."

"I don't-"

"Still not finished."

"Okay."

"I know you were thinking about yourself, and maybe especially about your relationship with Erica. That this is your internalized stuff, it's not about me. But. It still hurts to have you say it. And it makes me wonder what you think of me. Okay, now I'm done. You can talk."

Jordan took a slow breath. "I'm sorry I tried to interrupt you."

Leah nodded. "I accept your apology."

"I'm really sorry that what I said hurt you and made you doubt how I see you. Leah, I haven't sorted this all out, but I think this move, and the divorce, and the yartzeit and everything has stirred up old trauma and internalized ableism, and I'm having a harder time than I'd thought I would."

"Yeah, it does seem that way. I get that. So much change all at once. I'm in a time of change, and I'm struggling too."

"I truly don't believe that it's wrong for either of us to be struggling, or having meltdowns, or have mental health stuff get stirred up. It's just that in the middle of those things happening, I get these thoughts that say it's not okay. I'm sorry that I hurt you."

Leah nodded. "I get that. I get negative thoughts too. I'm not used to you saying them out loud like they're true, is all."

"Yeah, that was probably partly the martinis."

"Ah, yeah, I can see that."

"I'm thinking I need to go to therapy again. It's been a while, and it might help me sort through this stuff. I'm hoping you can recommend a kink-friendly queer therapist?"

"Yes, I'll email you a few names."

"Thanks. I'm going to try resting. Meltdowns wipe me out."

"Sounds good. Sundown is about 4:30 today--I looked it up--but we can do candles whenever suits you."

"And then the lesson."

"If you're up for it."

"Oh, I really hope I am."

"Me, too. I can walk you through some stuff about the lessons over dinner, see how it feels."

"A good way to test the waters. Thanks, Leah."

Leah smiled, and closed the door behind her, leaving Jordan to the quiet. She dropped into a heavy sleep, and dreamed of Leah kneeling before her, looking up at her with devotion.

22

SUNDAY EVENING, DECEMBER 22

LEAH

Leah could do this. She'd been getting ready for this conversation with folks that had more expectations, where it would come with a lot more baggage to sort through. This would be easy in comparison. She just had to get it rolling, and Jordan would probably help her get it out, even. It would be fine. Besides, she had dinner to futz with, if she needed something to do with her hands, or to take a minute to come up with words.

"So. Before we talk about the lessons more I wanted to bring up something specific." Her voice only quavered a little.

"Is this the thing you wanted to talk about a few days ago?"

Trust Jordan to keep track of stuff like this. "Actually, yeah it is."

"Okay. Would it be easier if you said everything before I talk, or do you want me to ask questions?"

"Questions would be good, actually."

"Okay. I'm going to turn off the music so it doesn't distract me."

Leah nodded. Good idea. Quiet was better. Easier to find words. She had the beginning ones planned at least. Here goes.

"So I've been going through a questioning process around my sexuality, and I recently realized that I'm gray ace."

Jordan nodded.

"I'm still sorting through all of what that means for me. One thing I know is that having sex and doing sexualized kink isn't something I'm up for all the time. It's not a fixed thing, it changes, so it's not predictable."

"Okay. I have a friend, RJ, who's ace, and sex averse. Ze is uncomfortable talking about sex or doing anything that feels sexual, or being around sexual dynamics. This sounds a bit different."

"Yeah, this is...more fluid than that. Sometimes I'm sex averse, sometimes

I'm into sex, sometimes I'm okay being around sexual things but don't want to have sex myself, it's more…gray. Hence the name, gray ace."

"Is it like, a spectrum?"

"I honestly am not comfortable calling my grayness a spectrum, because it doesn't really feel linear to me? And it'd be confusing, because gray ace is an identity on the asexual spectrum."

Leah took a breath, trying to word this next part. She ate a few bites as she thought. It took her a minute, and Jordan just gave her the space. Friends who know your speech patterns were gold. She continued, "Also, spectrum makes it seem like when I do feel sexual that my experience of that is the same as allosexual folks, when it's really not."

"Okay. Can you tell me more about that?"

"Well, like, I'm still figuring out all of the ways it works, but one of the things I know is that I don't sexualize most things, or assume they're about sex, or read sex into them, the way a lot of allosexual folks do. It's more than just the autistic thing of misreading cues, it's like…innuendo isn't part of my framework for seeing the world."

"So kink isn't automatically sexual for you, I take it."

"No, not at all, and a lot of the kinks I love I don't think of in sexual ways. It's kind of jarring to be in kink community spaces because there's so much allonormativity, where many people assume that everyone experiences kink as sexual."

"I mean, I knew that some folks did non-sexual kink, because you had introduced me to Tyler and Marcos, and I know their dynamic isn't sexual or romantic, but most of the books I've read talk about kink as if it's all sexual."

"Yeah, it's a problem," Leah said glumly.

"I'm relieved to hear that it's not true, because I'm not always up for things being sexual, either. Especially in public. Sex isn't an easygoing thing for me, that's part of what being a stone butch means for me. It's…I don't really have the words. What you told me about drop and how it feels? That happens to me when sex is part of things, even sex that respects my boundaries. Even when there's no kink involved. I mean, obviously, because I haven't done kink until recently. Does that make sense?"

It really did. Leah hadn't thought of it before this, but allo stone folks were not your typical allosexual. It was really cool to find connections in a conversation that she'd been afraid would make her feel alienated. Her throat felt like it had loosened when she responded, "Yeah, it actually sounds really familiar. For me, sex and sexualized kink feel like a huge emotional risk, and kind of like traversing in dangerous territory, where the stakes are high, and I feel very vulnerable."

"Oh, yeah, that does sound really similar."

"That's during. And afterwards, I am noticing that I get a much more intense drop."

"Did that happen after the party? And the class?" Jordan's questions were gentle.

"Especially after the party, but yes, after both."

"Can you tell me what it was like for you after the party?"

"I felt very thin skinned, for days, and like I was super hungry for touch and comfort. I had a few crying jags, including one at work. In general I was more emotionally sensitive and all over the place."

"You seemed to pull away from me," Jordan said cautiously.

"Yeah, I didn't want to dump all that on you. Plus I was feeling weird about stuff and trying to figure it out."

"Weird about stuff?"

"Well, just...weird about nudging Iris to teach you and wanting to teach you myself and weird about you two getting together after our scene without letting me know ahead of time. Like I said, thin skinned and emotional."

"Leah, is one of the meanings of weird jealous?"

She ducked her head. "Yeah, okay. I was jealous," she muttered. "I don't get jealous very often."

"Would it help to know that I felt weird about you pushing Iris toward teaching me instead of wanting to do it yourself? In my case the weird means insecure."

"Okay that does help, actually. How are you so good at this emotional processing shit?"

"Years of family therapy with Erica, probably. Plus, yknow, my job."

"Yeah okay. Fair enough."

"Leah, are you irritated that we are processing?"

"Not irritated, just...grumpy. But also, it's kinda nice? It makes me get in touch with how much I trust you."

"Right back at you. I'm very glad that you trusted me enough to talk to me about this. I know it's hard."

"Not as hard as I was scared it would be."

"What were you scared of?"

"I don't know. That you would personalize it or feel rejected around the sex stuff, or think something was wrong with me."

"I'm glad you trusted that I might not do those things, and took the risk to find out."

"And you don't?"

"No, darlin', I don't," Jordan said gently. "I actually think we have a bunch of things in common, including those fears. Often when I talk about being stone, folks react that way."

"Things in common is good," Leah said, feeling small. "Can I have a hug, maybe?"

"Absolutely," Jordan said, and stood, pulling her up into one of the most glorious hugs she had ever had. Jordan was wider, and a bit taller, and her presence felt so big that Leah was okay feeling small in her arms, it was like she was protected. Safe.

"Okay," she muttered to herself, when the hug was over and they were sitting again. "So I put together something flexible, where some lessons are non-sexual kink, some are ones that could be, or not, depending on how we feel, and a couple are sexual kink. I thought we could pick and choose based on how we felt, check in and see. It means less of a set schedule, but truly that's kind of how kink is in general, even if you have a plan for play, it often needs adjusting based on what folks are up for when the time comes."

"So it's like, a plan…but a loose and flexible plan."

"Yeah, I was actually going to talk about that tonight, because the lesson is about nuts and bolts of a scene, including planning."

"So this is just adding sex in as a thing that might be part of it or not, based on what we both are up for."

"Yeah. The other thing is…I might think that I'm for it but then realize I'm not."

"That's true for me, too, actually. I'm assuming that scenes need to be adjusted around those kinds of realizations sometimes, anyway. Or sometimes around stuff like disability flares. Kinda how any plan might need to be adjusted."

Leah sighed with relief. "Yes," she said smiling. "Exactly. Folks sometimes are more sensitive when it comes to a submissive taking sex off the table."

Jordan sat with that for a while. "I'm going to try not to judge them for that," she finally said. "But it's hard."

Leah just blinked for a moment, taking that in. "Can you say more about that, please?" she finally got out.

"Okay. I mean, I guess I start from the baseline that it's okay for anyone to take any activity off the table at any point. Submissive or dominant, sex or spanking or kissing or begging or whatever. I know that vanilla allocishet folks have all these normative expectations for partners, but I kinda thought kinky queers were at least trying not to work from frameworks like that but actually really centered and valued deep consent and doing what people actually mutually want. I definitely don't want to do something my partner isn't fully choosing to do. That's awful, and the opposite of hot for me."

"Some people like using their submissives for sexual service, and it doesn't matter if the submissive is into it."

"Okay. I'm not sure I know what that looks like, but given the context of our conversation, I am not imagining that you would be into that as a submissive. Am I wrong about that?"

"No, you aren't wrong. I am a bad fit for that, as I learned from experience. It's hard sometimes to tease out what aspects of D/s you're into, because they are often presented as if they are all linked together."

"Yeah, that makes sense. So let me say upfront: I don't want to do anything with you that you aren't also into doing, and openly choosing. It's absolutely fine with me for you to take anything off the table at any time, including in the middle of things, and to stop our play at any time."

"Thank you for saying that. I feel the same way about you. Please don't feel pressured to do any of these things or bluster your way through something you don't want. I'm only interested in teaching you what you want to learn, and doing play that you're interested in."

"Does that mean we need safewords?"

"I'd like to use a non-verbal signal, like before?" Jordan nodded, then Leah continued. "I think otherwise we can talk openly. We aren't going to play with consensual non-consent, so we can just say no or I need to stop doing x or whatever."

"That sounds easier."

"How do you feel about having a lesson tonight, after lighting the candles?"

"I'd like that," Jordan said gruffly.

"I thought we'd switch off who's lighting them, and that person could lead the songs and stuff."

"Sounds good, you want to do it today, and I can do it tomorrow?"

Leah nodded, and they moved into the living room where everything was already set up on a table. She walked herself through the steps, reminding herself that it was 2019, and she was in her house, far from her family. Her voice was hoarse as she sang the prayer, her hand trembling only a little as she lit the first candle and tried to settle the shamash without burning herself. When the prayers were done, she slid right into Maoz Tzur, which she loved, especially in Hebrew. She smiled at Jordan as they sang it first in Hebrew, then English. The she started Chanukah oh Chanukah and was puzzled that Jordan didn't join her. Maybe she didn't know that one. It made sense that they might have different traditions. She wasn't sure what to do next. Jordan looked so forlorn, like something was missing.

"So, is there something else you usually do on the first night that feels important not to miss?" Leah finally asked.

"My dad always told the story. And my first year of college, Chanukah was really early, remember? I had a big exam and couldn't get home in time for the first night. So he recorded himself telling the story, and sent it to me. After he died, Erica and I would listen to it together on the first night."

"Would you like to listen to it?"

"Yeah. I had thought maybe I would want to start a new tradition of telling it ourselves, but that doesn't feel right."

"Okay, it can be our new tradition to listen to it together, and maybe get Erica on the phone so she can listen with us?"

"Yeah, that would be good."

They ended up on the couch, with Leah putting Erica and her family on speaker, and Jordan using the living room stereo to play the recording. After a moment, Jordan reached for her hand, and they sat that way, Jordan's hand in hers, listening, Erica explaining to the kids who it was, and answering their questions about the story as it went on. Jordan would smile every time one of the kids broke in with a question, and pause the recording until it was answered. By the end, the kids were interrupting with what they remembered of the story, so it was like they all told it together as a family. When the recording was over, Erica prompted them, and Jordan's niblings chorused their thanks for the presents Leah and Jordan had given them.

"Thanks, Jordan," Erica said. "This was a really good idea. I don't know why we didn't include them in listening to dad before. I'm glad we did this."

"Me too," Jordan said. "Let's make it a first night tradition, ok?"

"Definitely. Okay, gotta get them into their baths. Love you both. Happy Chanukah!"

23

SUNDAY EVENING, DECEMBER 22

JORDAN

When they began the lesson, Jordan was surprised at how comfortable she was. Maybe because they hadn't gotten to the practice part yet. The lesson on structuring a scene was in the kind of chunks that felt right sized for her, and addressed a lot of her nervous thoughts about what to do and how to navigate things. It was super practical, and Leah was so sparkly, like she was into teaching it.

When they hit the stretch break, Jordan felt way more at ease about the upcoming practice part, too. Like she had the building blocks she needed. Leah had made little signs for the important ideas that she posted on the wall, with pictures and simple phrases to remember. A picture of ice cream in a cup with just a spoon, to remind her to start simple, with just one thing, and build the scene from that. A picture of a rocket coming back down to earth, to remind her to build in space into the scene for coming out of it with care.

For this next part, Leah had requested that she have her toybag, so she went to get it. When she got back, there was a new sign on the wall with an acronym. Interesting. She sat with the bag at her feet and picked up her notebook, writing DRASH vertically on the page, and each of the words associated with it (Dynamic, Requests/Boundaries, Activities, Safe Signals, Health/Body). What did kink have to do with midrash?

Leah smiled at her. "I made this acronym just for you, to help you remember the important pieces of negotiation. I thought you would appreciate how Jewish it is."

Jordan grinned. "I do. I'm eager to learn what kink negotiation has to do with drash."

"Well, I think of midrash as shared interpretations, folks riffing off the Torah together. That's how the rabbi who taught at my Hebrew school talked about it. He might've been trying to be cool, but I've always liked that idea."

"Yeah, that fits, it's a bit like fanfic in a way."

"Yes! So I think the body of kink is vast, and even without a single shared text it can sometimes seem official or set in stone, and like it needs to look a particular way. Some folks talk about kink as if there is only One True Way & their voices can be really loud sometimes, especially when you're new and wanting to know how to do things right."

"Oh yeah, I definitely saw a lot of that on the internet, and in fiction, too."

Leah nodded. "The reality is that when you negotiate, you collaborate with someone to put your particular spin on kink together, find the kink that suits the folks creating it. Kinda like drash. You get to decide what you want it to be, together. I think that framework helps you feel less hemmed in by what 'Official BDSM' is supposed to be, and create your own version."

"Yeah, I like that."

"Okay, here's a handout with a few suggested questions for each one of the letters."

Jordan looked at it, reading each section and then asking questions, or making comments, like "What's an honorific?" and "Oh I like that question about how to refer to their body." When she finished, she asked the question that had been bugging her. "So this seems rather one-sided. I only ask the questions?"

"Nope, this is where you also volunteer your answers, as relevant. Dominants often lead negotiation conversations, but it's not always the way it has to go. You're responsible for getting all the information you need to ensure consent, and this is a good framework for that, but the conversation can go a bunch of different ways."

"Can it happen over email? I think I'd like that better."

"Absolutely. You need to check in to see if anything has changed or come up right before, but most of the conversation can happen via email."

That was a relief.

"So I wanted to show you one simple way to do the activities part of the negotiation for a scene that involves SM. That's why I asked you to bring your toy bag. What you do is pick 3-5 toys that you'd be interested in for the scene, and lay them out on a surface. Then you ask the submissive to choose. At the beginning, I'd say they should choose just one."

"A scoop in a cup, no toppings."

"Exactly, I love that phrase from Mollena Williams-Haas--it's such a useful image."

Jordan opened the bag, touching each of the toys. After some consideration, she pulled out the wooden spoon, the clothespins, and the hairbrush. She wasn't ready for the quirt, so it didn't make sense to use it. And the ruler...she wasn't sure if she could wrap her head around using that.

"Okay, try leading me through the negotiation process. Try to lead without dominating, if that makes sense? That gets you better information, and you don't have consent for that until I give it."

"I get that, I think. It makes sense to wait to dominate until the actual scene."

"Exactly."

Jordan took a few slow breaths, and began with a question about dynamics. It was a lot to take in, she thought, as she focused on Leah's answers, but it did feel possible to put her own thoughts in after she took in what Leah was saying. By the time they got to discussing her own boundaries around touch and had taken sex off the table for the scene, she felt more grounded. She could do this. The acronym really helped. Then it came to the part where she asked Leah to select a toy for them to play with.

"So you probably aren't going to get a submissive play partner who would do this, but I'm going to share my internal monologue about the toys with you, so you get a sense of what might be going through their head."

"Thanks," Jordan said.

"I'm wondering if you put the clips because you already feel comfortable using them, but I'm not up for that kind of pain today. It's so intrusive, and I'd much rather have the sting from the brush or the spoon. I'd usually wonder if you were suggesting roleplay with the brush or the spoon, but since we already talked about dynamics and I made it clear I wasn't into that, I'm not worried. So I'm just considering the sensations each can give, in the different ways you might use it. If I were going to choose just for me, I'd choose the spoon today, but since this is also educational I'm going to choose the brush, because there are some things you can do with it that I'm not up for today, and some I am, and I think it'll be helpful to give you an opportunity to figure that out in scene."

Leah handed Jordan the brush. Jordan thought about it for a moment. This was supposed to be for learning. And it was good to know that even with this kind of negotiation there still might be places not to go. She grinned at Leah, stroking the bristles of the brush, and continued through the rest of the negotiation.

"So now, we can do the practice scene, if you're up for that," Leah said.

Jordan nodded.

"It's best to put aside student/teacher roles while we do that. We can unpack things later."

"Sounds good."

Jordan stood, and stretched, taking a moment to gather herself in the bathroom, to change into her boots. She thought about how that scene had begun at the party, with a particular song, and a ritual with kneeling, and rolling up her sleeves. How it had felt to sink into her dominance in that moment. Did she need those cufflinks again? No, that was organic, this could be organic too. She held that memory in her mind, though, just settled into her boots, remembering. Then she strode back into the living room. Leah had taken off her pants like they'd agreed. All she was wearing was a white cropped t-shirt that said Chub Rub Club in black letters, and red panties.

Jordan grabbed a large circular pillow from the couch, and settled herself into her favorite chair in the room, the one that felt a bit like it was made for a dominant. She wasn't even sure why it felt that way, something about how wide it was, how comfortable, how much space it took up in the room, how it was a viewpoint from which you could see everyone, and everyone's eyes would be drawn to you. She placed the pillow on the floor at her feet.

"Bring me the brush, and kneel there," she said, glad the words had emerged as an order without fumbling. Leah brought the brush, handing it to her, and kneeled. She was so gorgeous on her knees. Jordan just sat and enjoyed that for a moment, letting her gaze travel over Leah leisurely, like she had all the time in the world. When she was ready, she lifted her boot to brush Leah's hand off her left thigh. Then she leaned forward and placed the brush there, bristles side down, resting her boot on top of it to hold it in place, the heel digging into Leah's inner thigh. Leah gasped, and blinked, looking down at the boot on her thigh. Her left hand was fluttering, while the right one stayed still on her other thigh.

Jordan smiled down at her, and slowly began to roll up the cuffs of her shirt, drawing Leah's gaze. She liked how mesmerized Leah got by this, how focused she became on Jordan's hands. This was a good way to begin, she concluded, and slowed down her movements to savor it, noting that Leah bit her lip. Yes, this was good. This going at her own pace, this being attended to so deeply. She was glad there was no music to distract, so she was able to hear when Leah's breath caught as she finished and reached out a hand to stroke Leah's lower lip, wishing she'd remembered to ask about kissing. Since she hadn't, it needed to wait. She'd remember tomorrow.

24

SUNDAY EVENING, DECEMBER 22

LEAH

The bristles against her thigh were difficult to take. She was riding the edge of it, the whole time Jordan slowly rolled up her sleeves, so much so that when Jordan's thumb stroked her lower lip, Leah's instinct was to open her mouth and bite down on it. Should she say something? She could feel her jaw clenching. Both of her hands were fluttering.

Then Jordan lifted her boot and picked up the brush, and Leah sighed in relief. Jordan tilted her head, considering for a moment, before telling her to bring over a chair she could sit in for the rest of the scene. So she went to get her favorite chair on the other side of the room, the soft topaz one she'd built the room around. By the time she'd gotten herself seated, her hands were able to be still again.

Jordan was pressing the bristles of the brush into her own palm, and nodding. A good sign that she'd noticed Leah's discomfort. Then she slapped her own palm with the bristles and Leah felt her shoulders rise toward her ears. Perhaps she hadn't noticed, or hadn't understood. She needed to say something.

"Sir?"

"Yes?"

"I'm not up for any more of the bristles on my skin."

Jordan nodded. "Alright. Good job, telling me that."

Leah had never been praised for communicating about her limits before. It hadn't even occurred to her that it was something anyone would praise her for. Her throat felt all tight. She wasn't sure how to take that in.

Jordan stroked her cheek, gently. "What's going on for you right now?"

"I just was caught off guard, Sir. Nobody has ever said something like that to me before."

Jordan blinked. "Nobody has ever praised you for doing a good job?"

Leah gave a watery laugh. "No, they have. But not for that, specifically."

"But it's one of your most important jobs. Telling me what you're up for and what you're not, that's a really critical job you have as submissive. And I know it's not an easy one."

Leah nodded, at a loss for words.

"Does it feel bad, to get praised for that?"

"Oh. No, Sir. It felt good. Really good."

Jordan nodded. "Alright. No more bristles on your skin tonight. But this-" She stroked the back of the brush along Leah's thigh. "-this is just fine."

"Yes, Sir."

"Got it." She grinned at Leah. "Now about that warm up…" she said, as she began to lightly tap the back of the brush on Leah's thigh, just bringing the slightest warmth to the skin, more of a tease than anything else. She seemed so playful, almost mischievous, her eyes were sparkly and the laugh lines around them were all crinkly. Damn, she was handsome when she smiled. And so close, their legs were intertwined and Leah could feel Jordan's breath brush against her belly as she focused on bringing warmth to Leah's skin. It made her want to wriggle, everything about it, and she couldn't stop her body from doing that, even though she was trying to be good and stay still.

Except, had Jordan asked her to stay still? Leah thought about it, biting her lip, and realized that actually, she hadn't. Jordan was turning out to be a surprise in many ways, and she shouldn't assume.

"Sir?"

"Yes?"

"Do you want me to try to be still? I keep wriggling."

"No, I don't need you to be a statue. I like the wriggling. When I put my hand on your leg, keep that one still so I don't miss, and don't put anything in the path of the brush. But otherwise, feel free to move. And make noise."

"Oh. Okay. Thank you, Sir."

Jordan lifted her head and looked right into Leah's eyes for a moment. "I like seeing, and hearing, your reactions. It's my favorite thing." She held Leah's gaze until Leah was breathless, nodded firmly, and then refocused on her thighs, stroking them with her hand. Now that the brush had stopped those light taps, Leah realized that her skin was actually quite warm, in a yummy way that was just a bit itchy.

Jordan said triumphantly, "I think you're all warmed up," and used the brush for the first time in earnest. It had a gorgeous burn to it, the finished wood grabbing at her skin a bit as she lifted it off again, and the sound of it was a wonderful jolty thing all on its own. Leah let out a dreamy sigh. This was going to be delicious.

With Jordan clearly wanting her to react and not try to hide it or control it much at all, something loosened in her chest. She still didn't quite trust the invitation to let go like that, but she could try it. In a lot of ways, she felt freer because sex was off the table. Her reactions wouldn't be read in that framework, they could just exist. That was part of the point, to see what play would be like, if it was only sexual when she wanted it to be. She needed to try to lean into that, and trust it.

The brush was thick, and it made a truly sublime small paddle, packing a wonderful intensity to it, the blows driving into the meat of her thighs almost like punches, with an afterwave of sting. She let herself wriggle and writhe, savoring the throb that slid in behind the stroke. It was this gloriously slow burn that just built upon itself, and she groaned at the perfection of it, the coals stoked hotter and hotter. Jordan stuck to one area on each thigh, squeezing all of that burn into a small space, and it was going to bloom into the most gorgeous marks by morning, she was sure of it.

"Yes, I want your marks on me," escaped from her mouth, and Jordan responded by increasing the power of the blows. Leah groaned louder, the heat grabbing hold of her, and her hands started fluttering as her mouth just kept saying yes yes yes. They stayed suspended in that splendid place together for several luxurious minutes before Jordan slowed down, and then stopped, stroking Leah's thighs in wonder. "I did that," she murmured.

"Yes, Sir," Leah slurred. "You did that."

Jordan lifted her hand to Leah's face, and stroked the wetness under her eyes, groaning again. "I marked you," she said.

"Yes, Sir. Thank you, Sir," Leah said fervently.

"Can you move? I want to hold you close and cuddle on the couch."

"Luckily it's nearby," Leah said, and got herself there, not particularly gracefully. That didn't matter, though. Sir was going to hold her, and that was good.

Jordan pulled Leah into her body and held her tight, stroking her hair, and began to sing the Shehecheyanu softly, her husky voice full of reverence. Sir was so solid, and big, and in her arms Leah could let herself be as vulnerable as she felt, could be small and tender and in need of care.

Because she trusted that Sir would hold that space for her, would accept all of that from her, would be as big as she needed her to be.

That was what she'd felt, for so much of the scene, and she hadn't been expecting that, was still caught off guard by it. She was trembling, and Jordan just held her, stroking her back, her hair, as she continued to sing. That feeling, and the way the prayer wove through it, made the tears flow, and even when her sobs became audible, she didn't try to quiet them, just let herself weep in Jordan's arms.

When the crying subsided, Sir offered her some water, wiping her tears gently with a red hanky she pulled from her toybag. Then she cupped Leah's face in her hands. When she spoke it was to praise.

"You did so well, showing me your reactions, girl. It was gorgeous to see."

"Thank you, Sir. I like pain," Leah said.

"Yes, I see that. And I'm glad for it. I liked giving it to you. Marking you. I really wanted to mark you."

"You definitely marked me," Leah said, looking down at her thighs. "They will be even more intense tomorrow."

"Oh, really? I look forward to seeing that," Jordan said, stroking the marks.

Leah wriggled happily at the promise in that. Then Jordan led her into the kitchen and fixed her a pastrami sandwich that was basically the best sandwich on the face of the earth, so she devoured the entire thing, along with three full sour pickles and about a liter of water, with a grin that she could not wipe off her face to save her life.

25

MONDAY AFTERNOON, DECEMBER 23

JORDAN

It was going to be the second night of Chanukah, which meant Lesson Two. Just thinking about it made Jordan want to rock. She put on the Beauty and the Beast soundtrack, and just let the music wash through her as she stimmed. Leah had said Jordan didn't need any specific supplies or anything, but Jordan had been full of nervous energy and wanting to get out of the house. So she'd decided to use the Chanukah check from Erica's partner Caro to go shopping for something she'd dreamed about for a long time. She'd wondered if it was a betrayal to go to a different shop, if Leah would be mad she didn't go to Brazen. But she wanted to do this herself, without familiar witnesses to her fumbling around asking questions.

So she'd made her way to the shop, which had a different vibe from Leah's place. It was on the cheerful bubblegum end of décor, with smiling pixie-like young women greeting her. Jordan made a beeline for the small shelf of books, figuring it couldn't hurt to start in her comfort zone. She snagged a copy of a how-to-top book she'd never had the guts to buy when she lived with Dani, thought maybe she could grab lunch and do some studying after this.

Now for the next step. If she wasn't frozen on the spot. Her feet were made of lead, so she took out her phone and started crushing candy, one of her go-to in-public stims. She could feel her shoulders lowering and her jaw relaxing almost immediately. She began to run the next song on the Beauty and the Beast soundtrack through her head. It was one of those songs filled with action, all about revving things up and moving the plot forward. That energy would help her actually walk over to the other side of the store. When it got to her favorite part—the Macbeth quote—she grinned. There was something so satisfying about knowing references like this, the tiny moments that were hidden in songs that most people would just slide right through, having no clue what the song was evoking beyond the story itself. It was like having a secret treasure map. And really the Macbeth quote was apropos, she did need to screw her courage to the sticking place right now.

Jordan put her phone back in her pocket and strode over to the corner of the shop where they had harnesses and dildos. Luckily, the salesperson was busy with a different customer, and she could just take it in. From her research, she knew that they only sold one harness that was big enough to fit her, which was kind of a relief. (Fewer choices were sometimes a blessing.) So, she just had to choose a dildo, and had already ruled out anything that wasn't silicone. That narrowed things down, too. Especially when she realized that she wanted a more realistic shape. There was one that felt more right than the others and came with an option that included a vibrator. A roiling in her stomach just thinking about the vibrator version made her opt for just the dildo, which only came in two colors: gold and purple. Well, that was easy: purple was her favorite color.

Thirty minutes and two stops later, she was entrenched at a table waiting for her burger and shake to be ready, surrounded by her purchases. She'd picked up a cooked chicken for dinner, and there had been the donut place that Leah loved, just right there, so she'd gotten sufganiyot. It was the classic New York thing that happened to her when she was flustered-- she always stopped in at least a few stores. Just walking around them was grounding, somehow, even if she didn't buy anything. Besides, who could resist buying sufganiyot on Chanukah, especially with a marzipan glaze, and filled with blackberry jam? Even if it was from a fancy place with square donuts.

She had the new book, but she couldn't focus on it, not with last night's scene rolling through her head. How gigantic she'd felt when she was hitting Leah with the brush, how clear headed she'd been in the moment, like everything else fell away and the path was illuminated. She'd learned so much about Leah and her responses, and it had actually only lasted about 30 minutes. What would a longer scene teach her, about Leah? About herself? She could tell that she kept catching Leah off guard, but it felt like that was good, the ways it was happening. Though maybe Leah would give her different feedback.

If sex was on the table, or sexualized kink, she wanted to be packing. Even if it stayed in her jeans. She wanted to feel it there, the possibility of it, the in-your-faceness of it. Dani had vehemently objected to strap-ons, and Jordan hadn't felt up to the fight she'd face if she bought one for herself, for solo play. It was her body, damnit. She'd fantasized about this in a way she'd not even let herself fantasize about D/s, though the D/s had leaked into those fantasies, for sure. And yeah, she was butch enough without it, but. There was a part of her that felt like her particular cis butchness would feel even righter if she was packing. Gender feels: not just for trans and non-binary folks.

Her burger was ready, so she savored that, the beef tasting especially good, like she was specifically hungry for it. Which maybe she was, hadn't Leah said something about beef being good for drop? She'd gotten a black and white shake with malt, which should help on the chocolate front. The crinkle cut fries were perfect and the entire meal made her feel cozy and just a bit sleepy. Sated and content, she made her way home with enough time for a nap before it was time to light the candles.

Jordan loved lighting the candles, and tonight it was her turn. Last night Leah had sung the Shehecheyanu to a completely different tune and much less elaborately than Jordan was used to. She'd launched right into Maoz Tzur afterwards, then into a Chanukah song Jordan had never heard before that was super cheerful. Jordan had looked it up this morning and worked on learning the words so she could sing it with her tomorrow. Tonight, the prayer felt right in her mouth, and she rolled right into Haneiros Hallalu, which Leah didn't seem to know, but hummed along, clapping, and smiling at her. Jordan loved the repetition in this song, it was one of her favorites. When she finished with a flourish, she asked the question her dad had always asked on Chanukah each night: "What is one of the lights you have in your life right now?"

Leah smiled at her as she moved towards the table. "That's an excellent question. Let me think it over for a bit."

Jordan joined her at the table, making herself a plate. The chicken smelled amazing, and the mac and cheese looked wonderful. Comfort food hit the spot, just like she'd expected. And tomorrow she was going to make latkes to have with the rest of the chicken. She grinned at Leah and said, "Erica is definitely one of the lights of my life right now. It was really great to see her this weekend. She sent me pictures of the kiddos helping her make latkes, did I show you?"

"No! I need to see that."

Jordan opened them on her phone and handed it to Leah, who was properly appreciative, though she'd only met the kids a few times. She'd been the same with Erica, embracing her as family because Jordan was family, and that was just how it worked. It was one of the things that made their relationship feel solid. That, and close to thirty years of being friends who were family. Which meant they were going to be okay, no matter what happened.

"Dance is one of the lights in my life," Leah said dreamily. "I got to dance for a good long time today, and it was wonderful. I watched a movie about this woman songwriter who spends her whole life setting aside what she wants in order to support other people—her partners, really—and it was kind of depressing, but it has this great song that's sung by this minor queer character that seemed like it was from a Bond film, and it made me want to dance, so I did. What's cool is I found this article about how it was written by Lesley Gore, who was both Jewish and a lesbian, and was in a closet for much of her career, much like the lesbian character in the film."

"Okay now I want to hear this song. I had no clue Lesley Gore was queer."

So Leah put it on, and they ate sufganiyot to this wonderfully dramatic song with strings and dramatic proclamations about hiding love away. It was campy and hilarious and they couldn't stop cracking up. The doughnuts were delicious; the jam was beautifully tart, and Jordan felt calmer than she had all day, now that it was time for the next lesson.

26

MONDAY EVENING, DECEMBER 23

LEAH

Leah had taken a long hot shower after dancing that had left her all languid and made her skin ache for touch. So she'd put on a black satin gown that flowed over her skin like water, because it felt so damn good to wear it. She'd decided she was up for sexualized play and sex, and had chosen a subject for today's lesson that aligned with that. After she checked in that Jordan was up for the lesson she wanted to do (she was), she'd explained what she was up for in the practice scene. Jordan grinned and said she'd gone shopping for something today that might be useful, so Leah asked her to bring it.

When Jordan returned, she'd changed into a fresh shirt, a pin striped vest, and had put on boots, but she didn't seem to be carrying anything. She was walking with this delicious swagger, and Leah was enjoying that so much that she forgot everything else. Maybe she wouldn't need the first part of the lesson, after all. Jordan didn't seem to need help getting into dom space, if that swagger was any indication.

"Did you guess?" Jordan asked huskily, as she stood in front of Leah.

"Guess?" Leah had lost the thread of the conversation.

Then Jordan adjusted herself in her jeans, and Leah understood what she'd missed somehow. Jordan was packing. That was behind the swagger, and was perfect for the lesson, if she could manage to focus.

"Guess what I bought today," Jordan said teasingly, knowing that Leah had figured it out.

"Hmmm I seem to have noticed...something," Leah said. "I will see if I can work it into the lesson."

"Oh really? I'm looking forward to this lesson," Jordan said, and sat down, settling in.

Leah walked her through the first section on establishing headspace, talking about different strategies folks used, pointing out the ones she'd noted Jordan already using. This was more about making it intentional than teaching a new skill, as Jordan had seemed to grok this already.

She launched into the scenarios describing different kinds of D/s dynamics, doing a big brainstorm with Jordan as they read each scenario, writing down key words and things that charged the power dynamic. Then she picked up a blue marker and circled three words that would be today's focus: claiming, feral, and sexual. Jordan gave her the wickedest grin, and she got all breathless for a moment, before explaining how that kind of dynamic could look, and ways to might make it clear that's how you wanted to play, things you could do and language you could use in scene to deepen it. Just talking about it put her half in that headspace, and had her remembering Jordan's look of reverence as she stroked the marks she'd put on Leah's thighs. She lifted her skirt to show Jordan the marks, how they'd bloomed into dark red and deep purple. The awe and satisfaction on Jordan's face was basically the best thing ever. It made her all giddy and full of bubbles and she couldn't stop smiling.

She bubbled on through the next section of the lesson, talking Jordan through hair-pulling techniques, risks and ways things could go wrong, ways it could be a loaded or triggering thing for some folks. She got all flustered when she was trying to explain how it could be a hot button—in the good way—for some, and a direct link to submission. She was pretty damn sure she was blushing by the time she finished explaining that part. Now she needed to begin the hands-on piece of the instruction.

Leah grabbed a pillow, and knelt on it in front of Jordan, which was already feeling achingly familiar and right where she belonged. That thought had her heart racing as she talked Jordan through the basic technique on the crown of her head, and barely bit back a moan. Then Jordan practiced using both hands on the sides of her head, and she did fucking moan. But it was the grip at the base of her neck that had her slide right down into submission, her bones all languid, her voice dreamy as she tried to make words to explain how it would make her want to kneel if she was standing, and how this kind of response was fairly common among submissives. Jordan wanted to try using her hair to move her head, reciting the safety measures she'd gone over as she tried the first move, which had Leah staring at the bulge in Jordan's jeans.

When she explained that a tighter grip would help control her head better, Jordan seemed to get it fully. Holding Leah by the hair at the back of her neck, she exposed Leah's throat. Jordan stroked a thumb up from the hollow of Leah's throat all the way to her chin and Leah shuddered, a breathy "yes" escaping her lips. Jordan leaned forward, and her open mouth was shocking against the side of Leah's neck, so unwaveringly sexual that Leah gasped as sparks jolted into her. The hand twisted in the hair at the nape of her neck held her in place, and Jordan's mouth teased her throat with lips and tongue and the scraping of teeth, making promises about biting later on. Leah's hands clenched at her thighs, which only added to the heat blazing through her. This was so intense, even before the hand gripping her hair began to pulse pain there, insistent, rhythmic, making her moan from it.

When Jordan slowly lifted her head, then released her hair, smoothing it with a gentle caress, Leah tried to open her eyes again. She was panting, and liquid, full of want that she didn't want to wait on. She didn't want to shift back to teaching. She'd already sunk so deeply into submission, she wasn't sure it even made sense to try.

"Sir?"

"Yes?"

"I think I am done teaching for the night, if that's okay? That dropped me deep into subspace, and I'd like to just go forward with the scene, without the biting, if that's okay?"

"That's okay, girl. It's perfectly fine with me, as long as you promise to tell me if I cross lines or you need me to change or stop what I'm doing."

"I promise, Sir. I'm sorry I couldn't finish teaching tonight."

"Girl, you did very well. I think perhaps three things was a bit overly ambitious. You don't need to pack everything in, as far as I'm concerned. A scoop in a cup, no toppings works for the lessons, too, I think."

This was something to store away and think about. "Can we talk about this when I'm more coherent, Sir?"

"Yes, of course we can. I very much want you in my bed for this."

"Yes, please."

"Alright, you go ahead and get yourself there. Hands and knees, girl. That view will be delicious."

Ohhh. That felt exactly right, Leah realized. She didn't want to stand up, to put herself on the same level. It felt wrong, even the idea of it. But crawling in this gown would be difficult.

"May I remove my gown first, Sir?"

"You may," Jordan said, her voice a bit gravelly.

That felt better, too. She'd been wearing too many clothes. Her skin felt alive, sensitive, and as she began to crawl to Jordan's room, she could feel Sir's gaze on her body. It slid heat along her skin, and she felt sexier than she had in a long time. It was intense and surprising, scary and exciting, and she savored it.

27

MONDAY EVENING, DECEMBER 23

JORDAN

Jordan took the trip into her bedroom to fully sink into her dominance. She'd been really trying to hold onto learning mode, but it had been difficult once she was packing. Something about wearing a cock in her jeans just felt so right, so much like how she'd always seen herself, as a butch and as a dominant, that she'd been actively trying to hold the dom aspect back. And now she didn't need to. She could fully admire Leah's glorious fat ass, the way it swayed as she crawled, the line of her bare back, the feeling of bigness it gave her that Leah was crawling, and naked, and at her feet, while she was standing, and fully clothed.

She could feel her cock throb, and let her hand stroke it through her jeans, let herself fully enjoy the sight of her girl crawling, the movement of her body, the flush on her skin, the teasing glimpses of bruises on her thighs. She was going to claim her tonight, and a small part of her regretted not being able to bite her and leave those kinds of marks as well.

Jordan had this image of herself, all claws and teeth, biting into the meat of Leah's shoulder as she fucked her from behind, raking her nails along Leah's skin. She let that thought sit inside her and unfurl, and felt the rumble in her chest before she even heard the growl. Leah went still at the sound, like a prey animal would, and Jordan felt this intense satisfaction, and a deep desire to scare her, to bite down on the softness of her belly, to grip her throat with claws and soak up her fear. It was a delicious fantasy, and one she could not satisfy tonight. Tonight, Leah wasn't prey, and Jordan wasn't predator. Tonight, Jordan would claim Leah as hers, and that was an equally satisfying thought.

Jordan moved to Leah's side, and stroked along her back, leading the way into the bedroom. She laid some things out on the table by the bed and gestured for Leah to wait. When everything had been laid out, she sat at the end of the bed, and put a pillow at her feet. At her gesture, Leah kneeled there, and there was something about it this time that felt different. She'd been aware of it out in the living room during the practice session, but it was even more so now. This sense of rightness, of Leah belonging there.

She thought about the lesson, and the thing she'd guessed during it, that perhaps it wasn't just about pulling the hair at the nape of Leah's neck, but doing anything to that part of Leah's body that would sink her into submission. She decided to experiment, and, lifting Leah's hair, placed her hand at the back of her girl's neck. A small sigh of contentment. Hmm. She gripped the back of her neck, and drew her head down to rest on Jordan's thigh, where she'd be aware of, but not touching her cock. Leah groaned softly, and her eyes drifted shut, this peace sliding over her face and down her body, all languid limbs and slow sighs. Yes. This was exactly right. Just where Leah belonged. Under her hand, kneeling at her feet. Deliciously, perfectly hers. She savored that, let it sink her deeper into dominance, and thought about what she wanted next.

Leah had put a range of sexual things on the table for tonight, but her eyes had lit up at three in particular, and Jordan thought she might first tease her with one, before giving her the other two. She had mixed feelings about receiving a blow job, it was too focused on her own body, and to try it while her cock was still new felt too exposing. When she felt more solid as a dominant, she wanted to try it, but not now. But she could tease Leah with the possibility of it.

She gripped Leah by the hair at the nape of her neck, and drew her up so she was in her original kneeling position. Releasing Leah's hair, she ordered her girl to free her cock, with her left hand only. Leah's eyes got wide, and her right hand tightened into a fist on her own thigh, the knuckles digging into the bruise Jordan had put there last night, as her left hand fumbled with Jordan's fly. She bit her lip, focusing all of her attention on Jordan's cock, on getting the zipper down, and then working it out of her jeans.

"Hand down," Jordan ordered, and she obeyed instantly, her eyes still fixed on her dominant's cock. When Jordan began to stroke it, she whimpered softly, tongue coming out to lick at her lips.

"Stay still," she ordered, and Leah whispered "Yes, Sir," her eyes riveted on Jordan's hand.

Jordan closed her own eyes, and experimented with different kinds of strokes, focused on the sensory experience of it, finding the rhythm and motions that felt the best to her, focused on her own body, on the pleasure of this after so long. Leah whimpered, and the sound was delicious, not unlike the stroke of a tongue along skin. Jordan opened her eyes, and saw that Leah was breathing fast, her eyes filling.

"Tell me what you want," Jordan said.

"Please, Sir. Please. I want your cock. I want you to claim me. Please. Make me yours, Sir."

Jordan slid her fingers into the hair at the nape of Leah's neck, and drew her close, so her cock was brushing Leah's cheek.

"You want this," she said.

"Oh yes, Sir," Leah replied fervently. "Please. I want you to claim my throat."

Jordan tilted Leah's head back, and stroked her cock against Leah's neck, before leaning down to lick her way up Leah's throat, and spoke into her skin.

"This throat?"

"Yes, Sir."

"There are many ways to claim your throat, girl." Jordan lifted her head. "With my tongue. With my teeth. With my hand."

She stroked Leah's throat with her thumb, not pressing in, and just let her thumb rest there. Leah's eyes drifted closed and she whispered "Yes, Sir."

"I could leave a mark just here," and she stroked it again. "You said yes to that, to my sucking on your neck until I'd marked at as mine."

"Please, Sir. Claim me however you choose. I want to be yours."

Jordan lifted Leah up by the hair, arm wrapping around her to hold her close, as she claimed her girl's throat with her mouth, working at it hard, sucking in as much of her neck as she could, savoring the feel of her girl shuddering in her arms. "Mine," she growled against Leah's skin before going back to work, savoring the right to mark her submissive as she chose. Dominance surged through her, and she gripped Leah's hair in tight pulses of pain as her girl moaned.

When she lifted her head, the mark was raised and dark and beautiful. Hers. Her girl. Her submissive. Her Leah. Now she was going to fuck her, and she'd savor every bit of that experience, including all its sharp edges, which she could already feel working inside her chest. She released Leah's hair, and ordered her to bend over the edge of the bed, and put herself in the perfect position to get fucked. Leah asked permission to go get something to help with that, and Jordan gave it.

While awaiting her return, Jordan took slow breaths, reminding herself that she didn't have to do this, she could stop anytime. It was Leah, who she trusted, who wouldn't even think of trying to touch her without permission or convince her that there was something wrong with her for being stone. She sank into her boots, and reminded herself that she was fully dressed. That it was 2019 and she wasn't with Dani, but with her dearest friend in the world who got her better than anyone else. That she was going to get to use her cock for the first time, and could ride the excitement of that. That she was safe at home, nobody looking at her, not even Leah if she didn't want her to, nobody expecting eye contact or vanilla sex. That she was free to be in charge and ruthlessly take what she wanted because Leah was offering it to her, wanted her to take it, was meeting Jordan's dominance with her own submission, and that was a beautiful incredibly hot thing.

28

MONDAY EVENING, DECEMBER 23

LEAH

Now it was getting real, in a big way, and Leah's heart was racing a mile a minute as she went to grab the wedge pillow from her room. She took a couple slow breaths, checking in with herself to be sure she wanted this, and realized that she felt more like getting fucked than she had in a very long time. She wanted to be claimed like this by Jordan, all of her ached for it.

Sir's dick was beautifully thick, and she knew it would hit her in just the right spot in this position if Jordan could get in deep enough, so she was very glad she'd tested out the wedge last year and knew what a difference it made; it was her number one suggestion for fat folks trying to get deeper penetration. She hadn't used it since then, but there it was in the closet waiting for her. When she returned, she brandished it triumphantly at Jordan.

"Ah, you have special equipment, do you?"

"Well, there are some perks to playing with someone who owns a sex shop, and this is definitely one of them, Sir."

"I look forward to being enlightened. Before you get into position, I want to do one thing first."

Sir plucked the pillow from her hand and tossed it onto the bed, and then backed Leah into the wall, sliding her hands into her hair to grip it tightly, as her body held her in place, the wall cool at her back as Sir's mouth was hot against her neck, her tongue tracing along it. Then there was glorious pain from the grip on her hair, rushing into her in waves, and Leah cried out, the sound caught by Sir as she claimed her mouth, tongue thrusting, cock insistent against her skin. It was so much all at once, and the pressure of Sir's body was exactly right, the cool wall grounding her in the maelstrom of sensation. She opened to Sir, savoring the feel of her dominance around her, inside her, all over her skin and gave herself over to the kiss, wanting it never to end. She hadn't even known she was aching for this until it was insistently here and she was being subsumed into it.

When Sir gripped the back of her neck and led her to the bed, her cunt already throbbing, her head quiet, her whole being certain. She got herself into position, and it felt exactly right, presenting herself to her dominant, offering her body to be claimed. This was what she wanted. This was who she was. While she was in her desire—desire that was rare and fraught but also glorious—she'd offer this part of herself to Sir, and revel when she was taken.

"Well, your ass certainly looks delectable in this position. And you're exactly at the right height, aren't you?"

"Yes, Sir."

"Good job, girl."

"Thank you, Sir."

Sir stroked the length of her back with both hands, trailing them along her ass, and slid her hands under to find the marks on Leah's thighs and drive pain into them with her fingertips, making Leah writhe and moan. Jordan's cock was cool and slick, and insistently thick as she slid it home, sighing when she was fully inside. She stayed there for a moment, stroking Leah's ass, and once Leah was able to tune in over the feeling of fullness and rightness in her cunt, she realized that Jordan was murmuring the word "mine," over and over like a litany, and that her hands had a bit of a tremble in them.

This meant something to Sir, something important, this moment, and Leah felt her own body open further, felt something shift in her chest. She was giving Sir something she wanted enough to tremble as she took it. She wanted to meet that somehow, but her brain was all fuzzy and the sensation of fullness was so intense, the trembling touch so much to feel, that she couldn't think, couldn't try to guess at what would be wanted. Instead, she listened to that "mine" coming from her Sir's lips, and responded, "Yours, Sir. I'm yours," feeling her chest open more as she said it. Sir's hands were gripping her ass, and the "Mine," got louder, their voices intertwining in this gorgeous evocative song that slid into her. Then Sir was fucking her in hard thrusts, gripping her hips, and ramming herself deep and rough, and Leah was moaning around the word "yours," the sensation almost too much but riding the edge of that exactly right for several glorious minutes until it crossed over and she started begging, wanting Jordan to come, wanting that claiming too, and needing something, digging her nails into her arms before she realized she could ask for pain.

"Please hurt me, Sir," she begged, and Sir obliged, digging fingers into the bruises on her thighs, which canted her hips just a bit more and then Sir was hitting the spot that would make her come, so she started to beg for permission to do that, but she wasn't sure the words were working right because Sir just kept saying "Mine" and digging her hands into Leah's thighs, giving her the glorious pain that would only make her come faster, so she tried again to make words coherent, and she must have succeeded, because Sir growled, "G-d, yes, come for me," and moaned. The orgasm hit hard and sharp and stole her breath, making her shudder and gasp and grab onto Sir's cock, and Sir shouted, "Mine," and began to thrust in short fast digs that were all incoherent in their rhythm and clearly just about her own pleasure, which filled Leah so full of contentment that she floated to the fucking ceiling. She had pleased Sir.

Sir slid out and was rolling her onto her side, cleaning her up, and gathering her into the best hug she'd ever had in her life, all warm and safe and claimed. Sir stroked her hair, murmuring that now Leah belonged to her and that she'd been so good for her, that she was a very good girl. She was worn out and drowsy before long, and tried to get up and go to her own bed, but Sir said she'd like it if Leah stayed in her bed tonight. That sounded really good, so she stayed. The last thing she remembered before she dropped into sleep was Sir's thumb, stroking the center of her forehead, gentle as can be, as she sang the Shehecheyanu, and this deep sense of being cared for, protected, claimed.

29

TUESDAY MORNING, DECEMBER 24

JORDAN

When Jordan woke, she found herself spooning Leah, an arm wrapped possessively around her, still fully clothed from the night before, her cock insistent in her jeans, the leather straps digging into her uncomfortably. She didn't want to let go, didn't want to move, didn't want to break whatever spell they had going on. The only reason she was even awake this early was that her hips and knee were screaming that she'd pushed them way too hard yesterday.

It really sucked when it was both her knee and her hips, because walking helped the hips but made the knee worse. Swimming was good for both, but she hadn't joined a gym yet, was planning to wait for her insurance to kick in because there was a gym benefit. She had all these health things to take care of but that had to wait until the New Year. It was Christmas Eve, could she even get in to see an acupuncturist at the last minute? The flare was big enough that she'd be hurting for the next few days unless she did, or found a way to go swimming today. Was this going to happen every time she used the strap-on? Or maybe it was the position?

Jordan was torn between needing to get at least some NSAIDs on board and wanting stay in bed with Leah in her arms. They hadn't properly ended the scene last night, and while the pain had yanked her out of it somewhat, there were these lingering tendrils that ached to cling to her dominance. Was this how it usually went when you fell asleep in headspace? The pain felt like it was scraping against a rawness inside her, and she needed do something about it before it got worse. Decision made, she tried to remember where she'd left her cane, hoping that she'd at least brought it into the bedroom.

Ah, there it was, near enough that she could reach. Her backpack was on the chair, so she tugged it toward her using her cane. She might have a snack and naproxen in her bag, then she could wait until the pain was a bit more manageable. Damnit, there was no naproxen, and she only had an energy bar, which her entire mouth rejected the second she considered it. Some days she could get those down and some days the texture was too wrong.

When she got out of bed, Leah didn't even stir, so Jordan tugged the covers around Leah and let herself go as slow as she needed, grabbing naproxen off her dresser on the way. By the time she made it to the kitchen her knee was shrieking, so she pulled a chair over to the fridge and sat, staring at the contents and hoping something would seem eatable. Yogurt seemed okay. Was there fruit? Applesauce sounded good. And one of those lemon muffins Erica had made. She grabbed her lunch bag and filled it with the breakfast she'd figured out, and an ice pack, adding one of those energy drinks Leah had suggested for drop. Then she slowly made her way to the couch, so she could prop up her knee and start icing.

The pain was so loud, it didn't even occur to her to listen to music or watch something while she slowly made herself eat through the nausea and pain. The muffin was the most solid, so it was last, as by the time she got through the other things, the naproxen had kicked in. If it hadn't been one of her favorite things she wouldn't have been able to make herself eat it, but the scent grabbed her. Citrus made her mouth so happy, especially in the winter time, and the muffin was small, just a few bites really. She was sitting quietly, her head leaning against the couch, when Leah came in.

"Sir?" Leah said softly,

"Yes, girl?" Jordan murmured.

"Are you okay?"

"Okay enough. I'm in a lot of pain."

"Oh. I woke up and you were gone. I didn't do something wrong?"

"No, not at all. How about you come sit with me on my right side, and we can cuddle a bit. We didn't do proper aftercare last night."

"Yes, Sir."

It was weird to be in so much pain and still feel dominant. Jordan had thought that she wouldn't, that being in pain would push everything else out. But it hadn't. She probably should close the scene, though. They hadn't negotiated staying in role, and she wasn't sure either of them was ready for that, or even wanted it. She was pretty sure she didn't know enough to do it effectively, anyway.

The naproxen helped, but cuddling was hard, anyway. Every movement jostled her hips. So she tried a few different positions until she found one that didn't hurt that much where they could just be still and touching, and she began to sing "Bridge Over Troubled Water," one of her favorite self-soothing songs, that her dad used to sing her to sleep when she was sick.

As she sang, she felt this wave of helplessness and despair crash over her.

This wasn't supposed to happen this way. She was supposed to be able to be strong and help Leah come down slowly, but it was like the singing made her realize that wasn't strong at all, that she was weak and helpless and small. The dominance she'd thought was real a few moments ago was actually a wispy barely there thing compared to where she'd been last night, and it was fading fast. She felt like she hadn't just plummeted down to earth, but had crashed through the earth, was falling into an abyss, the walls closing in on her.

"Jordan?"

"Yes?"

"You trailed off in the middle of a word, there. It seems like you aren't actually okay."

"No. I don't think I am."

"Would space help?"

"I don't know. Maybe."

"Okay, I'm going to give you a bit of room, alright?"

Jordan nodded. Room was better than she thought it would be, she could feel her breathing slow down a bit. When had it gotten this fast? Was that why her head felt all floaty and weird? Why was her heart was racing so fast? Leah's voice felt far away, as it encouraged her to breathe slowly. She closed her eyes and counted breaths.

A panic attack. It had been a while since she'd had one, she was going to have to look at her notes on her phone to remember what comes next. She asked Leah to get it, and found the file. Ah. Get somewhere that feels safe. Water. Shower. Fresh clothes. Soothing stim. Take a break from emotional processing and trying to be productive. Well then, that was the plan for the rest of the morning, at least. She explained to Leah that she needed to come down from the panic attack alone, and get herself okay, and Leah got it. It wasn't the first time she'd been around for Jordan's panic attacks, it just was the first time Jordan had been doing D/s while it happened.

They would sort through that later, right now Jordan had to tend to herself so she'd be in a better place to sort through that. Leah offered to bring lunch to her room in a few hours, and Jordan accepted, grateful that Leah got how hard moving was for her right now. Then she made her way to her room, and closed the door, not feeling up for the shower, but hoping that after she hid in her blanket fort for a while she would be. For now, hiding sounded really good.

30

TUESDAY MORNING, DECEMBER 24

LEAH

Leah had never had aftercare turn into a panic attack before. But then, she also didn't fall asleep while still in subspace, hadn't in years. Not since she'd had that occasional weekend-long service arrangement with Ellie. And that was different. It was just service, for one thing, no sex involved, and romance off the table. Plus they'd explicitly negotiated that it was like a weekend-long scene, where they were both in role the entire time. This had just kind of happened, with Jordan. Leah realized that her own hands were shaking. Fuck. Why? She hadn't had the panic attack. Was she cold?

Well, actually she did feel cold, and more clothes would be good, but also, it was like she was cold all the way deep inside. Well, she'd figure that out, but she could start with warmer clothes. And tea. And something warm to eat. Oatmeal would be good.

Oatmeal helped, and so did warmer clothes. But it was like there was this aching bereft feeling inside her, and the only thing she could think of was that she needed touch, warmth. She thought it over as she finished her oatmeal, and came up with a plan. It was kind of experimental, but worth a shot.

When she got to her room, she grabbed what she needed from the closet, put on the space heater, and stripped down. It was better to be naked for this, with the kind of skin hunger she had right now. Her dominant wasn't able to help with that right now, but she could give herself what she needed. That was the best way to support Sir, she thought. Would have been a standing order if they had set things up with standing orders. It was comforting to let herself think of Sir as her dominant, as someone who would give her standing orders, to think of what she was doing as pleasing Sir. It brought Sir into the room with her, and that felt really good. She leaned into that, imagined Jordan sitting in the cozy chair in the corner, watching her with approval.

Leah had gone to a kink conference once that had this room where at the center, there was this huge red circular thing you could lounge on and watch other people play around you. Turn that way and see the queer men using the sling to do fisting, look behind you and watch a suspension scene, turn to the left and watch puppies wrestling. The big red thing was high enough off the ground that she felt comfortable getting on it, knew she would be able to get up again. She'd been wearing a rather small slip dress, showing a lot of skin, and when she lay on the red thing, she realized it was upholstered in velvet. She couldn't resist rolling around on it like a cat. The velvet had felt amazing against her skin, was this glorious sensual pleasure that brought her deep into her body and had made her feel sexy and alive and like she wanted to purr.

When she'd gotten home from that conference, she'd bought herself the most velvety sheets she could find, and a velvet blanket, plus several pillows upholstered in velvet. She stripped off her regular flannel sheets and put on the red velvet ones, got under the velvet blanket, and let herself writhe. It was intense, and amazing, and her skin soaked up all the lush sensation, reveling in it, imagining Sir watching her. She stroked her hands along her skin, savoring the feel of it, releasing any attempt at stillness, and rode the sensations, letting them lead. It felt amazing to let go like this, to give her body exactly what it wanted, to devour every drop of sensation that she'd been aching for.

It was so intensely sensual, and she found that it wasn't just that, sexual desire was there, too. She wanted to be under Sir's gaze, at Sir's command, and writhe against these glorious sheets not just for her own sensual pleasure, but to please Sir, from the deepest part of her submissive heart, she wanted to fuck herself for Sir, to come for Sir, to renew Sir's claim on every part of herself, including perhaps her orgasms, at least right now. She wanted that. She wanted that. Not because of any pressure or assumption or expectation. Not out of obligation. Jordan might never even know about it! It was her own fantasy, her own desire.

Yes, it might drift away, or fade, or not turn out how she wanted, or backfire. It didn't mean anything was fundamentally different about her sexuality. But it did seem to mean...something. Perhaps that when she waited to do anything sexual until she wanted to, that want might extend, might not immediately want to curl up into a protective ball afterwards every time. Perhaps that when she trusted her dominant to truly only want to have sex when it was fully deeply consensual, that foundation deepened her relationship with her own desire. It was too soon to conclude anything, but she grinned at the possibilities. And decided to dig out her toy box.

She'd fuck herself the way Sir wanted her to, told her to, and it could be slow and languorous and didn't have to follow any fucking rules or expectations or the needs of other humans. It was just about following orders, following her desire for Sir's eyes on her skin, Sir's control driving her actions. She took out her new plug, the lube she favored for anal play, a few small clips, and her nipple clamps. After a moment's thought, she also took out her favorite dildo. She wasn't sure she wanted that but she also didn't want to have to go rooting around for it at a crucial moment. Solo sex preparedness was key. She should get a badge or something.

The new plug was something she hadn't ordered for the shop yet, because she wanted to see how it worked as a plug, and think about how she wanted to display it. It was ace pride colors, part of a line of reasonably priced silicone pride-themed dildos. The texture was silky smooth, didn't drag along the skin like some dildos, and Leah really liked how pretty it was. The ace pride flag was one of her faves, and there was something really lovely about the recognition that some aces had sex and might like a plug in their pride colors. It made her a bit verklempt to think about the toy designers making that choice. Like they saw folks like her and wanted to honor them. She'd been waiting for a day when her desire was high and she wanted to do anal play solo sex, and today felt like the perfect one for it.

The solidness of silicone was comforting, the weight of it. And this was all silky, felt good in her hand and she slicked on the lube. Leah imagined Sir watching her intently, eyes on her hand as she told Leah to wait, to just stroke it for a bit, and think about what it was going to feel like, to stay with the feeling of wanting it before she got to have what she wanted. When Sir finally gave her permission, she groaned as it went in, the squirming slide of it, the feeling that rippled up her body. She always felt anal play all the way through, like a line of energy from her asshole up her spine that wrapped around her throat, delicious and teasing. This wasn't as hard as some plugs, it had more give, which was new and a rather luxurious feeling, like squeezing down on it created swirls inside her.

Leah lay on her velvet sheets, and rode the plug, feeling it respond to her body, warming up. She had this image of it painting ace colors in a swirling barber's pole up her spine, wrapping round and round. It made her shudder, to picture that, to imagine Sir's finger tracing along it. Sir was watching her, and telling her how gorgeous she was like this, how much pleasure she was giving her dominant right now. The words made her ass clench around the plug, and her clit pulse, and she moaned. She looked over to the chair where she imagined Sir was sitting, and in her mind Jordan had her own dick out and was stroking it as she watched, her eyes dark and intense as she ordered Leah to put the clamps on her tits.

These were clovers, her favorites, because they tightened when she tugged on them, and they had a chain between them. The chain was cool against her belly and she savored the burning pinch of the clamps. Then Sir ordered her to hold the chain between her teeth. She obeyed, and the tug of it tightened the clamps in a delicious way. The coolness of the chain in her mouth reminded her of the first time she kneeled for Sir, the way Sir's cufflinks had felt in her mouth, the shock of realizing that Sir's dominance was more intense than she'd predicted it would be.

Leah writhed against the sheets, the plug claiming her ass, the clamps claiming her mouth and her tits, and felt the ache in her cunt, and along her skin. She whimpered, her eyes begging, and Sir ordered her to touch herself the way she wanted, to give her body what she needed to give it, but not to come yet, to stop whatever she was doing if she was too close.

So she did, her hands stroking along her own skin, legs spread as wide as she could get them, so she felt the stretch in her inner thigh, and dug her fingers into the bruises Sir had put on her, had claimed her with. The love bite on her neck, the bruises on her thighs, her ass thrusting against the bed, her hands doling out the pain that would drive her closer to the edge. Then she stopped moving all at once, and felt the throb ride through her, forced stillness making it so intense, until it faded. That's when she grabbed the clamps, and placed two on each of her outer labia. Yes, that was perfect, the throb mixed with the pain and built it higher. She pressed down on each knee to hold her legs even further apart, push the stretch even more, her ass pumping against the bed, Sir's eyes fixed on her cunt. She leaned her head back, savoring the burn of the clamps on her tits, and moaned around the chain in her mouth.

Oh, this was glorious; her whole body was alive and aching, want filling her up and holding her open. Sir told her to drop the chain and let it fall, and she groaned in frustration. But then Sir ordered her get the dildo all slicked up, and work it in slow, stopping after the first inch so she could feel herself ache for it, want it. She felt her heart race; this was the edgiest thing she'd tried and she wasn't sure she could do it. Sir got that, though, told her they could stop at any time, stop any of the things they were doing, that it was about her trying things and seeing what she wanted, and part of what she wanted was to be a bit scared, to feel the edge, but in a safe way. She breathed that in. She could stop at any point, and there was no Sir to pressure or to disappoint, except the one in her head.

Her heart raced, and as she squeezed the plug in her ass, she realized Sir was right. She liked being just a bit scared, liked the adrenaline with sex, as long as there was no real pressure to perform anything. The dildo was ready and her heart was in her throat and she savored that, along with the tears that were threatening. Her hand was trembling, and she thought about how much Sir was enjoying seeing that, and she turned to look, and Sir was smiling proudly at her, watching with awe as she slid the dildo in just an inch, and bit her lip, so aware of how much her cunt ached, of the throbbing in her clit. Sir told her to press the heel of her hand down onto her cunt, to find the spot where that felt best, which turned out not to be directly on her clit, but on the mound above it. So she spread her legs wide, intensifying the stretch, as she held the dildo in place, and pressed down on her mound, and her mouth dropped open, because it felt amazing and made her want to scream in frustration all at once.

"Please" escaped Leah's lips before she even decided to say it aloud, and Sir groaned the word "Yes," and started stroking her cock again as she watched Leah insert another inch of the dildo. Now she was even more aware of how much she wanted that dildo deep inside her, how much she ached to be fucked with it, to feel the fullness of it inside her with the plug in her ass, how much she wanted Sir everywhere in her. So she started begging for real, pulling out all the language she could find as she stared at Sir jacking herself off, wishing that Sir would fuck her throat, would fill her in every hole that existed, would wrap her hands into Leah's hair and ram herself home.

She started begging for that along with begging for more of the dildo, and Sir told her to thrust it all the way in, to keep it deep inside and not let it go, to take it all, and hold onto it tightly. Once it was there, Sir stalked over to the bed, and told her to hold her legs as wide as she could. Then Sir grabbed the last clamp, and put it on her clit, telling her to take it, and not come yet, to wait until she was deep in Leah's throat before she came. Leah closed her eyes and took Sir's cock into her, aching for it, gasping around it as she came, and came, and came. And then let go of everything, feeling Sir take her throat for as long as she wanted, before removing all the clamps at once and thrusting her knee between Leah's legs, holding the dildo still and growling the word "Mine" as Leah writhed around it, that word making her come again.

With trembling fingers she removed dildo, and plug, and wrapped the covers around herself, holding her velvet pillow close, and fell into a deep sleep. She didn't wake until the alarm told her it was time to make Sir's lunch.

31

TUESDAY AFTERNOON, DECEMBER 24

JORDAN

Jordan always felt wiped out after a panic attack. That in combination with the pain, and it was like every movement took so much effort and went super slow, even after a nap. She wasn't just moving epically slow, her brain was made of sludge too. Food might help. She actually wanted some of that energy drink stuff, which told her how thirsty she was. She put on her coziest sweatpants and her super soft Fatties Against Fascism t-shirt, and trudged out to the kitchen.

Leah was wearing this electric blue satin thing, a camisole and short shorts that left none of her abundantly spectacular fatness to the imagination, and her hair was a tumbling mess of curls. Her wide thighs were still showing off those gorgeous marks Jordan had put on them, and her magnificent ass was basically only half covered by the shorts. She turned and gave Jordan the biggest smile with sparkling eyes, and it was like a jolt right through her. Jordan's heart literally stopped at the sight of her all flushed and gorgeous and happy, blue roses blooming across her chest, and then she said "I'm making you grilled cheese and tomato soup, Sir," and Jordan was filled with the most intense desire to kiss her. Being called Sir in that bright kitchen, with her submissive so happy to be serving her, at a time when she felt so low and shaken...she wanted to grab ahold of the surge of energy it gave. Her hands were trembling, she wanted to hold onto it so tight.

She lowered herself into a chair, letting herself be slow and deliberate as she placed her cane. She was reeling from the clarity of this moment, of how much she was in love with Leah, how she wanted so deeply to be her dominant, her lover, her partner, alongside being her friend, her family. To claim her. To keep her. She had no doubts. But to get there, they needed to do that deliberately. So she needed to draw a boundary now.

When she'd talked about it with Ruth over dinner last week, she hadn't thought it would be this hard. But it had been abstract, then. The question of whether she wanted to try to dom during a pain flare had been a thought exercise. And maybe in the future she might want to try doing it. But Jordan had listened to Ruth's stories and advice and had decided that while she was learning, that was too much to manage. This morning had only cemented that. The flare had fucked with her dom headspace. She might unpack that later, but that unavoidable fact made it clear that she needed to not try to mix flaring and D/s right now. She closed her eyes, and spoke. "That sounds delicious. Thank you."

Leah nodded, responding, "Glad to do it, Sir."

"Leah, I can't be Sir right now. I know we didn't do aftercare or close the scene, and I want to try to do both after lunch, but right now I need to just be Jordan."

"Okay. That's totally fine," Leah said. It seemed like she meant it, too. She hadn't stiffened and her tone was no less cheerful.

"Thanks for understanding."

"Of course. You get to consent, too."

Jordan blinked, because she hadn't framed it that way in her head, somehow. That was something to unpack, wasn't it?

Leah placed the soup in front of her and a platter of sandwich triangles between them. "Here you go. What would you like to drink?"

"Oh, I'd love some of that athletic drink stuff, if you don't mind."

"No trouble at all," Leah said cheerfully, and automatically prepared it like she had before, in a cup with a lid and some ice. It didn't even taste overly sweet, which told Jordan she really needed it. Soon Leah was sitting down with her own soup, wriggling happily in her chair as she ate. Wow, she was in a good mood.

"This is perfect, Leah. You used to make this for me after finals, and I always loved it."

"The secret is to use lots of butter," Leah said, and crunched down on a sandwich triangle.

"The Two Fat Ladies taught us that," Jordan agreed.

"They were very wise," Leah said, grinning.

"Yup, and the best thing to watch with a pain flare. Hmm. Maybe today we can do a rewatch."

"That actually sounds like great aftercare. Clarissa and Jennifer and cuddling on the couch, dreaming of something delicious covered in pastry, cream or butter."

"Then I'm going to want shepherd's pie for dinner, you know."

"That can be arranged. I know you were planning on latkes, but that's a lot when you're in pain. I'll make the shepherd's pie happen."

"You are an awesome friend, honoring my food whims this way."

"I will take any excuse to eat mashed potatoes. Plus I don't even need to shop, as I already have everything, I think."

"You are in an incredibly good mood."

Leah smiled, but it was more for herself than at Jordan, like she was hugging something delightful to herself and enjoying it. "Yes, I really am. Today is a happy day."

"Do you want to tell me about it?"

"Hmmm. Not right now. Maybe later."

After they watched a couple episodes of Two Fat Ladies and munched on some dark chocolate, Jordan felt more solid. And just...grounded in their friendship. Sundown was in a few hours, and she didn't want to just let this ride, so she asked if Leah was up for a check-in. Leah agreed it was a good idea, but suggested that they set a timer, so they didn't process for too long. She had a shepherd's pie to make, after all, and processing was a spoon suck, so maybe they could set an alarm for 45 minutes, and then wrap up?

Jordan blinked for a few moments, and felt some of the tension leave her shoulders. She'd never been able to get Dani to agree to setting limits on processing time, even though the longer it went on, the less Jordan was able to be present and attend and remember what was said, much less communicate clearly. She thought about it, and asked if Leah would be up for talking over text instead? Then she could lie down in the dark with an ice pack and be more up for the conversation. Leah grinned and agreed, requesting Twitter DM instead of text, so she could use her laptop. Jordan made her way to her room, and got settled into a position that was the most comfortable of her available options, and pulled up Twitter on her phone.

Jordan scrolled through her notifications, thinking about how to start. Then she opened her DM with Leah, which she hadn't used much since moving.

PanStoneButch: Hey there. I just realized we haven't been talking this way, when it used to be every day, basically.

LeahBlumensteinNYC: Yeah, I kinda missed it, actually. It's just...easier sometimes, yknow?

PanStoneButch: Yeah. Just because we're roommates doesn't mean all conversations need to happen face to face. Even if we're in the same room, we can still talk this way. It's easier to make words like this.

LeahBlumensteinNYC: It really fucking is. Ok then. I say we go back to doing this every day.

PanStoneButch: Make it so.

LeahBlumensteinNYC: Oh, Jean-Luc, I love it when you say that.

PanStoneButch: Do you, now? *stores that information away for later*

PanStoneButch: So I wanted to check in about our play, and stuff. I know that some folks do that after each scene, and we've had three, but it wasn't something you'd mentioned...

LeahBlumensteinNYC: Yeah, that was an error on my part. I should have made that happen. It's actually a really good idea with any new play partner, and even within ongoing play relationships. Often it's something you do a day or two after the fact.

PanStoneButch: Well this eight nights of Chanukah thing throws a wrench in that, doesn't it?

LeahBlumensteinNYC: *chuckles* Yeah, I don't generally play this frequently, much less with the same person. I got all excited about 8 lessons, 8 days. It made sense at the time. But really, we can postpone any of the lessons, or space them out more. I said that, right?
PanStoneButch: Yeah, you did. In all honesty, I don't think I'm up for a lesson tonight. Between the panic attack and my pain levels, it just doesn't seem like a good idea.

LeahBlumensteinNYC: I totally get that.

PanStoneButch: I would like to check in, though. But I'm not sure what that's supposed to look like?

LeahBlumensteinNYC: So, I think it depends on your style. Some folks have specific questions they want to discuss, kinda like a feedback form for a training?

PanStoneButch: Tell me people don't use a 7 point scale.

LeahBlumensteinNYC: *laughs* Nope, never seen one of those, but it could be funny to make a joke one.

PanStoneButch: I will leave that to the kink educator. So what kinds of questions?

LeahBlumensteinNYC: Like...what worked best? What would you change? What felt edgy? How are you doing emotionally & physically after our scene?

PanStoneButch: Those all seem like they are for the bottom.

LeahBlumensteinNYC: Not necessarily. There is this pesky thing where tops often ask all the questions and demand vulnerability from bottoms while rarely sharing information about themselves. But I absolutely invite you to break that tradition, because it's bullshit.

PanStoneButch: So what you're saying is that you didn't teach me about check-ins because you think they're bullshit?

LeahBlumensteinNYC: No. I made a mistake not teaching you about them in the first lesson. I do think checking in with each other is good. And sometimes I've liked doing the journal or scene report version of this, where I write the story of what it was like for me. I guess I think it's something that makes more sense as a mutual thing, where we both are vulnerable. Because play is like that, when it's good. And so is negotiation.

PanStoneButch: Ok...

LeahBlumensteinNYC: I just haven't experienced that before.

PanStoneButch: Well you don't have to push me for it. We can make it up together.

LeahBlumensteinNYC: You mean I don't have to be the expert who already knows, and neither do you?

PanStoneButch: Exactly. We're experimenting in a bunch of ways, this can be an extension of that.

32

TUESDAY AFTERNOON, DECEMBER 24

LEAH

LeahBlumensteinNYC: Well aren't you a breath of fresh air.

PanStoneButch: Am I?

LeahBlumensteinNYC: Yeah. You really are.

Had she really said that? It was what she'd been thinking since that first scene, but she hadn't really meant to blurt it out like that.

PanStoneButch: Can you tell me more about that?

LeahBlumensteinNYC: Ok. I've played with other novice dominants before. They don't usually...surprise me like you do.

PanStoneButch: I see.

LeahBlumensteinNYC: That's a compliment, in case that wasn't clear.

PanStoneButch: Oh, is it now?

LeahBlumensteinNYC: Yes. The surprises are good ones.

PanStoneButch: It would be helpful to have examples.

LeahBlumensteinNYC: Oh. Ok. I was being vague wasn't I?

PanStoneButch: A bit, yes.

She'd been avoiding. Because it felt...vulnerable to talk about. But she should.

LeahBlumensteinNYC: So I think part of it is that you seem to be pleased by things I wouldn't have anticipated, and they catch me by surprise.

Which isn't really about you being a novice at all.

PanStoneButch: *nods*

PanStoneButch: *waits for examples*
Right. Of course.

LeahBlumensteinNYC: Like, you praised me for telling you I couldn't take more of the bristles. You didn't expect me to be super still, in fact you were clear that wasn't something you wanted. And, you seemed pleased when I showed initiative and went and got the wedge. It's like...you value different things from most of the folks I've played with.

PanStoneButch: Those are good surprises?

LeahBlumensteinNYC: Yeah. It's exciting, keeps me on my toes, not knowing, and having a bunch of new stuff to learn. But also. I don't know.

PanStoneButch: *gently* I think you know. It's ok to say it.

LeahBlumensteinNYC: I think the stuff you value...it makes me feel safe in a new way. Like I can react how I react, and you want that. I don't have to try to act like a submissive is generally expected to act. I can have helpful ideas and expertise and offer them, and they aren't assumed to be challenging your dominance. My boundaries and sensory needs are seen as good and important and you want me to communicate about them.

PanStoneButch: *listening*

LeahBlumensteinNYC: Because, like, for some dominants the question isn't whether I'm up for a sensation or not, but whether I'm willing to tolerate intense difficulty and discomfort, or can't tolerate it. I don't think they get the way that works for me sensorily, to tolerate sensations my body is rejecting. Yes I can gut my way through it, I've got tons of practice at tolerating sensory awfulness, but it will be hugely draining and cost me so much for the next several days and make everything that comes after it unpredictable and hyperintense and often intolerable. I've tried to explain, but it's like they just don't get it, so I just stopped trying after a while. For them it's all about me using my will to submit to force myself to take things, as the ultimate value. And that kind of play changes how submission feels, to me.

PanStoneButch: Maybe they don't get it because they're allistic? (I'm just guessing.)

LeahBlumensteinNYC: Yeah. Probably. I haven't played with many autistic doms.

PanStoneButch: Leah, I don't want to push your edges in the way you describe, where you force yourself to tolerate sensations that your body is clearly shouting no to. I know what it's like when they make you wear something itchy or you can't get away from construction noise, or they make you look them in the eye. I know how draining it is, how much it fucks with you. That's not the kind of submission I want. Please do keep telling me if I happen upon stuff like that. You not only have my full permission, I am very clearly stating I don't consent to play like that, and need you to tell me if it goes there.

LeahBlumensteinNYC: Oh. I think I can do that. It's really a relief to hear you clearly say that you don't want that.

PanStoneButch: I did try eye contact once. How was that for you?

LeahBlumensteinNYC: It felt right. It was intense, but intensity fit in that moment.

PanStoneButch: Ok. That's good to know.

LeahBlumensteinNYC: I know flares just happen sometimes. I was wondering, though…do you think our play contributed to your pain flare today?

PanStoneButch: It might have. My hips don't often flare, so it might be the strap on. I really hope not.

LeahBlumensteinNYC: That could be a position thing. Maybe positions where you're standing for a long time are hard on you.

PanStoneButch: Yeah, that could be.

LeahBlumensteinNYC: Or standing and thrusting, which uses the knees and hips, really.

PanStoneButch: Good point.

LeahBlumensteinNYC: I have a handout on positions and different options.

I even have one that's specifically about adjusting positions based on bodies that talks about options around disability and fatness. I'll send it to you.

PanStoneButch: That would be great.

LeahBlumensteinNYC: Some folks really like cowgirl positions both because they're less of a strain on joints but also because the pressure of your partner's weight can feel really good.

PanStoneButch: I want to try that next, then. Leah, I really appreciate your expertise. I feel really lucky to play with a submissive who has this much knowledge to bring to the table.

LeahBlumensteinNYC: *blushing* Did you flare from the scene at the party?

PanStoneButch: Well, I actually started flaring a bit *during* the scene at the party.

LeahBlumensteinNYC: You did?

PanStoneButch: That's why I sat down. I didn't realize I was hurting until I suddenly did.

LeahBlumensteinNYC: Yeah, it can be a delayed thing with all the chemicals going on.

LeahBlumensteinNYC: So, um. I don't want it to be a thing where you play and then are paying for it the next day with pain. At least not without you choosing that.

PanStoneButch: I think this calls for experimentation. I need to try different positions, so I can figure out how to adapt things so I'm not as likely to flare. But since so much of this is new, the learning curve might be steep.

LeahBlumensteinNYC: This sounds like it might call for a seven point scale and a spreadsheet.

PanStoneButch: You would want to have it be organized.

LeahBlumensteinNYC: *folds hands primly in lap and looks at you over my glasses* Well it is an experiment, isn't it?

PanStoneButch: I propose that you make the spreadsheet/survey thing and it can be part of every check in.

LeahBlumensteinNYC: *bounces excitedly* Yay!

PanStoneButch: So, I have a question for you.

LeahBlumensteinNYC: Yes?

PanStoneButch: Tell me about how the sex aspect went last night?

LeahBlumensteinNYC: That's a good question. I'd love to hear your answer, too.

PanStoneButch: Fair. I will answer too. You first.

LeahBlumensteinNYC: That kind of kink generally feels sexy to me so it was a good choice to try this with. I loved how much it felt like you were claiming me. That dynamic was really strong, and I was with you every step of the way. In fact…

PanStoneButch: Yes?

LeahBlumensteinNYC: I feel like doing that, knowing I could stop it anytime and you would really be glad I did, choosing it from a place of honoring my desire, and really choosing it for myself…it feels like it opened something up for me.

PanStoneButch: Can you tell me more about that?

LeahBlumensteinNYC: Today, I was still feeling sexual. That doesn't usually happen. I often shut down, curl in on myself, get pretty damn sex repulsed for a while after I have sex. But that didn't happen this time. So I decided to follow that, push myself a bit with it, try some solo sex, and it was really good. Like, having the room to really say no and be met there made yes possible in a different way.

PanStoneButch: *nods*

LeahBlumensteinNYC: It's not like a thing where now I'm not gray ace. I still am. It's more a thing where I'm flowing more with my gray aceness, and not trying to put myself in an allosexual box anymore. And I have hope that maybe that will make the sex I do choose better for me. It seems to have made it better so far, anyway. Because damn last night was hot. And so was today.

PanStoneButch: *grins* That's why you were so happy?

LeahBlumensteinNYC: Yep.

PanStoneButch: Well then I guess I shouldn't worry about it being my first time using a strap-on and not being good for you.

LeahBlumensteinNYC: *fans self* Oh no I would say you don't have anything to worry about there. I, um. Tried to let go and really react. I hope that you could tell I was enjoying it.

PanStoneButch: I had a sense. But it's good to have that confirmed.

LeahBlumensteinNYC: And for you?

PanStoneButch: I really enjoyed my first strap on experience. I hadn't known how much it would feel like it was part of my body, but it really did. Combining that kind of claiming D/s was...wow. Even more intense and delicious than I'd fantasized it would be. Your responses were gorgeous. Also, it felt...less full of landmines than other sex I've had. Like, it didn't seem to be a thing that I kept my clothes on, or didn't want you to touch me, or was focused on your body and your reactions. Or at least...not a bad thing.

LeahBlumensteinNYC: It was a very *good* thing. Your rough jeans against my bare skin yes please. Knowing that the way to please you was to let you touch me and to let myself react...it's like a completely different way of giving over control and being vulnerable to a dominant, and it was glorious.

PanStoneButch: Well alright then. I'm liking this check-in thing.

LeahBlumensteinNYC: *chuckles* I'm glad. I'm liking it, too.

PanStoneButch: I did have reverb this morning, but I think it wasn't from the sex, but from not closing the scene last night, and then waking up in pain.

LeahBlumensteinNYC: Can you tell me more?

PanStoneButch: It just. I woke up and I felt so dominant and like you were mine and I was keeping you, and then the pain sent me plummeting right into drop. Because it makes me feel helpless.

Leah was reeling. She blinked several times to see if the words were actually real. Keeping you. Keeping you. Keeping you. She had to respond. She dug her nails into her thighs and reread the message, then focused on the part that needed an immediate response. It was almost time to wrap this conversation up. She could make it through a few more minutes.

LeahBlumensteinNYC: Fuck. Yeah. That sucks. Are you still feeling droppy?

PanStoneButch: I think the aftercare we did helped. I do think that I want to close scenes in the future, before going to bed.

LeahBlumensteinNYC: I agree, I don't think it's a good idea to play with more fluid D/s right now.

She'd already sunk into head space so fast during the lesson, and had a hard time coming up today. And you want to fucking keep me, so yeah, we shouldn't do that again. The thought was so loud she had to check to make sure she hadn't typed it.

LeahBlumensteinNYC: I think it's better if we keep it to scenes. Especially since you're still learning, and that's like jumping in the deep end without even any water wings.

PanStoneButch: Oh that reminds me. I need to go swimming.

LeahBlumensteinNYC: Well that's easy enough. You can even go tonight. I'll give you the guest pass for my gym.

PanStoneButch: Even though it's Christmas Eve?

LeahBlumensteinNYC: Damn, I'd forgotten. *checking* Oh, yup, they're open til 10. Not tomorrow though.

PanStoneButch: Oh wow, that would really help my pain levels, if I could swim. It makes a real difference.

LeahBlumensteinNYC: There's even a hot tub.

PanStoneButch: Yay! Oh, that's the alarm for wrapping up our check in.

LeahBlumensteinNYC: This actually seems like a great place to stop. I'm going to go lie down for a bit, but I'll email you the guest pass and all the info first.

PanStoneButch: Thanks, that would be great. Hey Leah?

LeahBlumensteinNYC: Yeah?

PanStoneButch: I'm sorry I didn't close the scene before we went to sleep.

LeahBlumensteinNYC: No, babe, it was our joint responsibility. I could have asked for that. I'm sorry I didn't.

PanStoneButch: I didn't wreck everything?

LeahBlumensteinNYC: No, not at all. Nothing is wrecked.

PanStoneButch: Oh good.

LeahBlumensteinNYC: I'm afk for a bit laying down. Hope the swim helps.

Leah closed her laptop and stumbled over to her bed, yanking the covers over her. She curled into a ball, hugging her velvet pillow, and rocked. The words on the screen were seared into her brain. I felt so dominant and like you were mine and I was keeping you. Fuck. Fuck fuck fuck fuck fuck fuckity fuck. What the fuck was she supposed to do now?

33

WEDNESDAY MORNING, DECEMBER 25

JORDAN

The swim and the hot tub had helped. So had rest, and taking a break from play. Jordan had even been able to sleep in, it was almost 10:30am. She was in substantially less pain, and also felt less droppy, and the panic attack had faded away, no more reverb. She was going to have leftover shepherd's pie for brunch, Jordan decided. She deserved the treat, and it was just the sort of thing that really worked for breakfast, in her opinion. Jordan grinned when she felt almost sprightly getting out of bed. Gonna get ibuprofen on board just in case, and not push it today, but things are looking good, she thought.

Leah had been in bed when she'd gotten home, and if she was home now, she was very quiet. There was no note in the kitchen. Maybe she'd texted or DM'd? Jordan sat at the table and checked her phone. Ah, yes. Leah was out for most of the day going out for Chinese food and a movie with Ellie's leather family. Oh, right. That was a Jewish tradition for her. Jordan's family tradition had always been to get Chinese food delivery and watch movies at home. Erica was probably doing that today. She should text her sister and see if they could maybe watch at least one of the movies together.

Leah hadn't invited her to go today. She had an ongoing play relationship with Ellie, maybe that was why? Maybe she just wanted some space. They didn't need to do everything together. This wasn't like when she'd visit and they would spend most of the time together. Jordan lived here now, and it totally made sense that Leah might want time with her people without Jordan around sometimes. She shouldn't read anything into it.

Something felt off, though. Jordan wasn't sure what, but it would have to wait. She wasn't going to try to ask about it over text while Leah was out on something that might be a date. Anyway, it might not even be anything. Jordan took out her phone and concentrated on planning out what kind of Chinese food she was going to order.

The sun was coming down and Jordan still hadn't heard back from Leah about whether they were going to do a lesson today. Maybe everything ran long. Maybe Leah's phone got lost, or the battery ran down. Maybe she would walk in the door any minute. Jordan couldn't shake the feeling that something was wrong, though. She checked her phone again. Nothing from Leah. But there was an email from Shiloh with a weird subject line. Wasn't Shiloh in Ellie's leather family?

She opened it, scanned, and then cursed, loudly, for ten minutes, before going to her laptop to respond. No way could her fingers deal with the tiny keys right now. The important thing to remember was that Leah was okay. She'd had a meltdown at the movies because they'd run into her mother. The meltdown didn't worry Jordan so much; though they sucked, they were part of life as an autistic person. But Leah's mother fucked with her head, bigtime, always had. So that had her worried. Probably too damned worried.

There was no reasonable reason that Jordan should be feeling this protective and frustrated that she hadn't been there, that she wasn't there now. Leah had been dealing with her mother her whole life. She was at a friend's house, away from the noise; her mother couldn't reach her. She was safe, and calmed down enough to take a nap. That's why Shiloh had emailed, because Leah was sleeping.

Jordan sent Shiloh her phone number, thanked zir for emailing, and asked if there was anything she could do. Would it help if she brought anything over? She was happy to do that if it would help. She didn't care if it was weird to offer. She wasn't going to invite herself over. But she'd come at the drop of a hat if they asked.

She decided to get dressed just in case. Then she'd be ready if they needed anything. Plus it gave her something to do as she waited for Shiloh to respond. When the response came, she had a hard time accepting it. She wanted to do something. She didn't want to let others care for Leah, she wanted to care for her. But Shiloh was right: Leah was sleeping, and what she needed right now was a quiet space to come down from the meltdown and tend to herself. Shiloh also said that ze wasn't even staying, ze was taking Judith to zir place so Leah could have Judith's room for as long as she wanted. Ernest, Ellie, and Gideon would care for her. Ze had given Ernest Jordan's number and he'd give updates, but she shouldn't expect Leah home tonight.

Jordan didn't even really get why it was so hard for her to not be there for Leah. It felt different than it had ever felt before, almost like a tug of war inside herself. Part of her knew she was good where she was; these were her people, they would care for her. But the part of her that thought of

Leah as hers was frustrated and wanted to tend to her, was angry at feeling helpless to do anything for her. As a dominant, she needed to tend to her submissive? Well, she certainly felt that way. Was that how all dominants felt? Did they feel that way about everyone they played with?

Several people had offered to be a resource for her in learning about kink. Perhaps one of them would be able to answer that question. She thought about it for a while, and decided that she really didn't feel comfortable texting anyone who celebrated Christmas on the holiday itself, so that left Iris off the options list. But Ruth was Jewish. She had answered some questions, and celebrated Jordan's new toybag with her when Jordan had come over for dinner. There was no harm in texting, was there? It was just 5 pm, not late at all. She read the text four times before sending. Within a minute, Ruth was suggesting that Jordan have dinner with her and Rebecca. Jordan took a breath and asked if they'd like to come over to her place, as she had a ton of Chinese food. That felt like a gutsy move, but she wasn't sure she was up to talking in a crowded restaurant. She went to the kitchen to get herself some water so she wouldn't stare at the phone. When she got back, Ruth had texted that they were on their way.

Okay then. Her first house guests in NYC. Jordan scanned all the public areas, murmuring the Shehecheyanu, picking up as she scanned, and then went into the kitchen to see what they could have for dessert. After a search, she concluded that there was nothing pareve, and Jordan wasn't sure how observant Rebecca and Ruth were. Maybe she could put something together quickly. There was lemon cake mix; she could use it to make cookies. Leah loved lemon cookie ice cream sandwiches. Jordan would pick up coconut ice cream for the sandwiches tomorrow. Baking would be soothing, too. Give her hands something to do, as she waited for R&R.

Leah wasn't really set up for cookie baking, she didn't have cooling racks. Jordan rigged something for now and pulled out her phone to add it to the list of kitchen items she needed to get. She hadn't thought about how Leah didn't really bake much, started putting together a list of staple ingredients. There was so much to do when you moved, and even with all of her organizational efforts, she still forgot stuff like this. Leah didn't even have confectioner's sugar, much less almond extract or cornmeal. The list-making soothed Jordan even more than the baking, and by the time two batches of cookies were out of the oven, she'd calmed herself down enough to realize that it might be good to make a pot of tea, as Ruth had favored iced tea with dinner last time. Though she'd offer the ginger fizzy drink as well. Oh, she should get the candles ready too.

Jordan was glad when the buzzer sounded, because at least she wasn't waiting anymore, and wouldn't be alone. Alone felt wrong right now.

Jordan focused on getting everyone situated, though she hadn't anticipated that Rebecca would want to get Jordan's plate as well as Ruth's, so there were a few moments of awkwardness as she adjusted to the idea that she was a dominant in a new social situation where she didn't know what was expected of her. When she blurted out as much to Ruth, at first Ruth just tilted her head, thinking for a moment, the teal streaks in her dark curls catching the light.

"Rebecca likes serving, and is used to doing so with my friends as part of her service to me, not just the dominant ones. But part of it too is that she's more physically abled than both of us and knows how many spoons it can take to do things like this. She likes to help me and my physically disabled and chronically ill friends save our spoons for other things, and doesn't always remember to ask their consent first, because it's a long-term habit."

Jordan nodded, considering this.

"But that doesn't make it okay. She should ask, especially with new folks where she doesn't already have consent. For both aspects of it, the service part and the aspect that's about helping you save spoons."

When Rebecca came in with Ruth's plate, she got a hand signal from her dominant, and knelt. Ruth quietly explained what they had been discussing, and Jordan saw Rebecca flinch, as she realized what she had done.

"I'm so sorry," she said quietly. "I should have asked for your consent first. It's not okay to give intrusive help as an abled person, or to give service that's non-consensual. I apologize."

Jordan nodded, acknowledging her words, and took the moment to breathe and consider what she actually wanted, and was okay with, before speaking. She was grateful that they both gave her the time without pressuring her for a response.

"Thank you for apologizing. I was surprised. I don't do especially well with surprises. You may ask my consent now, if you would like to."

"Thank you. I would like to serve you both tonight, if you will allow it. It would let you save your spoons for the conversation you wanted to have."

"Alright. Let's give it a try, tonight, and see how it goes."

"Thank you."

"I would be glad for you to light the Chanukah candles before we eat."

Rebecca grinned, and went to do just that, launching into Ner Li as soon as the prayer was over. Jordan joined her; it was the favorite of one of her friends in Boston, so even though she hadn't grown up singing it, she'd been singing along for years at his Chanukah party. Ruth then began a song in Ladino that it took Jordan a moment to remember, as it had been years since she'd heard it. Ocho Candelikas was a favorite of one of her father's friends from the Jewish Studies department at his university, and she hadn't sung it since childhood. She only remembered the chorus, and was glad for the reprieve during the verse as she tried to hold it together while they sang. But she couldn't, after all, so she made her way to the restroom, where she let herself cry for a few minutes, before pulling out her phone to text Erica that she missed her. The grief was just waiting to catch her at off moments, this year, and she wasn't even sure why now after all this time it was hitting harder, but it was like quicksand, damnit. She washed her face, humming Sevivon, Sov, Sov, Sov to herself as she did, trying to plant a new earworm.

As she ran through the song, she realized she hadn't played dreidel at all this year, and decided to suggest they play after dinner. When she got back, Rebecca was in the kitchen preparing her own plate. Jordan sat near Ruth in her favorite chair. She didn't want to watch the candles burn tonight. Rebecca sat on a pillow at Ruth's feet, and they ate quietly. She'd made it awkward by leaving so abruptly.

"I'm sorry. That song reminded me of my father. The grief is especially hard this year."

They both nodded, and Rebecca asked what was in the ginger fizzy drink, an easy question that seemed to smooth things out a bit. Jordan ate her beef with snow peas and gathered her courage, running the sentence through her head twice before speaking.

"So I've been learning D/s, and I'm still sorting through the way it works for me. I had some questions…"

"Feel free to ask, I'll help if I can," Ruth said, her tone warm.

"I did D/s that had a more claiming, feral kind of dynamic a couple days ago. And I'm having reactions that feel new and strange to me, ever since."

"What kind of reactions?"

"Like, this sense of protectiveness, this feeling that I need to tend to her when she's upset, even if she has support from others, that I need to be supporting her."

"Because you don't think they can do it?"

"I mean, I don't know they can, but I don't have reason to think they can't."

"Like her well-being is under your purview in a new way, and it feels wrong if you trust it to others when you aren't sure they are up to the job?"

"Yeah, maybe."

"Like she belongs to you in a new way?"

"Yes. Like she's mine, and I'm keeping her now."

"What kind of dynamic is this? Was it scene based or more ongoing?"

"It was supposed to be scene-based, but then we didn't close the scene before we fell asleep. So I think it's murky. We both woke up in dynamic, but then it got all messed up because I was having a pain flare, and had decided not to do D/s while flaring."

Ruth nodded.

"It sounds like the dynamic is lingering. Those feelings make perfect sense within the dynamic, but if it's supposed to be over now, it sounds like it's not really feeling that way to you. This is a pretty common issue."

"It is?"

"Yeah, the thing about D/s is that it eats the world. That's how my mentor put it when she was teaching me. Whatever space you give it, it will take up, it wants to take over everything. So if you give it room, it will take it."

"So what do I do?"

"Well, I think it depends a bit on why it's seeping out. It could be that you didn't close the scene effectively. That sounds possible. It could also be that this kind of D/s isn't driving things, but riding along with other stuff."

"Other stuff?"

"Claiming dynamics can hitch a ride on jealousy pretty easily. Or rescue. Both of which can go to super messy places. But I think they also can tag along with other kinds of things that are less potentially problematic. Well, I'm thinking of one in particular."

Jordan nodded, waiting.

Ruth put down her fork and put her hand on the back of Rebecca's neck. "How did I explain it to you, girl?" she asked.

"I believe you used the words love and bashert, Ma'am."

"Yes, you were the more poetic one, weren't you, girl?"

"Yes, Ma'am," Rebecca said, ducking her head.

"Is it possible that you are falling, or have fallen in love, Jordan?" Ruth's voice was gentle.

In love, yes. Bashert? As in soul mate? She'd never really believed in soul mates. If Leah was her soul mate, why had it taken them this long for her to feel it?

"Yes," she whispered. "I'm pretty sure I'm in love. I haven't told her that, though."

"We wouldn't break a confidence."

"Thanks. Bashert, though….it's not something I ever thought was real."

Rebecca smiled. "Bashert is like…there's a part of you that recognizes that you belong together, that whatever shape this takes, you will be in each other's lives. It kind of feels like bells ringing in harmony, all the way through your body. It doesn't have to be romantic, I don't think, or sexual. It can happen with friends, and chosen family, too. And you can have more than one bashert. It's that thing inside that says I'm going to keep you."

Oh. "I mean, I already felt that with her a long time ago, platonically. But now there are these other aspects of our relationship. Sex, D/s, romantic love. The I'm going to keep you has a different quality to it."

"Yeah, that might not be about not closing the scene effectively. I know even when Rebecca and I were doing scene-based D/s, that once I'd fallen for her, this part of me just…claimed her for mine and that feeling didn't fade between scenes." Ruth said ruefully.

"It was mutual, Ma'am." Rebecca said cheerfully.

34

193

THURSDAY MORNING, DECEMBER 26

LEAH

Leah wasn't ready to go home. She didn't want to overstay her welcome, though. Gideon, Judith, and Ernest had been so kind. She wasn't part of their family, but they treated her like she deserved care and kindness and respect. It made her ache, their closeness, the way they made space for her, made her welcome. Like if she stepped toward them, they would meet her there. But she never had, because she'd been keeping her distance with Ellie, and it hadn't felt right. Even after she'd struck up a friendship with Shiloh after an a-spec meetup and had hired zir at the shop, she still hadn't felt like she could let herself get close to Ellie's family.

Now, they'd all seen her lose her shit in public. They'd gathered around her. Shiloh had stared down her mother until she gave up and walked away, used zir size and ferocious energy to get her to go. Naomi had helped Leah pull herself together enough to get her out of the theater. Rena had brought the car around, and chauffeured Leah, Ellie, Nora, and Rachel while the others took the subway. Ellie had held her hand while she unloaded about her mother. Judith had given up her room so Leah to sleep there, had closed the blackout curtains for her so she could cocoon. Ernest had brought tea and a weighted blanket. Gideon had promised the house would be quiet for her, and had gotten everyone to leave her be and let her rest.

They'd been lovely, and as she lay there in Judith's cozy bed trying to work up the courage to go into the living room and face them, it was clear that she'd robbed herself of them and what they could've brought to her life, and had missed out, for years. She hugged a pillow close, and let herself cry and rock, because it was such a loss, and for what? To protect herself from building a deeper connection with Ellie? Ellie had never pushed, had she? She'd just kept inviting Leah to family gatherings, and been glad about her friendship with Shiloh. Leah was the one that had masked so much. Had avoided vulnerability with Ellie. Had insisted on casual, and casual meant no family ties.

Well that was blown to bits now. She'd had a meltdown, and they'd gathered around her, supported her, shown they cared, without hesitation or question, even though she'd been standoffish for years. Even though she'd given them no reason to want to. They'd still wanted to.

She got stuck on that, looping it around and around in her head. It didn't make sense. She didn't know how to make sense of it. There had to be a piece missing, somewhere, but she didn't know what it was. She rocked for a long time, hoping it would resolve and she would have clarity, but it didn't work. When her stomach growled, she decided to let it steep and maybe it would be clear later. Right now she needed food.

When she padded into the living room, Gideon smiled and greeted her. Ernest turned from the stove and grinned. Whatever he was cooking smelled amazing.

"You have excellent timing," he called. "The potatoes are almost done and I'm about to start frying the eggs. How many do you want?"

"Two would be lovely," she said.

"Two it is!" He was full of energy, and so damned adorable in his bounciness.

"Have a seat," Gideon said, gesturing to the spot next to him on the couch. She sat, unsure of what to do with her hands.

"You had a rough day, yesterday," Gideon said. "Would cuddles be nice?"

Oh. She blinked a few times, processing. It would never have occurred to her to ask, but she actually could really use them. But why was he offering? They'd never cuddled before. He did seem good at it, though. She'd seen him cuddle with Nora, and Judith, and Ernest, and even Octavia, once. Maybe he liked cuddling. Maybe he liked her, and wanted her to have what she needed.

"Um. Maybe. But. I don't get it. Why would you offer me that?"

"Ah. That's a good question, Leah. A few reasons." He numbered them on his fingers. "I like cuddling. I enjoy offering comfort to folks I care about, and I care about you. I get the sense that you really like touch and don't get as much of it as you might want or need, so it might be a good way to comfort. I know Ellie would offer them, but she's not here right now, and she entrusted your care to me when you were vulnerable."

Leah had trouble taking all of that in. She got stuck on the last one. "Can you explain more about Ellie, please?"

"Sure. I know you and Ellie play, she's someone you submit to, yes?"

Leah nodded.

"She asked me to look after you, when she went home. She felt responsible for your well-being, and trusted me to care for you as you recovered."

"But why would she feel responsible?"

"Perhaps she's better equipped to answer that than I. Most of the doms I know feel a responsibility to the submissives in their lives that extends beyond the bounds of a particular scene. Ellie has been playing with you for, what, a dozen years or so? You're important to her. She cares for you. She was worried about you, so she asked me to look after you while you were here."

"Oh."

"It sounds like this is new information for you."

"I guess I thought...I don't know what I thought. I'm all confused."

"You seem surprised that she would care. Or that I would."

"Yeah. I guess I am."

"Leah, I like you a lot. I always have. I know you've kept your distance from us, but I gotta say, it wasn't mutual. We'd be glad to have you in our lives more. You're great."

Ernest came into the room with her breakfast, which gave her room to think. He served them both, then got his own food, and sat on a pillow at Gideon's feet, humming to himself as he ate. It was really good, the potatoes were soft in the middle and crispy on the outside, and the eggs were perfectly fried, just a bit gooey, the texture perfect. After she ate, Leah's brain started working a bit better. It always took her a while to recover from a meltdown and shake off the fog that came with it.

Gideon liked her. Ellie cared about her and felt responsible for her well-being. Had basically appointed Gideon to act as her proxy dom because she wasn't able to be there but wanted Leah to feel safe and protected. She'd been scared that Ellie would just break off their play if she took sex off the table, but someone who did this didn't sound like a person who'd do that. Had she even seen Ellie clearly, at all? She decided to text her to see if she could get more clarity.

Leah: Gideon says you asked him to look after me.

Ellie: Yes, I did. I wish I could've stayed and looked after you myself, but I thought you'd do better sleeping alone, and there was no bed I could use. I'm a terrible nurse if I don't get enough sleep, and I have work this afternoon.

Leah: Oh.

Ellie: Are you hurt that I left you in his care?

Leah: No. I guess I just. I'm confused.

Ellie: What are you confused about?

Leah: I didn't know that you...would have wanted to care for me like that.

Ellie: Ah. Leah, what do you think I feel about you? What do you think your place is, in my life?

Leah: I figured that I was a casual play partner.

Ellie: And what does casual mean, to you?

Leah: That there's no commitment. Or romance. Or significant relationship. Just mutual interest. And when interest wanes, or if compatibility shifts, then it's over.

Ellie: I see. Is that what you want?

Leah: Um. I didn't know anything else was on the table. I thought that's what we agreed to, when we started.

Ellie: I see. That doesn't really answer my question, though.

Leah: What question?

Ellie: Ok, let's try this. Leah, I haven't pushed or been direct about how I see our connection because I've been afraid to lose you.

Leah: Oh. I've actually been afraid, too.

Ellie: Afraid?

Leah: Afraid to lose you.

Ellie: Given that we are both afraid to lose each other, I'd venture a guess that at least one of the things you said is inaccurate. That we *do* have a significant relationship. In that it's significant to us.

Leah: That does seem to be the logical conclusion, doesn't it?

Ellie: How about this: we both decide to be brave, and have a real conversation about who we are to each other, and what we want with each other.

Leah: I will if you will.

Ellie: *chuckles* Me first, eh?

Leah: I felt like I was being brave just texting you about this in the first place. I'm not in the best shape right now.

Ellie: True. So, do you want to have this conversation now? Over text? Or would another medium be better?

Leah: I communicate better over text, actually.

Ellie: Ok.

Leah: And I'm going to be anxious about it until we talk so I say let's do it now, if that works for you?

Ellie: That works. I will go first, if that would help.

Leah: Yeah. It would.

Ellie: Ok, I'm going to lay it all out in a longish thing. It may take me a few minutes to type, so don't worry, I'm still here.

Leah: Ok.

Ellie: So. I care about you. You're important to me. I love our D/s, and treasure your submission. I'd love to have a deeper friendship with you, alongside the play. I feel a connection that's about you as a person, not specifically you as a submissive. That's why I keep inviting you to family events, because you feel like you could be family, if you wanted to be. I know that we stopped doing service weekends and went back to more scene-based play, but I really enjoyed the focus on service, and would be glad to do more of that, if you wanted.

Leah: Oh. Wow. Ok, that's a lot to process. Give me a moment.

Ellie: Of course.

Leah read through it a few times, and once more, whispering it to herself, to try to get it into her head.

Leah: I didn't realize.

Ellie: I know. I wish I'd brought it up sooner.

Leah: You were scared.

Ellie: Yeah.

Leah: Because you didn't want to lose me?

Ellie: That's right. I don't want to lose you.

Leah: I don't want to lose you either.

Ellie: I hope you will tell me what you were scared about.

Leah: Oh. Yes. I should.

Ellie: I'm listening.

Leah: I realized recently that I'm gray ace.

Ellie: Ok. What does that look like for you?

Leah: Well, I'm still figuring that out. I do know that sometimes I'm into sex, sometimes I can take it or leave it, and sometimes I'm sex repulsed. It changes.

Ellie: Ok.

Leah: I was scared to tell you.

Ellie: Because we've been doing sexual play and having sex.

Leah: Yeah. And I thought you might not want to play with me anymore if I needed to take sex off the table for a while.

Ellie: Because you thought our play was about compatibility and nothing more.

Leah: Well, yeah. And maybe you wouldn't think we were compatible anymore.

Ellie: Was that the main thing you were scared of?

Leah: Well. I was also scared that you might be upset.

Ellie: What would make me upset?

Leah: Because a submissive should be sexually available to her dominant.

Ellie: I see. Leah, can I call you, instead of continuing on text?

Leah: Yeah, ok. Give me a minute to get to Judith's room.

She sat in the chair in the corner, figuring it was better to be sitting for this.

"Ellie?"

"Yes, I'm here. Leah, you just texted something to me that didn't sound like you."

"I did?"

"Yes. You said a submissive should be sexually available to her dominant. Leah, do you believe that?"

"I said that?"

"Yes."

"I must be triggered."

"It didn't sound like you. Is that something someone used to say to you?"

"Yeah, Bev used to say that. It was one of her rules."

"Leah, that's not a rule for all submissives. Not all doms need or want that."

"I know. I just...clearly this is triggering for me."

"How can I help?"

"Well, I'm maybe going to have a spotty memory of this conversation, could you write me an email summarizing it?"

"Yes, I can do that."

"I think it would help to be grounded in reality. I was telling you what I was scared of. If you have a response to those fears, it might help to hear it. Though I would want you to write the letter, too."

"Okay. First, I would never decide to stop playing with you—or anyone— because they took sex off the table. I don't need sexualized play or sex with my play partners. I really enjoy D/s and service that doesn't have a sexual component, and would be deeply satisfied by that sort of play. We did that for a while, and I really enjoyed it. So, just to be clear, taking sex off the table is not a dealbreaker for me."

"Okay."

"Also, I would never want you to push yourself to have sex you don't actually want to have or to tolerate sexual play when you are not up for it."

"Okay."

"Your consent and well-being are important to me and I do not consent to play that pushes in that way."

"Okay."

"I get the sense that you may have done that in the past, before you knew this about yourself, and I get that. I know figuring out this kind of identity stuff is hard, and everyone can only work from what they knew at the time. If we need to do anything to help heal from those kinds of experiences we can work on that."

"Um."

"Not something we need to figure out right now. I just wanted to say it."

"Okay."

"I care about you and want you in my life, Leah. We could stop doing anything sexual for the rest of our lives and I wouldn't be upset with you about that. I would be glad you drew the boundaries you needed to draw for your well-being."

"Oh."

"I can tell you that a bunch of times, if you want."

"That might be good."

"I'd like to take sex and sexualized play off the table for now. If you want it back on at any point, you can let me know, and we can talk about it. And it can just be for that scene, or in that moment. You get to change your mind at any point and take it off the table again."

That was this huge relief. Leah felt so light she was almost floating.

"Thank you, Ma'am."

"Did that help?"

"Yes, Ma'am, it helped a lot."

"I wish I was there to cuddle with you, girl."

"Gideon offered to."

"That's a very good idea. Perhaps both Gideon and Ernest can cuddle with you. They are very good at comforting."

"That does sound nice."

"How about this: you lie down in Judith's bed, and I will text Gideon and ask him to do that."

"Yes, Ma'am. Thank you."

"I'm glad we talked. Feel free to reach out again throughout the day if you need to. I'm here. If I'm at work it may take me a bit to respond, but I will."

"Okay. Have a good day."

"Thank you. I'll text him now."

Soon Gideon and Ernest joined Leah, offering cuddles, and this time she said yes. For a thin guy, Gideon made a really comforting big spoon, and Ernest was the snuggliest teddy bear she'd ever hugged. It was so grounding, to be there with them, even before Ernest started singing that song from Fiddler on the Roof about miracles. She drifted off to sleep before she got a chance to ask him what made him think of it. When she woke from her nap they were still there, holding her, protecting her with their bodies, showing her that she could count on them.

She was ready to go home. Steady enough. No longer triggered. Gideon made her promise to text that she got there safely, putting his number in her phone himself. Ernest wrapped up potatoes and brisket for her, and insisted on putting her in the cab himself.

35

THURSDAY AFTERNOON, DECEMBER 26

JORDAN

Jordan was making latkes. She was craving them, and the process of making them would give her something concrete to do. First, she dug her food processor out of the box of kitchen supplies she'd brought, grateful that it was enough of a big ticket item that she'd packed it, instead of planning to buy a new one. She had her dad's recipe, and half the potatoes she'd gotten would go to that. But Erica had sent her the recipe she'd used with the kids last night, and Jordan thought she'd give it a try. She'd also gotten sweet potatoes and was going to try to make latkes out of those. They could have a taste test.

She pulled up the recipe Erica had sent, and within a few seconds she was cracking up. It wasn't a how to cook video, it was a music video, because this recipe was sung by a Jewish boy band. She listened, noting the recipe on a piece of paper, and knew the song would be in her head all day. No wonder her niblings liked this version, it had a sing-along component!

She was going to try this recipe first, so she put the song on again as she prepped the ingredients. They did it by hand in the video, but she knew better. She'd only tried that once, the first Chanukah after her dad had died. Now she considered the food processor an essential tool for latkes.

She was singing along to the video as she put the food processor to work, and it wasn't until the potatoes and onion were shredded that she heard Leah talking. She stopped the video and turned, smiling.

"What are you doing?" Leah asked, her voice incredulous.

"Why, I'm listening to the latke recipe that Erica sent in the form of a boy band song as I make latkes, of course."

"Of course. I should have known."

"The acapella boy band is named The Maccabeats."

Leah giggled. "Oh really? That's fucking perfect."

"You have to see this video."

Jordan waited till Leah was sitting at the table and restarted it, watching her face light up with glee as she watched. Then she added the flour, baking powder, and pepper, waiting to mix until the video was over.

"That's High School Musical Jewish perfection!" Leah pronounced, when the video was over. "And it will be in my head all day."

"At least I won't be alone there," Jordan said, pouring oil into the pan and turning on the heat.

"I'm tempted to see what other musical offerings they might have."

"Beware the YouTube rabbit hole, you may not emerge for hours."

"Good point. So, latkes, huh?"

"Yup. Not sure what we'll have with them."

"Oh, perhaps this brisket that Ernest sent me home with?"

"I hope Ernest received proper gratitude for that," Jordan said, as she put the first few latkes into the pan, then prepped some plates with paper towels.

"Oh, he did, don't you worry."

"Have I met Ernest?"

"He's an autistic midsize fat white Jewish trans guy with curly red hair, who's bouncy and very service-oriented. He writes musicals."

"I think I'd remember meeting him."

"Well we did get invited to the Chanukah party at his place, for Saturday. You can meet him and his dominant then."

"And his dominant's name is…"

"Gideon. Gideon is a thin white Jewish trans guy who's rather quiet and calm. He's a kink educator, co-teaches with Octavia mostly. You remember her, she works at the shop."

"Yeah I think so. I'm going to need your help remembering names and pronouns. I've got this idea for a way to practice." They were golden brown so she flipped the latkes, and was proud she hadn't been splashed by the oil at all.

"Yeah, I can help. Do you want flash cards or something?"

"Oh wow flash cards would be awesome. Seriously? You would make me flash cards to help remember your friends?"

"Well, sure, if you want. I used to make them for myself, as part of my butler book, back in the day."

"Your butler book?"

"It's a service thing, especially for folks who are in service to dominants who have a lot of guests. A way to keep track of people's preferences and needs when they're visiting. I loved being able to do that, it was one of my favorite things about being in service to Bev."

"You haven't done it since then?" Jordan took the latkes out of the pan, then put in another set.

"No, I haven't been in that kind of service relationship since then. There were other things about it that I did not love."

Jordan nodded. Then decided to ask. "If you are up for telling me what you didn't love, I'd like to know, so I can avoid those things."

"Oh. Well the biggest thing was sexual service. I was expected to always be sexually available, was told that was an essential part of being a submissive."

"That seems like a really bad match for you."

"Yes. It was. I hadn't realized how much it fucked me up, until recently. Or how much I had internalized the idea that in order to do D/s, I had to be sexually available. Even though in my head, I know better."

"That sounds like trauma." Jordan winced as she flipped the latkes. She wasn't being as careful as she should, and had splashed the oil on her wrist. She finished flipping, then pulled aloe gel out of the fridge and put it on the burn.

"Yeah. I think it is trauma. I got triggered around it this morning, in fact."

"After a hard day yesterday, that really sucks."

"Yep it really fucking does. Ellie helped. So did Gideon and Ernest."

"I'm glad you had support. How are you feeling now?"

"Oh, I'm okay. It's stirred up, but I'm aware of it now, and talking back to it. It helped that Ellie was so great about me setting boundaries around sexual play."

"Oh, you had that conversation today? That was brave."

"Yeah, I feel like I worked really hard, emotionally, the past few days."

"It sounds like you have. If you need to rest, instead of doing the lesson today, I would understand."

"Actually, pain would be really good, today."

"What kind of pain are you thinking of?"

"How would you feel about learning how to use an impact toy?"

"Could I learn today and be able to use it on you right away without practicing much?"

"Depends on the toy."

"I did buy something when I was out with Iris."

"Oh? Can I see it?"

"Sure." Jordan put the latkes on a plate to cool, and turned off the heat. She washed her hands, and went to get her toy bag, sitting next to Leah at the kitchen table. Then she took out the toy.

"Ohhh. That's a beautiful quirt," Leah said. "May I?"

"Yes, of course." Jordan handed it to her.

Leah futzed with it for a bit, then hit her own hand with it.

"I love quirts. This one is wonderful."

"I'm glad you like it."

"So I'm not sure if you can learn how to safely use a quirt with a half hour's practice, but we can also take precautions and give you a big area to aim at. If it feels too hard, you can borrow a crop instead, which is easier to aim with. But if you want to try with this, I'd love that."

"Sounds good."

"It's not sexual for me. This kind of pain doesn't really hurt me. It's like...the kind of sensation that calms me, like I need it. Kind of how a weighted blanket works. It's a reset. I could definitely use a reset."

"Oh, I get that."

"Most tops aren't into it, because my reactions don't make sense to them. So I usually use quirts for solo play. It would be cool to try, and see how my reactions feel to you."

"Yeah, I'd be into that."

In that case, Jordan was only going to make one kind of latkes, and save her hands for later. She really wanted to see what the quirt did for Leah. A scene that was about giving her what she needed sounded like perfection after last night.

36

THURSDAY EVENING, DECEMBER 26

LEAH

There was something comforting about returning to this space she'd been creating with Jordan, of learning and practice and certainty that wherever either one of them were was okay with the other, and each time was in some ways a fresh start, a space for discovery. It already felt certain that Jordan was okay with whatever she brought to it, a solid knowledge that was deep in her body, not just something she knew in her head. She wasn't sure she'd ever felt this certain that it was okay to be herself, all of herself, in whatever space she was, with a play partner before.

Part of her that was giddy at the idea that Jordan might be someone who she could do quirt scenes with. She had stopped trying to find that, had accepted that it was a solo play thing for her. It would be fine if that's how things played out. But if they didn't, the idea that she could ask for the kind of pain that helped her reset, get to experience that with a partner…she couldn't really imagine what that might be like. She might just get to find out.

The latkes had been delicious, though Jordan wasn't convinced they were as good as her dad's recipe and said they should do taste testing one of these nights. The brisket was a dream, better than any her mom had served. Jordan had made her favorite ice cream sandwiches, and had even put a bit of lemon curd in them for extra zing. The candles had been so pretty, her mouth was extremely happy, her belly was full of comfort food, and she was going to teach her best friend how to beat her with a quirt. Life was immensely good.

Leah felt especially good about this lesson, because it felt like it would get them both back into the frame of mind she'd been trying for from the start. Best buds supporting each other, where it's all about teaching and learning in a friendly casual way. It wasn't messy like their last scene, which hadn't really ended and had Jordan saying things like she wanted to keep her. This wasn't about beginning a D/s relationship, or a romantic one, or a sexual one. This was about lessons between friends. And if quirts ended up being something that worked between them, it wasn't so different from asking a friend for a massage. No big deal.

Leah went through the basics of impact play, safe spots to hit with anything, spots you needed to only do light play, spots you needed special permission for. Then she demonstrated how to hold and use the quirt, and explained which part of the quirt to use for impact, went over wrapping. Jordan practiced with the pillow for a while, until she seemed comfortable. Leah talked a bit about what you did to go light, and how to use it to up the intensity. They reviewed the idea of warm-up, of unpacking what particular kinds of impact meant to the folks involved, and talked about different ways you could structure play of this sort, how it could intertwine with D/s. They talked through the aim of this particular practice scene, agreed that it was about sensation, and control, and that the focus would be Leah's back, so Jordan could practice reading her without seeing her face.

Then they moved to Leah's room, because she'd set the boundary that she didn't want to co-sleep afterwards. This way she could just drift off after they did aftercare. Jordan brought a chair, but decided to see what it was like to do it standing, and sit when she needed to. It was time, and Leah couldn't seem to be still. Her hands were twisting in knots as she kneeled on the rug by the foot of the bed, and she kept her eyes on Jordan's boots.

They were beautiful boots, oxblood with that distinctive Fluevog swirl that differentiated them from Docs. She hadn't realized that Jordan had such a wonderful collection of boots. But this was the third pair she'd noticed since Jordan had moved in, and each one suited a different piece of who she was. She wondered whether Jordan blacked them herself or if she took them to a cobbler. Maybe bootblacking could be incorporated into her plans for the boot play lesson. Leah loved that kind of service, and hadn't gotten to do it in a while.

Focusing on Jordan's boots had calmed her, she realized. Her hands weren't twisting anymore. She was ready to play. How long had she stared at Sir's boots? Was Jordan upset, angry? She looked up and Sir was smiling at her.

"There you are. I thought you would find your way."

What? Sir had just waited for her to find calm, and focus? Had given her the time to get there on her own? What kind of dominant was she? She blinked up at her.

"Sir?"

"Yes, girl."

"I'm not sure what you meant just now."

"Ah. I saw that you were struggling to get into headspace. But I knew you would find your way, if I gave you the room and time. And you did."

Oh. "Yes, Sir."

"I'm glad. Focusing on my boots helped, didn't it?"

"Yes, Sir. They are beautiful boots."

"I'm quite fond of them. They were a birthday present from Erica."

"I was thinking about how much I would enjoy polishing them, Sir."

"Oh really? That is good to know. I might enjoy that myself."

Leah smiled.

"Kneel up for me, girl, and raise your arms."

She just did it, without even deciding to. That was the best, when her body just flowed into obedience like that. Sir lifted her burgundy velour dress off in one fluid movement. Then she unclasped her bra, and Leah was naked from the waist up. There was something about just being in her polka dot tights, panties and Docs that made her feel more vulnerable than if she were fully naked. She barely stopped herself from moving her arms to cover up, clenching her hands at her sides as she settled back into her regular kneeling position and reminded herself to breathe.

Sir just stood there, looking at her, like she had all the time in the world. Leah tried to focus on her boots again but her mind skittered away. Then Sir began to move, making a slow deliberate circle around Leah, taking her time, until she came to stand in the same spot as before. The silence was so much. She could hear every foot step Sir took. When she stopped, Leah could hear her own breath. Then, a hand came into view. Sir was offering her hand to help her to her feet.

She took it, and Sir led her to the bed, told her to sit and remove her boots and tights, and lay over the big pillow. It took a bit of adjustment to get her close enough to the side of the bed, but not right at it so she felt like she'd fall onto the floor. Leah helped Sir place towels to protect her kidneys and neck, so the safe zone to hit was a clear target. And then she waited. Sir just stood there, looking down at her. And then she said the most devastating thing.

"I'm going to give you what you need, girl."

The scene had barely even started, and Leah was crying. Not even quiet tears, but loud desperate sobs, and Sir just stood there, stroking her hair, her bare back, and began to use the flat of her hand to warm up her skin. Light slaps, methodical, careful, building heat at the surface, drawing blood there, until she felt the warmth seep into her, and calm her a bit. She buried her face into the pillow, sobbing quietly, as Sir began to use the quirt.

Light teasing strokes at first, making sure of her aim, Leah thought, but soon they were harder, and the pain began to wash into her, to fill her up in the aching empty places inside. As it did, the sobs dissipated, and soon the strokes were deeper, harder, exactly what she needed, and oh so methodical, moving across her back in this glorious zig zag line, so every bit of exposed skin was full of sensation. She groaned, and gripped the pillow tight, sinking into the dark deep blue of it, letting herself submerge completely, trusting in the abundance. It went on and on, this glorious intensity that wrapped her up and filled her at the same time. It seemed like it might keep her submerged for a wondrous forever.

Then the rhythm changed, became a swirling water spout, building up and up and floating into the sky with her at the center, until finally she was flung out into the dark purple of a zillion stars. She floated out there for a good long while, savoring how free she felt, how calm and certain and right. She slowly sank back into herself, and found that Sir was laying on top of her, stroking her arms and hair, and laying small light kisses on her back. She must have made a sound, because Sir slid off of her and wrapped Leah up in her arms in the most wonderful hug.

Leah stayed in Sir's arms a long time, just letting herself slowly come back. There was no rush. Sir just kept holding her, stroking her hair, telling her she was wonderful and brave and a joy to play with and such a very good girl. Eventually she said yes to the water Sir was offering, and sat up to drink it.

"Thank you," Leah said. "Just...thank you."

Sir nodded. "I'm glad to give you what you need, girl. I enjoyed doing that tremendously."

Leah's breath caught, because those words just worked their way inside, and she couldn't stop them. She didn't even want to stop them, they were clearly the truth. Jordan was glowing with satisfaction, so damn content it just radiated off of her.

She didn't get it. Nobody else had ever been into doing that for her. Giving her what she needed? Was that a kink unto itself? If it was...could Leah do that on a regular basis, just receive like that? What could a dominant possibly get out of it?

"You really enjoyed doing that? Even though it wasn't..."

"It wasn't what, girl?"

"I don't know. It didn't hurt. I wasn't focused on serving you. It wasn't sexy."

Jordan blinked at her, and took a slow breath before responding. "I don't need for any of those things to be part of our play, Leah."

"But…what did you get out of that?"

37

THURSDAY EVENING, DECEMBER 26

JORDAN

Jordan spoke slowly, really wanting Leah to take it in. "I got to be in control. I got to create those beautiful reactions, from the nerves to the tears to the satisfied groans. I got to be the one giving you what you needed. Caring for you. Tending to you."

"I get the control part, I definitely felt that. It was a certain kind of surrender."

"Oh yes. It was beautiful, how much you trusted me."

"But the other stuff, about caring for me and giving me what I need...that's part of dominance for you?"

"Oh my, yes. It's why I like the aftercare parts, and also...it meets a need I have, that's wrapped up in the kind of claiming D/s we did last time. If you're mine, part of that is getting to meet your needs, care for you, protect you."

"Oh."

"I feel really good, because I got to do that. I like caring for you as a friend, but this has a different quality to it. It's like there's a contented leopard curled up inside me, basking in the fact that I gave you what you needed, with one paw outstretched, keeping you in exactly this spot."

Leah smiled. "I'm glad you are pleased, Sir. Even if I don't really understand."

"Can you accept that it's true, even if you don't quite get how?"

Leah took a moment to breath, and nuzzled Jordan's hand before answering. "Yes, Sir. I can accept that it's true for you."

"Not just me. I talked to Ruth and Rebecca about it yesterday, and Ruth said she had a similar experience, after doing that kind of D/s with Rebecca, back at the beginning of their relationship."

"Oh. I guess there are always new things for me to learn, even about stuff I know well enough to teach."

Jordan stroked her cheek, and smiled. "I guess so."

She wrapped up the aftercare, got Leah situated for bed and made sure her phone was charging, and alarm set. Then Jordan went into the kitchen and started clearing everything up. It was grounding to do, and gave her some time to think.

First, she sung the Shehecheyanu quietly, letting herself sink into the reverence of it. She'd decided to wait, not sing it in front of Leah this time. She wasn't sure why it felt private, but it did, and she wanted to honor that. The whole scene had been a miracle, so deeply satisfying. She'd gotten to take care of Leah in an entirely new way, and it had satiated the part of her that had struggled so much the previous night because she wasn't able to care for her after her meltdown.

Leah's tears after she said she'd give her what she needed were something to think about, especially given all these questions she had now. It seemed like even with all her experience, she hadn't met a dominant who wanted to care for her in this way. Was that because she hadn't allowed them close enough to do that? Because that wasn't part of how their dominance worked? Because they were doing D/s in a way that wasn't about meeting the needs of all the people involved?

Jordan didn't think that Iris was like that. Maybe she wasn't playing with Leah regularly enough to even get that she might need something like this, or maybe she was too allistic to get how quirts worked for Leah. But what about Leah's other play partners? Were any of them taking care of Leah? Had Bev taken care of Leah?

All this time she'd thought that Leah was so experienced, knew exactly what she wanted and was getting everything she needed. But what if that wasn't true? What did her relationships actually look like? It was something to think about. Maybe even ask Leah about. If she could figure out how to word the question.

She had her first appointment with a kink friendly therapist, Tal, tomorrow. She took out her phone and made a list of the things she wanted to discuss. 1. Therapy style and type; 2. Experience and approach working with autistic clients; 3. Grief and why it's different this year; 4. Leah; 5. Meltdowns and negative thoughts; 6. Erica.

It was a long list. Especially for a first session with a new therapist. She needed to prioritize. 1 and 2 were essential. So if she could pick one more... it would be Leah. Well, that was clear. She had poured everything she had into her marriage, and almost disappeared. She wanted to do things differently this time. Wanted to build towards something with Leah that was more balanced, that fed them both, that gave them room to be themselves, that honored both of their needs and also made space for their other relationships. Getting a therapist would help. She was glad ze could see her tomorrow.

FRIDAY MORNING, DECEMBER 27

JORDAN

The therapist actually seemed like a decent fit, would be flexible about phone sessions if Jordan was flaring, and could fit her in around Jordan's work schedule. Plus ze was Jewish! There was something really comforting about hir bluntness. Once they'd gotten through the compatibility negotiations, Tal had explained that ze was going to focus on the present, and only visit the past where it came up in the context of that. And then ze had turned to Jordan and asked, "What's going on right now that made you decide to seek out therapy?"

So Jordan had launched into the story about the yartzeit and her meltdown and the conversations with Erica and Leah. But she hadn't stopped there, had gone on to talk about the way she had disappeared in her marriage and how she wanted to do relationships differently now, wanted to do her life differently now, and thought support might be good.

Tal asked her to do a bit of homework. Which was one of her favorite things about therapy, getting homework, and she'd told hir so. She was supposed to choose a current relationship, and make two lists: a list of what she wanted to give in the relationship and a list of what she wanted to receive. It wasn't supposed to be about what was happening now, but what she wanted for the future, what she wished for. Tal suggested that she try to keep the lists fairly balanced, and notice if that felt uncomfortable.

It was a really good assignment, she thought, and decided to buy a new journal, take herself out to lunch, and start working on it. Her phone said there was a stationary store just a few blocks away, so she made her way there and then spent a really wonderful twenty minutes browsing through notebooks and pens before making her selections. She also picked up some Chanukah wrapping paper, plus a journal and some stickers for Leah, to add to her Chanukah gift. It couldn't measure up to the kink lessons, of course, but it would do.

Jordan wandered a bit in Union Square park, taking some time to rest on a bench for a bit before going to lunch. She pulled up Twitter and saw she had a message from RJ. Perfect. Maybe ze was online and would message with her while she rested.

EnbyAceCupcake: So I know I said you could settle in after you got here but seriously, radio silence for this long makes me antsy. Anyway, am thinking of you.

PanStoneButch: Hey there. I'm here. I'm sorry for the radio silence. Things have been pretty intense since I got here.

EnbyAceCupcake: I mean, you warned me. I get it. Your dad's death anniversary, Chanukah, moving, your work party, it's a lot.

PanStoneButch: Yeah it is. But I miss messaging with you.

EnbyAceCupcake: Mutual, my friend. I'm seriously excited we live in the same place now, but really, no pressure on meatspace meet up, ok? A month from now, six months from now, whatever.

PanStoneButch: Thanks. I am going to be dealing with all this new peopling stuff and peopling is hard. I do want to meet up. But it's so much change at once, and I just...I kinda need something to stay the same right now, for a while.

EnbyAceCupcake: I get it. Really, I do. Peopling is really exhausting and change is overwhelmingly hard and winter is fucking awful. Staying the same right now sounds good. I could use some steadiness in my life too.

PanStoneButch: Thanks for getting it.

EnbyAceCupcake: So in the interests of staying the same, movie night soon?

PanStoneButch: Yes! I need to rewatch Brave, had this new fic idea and wanted to soak myself in the canon first.

EnbyAceCupcake: I'm in. You know that movie is my most favoritest of all the favorites.

PanStoneButch: Yeah, I did think you might be into it.

EnbyAceCupcake: *sings* I will ride, I will fly, chase the wind and touch the skyyyyyy

PanStoneButch: I love that song.

EnbyAceCupcake: Ok now I'm all full of Brave energy. Thank you.

PanStoneButch: Glad to help.

EnbyAceCupcake: How may I be of help in return?

PanStoneButch: Oh actually, can you hook me up with resources about gray aceness?

EnbyAceCupcake: Of course. Just general stuff or was there something specific you wanted to know about?

PanStoneButch: Well, anything on gray aceness and kink or gray aceness and sex and consent.

EnbyAceCupcake: Ok, I will see what I can dig out for you. Do I get to hear why you are wanting resources?

PanStoneButch: Yeah, but it's kinda a complex story and I don't know how to tell you without talking about sex and kink.

EnbyAceCupcake: Ok. So I want to hear, but I'm not up for that story today.

PanStoneButch: Sure, of course. Not today then.

EnbyAceCupcake: Thanks for getting it. And not just launching into the story.

PanStoneButch: No need to thank me for that.

EnbyAceCupcake: Ok. So listen I'm on lunch break at work and I need to go so I can wash my hands before going back to my desk. We'll pick this up later.

PanStoneButch: Yes. I'll look at my calendar and suggest a night for Brave.

EnbyAceCupcake: Good. *rides off with the wind in my hair*

Jordan headed to the diner that Leah had told her about. Diners were one of the things Jordan loved best about New York, the way you could park yourself in a booth and read, study, or journal, for as long as you wanted, as long as you ordered something. She had so many fond memories of diners from her college years, of all night study sessions and talking until the wee hours of the morning with Leah.

She went for chicken souvlaki and curly fries, a personal favorite. Then she settled in with her journal and her new pen. Leah had been trying to get her to give bullet journaling a shot, and she'd watched a couple videos, studied the basics. Thought she might as well try it. So she did the bujo set-up, but left the calendaring aspect for later on, because thinking about the New Year and starting at her new job would completely distract her. It took long enough to do the set up that her hand was tired from all that gripping, so she put the notebook aside for a bit and just sat, drinking her egg cream, thinking about therapy.

The office was accessible, in the getting there, the getting in the door, and the seating, so it was definitely ahead of the other referral she had, which had stairs to get into the building. Tal seemed like a good fit in a lot of ways, didn't get weird about no eye contact, was trans, queer, and kink savvy, and had this bluntness that was paired with a gentle compassion that really worked for her. The homework was a plus, too. She'd never have asked herself both of these questions at the same time, but they balanced each other really well.

Jordan drew a line splitting the page, labeled each side, and began brainstorming the lists. She started with the list of what she wanted to give in the relationship. That list flowed pretty well, and was a nice mix of things that felt like friendship intertwined with things she associated with being a romantic partner, a dominant or a sexual partner. Often there was overlap, and she wanted to give things that had more than one flavor to them. Her food arrived, and she switched to reading for a bit, starting a queer kink romance that Leah had recommended. The pacing of the story was lovely, felt luxuriously slow, and she could see why Leah had thought it might be good for her to read, the way the dominant took things slowly, and was so careful about closing scenes in plenty of time. In the world of the book it felt like there was no rush, no urgency, and that sense translated to her mood in a real, tangible way.

She ate slowly, and savored each bite, the tang of the tomato, the garlicky tzatziki, the crispy outer layer of the French fries, the burst of egg cream bubbles on her tongue. When she finished, she felt fed on a number of levels, and more herself than she had in a couple days. Jordan turned back to the assignment, and when she tried to make a list of things she wanted to receive in her relationship with Leah, she soon realized that she felt stuck there, like she couldn't imagine what might go on that list, what it would look like.

Somehow that stirred this well of grief that felt so deep she might drown in it, so she turned to a new page and tried to siphon it off. What emerged was this rage she'd never touched before. At her father, for shaping her to tend to him from early childhood, and then fucking deserting her when she finally was starting to live free of that and for herself. He was the one who left her to care for Erica, it was her or the state because there was nobody else and she wasn't going to even think about Erica going into foster care and what it would've been like if she had. That anger just rolled right along to her ex-wife who provided security but never made room for Jordan to be herself or have needs, taught her every day for years that she needed to push herself down, make herself disappear, mask, in order to be in a relationship.

Of course she couldn't imagine receiving anything in a relationship beyond security, and she didn't need that anymore, it didn't have to be a priority now. What else was there, though? What would it even look like to need things, to have those needs met? What could those needs even be?

39

FRIDAY MORNING, DECEMBER 27

LEAH

Leah finished making the flash cards just as her therapist called for their regular session. It was usually in person, but since it was a holiday and he was visiting family, Xavier had arranged a phone session for the last couple weeks of December. She was glad he'd agreed to keep their sessions going even during the holiday. The routine really helped. Even if it did mean she couldn't hide shit the way she had with her last therapist. Xavier had this way of cutting through things and witnessing what was really there, and then reflecting that back to her so she could hear it, with this mix of bluntness and caring that felt completely genuine. It was what she needed in her life.

Xavier was the reason Leah had finally faced up to being gray ace. She'd randomly lucked out when her old therapist had moved away. She'd needed a queer kink aware therapist who actually got polyamory, and who wouldn't wind up at the same play parties. Xavier was a gay trans leatherman who was gray ace himself, and had an aroace queerplatonic partner who was a well-known leatherman instrumental in the leather fundraiser for AIDS research that her shop donated items for every year. They lightly crossed circles, but not in a way that made for discomfort in therapy, and that was hard to come by for someone like her.

Now she had to face the music. She'd avoided talking about the kink lessons with Xavier in their last phone session, had talked about her mom instead, and trying to prevent meltdowns, and cancelling her date with Ellie to go dancing. But there was so much news now she didn't even know where to start. How could so much have happened in a week?

She started by saying she needed to give an outline of the news, and walked Xavier through the main events: not going to her mom's dinner party, kink lessons, trying out sexual play, running into her mother and having a meltdown, talking to Ellie. She ended up rambling for several minutes about the quirt scene yesterday, and the things Jordan had said, how hard it still was to understand what Jordan got out of it.

"I think I'm getting in my own way. I can't get my brain to make sense of this."

"Mmhmm," he said, again. Like that was any help.

"Got any ideas why this is so fucking hard for me to grok?" she shot out.

He delivered the blow with gentle devastating clarity. "Leah, your first dominant did you a tremendous disservice in how she introduced you to D/s, and it's shaped so much for you. I think it is making it hard for you to get what's going on, even though you really want to."

"And here I was blaming my mother," Leah said dryly.

"Well your mother may have laid the groundwork, but that relationship had a big impact on what you think D/s can look like for you, and what you assume about dominants in your life."

"I don't feel like I can speak ill of her."

"You've mentioned that. There's a blanket of silence around that relationship. You lifted that blanket with me, with Ellie, and with Jordan this week."

"I guess that's true."

"I know it's uncomfortable to shine light on this, to approach it without that assumption of silence. But I think the idea that you cannot speak ill of her has translated to you not being able to look at the impact of the relationship, and the trauma that it has created."

"It does feel like there's trauma. I recognize that, because it's been shaken up, the way the trauma with my mom has been shaken up."

"Yes, I'm not surprised at all that you had a meltdown, and have been dealing with trauma symptoms. It sounds like you've been managing, and even accepting support, which is a big step for you."

"I did do that, didn't I?"

"Yes, you did. You keep getting surprised by folks in your life, recently. All these good surprises."

"I don't like surprises."

"I know. That's partly why I am attempting to offer a potential narrative that explains what keeps on surprising you."

"Is that what you're doing?"

"I'm trying to."

"Okay, what is the narrative? Be blunt, because I'm missing it."

"Alright. What if Bev was wrong about what she taught you about D/s? What if the expectations she set were her expectations, based on her own needs and wants as a dominant, and not The One True Way to Be A Submissive?"

Leah blinked. Was it really that fucking simple? Had she bought the One True Way bullshit and not even realized it?

Xavier continued, the gentlest steamroller just wrecking her fucking world.

"There are a lot of dominants out there who don't demand sex or even want sexualized D/s. There are a lot of dominants out there who want to take care of their submissives and don't see their own vulnerabilities, gentleness, or kindness as a threat to their dominance. There are a lot of dominants out there who want layers of relationship along with sex and kink and genuinely want to know their submissive partners as complex people. There are a lot of dominants who won't reject submissives that set boundaries with them or tell them that they are a failure as a submissive if the submissive sets boundaries or expresses needs of their own. There are a lot of dominants who don't expect their autistic submissives to mask in order to be a proper submissive."

"You know I'll never remember everything you just said."

"I know. Would you like me to write it down and send it to you in an email?"

"Um. Yes, please."

"What was it like, to listen to me say it?"

"It was hard. Made me feel like a fool. Because I know this stuff...for other people. I've said it, put it in handouts. But I somehow swallowed this bullshit, and have believed it for years."

"You aren't a fool. You were young, and had trauma that made this stuff feel true. And you were a novice. Novice kinksters often imprint, like ducks, yknow? Their first important kinky relationship has a deep impact, for good, or bad. Often both. There were good things about what she taught you, too. It's not black and white."

"No, it's not. But I haven't let myself see anything but the good."

"Seeing it isn't the same as speaking about it in public. Telling me, or Jordan, or Ellie, or any of your other friends and partners isn't the same as speaking about it in public. It's not disloyal to talk to the folks you are close to, or to talk to your therapist. That's part of what we're here for."

"See, and I'd say that, too, if a submissive friend said she couldn't talk about her relationship or ex because it would be disloyal to the dominant."

"It's more difficult to believe it for yourself."

Yes. It really was. The rest of the phone session was lighter, though Xavier did mention that perhaps they could revisit her experiment around sex the next time they talked. He knew it was too much to try to discuss that today, too. This was definitely enough for her to chew on.

Twenty minutes after the session, he sent her the email he had promised. She printed it out, and folded it up into a star. Then she placed it on her altar, choosing stones to anchor it. She would contemplate it later. Right now, she needed a nap.

40

FRIDAY AFTERNOON, DECEMBER 27

JORDAN

Jordan was meeting Shiloh at an ice cream shop right by the subway, so she just needed to go west a couple blocks and catch the local. She wasn't sure whether this was a date or not, but ice cream was always a good thing, and if it turned out to be a date, she could go with that. Shiloh seemed pretty great, and had Leah's thumbs up, so what did she have to lose, really? Plus, she had to know whether the Big Gay Ice Cream Shop lived up to its name.

It wasn't that big, but it sure seemed like the gayest thing ever, she thought as she crossed the street. Though Shiloh clearly matched it in sparkly gayness in zir leopard faux fur coat, slinky rainbow top and bright red corduroy pants. Ze had a huge smile for Jordan, and kissed her on both cheeks in hello. Ze had raved about the key lime pie sundae, so Jordan got that, but Shiloh got something called a Society Dame, which sounded amazing and aligned somehow with the way ze seemed almost like ze had burst in from a musical. Guys and Dolls, perhaps.

When Jordan said as much, Shiloh's laugh filled the shop, and ze checked zir watch, saying "Damn, it's not open yet. Let's go to the park instead."

Ze led her to this tiny sliver of park across the street that had benches. They sat right next to the gay pride statues to eat their ice cream, and Jordan was glad she'd bundled up. It wasn't super cold, but ice cream in winter outside still meant she needed a hat and a scarf.

"I was going to suggest we go to Marie's Crisis," Shiloh said, "Since you mentioned musicals. But it's not open yet."

"What is it?"

"A piano bar where they only play showtunes and everyone sings along." It was odd to watch zir eat the ice cream sandwich. Ze licked off the nonpareils coating the sides first, and it looked a bit like ze was eating pearls. It was distracting.

"Okay that sounds absolutely amazing, but I do need to get home by sundown, so not tonight."

"Another night, then," Shiloh said.

"Yes, I'd love that. Do they do Disney musicals?"

"Of course. Though some of the patrons are kinda snooty about them. They still sing along, though."

"I'm not ashamed of my love for Disney," Jordan proclaimed, daring Shiloh to judge her, as she tried her sundae. It was amazing, so perfectly tart.

"A fan, I see."

"I actually write queer fanfic."

"And would you be willing to share your fic with me?"

"Perhaps. Do you have some fic of your own to share?"

"Alas, I am more of a performance artist than a fic writer. But I'll get you a ticket to my upcoming show, if you want."

"Of course I want. Yes, that's a worthy exchange. I'll send you a link."

"Is it kinky?"

"Some of it. I can be sure to send that in particular if you want."

"Oh, I want. Do the kinks you write match the kinks you are into?"

Jordan took a big bite of the key lime pie sundae to give herself time to answer. But even after she was a bit stuck for words. "I...honestly don't really know yet. I'm too new to kink to be sure."

"Of course. I didn't mean to put you on the spot there. I'm so used to talking about it openly, pretty much anywhere."

"Yeah, I'm still finding my feet doing that."

"We don't need to talk kink right now. Unless you want to."

"I'm trying to sort something out that's kind of related."

"Oh? Feel free to ask me anything. I'll just tell you if I don't want to answer."

"Thanks. My new therapist asked me to make a list of the things I want to receive in a relationship, and I kinda don't know where to start, or what that could look like. I was hoping there might be a book or a blog post or something that would help."

"You mean, as a dominant?"

"Well, maybe? Ze meant more generally but that is one piece of it."

"Well. I can ask Gideon about a handout...I think he did one for a polyamory negotiation class. It might give you a place to start. But, I'm a switch. I can talk about what I like to receive as a dominant, if you want."

"Yeah, that would be great."

"Okay." Shiloh took a big bite of zir ice cream sandwich and sat for a moment, silent, before responding. "Well, I like receiving service, and I'm sexually receptive, so those are two easy ones."

Jordan pulled out her notebook and turned to a fresh page, writing "service?" and "blow jobs?". Shiloh smiled at her like she was being charming, and continued. "I give massages mostly, but I also receive them on occasion, and enjoy that with partners. Aftercare feels like a mutual give/receive thing for me in my play relationships."

"Yeah, I can see that. That might be one reason I got stuck, maybe a bunch of things I want to give are actually fairly mutual."

"That's definitely true for me, especially in relationships that include friendship, family, or romance. Stuff like emotional support, practical help, access intimacy, teaching and learning...those are all mutual."

"Yeahhh I think I got stuck. I'm more used to giving most of that, than I am receiving it. Though I'm not sure what access intimacy is."

"Oh, that does have a blog post, by the great Mia Mingus." Shiloh took out zir phone and after a minute, Jordan's phone pinged, presumably with the link. "It's basically about getting the other person's access needs, and supporting them in getting them met, but also just sitting with the awful reality of them not being met when that's what's going on."

"Oh, I definitely want to read about that."

"Okay, other things I want to receive in a relationship. I'm touchy feely, so I like receiving touch. I'm one of those people that if you bring me treats, or make me food, or even just remember my dietary restrictions or favorite restaurants, that feels especially good."

"Food is a great way to show caring, I definitely am with you on that. The thing you're describing about someone attending to what you need or what you like or the things that are important to you and the things you deeply dislike and want to avoid, that kind of caring attention...I've experienced that in a friendship context, and it's one of the best things ever. Is there a D/s version?"

"Oh yes," Shiloh said, as ze walked over to the trash can to dispose of the last few bites of the ice cream sandwich. When ze returned, ze continued. "It's often wrapped up in service, is sometimes called anticipatory service, when you receive that as a dominant. Where say you go to a party and the submissive will make you a plate that only has the things you love on it, and none of the things you dislike. Where they notice when your drink is getting empty and just refill it without you asking. Where they notice which outfits of theirs you especially enjoy, and wear those for you."

"Oh. That does sound very good. Like this sense that they are tethered to you by their own regard and attention, focused on you."

"That's a lovely way to describe it. There's a dominant version, too, of course. That's commonly shown in play and/or sexual activity, where you're attending to their reactions and using them to shape a scene that's about giving them exactly what they love the most, or need the most. Perhaps as a reward, perhaps because you choose to, want to."

"Ah, yes, that one feels very familiar to me, that's a central part of how my dominance works, probably because I'm a stone butch."

"See you do know some things about yourself as a dominant."

"Well, I've been taking lessons. Leah offered them, as a Chanukah present."

"That's a really great present. I'd love to hear about those lessons, if you want to tell me." Shiloh gave her a big grin, and then took out a hand mirror and began to refresh zir lipstick. The mirror said "There's No Wrong Way to Have a Body," and that sentiment made Jordan smile, and wonder where ze had gotten it.

"I would, but I don't want to shave it too close getting home. Maybe I'll send you an email. Or we could talk about them next time..."

"How about both?"

"I know it's maybe a betrayal of Disney but I've always believed in that Both is Good meme."

"Are you bi, then?"

"Pan, actually." Jordan said.

"Ah, yes. I'm one of those mythical non-binary folks who's actually bi. I bowed to pressure to use pan for a while, but then I said fuck it, and went back to bi." Ze lowered zir voice to a whisper. "We're said to not exist..."

Jordan laughed. "Well I'm a pansexual stone butch, pretty sure I'm not supposed to exist either!"

"Then we need to stick together, or in pride month we may disappear altogether!"

41

FRIDAY AFTERNOON, DECEMBER 27

LEAH

Time was all funky today (probably because her nap ate up so much of the afternoon), and Leah didn't even eat lunch until 3pm, which meant dinner was going to be later than usual and that would push everything later, and she couldn't find it within herself to care, except to worry that her food schedule would be all odd when it came to tonight's lesson and lighting the candles and that Jordan would want some kind of formal Shabbat Chanukah dinner at exactly the wrong time for her to eat. But it would be fine. Probably. What were they having for dinner anyway?

She'd pulled out her phone to text Jordan when she heard the door, and there she was, like Leah had produced her just by thinking of her. She was all flushed, her eyes were all sparkly, and when she pulled off her hat her hair fell in her face in that way that always made Leah want to touch it, and she just stood there in the kitchen doorway, eyes riveted on Leah like she wanted to devour her whole and pet her at the same time. Leah lost all words. It was like the kaleidoscope had turned, and she couldn't unsee Jordan as this really hot butch dominant that stole her breath and made her ache to serve. Leah blinked several times to see if the kaleidoscope might turn back and Jordan would be her best friend who she didn't think of that way most of the time, but instead it was like the Jordan that was her best friend melded with the Jordan that was her Sir and they were inextricable.

She just sat at the kitchen table and blinked up at Jordan, her mouth dry, her heart pounding, because she wasn't sure what to do with this, how to hold this new version of Jordan. Her hands started fluttering, and she looked down at her plate, which still had a bite of her sandwich, maybe she should try to eat that if her hand could be still enough for a moment. She was being all weird. She should say something. What the fuck was she supposed to do about this?

Jordan was quietly laying bags on the counter, and talking about how much she'd been craving falafel, so she'd stopped on her way home and gotten a few different things; they could pick and choose what they wanted for dinner. It would all keep, so they could eat whenever, though the zaatar bread was probably a bit better fresh, if she wanted some now. She turned and offered it, and Leah took a piece, putting it on her plate. She'd just drink some water before she tried talking.

The zaatar bread was amazing, the flavor danced in her mouth, and the texture was perfectly chewy. She grinned at Jordan and gave her two thumbs up. She still didn't feel like she could talk, so she stopped trying.

"No words right now, huh?"

She shook her head.

"Okay. No need for them," Jordan said, smiling at her.

Whoa that smile. It just wrecked her. She could feel the blush wash over her skin. Her hands had stopped fluttering, but the movement had taken over her leg now. That was okay, though, she remembered. She didn't need to try to mask that. Or the hand flutters, if they came back. In fact... Leah started off a rocking movement as she took another bite of the bread, and it felt really good, so she just sat, and ate, and rocked. Jordan was next to her, eating a piece of the bread too, and soon she was rocking, and humming Birdhouse. It felt like the most naked intimate thing to do with someone just then, and Leah could barely breathe. She was stimming with her dominant. She was stimming with her dominant. She was stimming with her dominant. And it was okay. It was more than okay, it was a way of connecting, of being close, of letting Jordan see her and know her, and for her to see and know Jordan in return.

Then it was too much, and she retreated to her room. She needed her weighted blanket, and hobbits on audiobook. She didn't need to figure anything out right now. It could wait. Right now, her world could narrow to familiar words and worlds and weight pressing into her and holding her safe.

Leah felt much more solid by the time Bilbo had left Gollum behind. She sat at her altar, and chose candles for needed change, protection, courage, clarity, and heart. She took several slow breaths, watching the flames dance, and picked up her favorite tiger's eye. She unfolded the star she'd made of Xavier's words, and read them to herself, slowly, willing each phrase to drop into herself like a stone in a pool of water, smoothly, deeply, with purpose and there to stay. She read the words aloud, listening to them as she did, taking them in, allowing herself to feel the way they unraveled things that had been strangling her.

Leah knew this wasn't going to fix it, that's not how things worked;

spirituality didn't do the emotional work for her, nor did it do the hard work of changing her thinking. But she also knew her will mattered, her intention mattered, drawing on the core magick inside of herself mattered. She'd made her peace long ago with the way that wiccan ritual fed her, bolstered her, and filled a space inside her that would go empty without it. She integrated it with the Jewish practices that felt good to her, but so much of Jewish religious practice was so trauma laden that she'd had to set it aside.

She'd tuck this tiger's eye into her pocket tonight, she decided, put it under her pillow while she slept. It was warm in her hand, felt almost happy. Leah folded the email back into a star, snuffed the candles, and placed the star in the center of her altar. A shower, she thought, and then she'd pick out something to wear that would knock Jordan's socks off.

42

FRIDAY EVENING, DECEMBER 27

JORDAN

Jordan knew it was best to let Leah come out when she was ready, and she wanted to wait to eat and light the candles until she did. She'd been out in the cold, and spending a lot of spoons being around people, so she took some time with a heating pad and watched one of her favorite Disney nature movies. The bear on the screen looked a bit like the winner of fat bear week this year, she realized, and looked over at the picture of Holly the fat bear queen that she'd posted over her desk. A ranger had said that Holly won because she had been single this summer and could devote all her energy to herself, and Jordan had made that her pinned tweet ever since. After her divorce, she'd decided to devote her energy to herself, and really consider what she wanted and needed out of life, and Holly was a great reminder to herself.

And yet, she'd gotten stuck even thinking about what she might want to receive in a relationship. Shiloh's ideas had made so much sense, but she had been stuck by herself. While she was thinking about it, she remembered that she'd promised to write to Shiloh about the kink lessons. Well, she had some time now, didn't she?

Shiloh,
So, this feels a bit like the letters I used to write Leah when my job sent me to conferences, where I'd talk about what I learned and what I was thinking about the con and how it might apply to my job. Except way more personal. Well, here goes.

The idea was 8 lessons, one for each night of Chanukah. Leah had me fill out this form about what I was into trying, which felt much easier in a lot of ways than when I'd seen similar forms, because I knew it would be okay if I thought I was into something and turned out not to be. It was like picking which workshops to go to at a conference. (I do a lot better when I pick things from a list than when I try to imagine possibilities on my own. That might be an autistic thing.)

Based on the form, she developed lessons, made handouts. We didn't decide on a schedule, went with a more flexible plan so we could pick what to do next based on what we're up for. The first lesson was about scene structure, and it was the most like school, except the kind of school I never had because it was geared to how I learn, with symbols to help me remember key points and an acronym to walk me through negotiation. Then came the practice. There's a lesson and then a practice scene, which is how I learn best.

Lesson one, I practiced leading negotiation, and then we did a short scene with a hairbrush, and then aftercare. The point was really the structure, doing each piece, being the one who led it all the way through. It was awesome. But then the next night I forgot to end the scene and do aftercare, we just fell asleep. So things got kinda wonky from that. It's such a basic thing, and I messed it up. I got back on the horse for the third lesson last night, though, and closed the scene, did aftercare.
So I bet you're wondering...if last night was the third lesson, why did it happen on the fifth night of Chanukah? We skipped the third and fourth nights. I woke up after that scene that wasn't closed with a huge pain flare that messed me up and led to major top drop. I just wasn't up for lessons or practice. And you know what happened on Christmas.

The second night was about a particular kind of D/s—feral, claiming, sexualized D/s—and hair-pulling. Biting was also supposed to be part of it but when she was teaching hair-pulling it put her into subspace, so we stopped the lesson and moved into practice. It was way more intense and scary and also really fucking cool to try that kind of sexualized D/s and pain play, it felt so different from the first lesson. In the first one, I was kind of stepped back watching myself, methodical. But this...I was deeply distracted by my own reactions and how they intertwined with her reactions and I kept needing to pause and take my time, be deliberate, because I wanted to rush forward and had these instincts to do things we hadn't negotiated and to move fast. So it was kinda like rushing forward and reining myself back, a dance between those things.

In all honesty, I don't have much experience with sex that engages my desire as deeply as that scene did. Mostly because I haven't had more than a handful of partners and they were all vanilla, and most weren't actually cool with me being stone, so I was pretty guarded during sex. This was new, and intense, and a bit sensorily overwhelming, and I'm very glad I didn't need to talk much. I'm sure I can do much talking during play, because my want feels so big in the moment it steals my words. Which I guess is good to know about myself. Though maybe it's too early to really know and more experimentation is needed.

I suspect all of that is why I forgot to close the scene or do aftercare, which means I need to be much more mindful until I build habits. Habits help me, a lot.

The third lesson was in using a quirt and it was a very different kind of play because it was completely non-sexual and focused on giving Leah what she needed, which felt really amazing to be able to do. I loved it. It felt like kink that really fed my stoneness, and this part of my dominance that's about protection, caring and claiming. Plus, it was physically satisfying to use a quirt, I liked the way the impact of it felt. I think it hit a sweet spot in my sensory needs, so I want to try other impact stuff.

Anyway, that's my report thus far, got another lesson tonight but I don't know in what yet...

Maybe we could hang out soon?

Jordan

Jordan was in the kitchen fixing herself a ginger lime fizzy drink when Leah emerged from her bedroom. She heard rather than saw her, and without turning around, asked if she wanted one. She did, so Jordan fixed it. When she turned, Jordan was glad she'd left the drink on the counter because she was certain she would've dropped it. As it was, she almost swallowed her tongue at the sight of Leah, who seemed to have stepped out of one of the crush-soaked summer dreams Jordan had as a teen that were set to the soundtrack of "Black Velvet". She was a Jewish Alannah Myles, wearing an outfit right out of the video where she'd been posing on the porch in her jeans, boots, chaps, and white button down shirt. Leah's hair was as big as any 80s icon, her lipstick dark, and she had a smirk on her lips like she knew exactly what the sight of her was doing to Jordan and she'd done it on purpose.

Damn, Jordan loved femmes. Leah was a spectacular gut punch in that outfit and even better, she knew it, and was posing in the doorway just for Jordan, like she was claiming Jordan in a way she hadn't before. Based on the way she strutted over to pick up her drink she had turned on the flirt to 500 watts, and it was all directed at Jordan. Mine, Jordan thought triumphantly, her dominance rising up to meet that strut head on. When a femme put on her fine feathers for you, she deserved every scrap of attention you could muster in her direction. Lesson? Couldn't they just play?

43

FRIDAY EVENING, DECEMBER 27

LEAH

Leah savored Jordan's reaction. She'd picked this outfit out just for her. It was one of her most powerhouse ensembles. Years ago Jordan had told Leah about her teen crush on Alannah Myles. So when Leah had gone down an 80s music video rabbit-hole the other day, she'd come up with the idea of dressing like her to please Jordan, and stored it in the back of her mind.

The outfit was a really good match for the lesson she'd chosen for today, as it put her in the center of her power, and would help her make the point that D/s wasn't about inherent submissiveness or dominance but the choice the people were making, and could be deliberately evoked with tools that had nothing to do with SM or service. This was one of the most important lessons to give newbies, especially novice dominants, as it helped cut off top disease before it really started forming, and helped dominants be able to carve out spaces where they could be vulnerable, have needs, not be in charge all the time.

Wearing this also helped her brave her way through flirting when it felt like it needed a nudge. She'd wanted to flirt, both as a femme and as a submissive. Wanted Jordan to feel wanted. She'd never set out to do that with Jordan before, and it meant something, was saying something. Something brave, about the possibilities between them.

She saw it register for Jordan, and let herself strut, the denim molded to her curves. She made her way into the living room with her drink, the chaps drawing attention to her gloriously fat ass, and put a bit of extra sway in her hips because she knew Jordan's eyes were on her. She set up the Chanukah candles, Jordan coming in close behind her, breath sliding across her neck. She took her time with the prayer so she could light all the candles before it was over, and slid into Rock of Ages immediately, leaning back into Jordan until their bodies met. They sang together as they looked at the candles, burning so bright, making the room glow.

Suddenly Leah was ravenous, and excited for shawarma and zaatar bread. She sat right next to Jordan on the couch, conscious of how their knees brushed against each other. Jordan told her about her new therapist giving her homework, and sitting in the park with Shiloh, eating key lime pie made into a sundae. She was full of energy and excited story and it was so nice to share a meal in the shine of candlelight and hear about her day. It fed something in Leah she didn't really have a name for. It felt so cozy and homey to talk about the food and Shiloh's outfit.

Leah found herself telling Jordan about her conversation with her own therapist, how it had shifted something for her. Jordan listened with her whole self, and it felt so good to have that kind of space held for her. She had no question in her mind that Jordan wanted to know everything Leah wanted to tell her, and it was surreal to know that about a dominant she wanted to submit to. The idea that Jordan wanted to see all of her, know all of her, cared deeply, liked her as a person…none of that was new, they were best friends. But the idea that a dominant felt that way…it didn't fit any of what she'd come to expect…or assume…about dominants in her life. This whole thing where Jordan the dom and Jordan her best friend were the same person was a lot.

She told Jordan about the flashcards she'd made for her, and her idea for tomorrow: she could be in service to Jordan at the party, as the practice part of the lesson on service. Part of that would be to attend to her socially, make sure she got help remembering before the party but also sitting at her feet ready to coach her if needed. It was her best idea for a lesson to match the event.

Jordan was into the idea, so they made a plan to do the lesson after breakfast and then negotiate what the service would look like. There was something about having that settled that made this twisting in her chest ease. She hadn't even noticed the twisting until it was gone, but its absence made it easier to eat.

When it was time for the lesson, Leah stood, and instead of posting an agenda on the wall, posted a blank piece of paper with the word agenda at the top. Then she asked Jordan whether she thought teaching was a dominant role.

"Yes, of course. It doesn't have to be, probably, but it generally is."

"So what's marking me as dominant right now?"

Jordan took a few minutes to think, then gestured to the blank agenda. "You know what the plan is, and I don't."

Leah noted that down on a different piece of chart paper she'd split down the middle, labeling one side "markers of dominance" and the other "markers of submission."

"What else marks me as dominant?"

"You're the authority on the subject, made the handout, and I don't know very much about it. That puts you in a position of power."

She noted that. "Anything else?"

"You're standing, and I'm sitting."

"Yup, that's another one. Let's riff off of that. Are there other dominant physical positions?"

"Sure. It's about having the high ground. So the dom could be standing over someone who's lying down. Or sitting up on a higher level like a stage or something. Or sitting on a chair while the other person doesn't get to use the furniture, sits or lays on the floor."

Leah praised those answers, and pointed out that the key with all of them was contrast. What other kinds of contrast could there be? They made a list, Leah adding things along with Jordan, until they had filled the paper. Then Leah talked about how any of these could be used to establish D/s or deepen a sense of D/s, and how they could be layered on top of each other.

They discussed the ways some were about control, and some were about privileges that folks had or didn't have, and how it felt to evoke hierarchy based on these things would depend on the people, on how loaded any of them might be, which was both individual but also something that potentially had oppression wrapped into it. That was why careful negotiation was a good thing, and being flexible about these things was very helpful.

She got a bit shaky when she said that, and Jordan asked about it. So Leah decided to be braver than she might even have been yesterday, and take it as an opportunity to give information about landmines.

"So, we're talking about D/s negotiations where any of these elements might be up for negotiation, but I'd be remiss if I didn't tell you that there are a large number of dominants who are very hardline about the expectations they have for submissives, and lay these things out more as decrees about what's expected from their submissive instead of as a thing that's flexible and can be altered depending on whether something might be loaded, triggering, unpleasant, or sensorily difficult."

"I see. I've seen that in fiction, but I thought it might be more about a fantasy than something folks do. But it sounds like a thing where either you agree to all or you don't get to be their submissive?"

"Yeah. It's a different kind of consent, sometimes called meta-consent. It's often top-down instead of collaboratively created by everyone involved."

"I wouldn't be comfortable doing that. It's not like a job where I write a job description."

"Ah well, for some folks it kinda is like that. You basically apply to be part of their household."

Jordan blinked at her for at least three minutes, then nodded. "I'm guessing that you've been in that sort of relationship?"

"Yes. My relationship with Bev was like that."

"Did you know there were other options, other ways to be a submissive, when you agreed to that?"

"No. No, I did not," Leah said, the words sour in her mouth.

Jordan nodded. "I'm sorry. That sounds like it could have gone some pretty bad places."

"Yeah, I realized recently that it's been fucking with my head all this time, in ways I hadn't really gotten."

Jordan nodded. "Do you want to tell me about that?"

"Well. I don't want to go into detail tonight. But the big picture is after that relationship was over, I decided to protect myself from being that vulnerable again. That's what my blue rose tattoo is about, a reminder to myself to not look for the moon in someone's eyes, you know, from the Pam Tillis song? I decided not to get close to a dom like that again, not to let myself need like that again, to keep things casual."

Jordan sat with that for a bit. Then she asked, her voice quietly neutral, "You blamed yourself for trusting her, for loving her, for needing her, and decided that was the problem?"

Those words…they got to the heart of the issue, didn't they?

"It felt like that was the problem. Some of that's probably my mother's fault."

"Blaming your mother is a good bet. She certainly deserves a fuckload of blame."

"You cursed!"

"Your mother deserves more than cursing, Leah."

"But you never fucking curse. I'm the foul-mouthed one. You don't use those words."

"I generally don't. Except when they're called for."

"Well okay then."

Jordan was gentle, but firm when she spoke again. "You're not actually to blame, Leah. Not for your mother's cruelty. Not for how Bev treated you, the choices she made that harmed you."

"I don't know how to characterize what happened with Bev, and I don't think she harmed me on purpose. I just know that I closed in to protect myself from it happening again. Because I couldn't give up kink, I just couldn't. I needed D/s. So I tried to find a way that felt safe enough."

"That makes a lot of sense. I just think it's important to say that you trusting someone, needing someone, loving someone in a relationship… that's not what caused you harm. Maybe it was a mismatch of needs and a clusterfuck of communication and nobody intended harm but harm was still done to you. That harm isn't your fault."

"Intellectually I get that. The rest of me…it's a harder thing. I'm working on it. I only recently got that this was still fucking me up, and that I internalized her idea of what a dominant expects as if all dominants would expect that. My therapist compared it to imprinting."

"Like birds?"

"Yeah, he said many people base their ideas about D/s on their first significant D/s relationship. It shapes them. That my relationship with Bev gave me a false idea of what D/s could look like for me."

"That makes sense. I'm probably doing that with you, you know."

Leah just sat with that for a few minutes, because it took her breath.

"I hope I'm not giving you a false idea of what D/s could look like," she finally managed to say.

"I don't think you are; I think you may teach it in a way that holds room for more possibilities than you were imprinted to believe in."

"You do keep on surprising me with how you see D/s and how you think it can look. It's part of what I was talking about when my therapist said that about imprinting. Because it felt like my head got stuck, and couldn't reconcile how you were as a dominant with what I thought D/s could be."

"Like what we were talking about yesterday, about how it feeds me as a dominant to care for you and give you what you need?"

"Yeah. Like that. Ellie surprised me, too. I think talking to my therapist helped me get unstuck. Plus I did a ritual this afternoon that I think helped too."

"Unstuck sounds good."

"Yeah. So, anyway, we got off track with the lesson and into processing. Wanna get back to the lesson?"

"Can I give you a hug first?"

Leah nodded. Jordan stood, and gathered her close, wrapping her in the warmest safest embrace that seemed filled with all the care and coziness in the universe. She just soaked it in, letting herself feel tender and tended to, like she maybe even could count on it, didn't need to be scared it might go away.

FRIDAY EVENING, DECEMBER 27

JORDAN

This hug felt different, made Jordan feel big and strong and so tender-hearted, like she was gathering Leah up and tending her wounds gently, like she was wrapping her in protection. The best part of it was the way Leah seemed to sink into it, to give herself to it, like the part of her that usually held something back had let go. There was new trust in it, and Jordan didn't think that trust came from anything she did, but more that Leah trusted herself more than she had, and it was rippling out.

She hoped she'd handled that okay. It was a lot of new information, and she'd take time to sift through it later, but right now wasn't about that. Right now she wanted to be in the moment with Leah. Part of that was about letting her pull on her teacher role again, because it would help her feel strong and safe, because it was what they'd intended for the evening, and because the lesson was actually really cool. So Jordan sat back down to listen some more.

"In my experience of lesbian culture, vanilla sex is often prized as mutual, and reciprocal," Leah began.

Jordan growled. "Yep. That's why folks often assume my stoneness is a problem."

"The assumption that good sex is reciprocal, that folks give and receive the same things and in equal measure, can be super intense and harmful."

"Don't I know it."

"With D/s, it can be fun to play with things being deliberately not reciprocal. Not just sex, of course, as D/s doesn't need to be sexual at all. Other things. Playing with that kind of difference can make D/s really charged. Especially if you draw attention to it, make it clear that it's deliberately hierarchical."

"Like kneeling."

"Yes, position is a fun one, especially when combined with things like a difference of access via touch. Where the dominant can touch the submissive and the submissive is not allowed to touch the dominant."

"Mmm, yes. That one is especially appealing as it solves a lot of what I worry about in intimate encounters with my stoneness."

"Yeah, this kind of thing can really work well for stone dominants. The hierarchy can create room to breathe and enjoy honoring your own needs and boundaries as a stone dom. Similarly, you could do something where the submissive is unclothed—partially or fully—and the dominant is fully clothed."

"So I can just integrate things that feel good to me into the hierarchy."

"Yes, as long as everyone agrees. Some submissives aren't comfortable with nudity, and couldn't tolerate it as a general expectation. Folks who are sensorily sensitive, who get cold easily, or who have dysphoria, for example. Some survivors have triggers around it, and some folks aren't comfortable with their bodies."

"Yeah, that makes sense. The sensory overwhelm seems like it could get really intense. You seem fairly comfortable unclothed but I bet not when you are sensitized."

"Yeah, I'm used to it. It's a common expectation and often safer for SM play. But I would never choose it again as an everyday thing."

Ah, this was probably one of the things Bev expected that Leah hadn't actually wanted. "I don't know why a dominant would want that as an everyday thing, anyway. I like seeing folks express themselves through their clothing. I definitely wouldn't want to miss out on an outfit like yours tonight."

Leah grinned at her. "I did select this ensemble for you especially, Sir. I thought it would please you."

"Oh you did very well indeed. It's like you stepped out of my teen fantasies."

Leah sang a few lines of Black Velvet for her, striking a pose. Damn she looked delicious. Then she stalked over to Jordan and knelt, asking Jordan to notice how it felt. The closest word she could come up with was right. She backed up and asked Jordan to stand, and notice how that felt. Intense, powerful. She lay on her belly on the floor, her cheek resting against Jordan's boot. Fucking sexy. She asked Jordan to place the sole of her boot on her cheek. Mine, like a ferocious yowl running through her. Then she asked Jordan to sit, and rest both her boots on her back, like she was a footstool. Uncomfortable. Itchy. She asked Jordan to sit like she usually would, and pulled herself up to sit just to her right, her back leaning against the couch. Right, again. Jordan couldn't resist petting

Leah's head, and was rewarded with a quiet groan. Then Leah stood, and walked back to where she'd been teaching.

"Yeah, I see what you mean about different positions having distinct feels," Jordan said.

"It may be that you have preferences, or that it feels different with each person," Leah said. "Let's try something else."

First, she unbuttoned the white shirt and tossed it onto a chair. She was wearing a plum tank top underneath, and her tattoos were glorious in the candlelight. Leah picked up some items and walked over to the couch, placing them down one by one. A collar. A leash. Wrist cuffs. A piece of chain you could use to link the cuffs together. They were clearly part of a set, and they looked beautiful, like they were perfect for Leah. The deep almost burgundy red would be gorgeous on her. Leah sat on the floor between Jordan's legs and lifted her hair.

"See what it feels like to put the collar on me," she said, her voice a bit hoarse.

Jordan took a moment just to run her fingers over the collar, imagine that it was her collar she was holding. Then she placed it around Leah's neck, buckling it. Her thumb caressed Leah's neck just above the collar, then she tucked it inside to be sure it wasn't too tight. That's what one of the books had said to do. Leah got up and knelt in front of her.

"Give it a moment to think about how that felt, what it feels like to look at it on me."

Right. It felt right. Leah looked stronger, more solid, more hers, with it on. Like she was confident. It had felt so good to put it on, was so satisfying to see her in it.

"Now attach the leash, see how that feels."

She attached it, slid her hand into the handle of it, and just held, noticing how energy thrummed along it between them, how connected they felt. Jordan had read this book, years ago. The heroine had gone to a masked party dressed as a tame bird, wearing a collar with a lead. The book described how once the lead was attached, the rest of the party had disappeared, all she felt was her dominant holding the lead, she could sense nothing else, remember nothing else. It was one of Jordan's favorite scenes in the book. She'd constructed so many fantasies around being the dominant holding the leash, had dreamed that scenario in a zillion different ways. Now, here she was with Leah on her leash, in her collar, and already she felt even more powerful, more deeply dominant, than she had in any of those fantasies.

She tugged at the leash, and Leah followed, going where Jordan pulled, using her hands to balance herself against the couch. It was the most delicious thing in the universe, and she didn't want it to stop. It took her breath, to see Leah move where she made her. She let the leash go slack and Leah returned to her original kneeling position, lifting her wrists in an offering gesture that needed no words. Jordan put the handle of the leash around her own wrist and buckled the wrist cuffs onto Leah, attaching them to each other by the chain. Leah's hands went into her lap, and this time when Jordan tugged her forward, she didn't brace herself, so Jordan was particularly careful, going slow, not tipping her too far off balance, just forward enough to rest her cheek on Jordan's knee. Once she was there, Jordan stroked her hair, tightening her grip on the leash and keeping her exactly where she wanted her. It was a miracle, this kind of control, this level of trust, and she marked it like she marked all the miracles she encountered, by singing the Shehechiyanu.

Then she released her grip on the leash, and guided Leah to kneel again. Leah's face was serene, and Jordan realized that yet again they had fallen into D/s dynamic in the middle of a lesson on D/s. This time, she asked if Leah could draw herself out of it, and Leah nodded, so she asked for Leah's wrists, and removed the cuffs, and then told her to lift her chin, and detached the leash. Then Jordan stood, and walked around Leah to unbuckle the collar. She stroked her neck, and went to the kitchen for water, telling Leah to sit, and drink, and see if she could draw herself out of subspace. Leah nodded, and Jordan saw the effort, and the shift, in her face.

"It seems that hands-on practice of D/s things isn't such a good approach mid-lesson," Leah murmured.

"A good thing to know. Is it meaningful that we move into D/s dynamic so easily and fluidly?"

"Well, it's not something that I've experienced since I was a hungry newbie. This isn't coming from hunger, it's something about us. We have spectacular D/s chemistry."

Jordan grinned. "And quite a foundation of trust. Maybe that's why we flow there."

"True, that foundation may be why."

"Was there more to the lesson?"

"Not much. Regarding the last bit with the gear, I was going to talk about bound/free and independent movement/directed movement, and symbols of dominance and submission, as other ways to evoke D/s. I got the sense that doing it gave you what you needed as far as that goes."

"Oh yes, in a lot of ways it's more clear from doing, especially as I was tuning in to my own responses, how it felt."

"So the last thing is to suggest you lead negotiation of a scene concentrating on a few, maybe three, of the elements we have discussed today, and build the scene from them. The idea is to try for a D/s scene that doesn't use SM or sex as a pathway, but plays with other aspects of dominance, control, and hierarchy."

"That sounds like a lot of fun. Do you need a break before we negotiate?"

"A bathroom break, yes. It's a different mindset, that'll help me shift gears."

Jordan nodded, and decided to take a few minutes in her room to ground and consider what she wanted from the scene tonight. When she returned, Leah was sitting on the couch. Perfect. She sat beside her.

"Which of these elements that we've discussed today are ones you want to do today?" Jordan asked.

"I've done pretty much all of them in the past. I'm open to you trying whichever you are especially into."

"Nope, that's not answering my question. Which do you want to do today? It's not about what you are willing to do, but what you want, or don't want. You can start with either thing."

Leah sighed. Took several slow breaths. "I don't want to get naked," she said, sounding a bit defiant.

"Alright. No clothes off today. And we already said no sex, and no SM."

"I don't want you to put your feet up on me like I was a footstool."

"I don't want that either." Jordan said clearly. She could see Leah's body relax slightly after she said that.

"I don't want to give you control over what I eat or whether I go to the bathroom."

"I don't want that either." Leah relaxed even more.

"I do want to give you control over other things, though. That can be fun."

"What other things?"

"Maybe I would need to ask permission before I talked?"

"That might be fun. You can make noises, if you want, but words you need to ask permission, unless I ask you a direct question. You can tap out to safeword. How does that sound?"

Leah ducked her head, smiling. "Good, Sir."

"What else do you want?"

"It feels weird to be sitting on the same level as you. I think being lower would be good."

"So, position is something that's a big one for us. We have already played with that some. We could do more. How would you feel about not moving from whatever position I tell you to take unless you get permission first?"

"I kind of instinctively do that anyway, it's ingrained at this point, in scene, because most dominants require it."

"Alright. Is there anything else you want?"

"Not especially."

"How would you feel about needing to keep your eyes lowered, or maybe focused on my boots?"

She actually blushed at that. "Yes, please."

"I'd also like to stick with I touch you, you don't touch me, which is something we set up from the beginning."

"Yes, of course."

"I'd like to put the collar back on, and use the leash, as well."

"I'd like that, too, Sir."

"Not the cuffs, just those for today, as part of directing your movements."

"Yes, Sir."

45

FRIDAY EVENING, DECEMBER 27

LEAH

Sir told her to kneel and Leah sunk into that, moving her gaze to the floor. She felt nervous all of a sudden. She hadn't played much with speech restrictions. If anything, dominants had insisted she talk at times when talking was near impossible. But now, she wasn't supposed to make words unless asked a direct question. What would it feel like? She liked calling Jordan Sir, liked reminding herself of the D/s every time she spoke. Now she had a different thing to pay attention to: not talking. Not looking away from Sir's boots.

"That's right, keep your eyes on my boots. You don't get to look at me, you aren't trying to anticipate me right now. You're trusting me to tell you how to please me."

Leah hadn't thought of that, of how much she focused on the face and body of her dominant to try to read what they wanted, to try to be pleasing. Her hands clenched. Sir's boots didn't tell her anything. All she had was what she could guess from sound, from the energy between them. She followed Sir's boots with her eyes as Jordan rose, and stood, on her left. Then the boots moved behind her, out of her view. Was she supposed to turn to watch them or stay in position? Both were standing orders but which was more important. She whimpered.

"Stay in position," Sir said. "Eyes on the floor if you cannot see my boots."

At least if she could see Sir's boots she had some connection. Now there was just what she could hear. Sir's motorcycle boots had a hard sole that tapped on the floor, and her ears focused on the sound, until it stopped, behind her.

"Lift your hair out of the way for me, girl," Sir said.

She stopped herself just before saying yes, Sir, and nodded, lifting her hair. The collar was still warm from her skin, and it felt so good, so right, to be wearing it again. Sir's thumb tested the tightness, and then her palm rested at the back of Leah's neck, just stayed there, lightly gripping her for a full minute before moving away. Even after it left, it was like the collar took up the charge, as if Sir had wrapped herself around Leah's neck, was holding her there.

"Let your hair go."

She did, and stayed oh so still as Sir lightly stroked her hand down it. She wouldn't lean into the caress, even though she wanted to. She wouldn't. Sir stepped away, removing her hand, and said, "I get to look my fill, and you aren't allowed to look at anything but the floor or my boots. Do you know how often I make myself look away from you? Not tonight. Tonight, my eyes will devour every inch of you, girl."

Sir's boots tapped on the floorboards as she slowly circled Leah, looking at her from every angle. She was fully dressed, and yet she felt vulnerable under Sir's gaze anyway. Not in a scary way, more like she couldn't hide.

"I can see you trembling. Do you like me looking at you, girl?"

She nodded, then shook her head. It was both. Sir chuckled. "A bit of both. Fair enough."

Sir's boots came into view and her eyes latched upon them, feeling better just to be looking at them. Sir leaned down and attached the leash to the collar.

"Hands and knees, girl. I want to try out this leash properly."

Oh. Leah had never been lead around on a leash before. She'd only been fantasizing about this for at least ten years, probably longer. Sir kept the leash in her left hand, using her cane with her right, so Leah got to the left to follow her. Sir waited for her to get in place, and then tugged on the leash, and it was as if her hand were on the back of Leah's neck, pushing her forward. She kept her eyes on Sir's boot, and followed, but she was perhaps a bit slow, or maybe Sir just liked tugging on the leash, because she got to feel it propelling her to follow for most of the way to Sir's bedroom. Sir had made sure there was a clear path, or maybe that wasn't even for this but was because Jordan needed it for herself, Leah should find that out later. Right now she just stopped when Sir stopped, at the foot of the bed.

She didn't really know what it looked like to be lower than her dominant when it came to bedroom furniture. It wasn't as clear. Where was her place? She whimpered, and then remembered that she was supposed to be where Sir told her to be. So she just needed to wait, and then she would know. She wasn't used to that. Sir stroked her hair, then tugged the leash so Leah's head was leaning against her leg, just above where her boot stopped.

"Just rest there for a moment, girl."

Waiting for orders was hard. Not being able to see what Sir was doing, just hearing rustling, made her nervous. She stared at Sir's boots, and tried to sink into hyperfocus, but this position wasn't comfortable on the hard floor, and Sir wasn't even still. How could she find a quiet place in herself if Sir wasn't still or quiet or touching her or telling her to do something? Did she even have quiet places in herself these days?

Sir moved away from her, the leash was slack, but out of the corner of her eye she could see that Jordan was sitting on the edge of the bed. Leah stayed where she was, trying to settle, her eyes on Sir's boots. It wasn't even a foot of distance but she felt so far away. She tried to sense Sir through the leash, their one point of connection, but there was a rushing in her ears and she couldn't, she just shook her head over and over trying to shake it off. Sir was saying something but she couldn't hear it, and then there was a tug on the leash, so she followed it. She was being tugged closer and closer, and then, down? The leash made it clear that she should rest her cheek on Sir's boot. The leather was cool, but Sir was radiating this warmth that seemed to surround her the second she touched her cheek to Sir's boot. Sir's hand was on her ass, pushing her towards the floor, and she realized what was wanted.

Lying on the floor at Sir's feet, her cheek resting on Sir's boot, helped her find calm again. She breathed, slow and even, taking in the scent of the leather. Her hands were clutching at the floor because she wanted so much to wrap her arms around Sir's boot but she wasn't sure she was allowed to. She ached to do it, though. So much that she felt tears rolling down her cheeks, a rawness in her throat.

"What do your hands want to do, girl?"

She was supposed to talk now. "May I wrap my arms around your boot, Sir?"

"Yes, girl, hold onto me as tight as you need to."

She did it instantly, squeezing her eyes shut as she held on with everything she had. Reassuring herself that she wasn't left alone, that Sir was there. She'd been panicking, hyperventilating, she realized. That's why there had been rushing in her ears. She could feel her heartbeat slowing, the warmth of Sir right there.

"I need you closer to me, girl. I'm going to sit on the bed, and I want you with me. Kneel up for me."

Letting go of Sir's boot was hard. So was kneeling. But she did it, her eyes on Sir's boots as Jordan got onto the bed, her legs out stretched, knees elevated on pillows.

"Get on the bed on your hands and knees."

She did that, the leash stretched tight. Sir tugged it, guiding her to a position that felt intensely intimate. She was sprawled on her side, her face buried in Sir's thigh, her head sharing the pillow with Sir's knee, one arm wrapped around Sir's calf, the other hand touching Sir's boot.

"Yes, this is where I want you to be," Sir said, her voice full of pleasure. She played with Leah's hair, winding curls around her fingers absently, humming with pleasure. Then she began to read aloud. The prose style was familiar, but it took Leah a bit to place it. Oh...it was from one of her most favorite kinky books, with a queer sacred masochist sex worker main character...who was also a spy. Sir was reading from the scene that had the leash, though she hadn't gotten to that part yet. Leah smiled and nuzzled Sir's leg, letting herself float on the words. Sir was right, this was her place, she felt safe and cared for and deeply submissive, like she could let go completely and it would be okay, because Sir was in charge. A very good place to be.

46

SATURDAY MORNING, DECEMBER 28

JORDAN

Last night's scene had felt like a balm, had left Jordan all cozy and content like a cat who'd gotten all the petting she'd wanted and now was just interested in a nap in a sun spot. She felt languid, sated, and even though she was going to a party that night, she was looking forward to it because Leah would be there, would be in service to her there. She had leftover falafel, baba ghanoush, and pita for breakfast, and the textures made her mouth really happy. She decided to reread the Jacqueline Carey book she'd read aloud last night, but from the beginning, and the familiar prose made her feel like she was wrapped in a warm blanket. Leah wandered into the kitchen and quietly set about making herself oatmeal, and she enjoyed just being there with her, imagining a long line of cozy domestic moments sharing space in the kitchen and languid kisses and D/s and occasional sex when their desires happened to align. She filled with this want for all of it, from the telling the story of her day to the feel of Leah in her collar under her hand, the friendship, the love, the living together, the claiming of Leah as hers to keep. Laughing with Shiloh, Ellie and Leah at the piano bar on a double date, Erica bringing her family to visit, proudly watching Leah as she got ready for a date with someone and put on her fine feathers, a future that perhaps included more private lessons from Leah, having Leah in service to her as she played with a new partner at a party, watching Leah and Iris dance, a Pesach feast surrounded by partners and friends and chosen family.

She hadn't ever let herself want this much, to imagine the life that would make her happy and cup that desire in her hands, shielding it, letting it glow and grow inside her. She wanted it all, and refused to try to tamp her want down, to only imagine what seemed likely to happen, to self-reject before she even tried to go for what she wanted.

"What are you thinking about?" Leah asked. "You have this odd smile on your face."

"Just dreaming." She started humming "A Dream is a Wish Your Heart Makes," and stood, offering her hand to Leah with a bow. Leah giggled, and Jordan began to sing as she drew her into a very slow waltz, enjoying the feel of holding her as she twirled them in slow circles. She had to go at half pace, couldn't do the fancy stuff like Iris, but she knew enough of the basics that she could dance with Leah if the occasion called for it. Leah grinned up at her as the song came to a close, and Jordan twirled her out, and brought her back, a bit breathless.

She leaned in, waiting to see if Leah would meet her the rest of the way. For a moment Leah just blinked, and then she seemed to understand, and lifted her lips to touch Jordan's in a whisper light kiss. Jordan drew her closer, holding the kiss, one hand stroking the nape of her neck, while the other held her firmly at center of her back. Leah's body seemed to melt, her mouth opening, and Jordan took that as an invitation to deepen the kiss. Their first kiss outside of scene, and she didn't want to push, but she also wanted to show Leah that she wanted her. Her hands were firm and still, her tongue sliding into Leah's mouth, savoring the taste of her for just a few moments, before lifting her lips, and smiling. "Good morning," she said.

"Good morning," Leah responded, sounding a bit dazed. Jordan released her, stepping back, and sat down again at the kitchen table, taking a slow sip of juice before asking, "How are you feeling after our scene yesterday?"

Leah didn't respond right away. She shook her head, then took her bowl to the sink and filled it to soak. She grabbed an orange and began to peel it, slowly.

"I wasn't anticipating going that deep into subspace," she said. "My neck feels...naked, now."

Jordan nodded. "Has that happened before?"

"Not since Bev removed her collar. But that was very different. I had this bondage set custom made for myself. It feels more like it's mine, usually. Like it's about my identity as a submissive, instead of belonging to someone, being claimed by someone."

"It felt different last night?"

"Yeah. It felt like I was yours, and the collar and leash were a symbol of that belonging."

"And your neck feels naked, now?"

"Like something is missing. We seem to go so deep, every time, almost right away."

"Yes, that's my experience of it, too. I don't know if it helps to know this, Leah...but I did think of the collar and leash as being about you belonging to me, when I put them on."

"Oh. What does that mean, to belong to you?"

"That's a very good question. One I wish that I had a clear answer for. I can tell you how it feels?"

"Yes, how does it feel?"

"It feels like...you know how cats mark you, claim you? You are their human now?"

Leah chuckled. "Yes. You feel like a cat?"

"Well, like a big cat, a very big cat."

"Uh huh. That feral play thing really resonated."

"Yes. It feels like...I've claimed you. You are mine. You belong to me. I'm keeping you."

"Oh." Leah looked uncertain.

"Not in an exclusive way. I'm not saying anything about monogamy. I don't think I could do monogamy again, ever. But yeah. Mine to protect. Mine to keep. Mine to care for."

Jordan thought about bringing up the romance part, too. It felt dishonest not to include it, so she tried to find the words. "It's not sexual, though it can be when we are playing that way, but that part can ebb and flow and isn't an essential thread. It does feel...romantic. Like, it's wrapped up with that, and I'm not sure I can imagine it without the romance part. They feel woven together for me."

"Oh I, Jordan we never talked about romance, I've been avoiding romance for a long time."

"We never talked about it, true. I know you've been avoiding it. Are you open to romance being part of what we are building together?"

"Building together?"

"Yes. It feels like we're building something, to me. A relationship of some sort. I maybe don't have the right words. But yes, it feels to me like we already have a relationship—we're best friends—and we're reworking that, reweaving it so there are other pieces of it as well as friendship."

Leah blinked at her, not saying anything.

"Maybe I'm not saying it right," Jordan said, because the silence was too hard to bear. "I don't want to make you uncomfortable. I'm just trying to be open about how I feel, what I think is happening."

Leah shook her head, and opened her mouth, but she seemed to be stuck, like she couldn't make words. Jordan's heart sank. Oy. She shouldn't have said anything. She'd pushed. She needed to back off now before she made it worse.

"It seems like you aren't able to make words right now," Jordan said.

Leah nodded.

"That's okay. You don't need to try to push that. It's okay to not be up for making words. Is there anything I can do?"

Leah shook her head, and then she got up and left the room. Jordan's eyes followed her for as long as they could. She went into her room. When she closed the door, Jordan flinched. Then she heard the sound of the lock, and it felt like a body blow.

Well that hadn't gone well at all, had it? Jordan took a ragged breath, her hands itching to do something. She stood, and focused on cleaning up her breakfast stuff, but it was like someone else's hands were doing it, far away.

What in the world was she going to do now?

47

SATURDAY MORNING, DECEMBER 28

LEAH

Sometimes when Leah went non-verbal it felt like she could communicate, just not with words from her mouth parts. She could at least shake her head yes or no or write out answers to simple questions, even if she couldn't make words about the thing that had led her to shut down. Sometimes it felt more like her whole brain almost powered off, like the stuckness she'd get sometimes where she couldn't think her way around something or figure something out, except it was like everything was shut down. At those times, the only thing to do was to get somewhere safe, and rest. Stimming sometimes helped.

She got herself to her room. That was safe. She locked the door. Safer. She got into bed and under her weighted blanket. Her brain was all swirly and frantic. She tried rocking, but it didn't slow it down. She didn't feel safe. She felt the opposite of safe. Her breathing was all funny. She screwed her eyes closed tight and hugged herself into a tiny ball and still didn't feel safe. She wasn't safe. She wasn't safe. She wasn't safe. What would make her safe? If she was a hobbit she'd be safe. She ran the words through her head, saying them slow to herself, as if she was detangling rope, the rope of words running through her fingers: "In a hole in the ground there lived a hobbit. Not a nasty, dirty, wet hole, filled with the ends of worms and an oozy smell, nor yet a dry, bare, sandy hole with nothing in it to sit down on or to eat; it was a hobbit-hole, and that means comfort." She kept going, the words worn and familiar like a favorite flannel shirt, soft and cozy and meandering, holding each in her hands before going to the next on the chain, pausing for a bit when she got to "you will see whether he gained anything in the end." Then she began again, from the beginning. The beginning was the very best part, the safest part, when we hadn't even really met Bilbo yet, mostly just his hobbit hole.

She ran through the words, rocking as she did, until it felt less necessary to curl up that tiny or screw her eyes that tightly shut, until the rocking itself felt less frantic. Until she wanted more of the story. Because it was nice to be in a safe cozy hobbit hole, it felt good and comforting and she needed that, but at some point she wanted Bilbo to go on an adventure, to learn that he was worth more than he thought, that he had more bravery in him than he knew, that people cared for him and valued him and saw him as more than perhaps he saw himself. You couldn't stay home safe in your hobbit hole all the time.

Right now, she wanted him to go on an adventure, so she restarted the audiobook from the beginning, reciting the first few paragraphs along with it just to try words in her mouth. They felt clumsy and odd, so she closed her mouth, curled up hugging a pillow, and just listened.

She must have fallen asleep while she was listening because when she woke, Bilbo was freeing the dwarves from captivity by shutting them into barrels, and she'd completely missed the riddles with Gollum and a whole lot more besides. She turned off the audiobook, and decided to try texting someone, to see if she could make words. She scrolled through her contacts, unsure of who to text, and somehow landed on Ernest. Was it weird to text him when they weren't really that close? He'd just been so nice to her, and she wanted to text someone who would be nice, and not assume things.

Leah: Hey, do you have a few min?

Ernest: Absolutely. Are you ok?

Leah: I am coming out of a meltdown. Maybe a shutdown is the better word.

Ernest: Are you in a safe place?

Leah: Yeah, I'm at home.

Ernest: Ok. How can I help?

Leah: I think I messed things up with my shutdown.

Ernest: What makes you think you messed things up?

Leah: Jordan's face. She looked like I'd kicked her in the gut.

Ernest: By shutting down?

Leah: By going non-verbal when we were talking about us.

Ernest: *nods* It's ok to go non-verbal. It happens.

Leah: Yeah, she was nice about it, said that.

Ernest: Then maybe you didn't mess things up. It's not like you did it on purpose.

Leah: True.

Ernest: I can't always catch that I'm overwhelmed until it's already gone too far. Most autistic people can't. I doubt she expects you to.

Leah: But. She looked so hurt.

Ernest: *nods* Can I ask more about what happened in the conversation? Do you remember?

Leah: I may not remember the whole thing. I remember a bunch. But I'm a little nervous that talking about it might make me shut down again.

Ernest: That makes sense. Do you want to try? It's ok to say no.

Leah: Um.
Leah: Let me think.
Leah: So basically. Jordan and I are best friends. And housemates right now. And then we started doing this sort of kink teaching thing, because she's a novice dominant and wanted to learn. I gave her 8 lessons for Chanukah.

Ernest: *nods*

Leah: Today, she asked how I was doing after yesterday when we did a lesson about D/s and a practice scene. Like a check-in.

Ernest: Good. Check-ins are a good thing.

Leah: So I told her that my neck felt naked without the collar. That the collar had felt like I belonged to her, and it was hard not having it after the scene was over.

Ernest: Makes sense. I know the feeling.

Leah: Then she said how it felt like I *did* belong to her, in a D/s way. That I was hers, and she was going to keep me.

Ernest: *nods*

Leah: And when I asked her to tell me what that meant, she started talking about cats scent marking, and belonging, and how it felt like we were building something, in addition to our friendship and being housemates. That we were building a D/s relationship, and a romantic one, that the sex part wasn't woven in but kinda ebbed and flowed but the romance felt intertwined with the D/s.

Ernest: *nods*

Leah: She was very polite and tentative, it wasn't like she was telling me how it was, she was just…telling me what she felt. It wasn't like those things where you have one date and they are UHauling, or the kink version of that.

Ernest: How long have you been friends?

Leah: Almost 30 years. Our whole adult lives, since college.

Ernest: Ok. What made you go non-verbal, do you think?

Leah: She said we were building a D/s relationship. And a romantic relationship. That she had romantic feelings. That she wanted me to belong to her, that she wanted to protect me and keep me and care for me.

Ernest: Ok. It sounds like that is a scary idea, that she wants those things, and has those feelings about you.

Leah: Um. Yeah.

Ernest: What makes it scary?

Well wasn't that the question. Did she even know the answer? Was the answer even about Jordan at all? Or just about the idea that anyone wanted that with her? Or that she could have that with Jordan, if she just met her halfway and said she wanted it.

Leah: I don't know.

Leah: I think it might be about my issues from my first dominant. Maybe. Signs point in that direction.

Ernest: First doms can mess you up, if they aren't a good fit. Or if they're assholes.

Leah: Yuppp.

Ernest: I don't think you need to know why you got scared. Or even to know what you want, right now. You can ask for time to figure those things out.

Leah: I can?

Ernest: Yeah, of course you can. You get to go at your pace. It doesn't have to match hers, even though she's a dominant. Your needs and your pace matter.

Leah: Oh. I might ask you to remind me of that again.
Ernest: Glad to do it. Right now, it sounds like it might help to tell her that you got scared and that the r words (relationship and romance, not the terrible slur) freak you out. And ask for time to figure out what you want and what got you scared. Also maybe to acknowledge that you think your shutdown might have hurt her feelings, that she was being brave telling you that and you wish that you had been able to hold it. I don't think you need to apologize for shutting down or going non-verbal, but acknowledging that it happened at a shitty time and inadvertently hurt her is a kind thing to do, if that makes sense?

Leah: Yeah. I gave her shit for apologizing for a meltdown, I def don't want to apologize for shutting down, but this is a good script for acknowledging the hurt. And the other pieces too. Thanks.

Ernest: Sure. Glad to help. Do you think you'll be up for the party tonight?

Leah: We'd planned to go with me in service to her. I need to think about whether I'm up for that.

Ernest: Yeah, makes sense. If you want it, I have a hug for you if I see you. But please don't feel pressured. Your well-being is important and parties can be a lot after a shut down.

Leah: I'll let you know, either way. Thanks for talking to me about this,

Ernest. I appreciate it.

Ernest: *smiles* I'm glad to do it. Sometimes I know I just need to talk to another autistic kinky person because other folks won't get it.

Leah: Yeah. I know a couple other autistic kinky people, but they're dominants.

Ernest: Well, I'm glad to be your autistic submissive friend. I like you.

Leah: I like you too, Ernest. Let's make a plan to hang out after the new year, ok?

Ernest: Definitely.

So she had a new friend, maybe. Or the beginnings of a new friendship anyway. That was a good thing. Now she needed to DM Jordan. She drafted it first. Careful was better. It took her a good twenty minutes to come up with the best words she could.

LeahBlumensteinNYC: I'm guessing that you might be worried about me. I'm ok now. I shut down, and went non-verbal, because I got triggered, and scared. I don't know all of the why yet, I'm hoping my therapist can help with that. I think that hearing you talk about a relationship and romance with me is what had me shutting down. I'm guessing that me shutting down in that moment hurt your feelings, especially because it was a time when you were being brave and telling me how you felt. I wish that I had been able to hold it better.

Leah sent the DM, not expecting a reply right away. She wasn't even sure if Jordan checked her Twitter that often, but she wanted to continue communication in the last place they had talked about things via text. Then she went to YouTube and pulled up the video Rena had suggested when she'd asked Twitter for recommendations of soothing music.

The voice was all lilting and soft, and the ukulele was a barely present accompaniment, but the striking thing was the words. The idea that everything stays. It was such a comforting idea. Things stay, even though they might change, but the things you leave behind stick around and are there waiting for you to pick them up again. They might not be the same, might fade or change with time, but they are still there. Kind of like Bilbo's hobbit hole, how it's there for him to return to, but different, and he's different in it. Like her friendship with Jordan, which had stayed and stayed and stayed throughout so much change, it was still there, and would still be there, even if it changed. It was a very comforting thought.

Leah walked over to the mirror, and looked at her blue rose tattoo, tracing her fingers over it, noting the places where it had faded a bit in the sun, the places where scars and wrinkles interrupted it, her skin changed so the tattoo changed with it. She had put so much intent into the tattoo, it was supposed to be like a protection spell, the thorns digging in to remind her not to make the same mistake again, not to look for the moon in someone's eyes. But was that even the actual mistake that had been made? Was she the one who had made the mistake? She felt like her certainty in that had been substantially shaken, and she was still trying to find solid ground to stand on, still trying to sort through the rubble to see what was real.

She sent a quick email to her therapist requesting an emergency call, something she basically never did but he'd been the one to fucking shatter this belief she'd held for over twenty years, so he was the one who needed to help her deal with all this destruction. Xavier responded pretty much immediately, saying that he'd call in an hour. She could wait an hour. Maybe have some lunch or something.

She was contemplating what to have for lunch when she heard the ping that was her Twitter notification. Maybe Jordan had responded?

PanStoneButch: Thanks for reaching out. I'm glad you're ok. I was worried about you. Do you need anything? I'm making myself lunch, can make you some too, if you want?

LeahBlumensteinNYC: I am hungry. What are you making?

PanStoneButch: I wanted a high tea kind of thing so I baked a Victoria's sandwich and made tuna sandwiches, lox and cream cheese sandwiches, and cucumber sandwiches.

LeahBlumensteinNYC: So basically a whole lot of tiny sandwiches? And a sandwich cake?

PanStoneButch: And tea, of course.

LeahBlumensteinNYC: Of course! That sounds amazing.

PanStoneButch: Sometimes you need to manifest the things you want.

LeahBlumensteinNYC: Yes, sometimes that's exactly what you need to do.

PanStoneButch: It's ok to just come eat, you know. No talking required.

LeahBlumensteinNYC: Thanks. I don't think I can talk about what we discussed this morning right now. I'm going to need to take some time before I can respond to what you told me. But I can make words now. Maybe we can talk about the party tonight.

PanStoneButch: Ok.

LeahBlumensteinNYC: I'm gonna take a shower, then I'll be out there.

48

SATURDAY AFTERNOON, DECEMBER 28

JORDAN

She needed time. Time was possible. Jordan had probably jumped the fences anyway, or whatever that metaphor was. Gone too fast, been pushy. If she needed time, she wasn't saying no, or yes, or anything. She was waiting to respond. Waiting was okay. Waiting was better than no.

Jordan arranged the sandwiches on the plate, adjusting them so they fanned out in a pattern. The cake was waiting on the counter. But she could get the tea ready. She put the kettle on to boil. She'd love to have a tea tray or one of those serving things with levels. It was early for afternoon tea, but it was the fiddliest food thing she could think of and she'd had to do something, had to focus on something. She hadn't wanted to leave the kitchen. Like if she'd stayed there Leah would come back and they could undo what had been done. Or something.

It couldn't be undone but it could be set aside, for now. What would that look like? What did Jordan want that to look like? Did she want to continue the lessons with this up in the air? Did she want to follow through with their plans for today, the preparation for the party, the lesson, the service at the party? What would that even be like? Could she do that and keep how she felt in her pocket? Could she stand the idea of not doing it?

Jordan tried to picture what it might be like to go to the party with Leah in service to her. She'd be sitting most of the time, Leah at her feet. Leah would fix her a plate, make sure her drink was refreshed, attend to her that way. Leah would do the thing that Anne Hathaway does at the party for her boss in Devil Wears Prada, making sure that Jordan knew who the people were that she was meeting and interacting with, knew their pronouns and something about them, where they fit in the constellation of relationships at the party. She'd be a buffer, would ease Jordan's way, in a different way than how she acted as a friend, and people would think of Jordan as belonging with her, as her dominant, her date for the party, would meet her that way with all the social things that came with that.

The idea of it ached, because she wanted it so much, and because it wouldn't be real in the way she wanted it to be. It would be for the night, and then maybe they wouldn't end up doing D/s for much longer, or at all. She couldn't be there proudly, her submissive in service to her, because Leah wasn't really her submissive. Not now, not yet, maybe not ever, except for a scene or two for practice.

The whole point of all of this was to honor what she wanted. This would feel a lot like betraying what she wanted, pretending she didn't want it. She'd had enough of that in her marriage. Well, that clarified things, didn't it? She wasn't really in a party mood anyway. Maybe she'd go swimming. Call Erica. See if Iris wanted to get dinner or something.

Leah did look less freaked out when she sat at the table, offering Jordan a small smile when she saw that Jordan had set out her favorite mug, which was bright pink and said Settle In, Babies. Jordan poured herself some tea, and decided to start with one of each kind of sandwich.

"You know, some folks in kink community do tea service," Leah ventured tentatively.

"Oh yeah?"

"Yeah, it's big with sissy maids, they have tea parties where they serve their mistresses. It's usually tea like this, except with those fancy tiered plate things and fancy china. It's not just sissy maids, of course. Ellie told me that Ernest does it, both for friends, and for one of his dominants, Nora."

"So it's tea like this but with a service component? Where the submissive makes everything and serves it?"

"Yup."

"Huh. I'll think on that."

"I can introduce you to Ernest tonight if you want to ask him about it."

"Ah, thanks for offering. I've decided to pass on the party tonight."

"Oh. Okay. Does that mean you want to cancel our lesson for today, then?"

"Yeah, I think that would be best."

"Oh. I. Okay. And tomorrow night? It's the last night of Chanukah."

"That's right, it is. I have presents for you. That's when I was going to give them to you."

"I like presents."

"I know you do. They all kind of go together so I wanted to give them to you as one thing, on the last night."

"I suppose, if I must wait until tomorrow…"

"Sometimes waiting can bring good things."

"True. Do you want to do a lesson tomorrow?"

"I'm not sure yet. Can we wait and see?"

"Yes, of course."

Jordan tried the cucumber sandwich first. This pumpernickel bread was perfect for it, and it was just the right balance of ingredients. She grinned, taking another. Cucumber sandwiches were the best thing ever. The lox worked really well on the 5 seed bread, not quite as good as a bagel of course, but still very tasty. The tuna on rye won the day, though, because she'd worked the tuna until it was soft and airy and put just enough celery in it to make a good crunch. Her mouth was happy, and Leah was making happy food noises as she munched, so Jordan was going to call this a success. Plus she'd gotten through that conversation without getting upset or sounding anything but neutral and friendly, she was pretty sure. She should get points for that.

"Thanks for lunch," Leah said softly. "These sandwiches are awesome."

"I'm glad you like them. I think they really worked. Are you ready for the sandwich cake?"

"Oh my yes. I watched GBBO with Ernest and Gideon the other day and they made Victoria sandwiches. I've been wanting one ever since."

"It's a pretty simple recipe, as cake recipes go. I didn't make my own jam, though. We're settling for the blackberry jam I got at Zabars."

"Blackberry jam! What would Mary Berry say?"

"That I was being resourceful given the limitations, I assume."

"You clearly haven't watched enough GBBO."

Jordan cut each of them a slice, and refilled their tea cups. Another cup of tea would be perfect with this. The jam was lovely and tart, and the sweetness of the buttercream balanced it really well against the barely sweet cake.

"Oh it's wonderful," Leah said. "It reminds me just a bit of those awesome sufganiyot."

"That would be the blackberry you are appreciating!"

"Okay you sold me on the blackberry."

"If there are sufgsniyot at the party, will you bring me some?"

"Of course. I'll text Ernest before I go and ask him to make you a plate and set it aside for me to bring it to you."

"That would be lovely. Thank you."

"Jordan?"

"Yes?"

"Are we okay?"

Jordan turned to Leah and took both of Leah's hands in her own. "Yes, we're okay. I'm not going anywhere."

"Okay good. I'd hate to mess us up."

"You could never mess us up by having a shutdown, Leah. They happen. I'm sure I'll have one myself at an inopportune time."

"I'm glad we're okay."

"Me too," Jordan said. It felt true, too. That yes, they were okay, and would be okay, regardless of where they ended up.

49

SATURDAY EVENING, DECEMBER 28

LEAH

Leah stood in front of the mirror, looking at her blue roses tattoo. She'd put on one of her favorite outfits: a knee-length teal tulle skirt, a slinky black shirt that showed off her collarbone, shit kicking black boots, and her signature burgundy lipstick. She was wearing the dreidel earrings with the burgundy beads she'd bought herself for Chanukah fifteen years ago. They matched her lipstick perfectly, and sometimes that was exactly what a femme needed to get herself out the door.

Now was when she usually renewed her blue roses vow. But after her conversation with her therapist today, she wasn't sure the vow made sense anymore. The protections she'd put in place were rooted in self-blame for something that at least two people she trusted had told her wasn't her fault. It wasn't looking for the moon in someone's eyes or giving someone her submission or her heart that had created the problem in the first place. It felt like it was, but that was trauma talking. The real story was more complicated.

Xavier had begun to create a different kind of safety plan with her today. One focused on looking for warning signs that a relationship was harmful to her, instead of assuming that having a relationship was automatically harmful. He'd apologized for asking her to doubt something she'd been using to keep herself safe without offering something in its place first. He said it made total sense she'd shut down given the situation. After the phone call, he'd emailed her the new safety plan, and she had it in the notes app on her phone. Plus a print out on her altar.

She looked at it. The first step was questions to ask herself to look for warning signs a relationship might be harmful. She could ask them at any time, including while she was on a date, but also every day or week, whatever helped her feel safe. If any of the answers to these questions was yes, she'd put things on pause, and get somewhere safe. Then she'd tend to herself, and not decide anything right away. Just take a break and think it over, write down which questions were yes in a safe place, in code if needed. Then check in with someone and talk it through before deciding next steps.

She thought about the ritual she used to do with the rose tattoo and knew she needed to change it. The question was how. She stared at the tattoo and realized that there were five big blooms, where the roses were open. The rest of the roses were more bud-like. She hadn't planned that, it had just happened. But it felt like a sign. She was going to try asking the questions out loud, as she traced each bloom with her fingers.

Ellie would be there tonight, so maybe she could start with thinking about her.

"After contact/spending time with Ellie, am I often triggered, feeling bad about myself, wanting to hurt myself, or feeling more depressed?" She thought about it, and it really didn't feel like it was true.

"Does it feel like my body or physical health are being harmed?" Nope, that was clear as day.

"Is my full consent being honored and respected?" After their last conversation, it really felt like it was, like they were being open enough about what they wanted to make that happen in a full way.

"Am I being isolated from others?" Definitely not, if anything she was more connected, making new friends.

"Does it feel like I need to hide, mask, or change who I am or what I feel?" She hadn't tried to show Ellie her full self as much as she'd like to try, or tell her much about how she felt, but everything she shared with Ellie had been embraced, accepted, held.

She'd thought it would be harder to answer the questions, but actually it really wasn't. At least not as far as Ellie was concerned. That was reassuring. Maybe she could spend some time sitting at Ellie's feet tonight. She wanted to reconnect, and needed comfort. Today had been a lot. Sitting at Ellie's feet for a while might be exactly what she needed.

She could see how even if she answered yes, it still might not be that the relationship was harmful but maybe that she hadn't shared herself, her feelings, hadn't honored her own consent. So a yes might not mean actual danger, just that she'd been closing herself off to protect herself. Or she could be instinctively not trusting them because they really weren't trustworthy.

It was fucking complicated. Unlike her original vow, which at least was simple, damnit. But she was going to give this a try. Because she'd be damned if she was going to let the thing with Bev mess up her entire life. Or make her hurt Jordan worse than she already had.

50

SATURDAY EVENING, DECEMBER 28

JORDAN

It surprised Jordan a bit that Iris was free, and wanted to do a last minute dinner with her. From her texts, it seemed she'd gotten back into town yesterday and had spent all day at the office dealing with some emergency thing. She needed to get away from all of that and decompress and talk about anything but work. So Jordan had great timing. She'd really been looking forward to latkes so she searched on yelp and checked out the top ten restaurants in Manhattan, settling on one in the East Village. She'd walk through St Marks on her way there from the subway, maybe stop at the sock shop and get a pair to add to Leah's present.

Walking along St Marks used to be one of her favorite things when she first lived in New York, and it was nice to be back. She caught sight of a store that had tumbling stones, and since she had some time, she went in. It felt really good to sort through them with her hands, the smooth stones cool against her skin, and pick out ones that she wanted to take home. This rose quartz and that unakite, a tiger's eye, a snowflake obsidian, an ocean jasper, and a bloodstone all needed to go home with her.

When she got to the front, she spotted a case of pendants, and could not take her eye off of a lapis lazuli one. It was almost an exact match for her cufflinks, and had this lovely feel to the oval design, like it was an antique. She asked to see it, and as soon as she'd held it she could picture it on Leah. Well then. A perfect addition to her Chanukah present. She got a black silk cord and swept away the thought about chains and collars she kept having as she held it. That was getting ahead of herself. The point now was the pendant, not whether it might hang from a collar someday. Regardless of what might come in the future, the pendant would look beautiful on Leah. The rest could be kept in Jordan's pocket for another time.

She had a lot of stuff to keep in her pockets right now, and moving forward while doing that felt weird and confusing. She was much better at keeping silence about unspoken things when they were actually unspoken. She'd done that for years with her dad, and with Dani. But a situation where something was spoken but now we were going to just slip it into our pockets and pretend it hadn't been? She didn't know how to do that, or even if it was a good idea to try.

She sorted through the stones and decided to put the tiger's eye in her pocket, she'd fidget with it at the restaurant or on the subway home if she needed to. The rest went into her bag, and she stepped back onto the sidewalk, glad it wasn't snowing. She was enough of a fall risk without dealing with snow or ice. She stopped at the sock store and after some deliberation, selected two pairs: navy with orangey red octopi and green and black with raptors. The sock man drew her in with his buy two get one free offer and so in the end she also left with black socks that had flying pigs. She might not put all three pairs in the box.

Jordan liked to buy gifts for the folks she cared about and store them away for the right time, which presented itself eventually. She also liked to give everyday small things to the folks in her life just to say "I was thinking about you today." It was something Dani had never gotten; she'd thought all the little presents cluttered their home and were a waste of money. Even when they were just a buck or two. So Jordan had stopped getting them for her, saving all her present-giving desires for Erica and Leah instead.

She'd wished so many times as a kid that her dad would just notice her. Do something that said he'd been thinking about her when she was at school, that she was important enough that he held her in his mind. But that wasn't how he was. He'd brag about her grades to other professors they had over for dinner, or play chess with her and be full of praise when she beat him. He'd take her to study for her Bat Mitzvah and ask her about it all the way home, what she thought her torah portion meant, what she might say about it when she gave her speech. When she was right in front of him doing something he understood and cared about, he'd notice her. But he never once seemed to think of her otherwise, had no clue that the blender her mom used every day was intolerable for her to hear, didn't see the way she shut down when Joanie Fineman broke her heart or notice when she came home bruised from the girls who'd pinched her to show she wasn't the right kind of girl.

She knew why he didn't see her or think of her, the therapist she'd gone to with Erica after his death had explained the way depression could do that, could take up so much room that the person barely saw other people. But knowing it didn't make her less sad and angry and hurt, even now. She'd never gotten to confront him about it, to tell him how it had fucked her up, had contributed to her choosing a marriage that encouraged her to disappear.

She needed the people close to her to show her that they'd been thinking of her while they were apart, to notice her, to pay attention to her, to hold space for her experience and feelings. That was something she wanted to receive, so she should put it on the list for her therapy homework. Not just wanted, needed. That was why she had stepped back when Leah hadn't been able to hold what she'd told her. That was why she felt lost as to what to do next, how to move forward. She'd counted on Leah to do those things, because Leah usually had. Not when her depression was flaring, but even then, she'd been upfront about that happening and letting Jordan know that she was dealing with that and might act differently.

Hadn't she basically done the same, only this time it was about trauma? That was what her DM had said. She'd acknowledged that she wished she'd been able to do different. Jordan stopped short, no longer walking, and someone almost bumped into her. It was the same, only Jordan hadn't framed it that way in her head. Now that she was, something that had been twisting in her gut eased. She'd walked too far, she realized, and turned back.

The restaurant was warm, and small, and Iris had already snagged them a table. She gave Jordan a smile that was weary but warm, and said that a co-worker had raved about the borscht here. Well that made things easy. Borscht, latkes, and an omelette. Maybe blintzes for dessert later. Iris got a whitefish salad sandwich, and launched into a story about her mother-in-law's famous family recipe and how she'd had to learn to make it in order for her mother-in-law to give her approval for them to get married, because it was her husband's favorite thing. Dani's mom hadn't pulled anything like that, and Jordan was feeling like she'd gotten off easy by the time the story was over, and said as much, making Iris laugh.

"David explained it to me like this: she's the matriarch. She calls the shots. If she hadn't tried to push me around, but had been all distant and polite, that would really be rejection."

This had Jordan's head spinning a bit, because Dani's family had been unfailingly polite and never seemed to get less formal around her. She hadn't thought about it that way, though. She hadn't had a matriarch in her family, and this was the kind of thing she often didn't get about family dynamics, because it seemed one way on the surface but meant something different underneath.

Jordan nodded, not knowing what else to say. Iris just jumped to the next thing smoothly. "Soooo, you texted that Leah was giving you lessons. How is that going? Did you get to try any of your new toys?"

Jordan focused on the last question first. "Yes, I did, I got to use the hairbrush, and the quirt, so far."

"Nice. How did it go?"

"I think it went well. I want to practice more with the quirt, but I really liked using it. I think I might like other impact toys that feel similar to use."

"A crop could work and they are inexpensive, so you can experiment more and it's not as big a deal if you buy one you don't like. But I'd recommend a flogger or a cat. They are pricier, so you want to find ones that really suit you, and are the right length for you. The store I took you to has a decent selection and it's nice to try them out, but there are also some folks in the area that make floggers and cats. My husband is actually one of them."

"Oh that's good information to have."

"Here let me give you a card with his site. You can take a look. You would get the friends and family discount, 25% off, and if you're going to be at the New Year's party, I can ask him to bring a few for you to test out and see how they feel. Given that you liked the feel of the quirt, I'd recommend trying out a medium length cat with flat braids, maybe a bootlace flogger, and maybe one in bullhide. Those are some go-tos for more intense sensation, and I'm betting that folks who like your quirt will like them."

"Okay. I'll take a look."

"If you were thinking of flogging Leah, I can tell you that the flat braid cat is a winner."

"Good to know."

"Are you thinking you might flog Leah?"

"I'm thinking I want to know what it feels like to use a flogger, because it felt good to use the quirt. It might be an autistic thing? I really enjoyed the sensory experience of the impact, as a top. I want to try something in a similar family and see if I get the same kind of enjoyment."

"Oh, then you might want to test out the toys before you buy, see how it feels. David will gladly volunteer to be the testing bottom. He's a pain slut, and loves being flogged, it's how he got into making them. He found out it was really good for his anxiety, but that's not why he started."

"Thanks. I might take him up on that." Did people often volunteer their partners for stuff when they weren't even in the room? Or use the word slut with such fondness?

"You may also consider going even simpler and using your belt. Though I'd caution you to negotiate about belts specifically as they may be loaded with trauma for some people. There is something very hot, though, about removing your own belt and beating your submissive with it."

Their food arrived, and Jordan thought about all the fantasies she'd had years ago about using her belt on Leah. She thought about getting a flat braided cat and seeing Leah's face when she brought it home and showed it to her. She thought about going to the New Year's party, and whether Leah would be with her, whether Leah would want to play. Not as part of a lesson. Without the excuse that she was doing it to teach. Just because she wanted to.

51

SATURDAY EVENING, DECEMBER 28

LEAH

Ernest gave Leah the biggest hug when she arrived. Then Gideon wrapped her up in his arms, and she thought Ernest might have told his Daddy she'd been having a bad day. Gideon led her to a room she hadn't been to before and told her it was the quiet room for the party, showing her the mini fridge with drinks and snacks, the books, fidgets, and weighted blanket, and the laptop with the guest password written on a sticky note. He made a point of saying she should feel free to come in here anytime during the party and if anyone else joined her it would be because they also needed a quiet room.

Then he led her into the main party space, and Ellie stood and greeted her with a big warm hug. She almost burst into tears, it was so much kindness all at once, but she really didn't want to do that, so she just tucked her face into Ellie's neck and hid until she had it together. When Leah whispered her request in Ellie's ear, her Ma'am said "Of course, girl. Here's a good pillow to sit on," and sat down again, placing the pillow on the floor in Leah's spot. Leah looked around for Rena, who had shifted a few years ago from being Ellie's submissive to being her QPP. She'd gotten in the habit every time she took this spot at Ellie's feet, because for a long while, she'd shared it with Rena. Even though Ellie didn't have another submissive right now, and hadn't for a while, she still felt like it was a shared spot, somewhere inside her, and she tried to be good at sharing. Rena was in the kitchen helping Ernest with the food, and grinned like she knew why Leah was looking for her. She probably did. Leah had never met anyone as good at reading people as Rena.

Ellie's hand was gently stroking Leah's hair. It was the best thing ever to be in this spot, cocooned a bit by her legs, attuning to her and the minute shifts in her body and energy, listening for her voice. "I'm glad you're here, girl," Ellie murmured, and she felt lit all the way through with sunshine. She nuzzled against Ellie's hand, whispering "Me too," against her skin.

Nora had sat down next to Ellie and was asking her about something Leah hadn't quite caught. Oh, Nora had asked Ellie to come talk to the GSA she was advisor for about the importance of reproductive healthcare and ways to advocate for and find queer and trans sensitive care. As a queer trans nurse she was perfect for that. Leah closed her eyes so she could hear them set the agenda for the talk. She loved hearing Ellie speak from her expertise. Was there anything more attractive than competence?

Leah should have Ellie give a reproductive and sexual health talk at her shop again. It had been at least a year, she thought, trying to remember. Ellie tugged her hair gently and she opened her eyes, focusing. Someone said her name, and she realized that Nora was looking at her.

"Leah, I was hoping you might come to the GSA next month and do a binder and packer options talk."

"Sure, I can, or if you want I can get Shiloh to do it instead? Ze is doing more teaching these days as part of zir new role at the store, and maybe they'd prefer a non-binary person to do it, feel more comfortable that way?"

"Hmm. I was going to tap Shiloh to talk about queer and trans performance art. Though you do have a point. If you have a trans guy who does this, that would be especially good, we have several new trans boys in the group this year."

"Tyler has started doing more education recently; he might be perfect."

"The demo bottom from your fisting class? I didn't know he worked at the store."

"He keeps his hours low, it's just a side gig for him, and he mostly works in the back."

"Well he sounds perfect, let's make this happen."

"Absolutely. I wish we could do sex ed. I would've loved to have access to a strap on class when I was a teen. Of course we didn't even have a GSA at my high school then."

"I wish we could, too! My teenage sex life would've been vastly improved if I'd known about lube."

"Yknow, I'm thinking about developing a set of classes about ace spec and aro spec identities and relationships. Maybe I could come out and do one of those."

"That would be awesome. Honestly, we need ace spec and aro spec 101. Or, one of those old-school panels like we did in the 90s, but focused on a-spec identities."

"Well if you want to start there, count me in as your gray ace panelist," Leah said, trying to keep her tone light.

"Great. Ernest will talk about being demiro, I bet. Lemme see what I can put together."

Nora headed right for the kitchen to try to tap Ernest. Leah's ears were ringing.

"Just breathe, girl," Ellie said.

She breathed, concentrating on the feel of Ellie's hand on the back of her neck, anchoring her.

"I'm proud of you, girl."

"You are?"

"Yes. Not only were you brave in coming out, but you also did that when I was here to support you. And you're letting me support you now."

"Oh. I am, aren't I?"

"Yes. Thank you for that. It's a thing us dominants like to be able to do, when it's wanted."

"It is?"

"Maybe not all dominants. But many of us. It's definitely something I like to do, for you."

"Oh." She tilted her head to look up at Ellie, who was smiling at her with such fondness it stole her breath. And made her wonder. What did Ellie want, with her? If Ellie wasn't worried about scaring Leah away, how would she answer that question? She'd never wondered about that before. She'd never been brave enough to let herself wonder about what could be.

"What are you thinking, girl?"

"I'm not sure I'm ready to talk about it."

"Okay. Perhaps when you're ready."

Leah nodded. She'd like to be ready someday soon. The idea that she'd foreclosed possibilities—with Ellie, and Jordan, and who knew who else—was really fucking frustrating.

"So I've been thinking about the Chanukah story, and how it's all about fighting back against assimilation," Ernest said, and the room got quiet, listening. He continued, "Fighting back against the forces that try to erase us, and how if we stick together, and hold onto who we are, we can survive as a people."

Ellie nodded, and chimed in. "There are so many forces trying to erase each of us, including anti-semitism and the pressure to assimilate in that way, but on every axis of oppression. Every day I go to work I'm dealing with a medical system that doesn't make room for who I am as a trans woman, that doesn't even research the long term impact of the medical interventions I'm given, and offer our trans clients. If I didn't have trans colleagues and friends, it would wear me down."

"This hits each of us in so many ways," Gideon said. "And we support each other to remember who we are, to hold onto it, even as we get pushed to blend in or hide or disavow ourselves."

"For me the pressure to assimilate feels especially strong around being autistic," Leah said softly.

"Yeah," Judith said. "There's so much pressure. It helps me to spend time with other autistic people who aren't trying to mask. It's like it helps me remember to be myself."

Leah nodded. "Stimming with other autistic people helps me a lot. I was realizing today that I need more autistic kinky people in my life. Especially folks who are submissives—including switches who submit, of course."

"Maybe we could have an Autistic Submissives Tea, or something," Ernest said.

"You just want an excuse to make tiny cakes," Judith teased.

"Well of course!" Ernest said. "But that excuse can just be that it's Tuesday. I thought tea might be nice for a small gathering, with lots of stuff to do with your hands."

"It's a good idea," Leah said.

They lit the candles, and sang Chanukah songs. Leah ate latkes, cucumber salad, garlicky string beans, and this amazing poached salmon Ernest had made with dill that had the best texture ever. She told them about the latke recipe song and then Ernest pulled it up on the tv and they all sang along. Which led to karaoke, of course. She hadn't sung this much in a long time, or laughed this much, and she'd needed both more than she could measure.

She left feeling fed in places she didn't know she'd been hungry, and grounded in a way that made her feel brave. So she messaged Jordan on the train home, talking about the party, and how it was like she'd slid into place in a family that had wanted her there all along, but she'd been too scared to see it or let it happen. She'd been too scared to see so much in her life. And she didn't want fear to be in charge anymore.

It wasn't a promise, she wasn't up for promises or answers, but it was a true thing. She hoped it would make a difference to Jordan to read it. She hoped, and hoping felt like the bravest thing ever.

52

SATURDAY EVENING, DECEMBER 28

JORDAN

The borscht was wonderful, and Jordan closed her eyes and just savored the earthy grounding taste of it. She'd never had vegetarian borscht before and that meant lots of sour cream as a tangy counterpoint, which made her mouth zing in the best way. Then she tried the latkes (also with sour cream) and they were amazing crispy fried oniony deliciousness. The omelette had this awesome texture with the apples still a bit crunchy and the cheese all melty, and this was clearly a stellar restaurant choice.

She looked up from the awesome food and grinned at Iris, who gave her a fond smile and said the whitefish salad was pretty great. Then she said, "I'd love to hear more about the lessons, if you want to say. I know it's maybe a bit odd because we know each other through Leah. I'd never share what you told me with her. If I thought she needed to know something, I'd suggest that you tell her."

Jordan nodded. That was a bit reassuring, though it hadn't been a big worry. It would be good to talk this through, see if she could get more grounded in what she needed. "I guess I'm trying to sort through the strands of how I'm feeling, and it's all kind of new," she said slowly. "I know the thing we talked about was 8 lessons for Chanukah, but it feels like what we're doing is something else. At least from my end. The D/s doesn't feel like it's only about learning, it feels like we are building another aspect of our relationship. It has all this stuff wrapped into it, all this caring and tenderness and wanting to protect her and wanting to keep her, claiming her for mine, wanting to make sure she has what she needs...it feels like D/s and romance all wrapped together."

Iris nodded, and took a bite of her sandwich, clearly thinking about what Jordan had said. "Are you polyamorous? I don't think I ever asked."

Jordan nodded. "I mean, I think I am? I was in a monogamous marriage but I really don't want monogamy now. I don't have experience with polyamory, though. Oh, did I say something that was inappropriate, because Leah's your play partner too?"

"No, no, I didn't mean that, I was just trying to get a sense of what you mean, if anything that you were feeling was about wanting monogamy with Leah."

"Nope. The claiming D/s thing doesn't have that kind of possessiveness in it for me. I like the idea of Leah having multiple folks in her life to care about her and build relationship with and help support her and give her what she needs. I want that for myself, too."

"So I think there's a kind of polyamory where folks go into a connection with someone and they already have a sense of what it can be or should be, they've foreclosed possibilities and are trying to shape it into a mold."

"Huh. Okay. Not sure what you mean by that."

"So like, they have a primary partner and see the new person in their life as a potential secondary partner, for example. Often there are rules, boundaries, and expectations that try to shape that relationship to be smaller in some way than the primary partnership."

"Ah, okay."

"Other folks approach polyamory seeing potential relationships as things that grow organically and shift and change as the people change. They might try to be careful and intentional to make sure they grow strong and are balanced, but they aren't trying to fit them in a box they decided ahead of time."

Jordan nodded. "That seems more my style."

Iris smiled. "Yeah, you didn't seem worried that the relationship was shifting and not fitting the original expectations or framework."

"No, I kinda think it's exciting. Or at least I would, if Leah were also into seeing what was possible."

"She isn't?"

"I mean, I think she doesn't know. But the idea seemed to scare her, catch her off guard. She's mentioned multiple times that I keep surprising her."

"Ah, yes. For most of the time I've known her, Leah has done a version of what some people call solo polyamory, where she's her own primary partner, and she mostly just does secondary or tertiary relationships with folks who already have primary partners, or keeps her play connections casual. She's been working from the model of deciding ahead of time what something is and shaping it to go inside that box."

"Huh. That explains...a lot."

"Yeah, I haven't seen her try a relationship that had romance and D/s in it since Bev."

"Oh, you were around for that?"

"The last year of it, only. Bev and I were metamours—my first submissive was a girl she'd trained and was mentoring—so I got to know Leah that way."

"Were you at the party when Bev dumped her?"

"No, I was out of town on business. I'm grateful I missed that; my girl told me what happened. She was the one who suggested that I reach out to Leah and see if she was okay. She thought Leah might need a dominant in her life who was trustworthy and not trying to get in her pants, because the wolves would start to circle."

Jordan shuddered. She didn't often think about that time in Leah's life, because it scared the shit out of her. But it hadn't occurred to her that Leah was vulnerable to predatory dominants then, though it made sense once Iris said it.

"You watched out for her?"

"Yep. And my girl was right; I wasn't trying to get into her pants. Leah and I didn't do anything like play or sex for the first dozen or so years we knew each other. I was kind of a protector for a while after the breakup—I vetted the folks she played with, watched the scenes if she wanted me to, was a safe person to go to social events with. Then we transitioned into being friends for a while. And then, I became her dance partner, and that was the main thing we were together for many years."

"Thanks for watching out for her, for protecting her."

They exchanged a classic butch nod, and there was something about the gesture that made Jordan feel like she'd just leveled up.

"Glad to do it," Iris said quietly. "What you're talking about, with the D/s feeling protective, and tender, and claiming, and like you want to see that her needs get met, like you want to keep her...that's how I am, with my husband. It gets wrapped up in romance for me too."

"Yeah, when I mentioned it to Ruth, she said that was how she was with Rebecca."

Iris nodded. "It can be really beautiful, that kind of D/s. Building that on top of decades of being best friends...it could be really solid, because you know each other."

"You don't think I'm rushing things?"

"I mean, if you were twenty, and she was a stranger, I'd say you were. If you were raving about how she's the perfect submissive, or how powerful she makes you feel, I'd say it was the sparkle of D/s. But that's not what you're talking about."

"True."

"The thing is, this wasn't made for casual. You know each other, have supported each other, been the kind of friends that are family for years. The idea that it feels like building another layer of relationship...I kinda don't see how it wouldn't. You're already in a very close intimate relationship."

"True. And we're trying new stuff, taking risks. Not just me...she's doing that too, with the lessons. The structure of them, and I think the fact that it was me made it feel like she could. Just like I felt much more comfortable trying D/s where there was already a foundation of trust and friendship."

"Sounds like the recipe for a lot of emotional intimacy and intensity, which also doesn't lean casual."

"Yeah. It's intense stuff."

"Leah's usually a lot more careful to avoid anything that's not strictly boundaried. But she didn't do that with you. And she decided to push herself to take risks with you, too. Because she trusted you. Maybe on some level she was wanting something different with you. Even if she wasn't fully aware of it."

Jordan hadn't thought of it like that before. It made her feel hopeful, somehow.

SUNDAY MORNING, DECEMBER 29

LEAH

Leah woke at 6am thinking one thing: it was the last night of Chanukah. Which felt like a deadline of some sort. Because in her head, the eight lessons were supposed to end tonight, probably. But they'd only done four of them. She'd said that they could postpone some of the lessons, because that was just realistic, but tonight felt like the end of something somehow anyway. Something she didn't want to be over.

She curled up in bed, hugging herself, and rocking, as it all caught up to her in a wave. This was how her brain worked. It stuck with things as long as it can, but if they got unmoored or doubts began, they'd build in the background until something would set off a wave of clarity, usually in the early morning, like it had built all night long, and was now ready to flatten her. There was no slowing it down, she just needed to hold on and stim her way through it.

She'd had these ideas in her head about what these lessons would be, and how the structure of them would protect her, but now that she was staring down the last night of Chanukah that all felt like a fucking joke. Protect her? From what? She'd jumped into sex and play with her best friend and somehow thought it was going to be like it was with everyone else! As if Jordan wasn't already inside most of her armor already. As if Jordan wasn't someone she'd loved for thirty fucking years. As if Jordan didn't already know her down to the fucking ground, and still wanted her, still stuck around, never tried to make her be anything but herself, seemed completely delighted with who she was, even when she didn't mask a fucking thing.

She'd made all these choices about not getting into relationships to protect herself from another devastating relationship like she'd had with Bev, but Jordan wasn't like Bev at all. And she wasn't the same Leah that she'd been when she'd signed the contract with Bev all those years ago, either. She owned her own business, was entrenched in kink community so deeply there was no way she could lose it, wasn't young and naïve like she'd been back then. She wasn't trying to wrest herself out of the control of her family or prove that she was an adult. She wasn't afraid of her own power.

Leah had already stood up to Bev eleven years ago and gotten her to back down on the TERFy awfulness, even though it had scared the shit out of her. After that Bev hadn't seemed as right and perfect anymore, her judgment and rejection hadn't seemed devastating in the same way. The idea of running into her at the New Year's party, even in a clearly submissive headspace, didn't scare her anymore. Even if Bev thought she wasn't a good submissive, a real submissive, and might say that or imply it. She wasn't the arbiter of that. She never had been, except in Leah's mind (and her own).

So if Leah was different, and Jordan was different, and the situation was different...the relationship would be different. That was logical. The problem wasn't that she was actually in danger of going through that again. The problem was that she was scared shitless at the idea of taking the leap. Because the breakup with Bev had made her feel even more worthless, useless, and shattered than her mother ever had, and her depression had spiraled down so bad it had terrified her.

You survived, a part of her insisted. You were way more isolated and vulnerable and you still survived. It was true. She had survived, despite the ideation. She'd gone back to therapy, had stayed with Rebecca until she found her own place, had refused to give up kink and instead had Iris vet all her play partners until she felt like she could do it herself. She had poured all of her energy (and half of what her grandmother had left her) into starting the shop, and had made it into a place where people could learn all the things she'd needed to know as a novice. She had scraped together a life for herself, and there was a lot in that life that was good.

She already knew she could survive being shattered, because she already had. She already knew she could survive another depression flare that bad, because it might have been the first, but she'd had at least four that had rivaled it, since, and she was still here. She might be scared of those things, but the real fear wasn't there, after all. The real fear was that Bev had been right. The real fear was that if she tried to build a D/s relationship again, let herself fall in love with a dominant again, she'd discover that she wasn't good enough, that she'd never be good enough, that she could never be a good submissive.

Leah curled up into a ball and wept, as the last of the wave flowed over her, that terrible terrifying question circling in her brain: what if I'm not good enough? The same question that had haunted her for as long as she could remember, that always grew louder when her depression flared. She sobbed for what seemed like forever, until her head throbbed and her throat was raw, and she fell back asleep, exhausted from the sobbing and the wave that had brought it on.

That terrible day returned in her dreams, of course. The dream began a bit earlier than usual, not a partial memory looping repeatedly like usual, but the whole day played through in detail, herself in a movie theater watching it, Ellie on one side, Jordan on the other, with Rebecca and Ruth in front of her, Ernest and Gideon next to Ellie, and Iris next to Jordan. It had never happened like this before, and it was both terrifyingly exposing and also really comforting to be surrounded by folks who cared about her, who wanted her to be safe. Their reactions were astounding. The way Jordan snarled, the way Ellie squeezed her hand, how Iris seemed to be in a slow boiling rage as they all watched Bev put her off when she asked to renegotiate that morning, as they saw how Bev had refused or ignored her service after that. From this angle, she could see how red Bev had gotten, how petulant and small she looked. "That's not what love looks like," Ruth murmured to Rebecca at a moment of rejection that had been accompanied by a sneer and derisive comment. It was so clear that she was right, too. That Bev had felt threatened, and was lashing out, in a way that made it clear that there was no care or love in her dominance.

When the movie got to the part of the day that was at the party, Leah was already angry, on her own behalf, in a way that she hadn't been back then. The worst moment, the public rejection and derision and removal of her collar in front of everyone, filled her with rage, and she felt like she saw it for what it really was for the first time, as the folks who loved her started ranting and cursing at the screen on her own behalf: Bev hadn't been declaring a truth about her, she'd felt rejected by Leah's request to renegotiate and had lashed out at her all throughout the day and when that hadn't broken her, had done it in public, in the most humiliating way she could find, out of her own hurt feelings and insecurity.

When she woke from the dream she immediately wrote down what she could remember of it. She didn't want to lose it. It felt like the answer to the question that Xavier had asked. Her head was still pounding, so she went into the kitchen to get some water, and tea, and figure out food. She felt like she'd been trampled by a herd of dinosaurs. Was that the name for a group of dinosaurs? Maybe each kind of dinosaur had a different group name, like other animals did.

The headache made her feel queasy, so she decided toast was the first step foodwise, and moved around the kitchen without turning on the light, standing by the sink as she downed her first glass of water, before pouring another, then filling the kettle. She sat at the table and made herself finish a triangle of toast before grabbing ibuprofen from the drawer and downing it. She put honey in the green tea, and it helped her throat feel less raw. She really hoped she wasn't getting sick. Then she made herself finish the rest of the toast, even though it hurt her throat.

Her eyes were swollen from the crying, and she just wanted to curl up and have someone hold her and read her a story. Maybe make her soup. Fuck, she probably was getting sick. She never daydreamed about that kind of stuff unless she was sick. She didn't want to be sick on the last night of Chanukah.

She rested her face on the table inside the circle of her arms. The table was cool and smooth, and it felt good not to keep trying to hold her head up anymore. That was a bad sign too, she realized. Then the light came on, and she was pretty sure she yelped.

"Sorry," Jordan said. I didn't think anyone was here. Why was the light off?"

"Because everything hurts and it would just make it worse," Leah said miserably.

"I will turn it off as soon as I can, okay? I need it to get around the kitchen."

"Yeah, it's fine," Leah said, and went into the living room to hide from the light. The velvet pillow felt really good against her forehead when she buried her face in it. It wasn't long before Jordan came into the living room, bringing Leah's tea, and water glass, which she'd refilled.

"Are you sick?" she asked quietly.

"I don't know. Probably."

Jordan got up, and was back in a couple minutes with a thermometer. Leah sat up grumpily and put it in her mouth. She got up again and left the room for a minute. Jordan came back with a blanket just as the thermometer beeped. She handed Leah the blanket and looked at the thermometer, nodding.

"It's not bad, but it's a bit high. 99.8. Since you had ibuprofen, it might have been higher. We should keep an eye on it. I'm assuming you have a headache. What else hurts?"

"Everything. Especially my throat."

"Okay. Have you been coughing?"

"Not so far."

"Congested?"

"Yeah, maybe."

"Okay, so maybe a cold, with a sore throat. Know anyone who's been sick?" Jordan stroked her hair, giving her a soft smile. Jordan was here for her, caring for her, even though things were strained, even though her feelings were hurt. Because Jordan's love wasn't conditional, wasn't about exchange, didn't need to be earned. It just was there, in the warm sunshine of her regard, in that soft smile and gentle questioning.

"Nora said she was getting over a cold when I saw her last night."

"So then unless the fever goes up let's assume you got the same cold."

Leah nodded glumly. "But it's the last night of Chanukah."

"We can still light candles. You still get your present."

A present was good. But.

"But I wanted to do Chanukah wax play."

"Oh, really? Well, perhaps we can do Chanukah, observed, later on this week, and do waxplay then."

"Okay, fine. But only if we get to do Chanukah waxplay next year on actual Chanukah, too," she said grumpily.

"You drive a hard bargain," Jordan said, her voice a bit hoarse. Was she getting sick too? "You have yourself a deal."

Jordan sat next to her on the couch, and pulled her close. "How about I hold you for a while?" she asked.

"And read to me?"

"Yes, of course. What book?"

"Hobbit."

"I can do that," Jordan said. "Just give me a minute." Leah turned a bit so she could get more comfortable, and pulled the blanket to cover them both, while Jordan presumably downloaded the book onto her phone. Jordan's hand was stroking her back as she began to read, the familiar words cozy comfort, and Leah closed her eyes, letting herself sink into it. She felt Jordan kiss the top of her head oh so gently before picking up the next paragraph, where Gandalf appeared, and even though her head felt like it was full of water, the kiss was warm and made her feel loved in a way that snuck into her and settled.

54

SUNDAY AFTERNOON, DECEMBER 29

JORDAN

Once Leah had settled down to nap, Jordan ordered Leah's favorite sick foods from the Thai menu clipped to the fridge. It had stars next to a few things that Jordan would eat regardless, so she got a range of things that included both the soup and the curry that Leah favored when she had a cold. She felt more settled once she'd done that, and gotten the candles ready, set out Leah's Chanukah present. So she texted Erica.

Jordan: I had borscht last night! It was vegetarian, so so good. Remember when you tried it for the first time and said it tasted like dirt?

Erica: I was 11. And I stand by that.

Jordan: Well, some people like earthy tastes, you know.

Erica: I know, I know. Thanks for not making me eat it.

Erica: A lot of my friends, their parents made them eat stuff, but you never did.

Jordan: There's so much I can't stand to eat, I'd never do that to you.

Erica: I know. You let me be who I was, and didn't try to make me into anything else.

Jordan: Who you are is perfect.

Erica: Holidays have you all sentimental!

Jordan: I miss you, okay? It's weird not to see you for Chanukah. Don't forget to wear your gloves. You always forget your gloves.

Erica: I won't forget my gloves, I promise. *eye-rolling emoji*

Erica: I miss you too. But I'm glad you're there, getting settled. And you have Leah to celebrate with.

Jordan: At least for some of the nights. We're celebrating tonight.

Erica: That's good. What's wrong? It feels like you aren't saying something.

Jordan: Me and Leah…it's complicated right now.

Erica: Complicated how?

Jordan: Complicated like I'm in love with her and she's scared of being in a relationship.

Erica: Did you tell her how you felt?

Jordan: I tried. She freaked out.

Erica: I'm proud of you.

Jordan: What?

Erica: You don't tell people what you want. You never have. But you told her, didn't you?

Jordan: I started to, anyway.

Erica: Good. She'll come around, I bet. You two would be great together. You deserve to be happy. You spent so much of your life making other people happy. But I think she actually cares about you being happy too. You just need to be honest about what you want.

Jordan: Oh just that, eh?

Erica: You've got this. Nobody is better at loving than you. As long as you work on letting her love you back, you're gonna be fine.

Jordan: Thanks. Happy Chanukah.

Erica: Happy Chanukah. I'll send pics of the kids tomorrow, with your presents. Maybe have them call to thank you.

Jordan: I'd love that.

It was snowing outside, which explained the ache in her knees since this morning, and Jordan stood by the window watching it come down. Her first New York winter in so long. It looked so pretty from a distance, but it was going to make walking risky. She felt bad for the delivery person, being out in this. She grabbed a few extra bucks to add to the tip, and it was like she'd summoned him, because there he was. It smelled wonderful, but she wasn't hungry yet, so she decided to get some heat for her knees and rest a bit.

There was so much to think about, and it was all muddled, she didn't know what to do about any of it, so she did what she usually did in those situations: put things aside and give her brain something else to do. She'd been working on training the speech to text software she had to understand her voice, because her hands had been flaring more, and she wanted options for writing that were at least somewhat usable. So she'd started a fic series that she wrote using the software. It was a comfortfic D/s series where a certain icy queen was rather softhearted with her service submissive, a girl who had run away from her sheltered tower to live in the ice palace to be with her. It was soothing to describe the servant baking delicious things for her, or making art for her, and the queen having her girl brush her hair.

When she finished drafting the next chapter of her fic, she felt less weighed down by confusion, and she sang the new lyrics she'd written for "When Will My Life Begin," tweaking a lyric or two before singing it again. Yes, perfect. Writing comfortfic always soothed her. She loved all those quiet domestic moments, the way each character showed the other how much she loved her, how devoted she was. Love wasn't about what you said, but what you did, she'd always thought.

Time to check on Leah. She peeked into her room, and saw that Leah was tossing and turning. A nightmare? She was muttering the word "please," but it sounded desperate, wounded, not like she'd ever heard her use it. "Leah," she said firmly. "Time to wake up." Leah stilled, then her eyes opened, found Jordan. She didn't say a word.

"I think you were having a nightmare. You're safe now. Try sitting up for me, okay?"

Leah sat, but she had that intense still quality. Like a possum that froze around a predator.

"Leah, you're home, in your room. Would you like me to sit next to you?"

Leah nodded, and when Jordan sat next to her, she started trembling, and then reached for Jordan with both arms, and clung. Jordan wrapped Leah in her arms and stroked her back, murmuring "I'm here, it's okay, you're safe now."

Leah let out a shuddering sigh. "I shouldn't have gone back to sleep."

"You need your rest when you're sick."

"I mean, yeah, but. I didn't need to have that nightmare again."

"Again? You had it already once today?"

"Well that time was different actually. This was like it used to be, the old way."

"Would it help to tell me about it? I can listen, if you want to."

"I mean, maybe? I don't know. I was back there, that day Bev took her collar back."

Jordan nodded. "I know that was a very hard day, I remember what you were like the next day when I came to visit you at Rebecca's place."

"Yeah. It was the worst day," Leah said, sounding so small.

"I'm here if you want to tell me more. It's also okay not to."

"She said some things that really hurt, in front of a room full of people, at a party. And I realized, this morning, that part of me still believes she might have been right."

Jordan nodded, and held Leah close. If she wanted to say more, Jordan would listen. She could hold it, whatever it was.

"She said I was willful, like it was the worst thing in the universe to be. That I was useless--" Leah took a jagged breath, "and that I'd never be any good to a dominant. And then she took off her collar, grabbed her safety scissors, and cut it up, dropping the pieces on the floor in front of me."

Jordan felt a white hot rage surge through her. She took a slow breath, digging her boots into the floor, driving it out with that motion. There was no room for it right now.

"She had no right to say those things to you, to hurt you in that way, to try to shame you like that in public."

"Oh I know," Leah said. "Iris told me she's banned from those parties for doing that. I didn't really get it for a long time, though. I thought she was banned for making a messy public scene, which of course she'd blame me for. I didn't know that the dominant who ran the party thought Bev had acted terribly toward me, that she felt it was dishonorable to end a D/s relationship like that. Nobody told me that until recently. Of course, a lot of the folks that were there aren't around much anymore."

"I'm glad there are folks in the community who get that the way she acted wasn't okay. I wish they had been more clear with you about that."

"Yeah, me too. It's possible some people tried, and I wasn't hearing it. I refused to discuss her or that night with anyone, basically. It was too painful, and I felt too ashamed. Even thinking about it felt like it might trigger my depression again."

"Yeah, that makes sense. I'm sorry you've been dreaming about it. Have the dreams triggered your depression?"

"Actually...no. I seem to have belatedly found my rage about it."

"Well considering I have some rage on your behalf, may I say how glad I am that you have?"

Leah gave a watery chuckle.

"Let me know if you want to do some cathartic rage stuff. I'd be glad to join you. I seem to be finding my rage at my father after all these years, so I've got plenty of my own."

"Ah. Don't get me started on my mother."

"Fair enough. How does soup sound? Your throat seems pretty raw."

"Soup sounds like the best thing ever."

"I want to take your temperature first," Jordan said, as they walked towards the kitchen.

"Of course you do. You can't resist your chance to take care of me, can you?"

"Nope. Thanks for letting me. It means a lot that you trust me to care for you, Leah."

"Honestly, one of the first things I thought of when I realized I was sick was that I just wanted to curl up in your arms and have you read to me. I'm becoming a fucking sap, too, because it felt perfect."

"Okay, sick Leah has no filter, and while I'm appreciating it, a lot, I really don't want you to regret what you say to me later and wish you could take it back."

Leah took a moment before responding. Jordan was glad she didn't automatically argue, but was thinking about it. "Okay. I'll try not to say cheesy stuff until I'm better," she promised. "I don't want you to doubt that I'm choosing to say it."

"That sounds fair," Jordan said slowly. "I swear I'm not trying to get you to tell me things you wouldn't normally tell me."

"Oh, I know that," Leah said. "You're all about my consent in a way that most people don't even think about. I trust you."

"Okay. I'm glad you trust me. Now. Temperature." She handed Leah the thermometer. Leah was listing to the side a bit, so Jordan stood on that side as a sort of support beam. "Still the same, 99.7," Jordan said. "So I'm thinking maybe you want some cold medicine along with ibuprofen after your soup."

55

SUNDAY LATE AFTERNOON, DECEMBER 29

LEAH

Leah nodded, and made her way to the couch without falling over. She proceeded to put pillows on either side of herself to keep upright, and Jordan put a pillow with a towel on it on her lap, so her soup was closer to her mouth. Helpful, and she'd never have thought of it. She could barely taste the soup but it made her mouth tingle and she could kind of smell it. It was her favorite spicy Thai soup, and she hoped the chilis would help clear her congestion. She managed to eat a few chive dumplings, and a bit of rice, too.

Then Jordan took away the soup and brought her meds, and lit the candles, singing the prayer slowly, her voice warm and familiar. She sang Rock of Ages next, in Hebrew and then again in English, and Leah knew that was because Leah loved it so much. Then Jordan brought over a rather large present. It was heavy, and solid, and the paper tore away to reveal a beautiful wooden box, with an image of a couple ballroom dancing inlaid into the cover. She lifted the cover, and found a bunch of smaller items. A journal, again with ballroom on the cover, a dreidel, gelt, stickers for her bujo, a DVD of what was clearly an independent film with two women dancing on the cover, a pair of socks with raptors on them, and a small velvet bag. When she opened the bag, there was a pendant on a silk cord. It looked like an antique, with an intricate design in silver around an oval of lapis lazuli. It was gorgeous, and she put it on immediately, thinking of Jordan's cufflinks, which she thought were almost an exact match for the stone in the necklace.

The presents were thoughtful, and useful, and showed that Jordan paid attention. The box would go perfectly on her dresser and hold her jewelry, the pendant exactly right for her but also felt like a gentle reminder of that first scene. It felt like with the pendant, Jordan was offering herself, and her sense of that only strengthened when she looked at Jordan's face, saw the light in her eyes and the yearning as she looked at the pendant. The rest of the gifts were for Leah. The pendant was for Leah and from Jordan. Not pushing, not presuming, but...putting it out there.

"I love all of them, but especially this," she said, tracing her finger along the stone in the pendant. "Thank you."

"I love giving presents, you know that. I'm so glad you like these."

"I really do," Leah said. "Can I give you a hug?"

"I'd love that," Jordan said, and moved the presents and the pillows, joining her on the couch for the hug, which was a better idea really. It felt good to hold her, and to be held, and Leah sighed contentedly.

"I'd suggest we watch the movie but I don't think it's a good one when you're sick, because it has a controlling mother."

"Yeah, that's no good. It will have to wait for another day. I could watch the Two Fat Ladies, though."

"I'm always game for the Two Fat Ladies. Can we watch the one where they walk too far and Jennifer decides she can't go another step?"

"Of course. I know how much you love that one."

"It's my favorite. I love that she refuses to push herself anymore."

"Yeah, it's good."

Jordan queued it up, then asked "So Jennifer is the femme and Clarissa is the butch, right?"

"Definitely. I love that the femme is the one driving the motorcycle."

"Honey, I'd totally ride in your sidecar if it wouldn't completely mess with my knee."

"Aww, thanks. We just need a more accessible sidecar. And to be in the British countryside where we aren't worrying about the dangers of New York City traffic."

"We could travel all over the country and I would cook for people and you could teach them about kink and sex toys."

"Hmm. That would definitely get us a TV show, wouldn't it?"

56

MONDAY AFTERNOON, DECEMBER 30

LEAH

Leah was sick of being sick, and full of grumpiness about everything, including being taken care of. She wasn't helpless, damnit. She just had a fucking cold. She hadn't gone to work in over a week, and while the shop was doing just fine without her, she missed being there. Missed her employees. Missed leaving the fucking apartment.

She couldn't wait to spend New Year's Day there all by herself, cleaning, rearranging things, starting the New Year off with something new. Maybe that's what she needed around here, too. A deep cleaning, and a rethinking of the space. Starting with her room. Maybe even starting with her closet. At least that way she'd feel like she was getting things done. She just couldn't be still for another fucking second.

She put on cleaning clothes—yoga pants and her Fat Bitch t shirt, a red and black handkerchief to pull back her hair—and filled up her water bottle. Okay, she was ready. Leah stared at the jumbled tangle of her closet and felt a bit overwhelmed. There had to be a place to start. Something that was doable. Accessories, she could organize those. Sort through them, get rid of the ones she never used, make a system for storing them so she could find them. Ages ago, she'd fallen hard for these hatboxes. They were so pretty. She'd gotten a bunch of them at a thrift store, thinking she'd find some way to use them for a display at Brazen, but she never had. They'd wound up on the top shelves of her closet, gathering dust. Well, she had a use for them now. She just needed to get them down, and see how many she had, think about how she was going to organize them. Did any of them actually hold hats?

Leah had gotten stuff to dust them with, but she couldn't dust them before getting them down because they were just too high up, so she tried to take them down without getting dust everywhere. That hadn't worked out so well. There was just one more stack to grab, and then she could really begin. She tugged, but it was unwieldy, was there actually something in one of these?

Yes, it turned out there was, because it all spilled out on the floor of her closet. Letters and mementoes she hadn't seen in years, photos too, most of this stuff was at least twenty years old. And amidst the mess, the pieces of the collar that Bev had tossed at her feet. Because of course she'd gathered them up and taken them with her, and then tucked them away, unable to look at them or think of them, but also unable to let go.

There was a photo of her wearing the collar, sitting at Bev's feet, so so young, and happy to be serving. That poor girl, she thought as she looked at the image of herself from all those years ago. All she wanted was to be good, to be useful, to please. Her heart had been so open, so full of yearning and hope. And was that so wrong, really, to hope? To want to be useful? To ache to submit? Had that girl actually done anything wrong?

Leah picked up the photo, and the pieces of the collar, and stood, taking them to her altar. She picked up her scissors, and cut a circle of herself, out of the photo. That was what she wanted to keep, that younger Leah who was full of hope and love and desire to submit. It wasn't about how Bev saw her or even what Bev did to her. It was about her, and how she saw herself, how she saw this part of who she was. That was what she needed to contend with, to honor, to accept. Her own submission. The rest of the baggage around it needed cleansing, starting with the scraps left of this photo. She sat and planned out the ritual, wanting to be really intentional about it. To create a new beginning with it.

TUESDAY LATE MORNING, DECEMBER 31

JORDAN

Jordan had spent the previous day in a lot of pain, and doing her best to still care for Leah while not pushing her body too much. She'd watched Brave with RJ that night, back to their Monday movie schedule, and they'd talked about Merida clearly being aroace and how awesome a QPP she'd be for Rapunzel. She'd woken up in considerably less pain, and almost felt spry after using heat on her knees and hips. She'd started outlining the Merida/Rapunzel QPP fic she wanted to write, and her hands were still doing okay afterwards. She'd be fine to go to the party, unless the weather changed dramatically.

Leah seemed to have recovered from her cold for the most part, and was much less grumpy than she'd been the day before. She always got especially grumpy when she was sick, so Jordan was used to it, but it was nice to see her smiling a bit. Leah had offered to bring her brunch in bed, make her cheddar scrambled eggs and French toast, and to help her practice with her flashcards this afternoon, before the party. She was singing along with Tracy Chapman in the kitchen as she cooked, and Jordan was trying not to read too much into the lyrics, which were all about trust and giving her a chance and living as if only love matters.

Leah brought in the tray table with her food, and it was beautiful. Leah had arranged the plate just so, and had lightly fried an apple with some cinnamon and sugar and made it into a flower to garnish the whole thing. She'd folded a napkin into a star, and fixed Jordan's tea exactly how she liked it, and had the best smile on her face when she placed it in front of Jordan. It made Jordan's breath catch, just seeing the way she'd put her whole self into it, and how much joy it brought her.

"Thank you," Jordan said hoarsely. There was something happening, she could feel it, and this food was part of it. Leah was trying to tell her something. But she wasn't speaking, she just stood there, smiling, so Jordan began to eat. The food was wonderful, the eggs how she'd always loved them, the apple crispy with just a hint of caramel flavor on the edges of the flower, and the French toast was this amazing soft texture and carried exactly the right amount of cinnamon. Simple, delicious, beautifully presented, created with such care and attention.

"Are you going to have some?" she asked, when she realized that Leah was just standing there watching her eat with a smile on her face.

"I will, in a bit. I need to finish making mine," she said.

Jordan nodded, and closed her eyes as she savored the food. When she was finished, Leah took the plates away, and there was a letter there waiting, underneath, with Jordan's name on it.

Leah left with the dishes, closing the door after her. Ah, she wanted to give Jordan space to read. Jordan's hands trembled as she opened the envelope and drew out the pages. This felt important. Scary. She closed her eyes for a moment to try to gather herself before reading, tuning in to the sound of Leah in the kitchen. She was doing the dishes, Jordan thought. And probably making her own food after that. There was time to read slowly.

Jordan,

I know it must have been hard to tell me how you felt, and for me to shut down like that. I'm sure that hurt, to get that response. I still ache, knowing that I hurt you with my reaction, and I worry about hurting you again, because I know I'll get scared again. The wounds I have are deep, and I patched over them as best I could at the time, but the patches I used cut me off from so much possibility. I've come to realize that I want to be brave. That I want to try to live into the fullness of myself even though it scares the shit out of me. That's the thing about being brave. It means fear is coming along for the ride as you take risks. I worry that I'll hurt you again out of fear. But I figure risking that is your choice. I don't want to take it away from you. After all, you have been so wonderful about supporting me to make choices for myself, for as long as I've known you. It's one of the reasons I trust you so deeply.

And I do, I want to be clear about that. My fear wasn't about not trusting you. It was about my own trauma, and the ways I'd tried to keep myself safe from harm. But I know now that I need better ways to keep myself safe, and I've been working with my therapist on building that. I'll tell you about them sometime, if you want. It's the kind of thing you'd totally geek out about.

It turns out, underneath, I do want relationships. I told myself to never look for the moon in someone's eyes, but I think about all the yearning to love and submit and build connection that I had when I was young, how much I hoped and wanted and let myself need...and I want to hug that Leah, and tell her to be brave and try for that again. I found an old picture of myself from back then, and I spent a long time looking at my own face and sitting with the way submission filled me with joy. I was so hopeful and happy and fucking gorgeous, when I was looking for the moon in someone's eyes.

Doing D/s with you has given me a taste of that, because everything in me wants to give myself to you, to belong to you, to have you claim me and protect me and love me and keep me. I've been scared to let myself want that, to tell you that I want to be yours. So so scared that if I really let myself submit again, that I'd realize I was a bad submissive, in all the ways Bev told me that night.
But the thing is, that's the same self-worth bullshit that I've been dealing with my whole life, courtesy of my mother, and society and misogyny and fat oppression and my good buddy depression. I just found a pocket of it that had been festering for years, hidden away in the dark. I know what to do about it, have a fuckton of practice, and a bunch of tools. It's going to sneak up on me every once in a while, of course. I think it's important to tell you about it going in because it might rear its head in our D/s relationship. I also want to say, very clearly, that this is a me problem that I'm bringing to therapy, not a problem that can or should be solved by D/s or taken on by you.

So, now that I've shared all my disclaimers about how I'm a 51 year old work in progress and that's going to bite us both in the ass sometimes, I want to tell you the real point of this letter that's already way too long. Which is to say yes, you're absolutely right, we have been building relationship, and yes I want that with you.
I want to be yours, to belong to you, to build relationship with you in all these new ways that still honor all the ways we were already intimate and family and love each other. I want to build D/s with you, and be claimed by you, and have you keep me. The word keep makes me all nervous and swoony and I love hearing you say it. So please if you could say it again, I'd really like that. I love the sex we've had, more than I've even said, and I'd love for our kink to sometimes include sex when we both want that, but also I love the ways it doesn't need to be sexual, and how safe that makes me feel to embrace the times when it is. I love living with you, and the small domestic ways we share our lives, and want to continue to do that. I want to work out how to navigate all the layers of who we are to each other, and make all of them shine, and that absolutely 100% includes the fact that I'm in love with you, and see the moon in your eyes, and want so so much to be yours. If you will still have me, that is.

(hopefully) your Leah

Jordan just sat there after she read, hands fluttering, letting it sink in. It was so much more than she'd even thought was possible, really. She hadn't even realized how convinced she'd been that Leah was going to back away until she read this. She needed to reread the beginning because most of it had felt like a lead in to exactly that, on first read. But it was totally Leah's way, to begin with disclaimers and worries and end with the hopeful thing. If she'd been able to step back enough she would have realized that's what she was doing. She just was too close to it to do that. Damn, she was glad it was in letter form, not just because it was something to hold in her hands, but because if Leah had begun that way in a conversation, even if it was over text, Jordan would have been so upset and anxious she might not have even been able to take in the real message. Being used to this as Leah's way didn't mean she was better at navigating it when the stakes were high.

Jordan took several slow breaths, and read the letter again, from the beginning. Then she sipped her tea and thought about what to do next. There was a limited amount of time before the party, after all. When she had it set in her mind, she went out into the living room. Leah was just finishing her French toast, which Jordan figured was perfect timing.

She moved the food out of the way and settled herself over Leah, cornering her on the couch, her hand cupping Leah's cheek, her thumb stroking Leah's lower lip.

"Mine to keep?" she asked.

Leah's eyes widened, and she let out a shaky breath. "Yours," she confirmed.

Jordan leaned forward, holding her face still as she kissed her girl, putting all the tenderness and claiming she had into it. When she lifted her lips from Leah's she said. "We have things to negotiate, don't we girl?"

"Yes, Sir."

Jordan moved to sit next to her on the couch, pulling her close. "Before we do, I need you to know how proud I am of you for being brave."

"Thank you, Sir."

"And how much I believe in you, and trust you. You're wonderful, and I'm lucky to have you as mine."

Leah seemed to freeze for a moment, as she took that in. "Thank you, Sir," she whispered.

"Oh, and one more thing you should know."

"Yes, Sir."

"I'm in love with you," Jordan said softly, right into her ear.

"That is a very important thing to know, Sir."

"Yes it is."

"I'm in love with you, Sir."

"Good. At least that part is already settled. Now we need to figure out what we're doing at this party."

They decided against a lesson before the party, wanting to try a longer scene that wasn't about practice. It felt like the right next step, along with arriving at the party already in D/s dynamic. It claimed the experience for them as a couple, and declared that Leah belonged to Jordan in a public way, something they both cared about.

So, before they left for the party, Leah had knelt, and Jordan had placed a collar on her neck. It was the same one Leah had bought for herself, that matched the cuffs, but this time Jordan had locked it, and pocketed the key. And she'd added her own flourish to the collar. Instead of using the ring at the hollow of Leah's throat to attach a leash, she'd attached the pendant she had given Leah for Chanukah. It was both decorative and claiming, and Leah had admired the look of it in the mirror for several long minutes before they'd left for the party.

58

331

TUESDAY EVENING, DECEMBER 31

LEAH

Leah had chosen her clothes deliberately, so as to show off the collar, and as a declaration to herself. She was wearing her stretch jeans, chaps, and boots. She'd tucked the picture of herself full of yearning and joy in submission into her right side back pocket, a silent reminder to herself that she'd flag with it if she could. After considerable thought, she'd chosen to wear a tank top that just said "brazen" in red curvy script on the black fabric. It was her favorites of the first set of store tees she'd ever had made, but it hadn't been a popular cut, so she'd just kept a few for herself in different colors. It was soft and cozy, a remembrance of how she'd reclaimed her life and declared that she wasn't ashamed of who she was. Wearing it tonight, with her collar, was about reminding herself that she could be in her own power, be in her own submission, and allow herself to choose clothes that felt good sensorily, all at the same time. That she could be her full self, and none of it was a contradiction.

She'd geared herself up for potentially running into Bev, but when they'd arrived at the party, Iris had told her she'd heard Bev had been banned from this party, because one of the hosts was the same person who'd disapproved of how Bev had treated her all those years ago, and had insisted upon it. It made her shiver, thinking of it, and she got angry all over again that the host had done that, but never said a word to her about it being wrong. She snapped something about it at Iris, who had recoiled at her sharp tone, then gone quiet for a minute, before nodding, and agreeing it wasn't right. Iris apologized that she hadn't put that together until now, and asked Leah if it was okay for her to mention it to the host, to see if it might be remedied. Jordan took her hand, but didn't say anything, offering support while she decided. Leah took a few breaths, considering, before she nodded that it was okay.

Jordan drew her into a hug, and she clung to her Sir, feeling a jumble of things all at once. When she realized what she needed, she whispered it in Jordan's ear. Jordan nodded, and sat on a couch, in the circle of Leah's friends, and Leah sunk to the floor, glad to be in her place at Sir's feet. Sir's hand went to the back of her neck, tracing the edge of the collar, and she leaned in to whisper that Leah should focus on her boots. Glad for a clear direction that let her stop scanning the room, she sunk into the gradations of color swirling on Sir's oxblood boots, and focused on the music. Piano and strings and not much else except a lilting voice she didn't recognize, singing about counting on your partner to catch you, being brave, belonging. When the words "I am yours" came, they rang through her, making her smile. She was Jordan's.

Someone sat by her, introduced herself as Robin, and asked Sir if she could speak to her submissive. Sir gave permission, and told Leah she could use her gaze freely now, and make her own choices about speaking to Robin. So Leah looked up, even though she could feel her heart racing. Because if Robin was the host, and she thought she was, then she'd seen Bev do that to her. Leah wasn't sure she wanted to see that memory in her face.

But when her eyes got to Robin's face, she couldn't see it there. She blinked, trying to get her eyes to focus better. Robin was butch, fat, and white; she had grey hair that was styled like KD Lang under her leather cap. She was handsome, with all these amazing laugh lines around her eyes and mouth. She wore well-worn leathers from head to toe, her vest full of patches and pins, held her cane in front of her, leaning her chin on her hands. She looked almost deferent. Not at all like she was holding a memory of Leah's humiliation she might use as a weapon. More like she wanted to really connect, but only if Leah wanted that, so she was holding back.

"Leah, may I speak with you?" she asked gravely.

Leah nodded.

"I have come to recognize that I owe you an apology, and have for quite a long time."

Leah waited, didn't respond. Just tried to be present. Sir's hand at the back of her neck helped. So did the hardness of the floor under her.

"I was there when Bev behaved reprehensively towards you at that party. I took action against Bev afterwards, making sure she was banned from future parties, and that she knew why. But I took no steps to attend to your safety or well-being that night, or to make sure that you knew that there were people in our community who found her behavior deeply dishonorable and a betrayal of the lifestyle we share. You deserved so much better from her, and from us."

Leah found that she had things to say. "Yes. I deserved better. And our community deserved better than for you to push the problem out of your own personal circle and do nothing to address it otherwise. One of the consequences of your actions was that I believed, for many long years, that it wasn't safe for me to form D/s relationships because I was scared that all dominants would end up being like her. After all, no dominant had ever spoken against the way she treated me."

Robin nodded, listening, all of her attention on Leah.

"I am so sorry, Leah, for my part in this, for the way it has made you feel that you could not be who you clearly are. I saw it then, all those years ago, how your submissive heart glows, how much you want to serve. I apologize, for the ways my inaction has contributed to robbing you of that joy in your life. I want to make amends, if you will allow it."

Leah thought about it. She realized that she didn't want to decide what amends she needed right now. And there was no reason that she had to.

"We can discuss it," she said, and pulled out her card. "You can find me at this email. I want to be clear, though, that this is not just about making amends to me as an individual. The community needs this addressed as well."

"I understand. Thank you, Leah."

She nodded.

"If I may be permitted to say..." Robin ventured quietly.

"Alright."

"I'm glad to see that you have found a dominant worthy of your trust and submission, Leah. You deserve to shine like this, to be cared for like this."

Leah turned to look at Jordan, whose hand hadn't left her nape this entire time. She was done with words, now. Jordan raised a brow, asking if it was okay to respond. Leah nodded.

"I'm very lucky that Leah has chosen to offer her submission to me," Jordan said simply.

"I hope you all enjoy the party. I'm glad you're here," Robin said to the group, then she left.

Leah leaned against Sir's leg, relieved that conversation was over. Confrontations were hard, even when people were appropriate. She just didn't want to think about it anymore. She felt herself retreat inward, and tried to stay connected to Jordan. Being in public was the point of going to a party, but right now, she just wanted to sink into the floor. She decided to ask for what she needed.

"Sir, may I please lie on the floor and rest my head on your boot?"

"Yes, my wonderful girl. That would please me very much. Wrap your arms around my boot as well."

She sunk to the floor, and laid her cheek against the glossy shine of Sir's boot, her arms wrapping around and clinging as tightly as she could. She felt everything melt away, until it was just her and Sir's boot, and the floor holding her. The music shifted to "At Last," one of her favorite waltzes, and it was like she was dancing with Sir.

The music was evocative and familiar, the song one she'd danced to for years, and the steps flowed in her mind, as she twirled round and round, surrounded by Sir's dominance, floating on their dynamic. They had a scene planned for later, and she had been looking forward to it, but right now, she felt like she could float in this waltz of submission forever, and that would be perfection. Sir reached down and stroked her hair, and she nuzzled Sir's boot contentedly, drifting happily.

They'd decided to play in this room because it had this amazing chaise in it that Jordan said was the most comfortable thing she'd ever sat on. The door was closed, this was just for them. It was their first full scene, and they neither needed, nor wanted, witnesses to it.

Leah removed her clothes and knelt for her Sir, smiling so wide she could feel the stretch of it in her cheeks. Sir stroked her cheek, and lifted her chin to take a long look at the collar around her throat. She caressed the lapis pendant, growling softly, and her smile looked satisfied.

She offered Leah a hand up and gripped her by the hair, kissing her roughly, and then used her hair to lead her over to a huge circular padded bondage bench that faced the chaise. She buckled the wrist and ankle cuffs onto Leah, and then drew her down to lie on her belly, attaching the cuffs to the bench so she was spread eagle. She sat next to Leah on the bench and just caressed her ass gently, running her fingertips along the curves of it, tracing spiraling patterns over her skin, before she began to slap it, warming up the skin methodically. Leah was deeply aware that Sir seemed to be taking her sweet time with this, more than she ever had before, and it made her squirm, and tug at the cuffs, not wanting to be free, but wanting the reminder that she was naked, and bound, and there for Sir's pleasure.

Her ass began to heat up, and she ground into the table, her clit pulsing as she thought about Sir marking her. She wanted that, so much. Wanted to carry Sir on her skin. Wanted to know that every time she sat down she'd remember this. Then Sir stood up, and she heard her unbuckle something.

It wasn't the cuffs. Sirs voice floated towards her, fervent and low.

"I need this, girl. Take it, for me. I need to mark you with my belt."

Leah shuddered. "Yes, please, Sir. I want to take it for you."

The blows were like fire, and she welcomed the burn of them, writhing in her bonds. The flames drove into her and slid inside her and devoured her and she took each one like the gift it was. Sir needed her to take this, her voice had sounded like a prayer when she'd said that. Leah was filled with joy that she could give this to her. The pain licked at her skin in a glorious conflagration, and she soaked up every bit of it, holding it close to her heart, writhing on the table as Sir marked her with her belt. It was wondrous and made her shudder with her desire to please, filled her with the need to give Sir everything she could. She throbbed with it.

Then Sir's hands stroked along her skin, and first her ankles, then her wrists, were freed. She blinked, and Sir's hands urged her to turn onto her back. When her ass made contact with the table she yelped, and Sir laughed delightedly. Pillows were placed under her head, and the belt was offered to her lips for a kiss, which she gave, shuddering. Sir put some clips, a bottle of lube and Leah's new favorite plug near Leah's hands and said, "Now I get that show you promised me, girl."

She walked over to the chaise, and got comfortable. Leah had asked for this, had told Sir the story, said she wanted to try it for real. She was glad that Sir had given her pain first. It made it easier to close her eyes and focus on Sir's words.

"Show me how you touch yourself when you're alone. When you are feeling all hot and sexy and like you really want to get off. Show me what that looks like."

Leah put the lube and plug down and focused on her clit for a while, one hand adding clips to her nipples. She bit her lip, pain soaring through her, and pinched her clit. Yes, that was good. More pain would be better. She started adding clips to her labia, shuddering. Yes, shuddering was good, it made the welts on her ass throb. She was panting now, grinding her sore ass against the table to feel the welts again, and she could hear Sir in the background telling her to keep going, she was giving her such a good show. She yanked one of the clips off really hard, and rode the pain in waves, her hips thrusting, pinching her clit tight, and then she attached the clip right there, the sharpness making her gasp, and say "Yes!"

"That's perfect, girl, you're doing so well. Now I want to see you use that plug," Sir growled, and Leah could hear her unzipping her fly, and knew she was taking out her cock, that she'd pleased Sir enough that she wanted to jack off at the sight of Leah doing exactly what she said. Leah's hips kept working as she lubed up the plug, and Sir groaned when she started playing it around her hole, working herself open with it. She went slow, enjoying the slide of it into her, the way it opened her up. It felt amazing, was exactly what she needed, and she said "Thank you, Sir," fervently, as it settled inside her.

Then she returned to playing with the clips, loving how the pain made her writhe and clench, and the way Sir kept murmuring "good girl, my good girl," over and over as she watched. Leah was moaning now, and aching to come, but she wanted to be good, and Sir was enjoying this so much, and she ached to give Sir exactly what she wanted.

"Get your ass over here, girl. I need you on my cock," Sir growled, and that was clear enough, wasn't it, so Leah sat up, carefully, and opened her eyes, saying "Yes, Sir."

Sir was stroking a condom onto her cock, and had this ferocious look on her face. Leah made sure her legs were steady before she rushed to follow orders. She lost a couple clips in her hurry, yelping at the pain, and realized that there was little chance of the clips on her cunt staying on once she started riding Sir's cock. Well, they'd come off when they came off, she thought.

The chaise gave her awesome leverage for the cowgirl position, so she climbed on with relative ease, and slid slowly onto Sir's dick, each inch of it feeling more intense. When it was fully seated inside her cunt, she grinned in triumph at Sir, who was staring at her in awe.

"Fuck you are the hottest thing in the fucking world," Sir growled, and ground up into her, holding her hips in place. She gasped, and Sir grinned, and twisted the clips off her nipples, setting off a wave of pain that was so strong she began to beg instantly to come.

"Not yet, girl, not yet," Sir said. "Ride me."

So Leah did, each thrust building the ache inside her, savoring the way Sir groaned when she rocked onto her, Sir's hands pressing into the delicious welts on her ass.

"Tell me you're mine," Sir growled.

"I'm yours, Sir. Your girl. Your submissive. Yours to keep, please please please Sir I'm yours!" she moaned out the words as she swiveled her hips, grinding into Sir, and felt the first clip pop off, setting off a yowl of pain.

Sir reached up and gripped both her nipples, driving pain into them in delicious bursts, and ordered her to come.

The orgasm rolled over her in giant spasms of swirling sensation. The plug was so fucking insistent in her ass, Sir's cock impaling her, the pain rushing into her in waves, and Sir's voice wrapping around her in a growling litany of "Mine, yes, you are all mine, such a good girl for me, my girl, mine to keep." When she was shuddering through the last shocks of her orgasm, Sir grabbed her hips and thrust up into her in short shuddering stabs, her head thrown back on the chaise, eyes closed. Just the sight of her coming set Leah off into another spiral and she exploded into a zillion stars on the ceiling, before collapsing onto Sir in a heap, trembling.

They lay like that for several long moments, before Sir urged her to sit up again, making her groan with renewed awareness of the way her cunt and ass were both so damn full, and throbbing. Then Sir twisted each clip off separately, telling Leah that she could come as much as she wanted, as long as she said "I'm yours to keep, Sir," after each orgasm. Leah found that she actually had several more orgasms in her, as the pain drove through her and Sir twisted her fingers into her hair and ground her hips up each time she took off a clip.

The most intense was the one that had somehow stayed on her clit, which Sir ordered Leah to remove herself, an entirely wicked grin on her face as the orgasm slammed into Leah like a fucking freight train. She said she wanted to be the last thing inside her so she made Leah remove the plug while still riding her cock, and once it was free, she pulled Leah down for the filthiest kiss, holding onto Leah's ass and thrusting her cock up into her slow and insistent. Jordan whispered against Leah's lips that she loved being inside her, claiming her this way, that Leah belonged to her now, and she was enjoying every bit of her delicious cunt, that Leah was going to make her come because she felt so good on top of her, her weight was delicious and wonderful and exactly what Sir needed right now, her weight and her skin, and her cunt and those little gasping sounds she made and she was being so good, such a very good girl. Then Sir came, gripping her tight, shuddering under her, and she took it into her heart to hold onto forever.

Afterwards, they curled up together on the couch in the common room, and Sir stroked her hair and made her drink so much fucking water until she thought she'd burst, and wrapped her in a blanket and told her how much she'd pleased her. Nina Simone came on singing "Here Comes the Sun," and Sir told her how much she loved this song, and they lay there, listening, wrapped up in the music and each other, slowly coming back down to earth.

"You know, you still owe me four lessons," Sir murmured.

"That's true," Leah said. "I liked getting to play without a lesson, though."

"Oh yes, me too," Sir said and kissed her cheek gently. "I think we can find a way to balance both."

"After all, you do have a kink educator for your submissive. You should use every ounce of her skills, don't you think?"

"It is important to give your submissive opportunities to be useful," Sir agreed. "An extended study is an excellent idea. And of course, there's Chanukah next year. I'm guessing I might be able to get some more lessons then."

"We mustn't forget Chanukah wax play. You promised."

"I wasn't sure you would remember that."

"I never forget promises of this sort, Sir."

"Excellent. I'm looking forward to next Chanukah already."

A NOTE FOR READERS

Thank you for reading this book! I hope you have enjoyed it, and you are very welcome to leave a review or recommend it to a friend; recommendations and reviews mean the world to indie writers and I am grateful for anything you might want to say about my work to other readers.

I would like to insert a brief note about gender and ways to discuss this book and craft reviews without harming other readers. I am grateful to Ana Mardoll for modeling this idea in xer lovely collection No Man of Woman Born, which xie has graciously granted me permission to borrow from in writing this note. (Xie also helped spark the idea for the note about non-binary terms at the beginning of this book.)

Some of the characters in this book are transgender people; that is to say they are folks whose gender does not match the gender assigned to them at birth. Many trans and/or non-binary people prefer that their gender assignment not be discussed all or most of the time. There are several non-binary secondary characters in the book; their gender assignments are not discussed and do not need to be referenced in reviews. While Erica's gender assignment is obliquely referenced, it is unnecessary to state that Erica is AMAB in your review. Instead, it is best to refer to both her and Ellie as trans women. Similarly, Ernest was not "born a girl", nor is he "female"; please do not refer to him using that language. It is both inaccurate and may also be harmful to trans and non-binary readers of your review.

When discussing the story, please use the pronouns that characters use in the story. In determining which pronoun form to use, the note at the beginning of the book may be helpful. When discussing the author, please use singular they/them pronouns.

None of the characters have genders that should be considered a spoiler; there is no need to conceal their genders with incorrect pronouns or terminology.

Thank you for being considerate; sensitive reviews for books with trans and non-binary characters and authors are easier for trans readers to navigate.

More resources on transgender characters and how to write about them are available at GLAAD.org, Nonbinary.org, and https://ifoundmyselfreading.wordpress.com/2016/10/23/how-to-review-a-trans-book-as-a-cis-person/ . I am very grateful to Ana Mardoll (@AnaMardoll), Vee (@findmereading) and Avery (@BookDeviant) for sharing their thoughts with me regarding the ways trans characters are discussed in book reviews.

CAST OF CHARACTERS

Protagonists

Leah Blumenstein (she/her): protagonist

Jordan Stern (she/her): protagonist

Leah's friends and connections

Bev (she/her): Leah's first dominant

Tyler (he/him): Leah's play partner, Marcos' QPP and submissive, works at Leah's shop Brazen

Marcos (he/him): Leah's friend, Tyler's QPP and dominant

Iris (she/her): Leah's dance partner and occasional play partner. Her husband: David (he/him)

Rebecca (she/her): Leah's friend, Ruth's submissive

Ruth (she/her): Leah's friend, Rebecca's dominant

Xavier (he/him): Leah's therapist

Jordan's friends and connections

Dani (she/her): Jordan's ex-wife

Erica (she/her): Jordan's younger sister. Her spouses: Avery (they/them), Caro (she/her)

RJ (ze/hir): Jordan's friend from Twitter

Tal (ze/hir): Jordan's new therapist

Gideon's Leather Family

Ellie (she/her): Leah's play partner, Rena's former dominant, now her QPP

Gideon (he/him): Ernest's dominant, Nora's dominant, head of the leather family

Ernest (he/him): Gideon's submissive, Nora's submissive

Nora (she/her): Gideon's submissive, Ernest's dominant

Judith (she/her): Gideon and Ernest's housemate, Gideon's ex, Shiloh's BFF

Shiloh (ze/zir): works at Leah's shop Brazen, Jordan's new friend, Judith's BFF

Rena (she/her): Ellie's former submissive, now her QPP

Naomi (she/her): Rachel's dominant

Rachel (she/her): Naomi's submissive

At Jordan's new job, Safe Haven

Jax (he/him): Jordan's close colleague

Zak (he/him) Jax's submissive, works at Safe Haven

At Leah's sex shop, Brazen

Amaya (she/her): manager

Octavia (she/her): manager, co-teaches with Gideon

Community connections

Violet (she/her): Hosts Femme Brunch, Liliana's dominant

Liliana (she/her) Hosts Femme Brunch, Violet's submissive

Robin (she/her): play party host

DRINK RECIPES FROM EIGHT KINKY NIGHTS

When I was wrapping up the first draft of this book, I remembered the holiday romances I loved from my early romance reading, and how many of them had recipes in the back, of things characters made in the book. I wanted to do something like that for Eight Kinky Nights, so I asked my mixologist friends on Twitter to help me fulfill my fantasy of publishing my own holiday romance with recipes in the back.

I'm especially excited to be doing this as Leah and Jordan are all about taste stims, and it's rare to get recipes that are going for that kind of experience.

I'm thrilled to include four non-alcoholic drink recipes drawn from things Leah and Jordan drink in this book!

Recipes included:

- Ginger Lime Fizzy Drink created by Alyssa Palomares (Twitter: @cfmvirus). This is the drink Jordan makes at home.
- Cherry Lemonade created by Lucy Eden (https://www.lucyeden.com/). This is one of the drink options Leah brings to Jordan at her work party, the one she ends up drinking.
- Grapefruit Ginger created by Lucy Eden. This is the other drink option Leah brings to Jordan at her work party, the one Jordan decides to drink.
- Ginger Lime created by Lucy Eden. This is the drink Jordan makes at home.

GINGER LIME FIZZY DRINK RECIPE

Equipment needed

- Citrus zester
- Vegetable peeler
- Small saucepan
- Your favorite drinking vessel

- A spoon OR a cocktail shaker

Ginger-Lime-Honey syrup

- 1 oz. (2 Tbsp.) of peeled, minced ginger OR 1 tsp. ground ginger
- Zest of 1 lime
- 4 oz. (½ cup) water
- 6 to 8 oz. (3/4 - 1 cup) honey
- 1 ginger teabag

Zest lime. Peel and mince ginger, OR measure out ground ginger.

Combine everything in a small saucepan over medium-high. After it reaches a boil, reduce the heat to medium and simmer for two minutes. Allow to rest for at least an hour. Strain the syrup of solids, but keep teabag submerged in syrup. Using a funnel, pour the syrup into a squeeze bottle. Refrigerate for up to two weeks.

Ginger Lime Fizzy Drink

- 1 part Ginger-Lime Honey Syrup
- 1 part ginger ale
- 1 part lime soda/flavored seltzer
- 2 – 4 fresh lime wedges OR lime juice, to taste
- Ice (shaved is ideal, but crushed or cubed will do too!)
- 1 lime wedge (for garnish)

Combine syrup, ginger ale, and soda in preferred container. Squeeze juice from a fresh lime wedge on top, or pour lime juice. Stir. Add ice and garnish with a lime wedge. Add more lime juice (fresh or otherwise) or syrup to taste.

Recipe by Alyssa Palomares

CHERRY LEMONADE RECIPE

The Drink:

- 1 cup frozen black cherries
- 1/4 cup fresh lemon juice
- 3 tbsp honey
- 1-2 oz. seltzer water (as needed)

Blend all ingredients except seltzer until smooth, adjust honey to taste. Slowly pour into pre-rimmed glass. Float a thin layer of seltzer over mixture. Garnish. Serve immediately.

The Garnish:

- Lemon slices
- Fresh pitted cherries
- Honey
- 3 parts sugar/ 1 part citric acid mixture.

Rim the glass with honey, dip into sugar mixture. Garnish with cherries and lemon slices to your preference.

Recipe by Lucy Eden

GRAPEFRUIT GINGER DRINK RECIPE

The Drink:

- 1/4 oz. fresh ginger peeled/chopped
- 5 oz. ruby red grapefruit seltzer water

Muddle ginger together before straining. Pour 1/4 teaspoon into chilled martini glass. Pour seltzer slowly into glass.

The garnish:

- Long thin slice of fresh ginger.
- Large slice of ruby red grapefruit.

Add the ginger to the drink then carefully float the grapefruit on top. Serve immediately.

Recipe by Lucy Eden

GINGER LIME DRINK RECIPE

The Drink:

- 1/4 lime peeled/ chopped
- 1/4 oz. fresh ginger peeled/chopped
- 5 oz. seltzer water

Muddle the lime and ginger together before straining. Pour 1/4 teaspoon into chilled martini glass (pre-rimmed with honey). Slowly pour seltzer water into the glass. Garnish. Serve immediately.

The Garnish:

Rim the glass with honey. Garnish with lime slices

Recipe by Lucy Eden

SONGS REFERENCED IN EIGHT KINKY NIGHTS

A playlist of all of the songs referenced is available at the following link: https://www.youtube.com/playlist?list=PL7Y3eKgacbkOse1pC1YPvsFiL01O1QfqY

1. Perhaps, Perhaps, Perhaps-Doris Day
2. Glory Be-Coyote Grace
3. Ghost Boy-Coyote Grace
4. Blue Rose Is-Pam Tillis
5. Killer Queen-Queen
6. Fat Bottomed Girls-Queen
7. Leaving on a Jet Plane- Chantal Kreviazuk, Armageddon soundtrack
8. Iris-Goo Goo Dolls
9. As the World Falls Down-Lena Hall
10. Until-Sting, Kate & Leopold soundtrack
11. Ain't Got You-Alicia Keyes
12. Goldfinger-Shirley Bassey, Goldfinger soundtrack
13. By Your Side-Sade
14. Firewood-Regina Spektor
15. She Used to be Mine-Sara Bareilles
16. Angel-Sarah MacLachlan
17. Stay-Rihanna ft Mikky Echo
18. Skyfall-Adele, Skyfall soundtrack
19. The Misty Mountains Cold- Richard Armitage, soundtrack for The Hobbit-An Unexpected Journey
20. Closer to Fine Indigo Girls
21. Less Can Be More (Samwise's Theme)-Glenn Yarborough, sound track for The Return of the King (1980)
22. Miss You Much-Janet Jackson
23. You-Janet Jackson
24. Birdhouse in Your Soul-They Might Be Giants
25. Clever Girl-The Doubleclicks
26. Clifford is Not Too Big-The Doubleclicks

27. Red Light-Linda Clifford
28. If I Was Your Girlfriend-Prince
29. I Am A Rock-Paul Simon
30. Perfect Day-Lou Reed
31. The Kiss Waltz-Ruth Etting
32. Maoz Tzur / Rock of Ages-Mostly Kosher (as part of a medley)
33. Chanukah oh Chanukah-Jay Levy
34. Shehecheyanu-Cantor David Propis
35. The Mob Song-Beauty and the Beast soundtrack (1991)
36. Haneiros Hallalu-Judy Kaplan Ginsberg
37. My Secret Love-Lily Banquette, Grace of My Heart soundtrack
38. Bridge Over Troubled Water-Simon and Garfunkel
39. Ner Li-Abigail Lapell and Laura Spink
40. Ocho Kandelikas-Kenny Ellis
41. Sevivon, Sov, Sov, Sov-Dafna
42. Miracle of Miracles-Austin Pendleton, Fiddler on the Roof OBC album
43. Latke Recipe-The Maccabeats
44. Touch the Sky-Julie Fowlis, Brave soundtrack
45. Black Velvet-Alannah Myles
46. A Dream is a Wish Your Heart Makes-Lily James, Cinderella soundtrack (2015)
47. Everything Stays-Rebecca Sugar, Steven Universe
48. When Will My Life Begin-Tangled soundtrack
49. At This Point in My Life-Tracey Chapman
50. Yours-Ella Henderson
51. At Last-Etta James
52. Here Comes the Sun-Nina Simone

BOOKS AND MOVIES/TV REFERENCED IN EIGHT KINKY NIGHTS

Books

- That Kind of Guy by Talia Hibbert
- Chapter 10: Harry Potter and the Prisoner of Azkaban by JK Rowling
- Macbeth by William Shakespeare
- Chapter 25: The New Topping Book by Dossie Easton and Janet W. Hardy
- The Hobbit by JRR Tolkien
- Chapter 46-48: Kushiel's Dart by Jacqueline Carey

Movies:

- Becks (2017)
- Chapter 5 Goldfinger (1964)
- The Princess Bride (1987)
- Chapter 10: Lord of the Rings: The Fellowship of the Ring (2001)
- Leading Ladies (2010)
- Chapter 57: The Two Fat Ladies (Season 1, Cakes episode, 1996)
- Tangled (2010)

ACKNOWLEDGMENTS

I could not have done this by myself. My deepest thanks...
to Hannah Zayit, who created a gorgeous cover
to Shira Glassman, who helped me see what was missing
to Hillary and Ali Thompson who offered some needed reality checking
to Melissa Blue for a very useful first page critique
to Cole McCade for support when I was struggling
to RB, whose friendship means the world to me
to my therapist, who shored me up when I really needed it, more than once
to my sprinting buddies who helped me get this draft done
to all who sent gifts, offered practical help, or said kind things during the power outages
to Em, who kept encouraging me to write (and finish) this story
to RoAnna Sylver, for their truly wonderful editing and support
to Edith, whose support was instrumental
to May Peterson, who was a great help
to L. Anthony Graham, Brooke Winters, Ren Basel and J. Emery for their tremendous assistance with important matters
to Gayathri, S. Jet Pak, and Andrea who gave such useful feedback
to Lucy Eden and Alyssa Palomares for donating their mixology expertise
to Janani, whose proofreading help made this book more accessible to readers
to Ceillie for last minute formatting help
and to the QWC for your support as I worked through my process on this story.

I WANT TO EXTEND PARTICULAR THANKS...

to all the kink educators I have learned from, and in particular to the submissive, bottom, and switch kink educators I've had in my life

to the stone folks who came to my stone classes, and who have talked stone identity and sexuality with me over the years; you made me feel less alone and more able to write characters like Jordan

to the ace spec folks in my life who helped me think about my own ace-spec identity and about ace-spec representation in stories

to the kinky a-spec folks I know who helped me tease out ways to think about kink and the split attraction model

and to the ace spec folks in my life who cheered me on in writing fiction depicting non-sexual kink.

You helped shape the thinking that went into this book, and made me believe there were readers who wanted (and needed) stories like this one.

ALSO BY XAN WEST

Books
Nine of Swords, Reversed
Their Troublesome Crush
Show Yourself To Me: Queer Kink Erotica

Selected Stories in Anthologies
"Tenderness" in Queerly Loving, Volume 2
"Crave" in Best Lesbian Erotica of the Year, Volume 4
"Trying Submission" in Best Lesbian Erotica of the Year, Volume 3
"Building Something New" in Big Book of Submission, Volume 2

Free Erotica Stories:
"A Good Beating" on Sugarbutch.net
"The Tender Sweet Young Thing" on Sugarbutch.net

PRAISE FOR XAN'S WORK

For Xan's contemporary fantasy romance Nine of Swords, Reversed

"A warm and uplifting tale, satisfying and sweet." —A. Merc Rustad

"There is a feeling when you read good representation of yourself. 'Other people feel this, too.' Or sometimes, 'Who looked inside my head and wrote down what I was thinking?' This is what I felt when reading Xan West's Nine of Swords, Reversed." —Liminal Nest

"This novella is such a genuine and honest look at a very tender relationship, and I am glad this is my first book of the year." —Mehek Naresh

"very sweet comfortfic about two genderfluid individuals in a D/s relationship navigating their relationship."—Psygeek

For Xan's cute foodie contemporary polyamorous romance Their Troublesome Crush

"THEIR TROUBLESOME CRUSH has a demiromantic MC dealing with the realisation that he has a new romantic crush, and the upheaval and possibilities this opens, and I absolutely adored Ernest's evolution through this storyline, how much discussion happens around different attractions, how he has other arospecs to talk with. It's incredibly validating and thoughtful rep, and there's a bit where he writes a love song from an aromantic perspective that was just -amazing-."-Claudie Arseneault

"A lovely, intimate portrait of kink, autism, and romance. For so long I have longed for representation like this in media, and this book such a delightful read. Plenty of queer and trans characters that just are. It's so freaking adorable how they connect and process and make space for each other."
- Michón Neal

"I loved this book. I loved the representation and I love how seen it made me feel and I loved the queerness and I loved how soft and tender it was. My heart feels so good after reading this book." –Ash

"This is an absolutely adorable book—which is not something I ever thought I'd say about a book featuring Daddy/Good Boy, D/s, and rope kinks...Did I mention the protagonist of this book also loves show tunes, and is writing a(n even) queer(er) musical version of Yentl? Yeah. You want to read this."

–Jess at Book Riot Kissing Books

For Xan's queer chosen family love story "Tenderness"

"So poignant and sad but uplifting at the same time. I love seeing a queer found family coming together to comfort one of their own." –Small Queer, Big Opinions

"Engulfing and warm, 'Tenderness' is a thoroughly enjoyable read, and was gloriously inclusive...watching Judith become more herself was the truest gift of this story." –Dena Celeste

"Made me feel safe, accepted, and loved. I will be treasuring this story for the rest of my life."

–BookDeviant

"Gorgeous, gentle, and hopeful in exactly the ways I needed." –Mo

ABOUT THE AUTHOR

Xan West is the nom de plume of Corey Alexander, an autistic queer fat Jewish genderqueer writer with multiple disabilities who spends a lot of time on Twitter.

Xan's erotica has been published widely, including in the Best S/M Erotica series, the Best Gay Erotica series, and the Best Lesbian Erotica series. Xan's story "Trying Submission," won the 2018 National Leather Association John Preston Short Fiction Award. Their collection of queer kink erotica, Show Yourself to Me, will be rereleased soon.

After over 15 years of writing and publishing queer kink erotica short stories, Xan has begun to also write longer form queer kink romance. Their recent work still centers kinky, trans and non-binary, fat, disabled, queer trauma survivors. It leans more towards centering Jewish characters, ace and aro spec characters, autistic characters, and polyamorous networks. Xan has two other queer kink romances currently available: Nine of Swords, Reversed and Their Troublesome Crush.

Website: https://xanwest.wordpress.com

Twitter: https://twitter.com/TGStoneButch

Newsletter: http://eepurl.com/cj-Lub

ABOUT THEIR TROUBLESOME CRUSH

In this queer polyamorous m/f romance novella, two metamours realize they have crushes on each other while planning their shared partner's birthday party together. Ernest, a Jewish autistic demiromantic queer fat trans man submissive, and Nora, a Jewish disabled queer fat femme cis woman switch, have to contend with an age gap, a desire not to mess up their lovely polyamorous dynamic as metamours, the fact that Ernest has never been attracted to a cis person before, and the reality that they are romantically attracted to each other, all while planning their dominant's birthday party and trying to do a really good job.

Content Warnings for Excerpt:

- References to fat oppression, trans oppression and ableism.
- Oblique reference to being a survivor and managing PTSD.
- References to BDSM, including Daddy/boy dynamic, D/s, service, and bondage.

THEIR TROUBLESOME CRUSH EXCERPT

Ernest had the best idea for Daddy's birthday and he couldn't wait to share it with Nora. When would she get here? He was so excited that his hands were fluttery, and he was bouncing a little. They were going to throw Gideon an amazing birthday party, and Gideon was going to ruffle his hair and call him a good boy, and cup Nora's cheek and give her that sweet smile he had just for her, and he would tell them both they did a good job. There was nothing better than doing a good job.

Ernest was getting ahead of himself, he knew, but he couldn't help it. He always got giddy at the beginning of tasks; this was their first joint task doing service for Gideon as metamours, and that was exciting, and Ernest was rather bouncy in general, anyway. Luckily, Nora was more grounded and moved slowly and deliberately, so they would balance each other out, he thought. Ernest had this image in his head, of himself tugging on Daddy's hand, racing forward, unruly short red curls going every which way, and Nora holding Gideon's other hand, moving slow and steady, gazing up at him like he hung the moon, her tight dark curls framing her face in a somewhat controlled cloud. Maybe there was a song in that, he thought, the two rhythms dancing around the melody, balancing it. His fingers moved on his thighs, building the rhythms, as his head started to fill with the melody. Then two women sat right next to him, talking loudly about the bat mitzvah they were planning, and he lost the song altogether. He should have sat in the corner.

Ernest moved to the corner table, which was quieter, thankfully, but he couldn't get the song back, so he sketched out the idea in his notebook and turned his attention back to the party planning. There were a ton of cupcake shops in NYC, but Nora favored this one on the Lower East Side; they were meeting there so Ernest could try them out. He still wasn't sure cupcakes were the right choice. They would be perfect for his own birthday, but perhaps Gideon would want something more dignified. He had his eye on a pie shop in Brooklyn. But it made sense to at least try the cupcakes, didn't it? How could he resist a chance to try cupcakes?

Maybe they should get a half dozen and sample. It would give him a chance to take leftovers home and see what Daddy thought. But he knew Nora was diabetic and that made it thorny to fill the table with cupcakes. What if it was a mean thing to do, since she probably could only have a few bites? At least, that was what she generally did with desserts, when they had gotten them in the past. They always shared so she could have a taste but not mess up her blood sugar. But maybe it wasn't right for him to not ask just because she was diabetic? He didn't want to act like he was in charge of her food choices.

He thought it through, considering it from a few angles, trying to figure out what would be the most considerate and the least intrusive and the most respectful of her autonomy, his brain filling with these spiraling thoughts that contradicted each other, until he remembered what his play partner Jax had said to him once: "People think they are being so caring when they comment on what you eat, when you're a fat diabetic. They don't see the way our food choices are constantly scrutinized and judged, the way we're so often blamed for having diabetes, how we have unhelpful non-consensual help pushed on us all the time. What I really need is to be left alone...unless I ask for information or help."

Well, that cleared things up. He would do the sampler thing and try a few flavors, and let her do what made sense for her. Ernest got enough shit from the world as a midsize fat not-really-passing-most-of-the-time trans guy, for eating sweets in public...it seemed likely that as a larger fat diabetic femme cis woman, she got a whole lot more. He definitely didn't want to add to that. Once he connected those ideas, a whole bunch more slotted into place, as he thought about unhelpful non-consensual help, and all the ways it messed things up, about the ways that kind of help interacted with ableism and fat oppression and misogyny. He started mapping it out in his notebook, connecting the dots for himself. Writing it, mapping it, helped make it stick when there was a gap in a pattern like this, like it was reinforcing a piece of the puzzle that had been missing but was now in place. He didn't want to lose this piece again.

Ernest traced the pattern he'd drawn in his notebook and felt his brain ready itself for a leap to another connection, just as he heard his name being said in a husky musical voice that held tones of humor, like perhaps she'd already said it a few times and he'd missed that. So he looked up, and Nora was there, taking off her adorable raincoat, which was bright pink and had white polka dots. She was wearing purple tights and a short black dress. Her dress had cupcakes on it! Nora managed to look both powerful and cute at the same time; it was something about how her clothes suited her pear-shaped fatness perfectly, and something about how she held herself. Her face was flushed, she was smiling, and her chin-length dark brown hair was all wild frizzy curls today. So was his own hair, come to think of it. He actually had a curl in the center of his fucking forehead, which of course put his mother's voice in his head, exactly where he did not want her. He dug his nails into his thigh to try to get rid of her and focus on the present.

"You were in your own world," she said.

He ducked his head. "Um, yeah. I do that."

"I do it too, when I'm writing. My world is a pretty good place to spend time in."

He smiled. His world was pretty great too. "I know what you mean. My world is a lot better than most places in NYC. Maybe you could tell me about your world sometime?"

"You want to hear about the world I'm writing, the novel I'm working on?"

"Yes, please," he said firmly. He definitely wanted to hear about that.

"Hmm. That rates a please, does it?"

Ernest blinked, trying to figure out what she meant. Was he not supposed to say please? Was he not supposed to want to hear about her world? He didn't know what to say, so he just nodded.

She was still standing over the table, though she'd draped her raincoat over her chair, and moved closer to him, so it wasn't that she was going to leave. Was he supposed to be standing too? She made him nervous, looking down at him, standing so close. His heart was racing. Why did he like being around her so much if she made him nervous like this?

"Come on," Nora said, and her hand appeared. He was supposed to take it, he knew. But they hadn't ever touched, so it was a shock to be suddenly faced with it. Did he want to take her hand? After a moment the answer came: yes. So he stood up and took it. She tugged him over to the display case of all the cupcakes and then stood next to him, reaching over his body to point out her favorite flavors, closer than she had ever stood before. It made him a bit dizzy, but not in a scary way. It was like being filled with bubbles; he was unsteady, almost floating, definitely not firmly planted on the ground.

He dug his boots into the floor, not wanting to fall, as her voice filled him up, talking about why she loved these particular flavors. The scent of sugar and butter was so strong in this part of the shop. But that wasn't all he smelled. Her raincoat had a hood but he didn't think she'd been wearing it, because her hair, which was so close it had brushed his face, smelled like rain. He closed his eyes for a moment and breathed in, concentrating on the smell of rain. He'd always loved the rain, would stand outside in it every chance he got, savoring the sensation of it on his skin. There was nothing like spinning in the rain. He'd tried spinning in the shower but it wasn't the same. "Singin' in the Rain" came into his head and he hummed it, knowing that he couldn't sing, not in a bakery, even though he wanted to. Humming would have to do.

He didn't even get a chance to suggest getting an assortment. She suggested it first, though she was going to leave out the lemon, and he knew Gideon loved lemon sweets. So it wasn't like he made no contribution at all or anything. They got a half dozen of the regular sized cupcakes and returned to their seats, Nora taking out a half frozen bottle of water wrapped in a grey handkerchief and putting it on the table. Ernest expected the half frozen water bottle; she carried them everywhere, no matter the season, but the grey hanky, that was new to him.

Ever since Jake, Ernest had been wary about Gideon's partners assuming he was also part of a package deal, that if they got together with Gideon they were automatically going to be playing with Ernest too. As he and Nora had been building their metamour relationship, he'd been so worried that she might think he was hitting on her that he hadn't talked about his kink life or his relationships, and hadn't asked about hers. Which meant he actually knew very little about her kinks. That made the grey hanky completely distracting, because he knew Gideon didn't like bondage and in Ernest's world, if you owned a hanky, there was a good reason for it.

"That's a grey hanky," Ernest said, before he caught himself.

Nora grinned at him. "Why, yes it is."

Ernest waited for her to say something more, but she didn't, just kept smiling at him. This was going to completely distract him if he didn't find out, but maybe it was rude. Maybe she didn't want to say, and that's why she didn't. She was smiling. Was that friendly, or teasing, or maybe she thought it was funny that he just blurted that out?

"You aren't going to ask, are you?"

"Um. Did you want me to?"

"Ernest...do you think you can't ask me stuff?"

"I don't want to presume..."

"Okay, here's the deal. You can ask me anything, as long as you are okay with me refusing to answer," she said firmly.

"That wasn't you refusing to answer?"

"No, that was me teasing you."

"Nora, you know I'm autistic, right?"

She nodded.

"I don't know how to parse a lot of stuff, especially indirect communication. I didn't know if you didn't say because you didn't want to answer, or were teasing, or what. I'm not gonna know that stuff, unless you're direct.'"

"Okay." She thought about it for a moment, then continued. "Then if I don't want to answer, I'll say that. And then you leave it alone. Sound good?"

"Well. I won't know if it's a rude question sometimes. Or too blunt. I'm often too blunt for people."

"That's okay. I like blunt. And I just gave you permission to ask any question you have. So, none of them are rude."

Ernest blinked at her for probably a minute. It felt more like five. He'd never had an allistic person say that to him before. No rude questions, and she liked blunt? If only he was into cis people. She'd be perfect for him. Except of course for the whole metamour thing that was going so well.

Made in United States
North Haven, CT
23 November 2024